I0761121

ESCAPE!

ESCAPE!

A NOVEL

STEPHEN FISHBACH

DUTTON

DUTTON

An imprint of Penguin Random House LLC
1745 Broadway, New York, NY 10019
penguinrandomhouse.com

Portions of this work were originally published in 2021 as "To Sharks" in the online journal *One Story*, https://www.one-story.com.

Book design by Daniel Brount

LIBRARY OF CONGRESS CATALOGING-IN-PUBLICATION DATA

Names: Fishbach, Stephen author
Title: Escape!: a novel / Stephen Fishbach.
Description: New York, NY: Dutton, 2026.
Identifiers: LCCN 2025040597 (print) | LCCN 2025040598 (ebook) |
ISBN 9798217048151 hardcover | ISBN 9798217048168 ebook
Subjects: LCGFT: Thrillers (Fiction) | Psychological fiction | Novels | Fiction
Classification: LCC PS3606.I7684 E83 2026 (print) | LCC PS3606.I7684 (ebook)
LC record available at https://lccn.loc.gov/2025040597
LC ebook record available at https://lccn.loc.gov/2025040598

Printed in the United States of America
1st Printing

The authorized representative in the EU for product safety and compliance is Penguin Random House Ireland, Morrison Chambers, 32 Nassau Street, Dublin D02 YH68, Ireland, https://eu-contact.penguin.ie.

For Margot and Prue

We are what we pretend to be, so we must be careful about what we pretend to be.

—KURT VONNEGUT, *MOTHER NIGHT*

Life can only be understood backwards; but it must be lived forwards.

—SØREN KIERKEGAARD

AUTHOR'S NOTE

This novel is a work of fiction informed by my extensive interviews with hundreds of reality contestants, producers, camerapeople, audio professionals, and TV executives across dozens of reality shows. While I'm primarily known for my two times playing *Survivor*, all the characters, dialogue, and events in this book are fictional products of my own imagination.

What the book has taken from my personal experience is what it *feels* like to be on reality television. The characters are animated by my experiences, my thoughts, my joys, and my frustrations. I feel myself deeply in Miriam, the naive contestant stepping wide-eyed onto the show for the first time; and also in Kent, the old has-been, who returns to the reality TV circus too cynical and too knowing, with too much of himself on the line.

I've touched almost every part of the reality TV world, not only as a contestant, but as a television network executive, in my work for the Nonfiction Producers Association, and through fifteen years writing and podcasting about the genre. I've heard countless stories of manipulation, duplicity, and dangerous behavior. Almost anything can happen on a reality show, and many of the most outlandish, extreme events depicted in this book are informed by actual occurrences. However, I never encountered any of that from the extraordinary professionals on the *Survivor* team, who are truly the best in this business. Nothing in this book should be taken to impugn them. They gifted me the adventure of a lifetime, twice, and for that they have my eternal gratitude.

ESCAPE!

ACT ONE
CASTING

CHAPTER 1

KENT

When the phone rings, Kent Duvall is in the Memorabilia Room watching himself on the reality show *Endure.* On days when he is feeling his age and the slab of gut hangs like an anchor at his waist, he will pop the disc into his DVD player, which clicks and snaps like an arthritic joint. He doesn't need much. The show's intro features a three-second slow-motion shot of him pounding his chest in the tropical light, hair billowing around his face. God, he had epic hair, long blond locks that in the island's unreasonable humidity looked like they belonged to the lead singer of an eighties metal band. Last year, his wife, Margaret, insisted he shave his head. "You're starting to look like you have a comb-over," she said, walking her conversational tightrope between loving joke and withering insult. He'll watch that three-second clip again and again, rewinding and replaying, rewinding and replaying, and think to himself, *That is me.*

He still calls it the Memorabilia Room, though most of the memorabilia has been auctioned off on eBay. He argued that they were selling his treasures for much less than they were worth. Margaret said they were only "worth" what someone was willing to pay. What's left behind are the discolorations on the wallpaper to mark where he mounted the dull machete (fifty dollars), the necklace he carved out of driftwood and strung along a circlet of woven grass (seventy-five dollars), and the single set of clothes that he wore throughout the show's forty-five days, which reeked of sweat and woodsmoke even through the pane of protective glass (thirty dollars). The lone piece of memorabilia remaining is a photograph of him holding his one-hundred-thousand-dollar check and smiling into the universe.

Kent pauses the DVD to answer the phone. A woman with the improbable name of Gita Seuss is on the line. She's organizing a charity event, she says in a voice like a cowbell, where former reality television contestants will sign autographs and mingle with paying fans. The signing will benefit . . . He misses who exactly it is supposed to benefit.

"I asked the fans who they wanted to see," Gita Seuss is saying, "and your name came up again and again. I said, Kent Duvall? He was on over a decade ago. But your fans *love* you, with a devotion that transcends time."

Kent rolls his eyes. "I'll need some kind of appearance fee."

"We can pay for your travel and lodging, which is what I've offered all our guests."

"My appearance fee is fifteen hundred dollars."

"This is for *charity*," she says.

"You have to understand, I get a lot of invitations—"

Gita rattles off a list of other reality TV contestants who will attend. Most are names he doesn't recognize or wishes he didn't. A survivalist from *Naked and Afraid*, a finalist from *The Bachelor*, two *Amazing Race* winners, a longtime participant on MTV's *The Challenge*. Some are from television shows he's never heard of, shows he isn't even sure exist. *Beauty and the Geek. Extreme Pregnancy.* But Kent stands firm, and eventually Gita relents.

"The fans really want to see you," she says, the cowbell clanking mournfully.

Fifteen hundred dollars off the top—what will it even matter to the diabetic orphans or homeless pets? Kent was once a mainstay on the reality charity event circuit, and he remains mystified by the economics of these affairs. A few hundred fans pay what—thirty dollars? fifty dollars?—for the privilege of getting drunk with contestants from their favorite shows. Out of that, the event organizer covers airfare and lodging for fifty-some reality stars. What could possibly be left for charity? He imagines Gita Seuss proudly handing an oversize novelty check for $23.57 to a group of confused kids from the children's hospital. But then, he thinks, the economics aren't the point. He and his fellow has-beens can recapture for a few fleeting hours the feeling of being famous; the fans get to fill the void in their lives that can only be filled by the autographs of former reality TV stars; and Gita Seuss can ascend to heaven for her efforts.

"It's for *charity*," Kent says to Margaret over dinner that night.

"You're not digging wells in Africa. You're getting drunk at a bar."

"Why don't you come? It'll be fun. I bet I can get them to pay for—"

"No way, buster. I end up taking pictures while you play celebrity." Margaret has just come home from her shift at the hospital, and her face looks like a bruised orange.

"That's not true," Kent says.

"You *hate* these things. You come back miserable and talk about how annoying everybody is. They spend the entire time either explaining why they really deserved to win their show, or making alliances for a future season, so you drink too much and come home with a massive hangover. Then I have to spend the next day nursing you like a wounded bird."

"It's fifteen hundred dollars," he says, holding out his hands. The truth is, even more than they need the money, *he* needs the money. He's tired of being a freeloader, tired of watching his wife drink day-old coffee. Kent Duvall's wife deserves five-dollar lattes! Most of all, Kent is tired of the way Margaret looks at him. Like she doesn't expect anything more. Like she's resigned herself to life with a lump.

When he won the show, he quit his job to travel the country on the speaking circuit. His last paid speech was over four months ago. They gave him travel expenses and a five-hundred-dollar honorarium, and for that he rode a bus twelve hours to Shamrock Lakes, Indiana, on a frigid December afternoon. Seven bored kids swiped on their phones while he clicked through his PowerPoint and told them that if they believed in themselves, they could accomplish anything. Afterward, the tweedy professor who had organized the event drove him to the bus depot.

"It's *very* cold," the professor offered. "I can think of quite a few people who said they would come, but it's very cold."

Kent nodded.

"And the students have finals next week."

"Bad timing," Kent agreed.

"Well, *I'm* a huge fan," the tweedy professor said, bristling as if Kent were blaming him. "But I have to get back to campus. Do you mind if . . . ? The bus should be here any minute." And Kent waited for an hour in the bus depot, which was nothing more than a ticket kiosk and an out-of-order toilet that stank of piss, watching two meth heads bicker over which of them was at fault for ruining the other's life.

Margaret used to come with him, back when he could still fill auditoriums. While he spoke, he would find her in the first row of the audience, and they would lock eyes and share a little smile that said, *Isn't this all so silly?* She'd drive him home, his right leg still jackrabbiting from the adrenaline, and she would mock the tweedy professors and the pompous administrators who were *so honored to introduce*—"Honored? Really? No offense, babe, but you're not the president"—and he loved it because he could see her pride. He would see it in the twist of her mouth when people stopped him on the street, or that time he was on the cover of a magazine. Sure, it was his college alumni publication, but still, a glossy object you could hold in your hand. She had the look of a skeptic waiting for the two-bit magician to reveal the wrong card, when suddenly he pulls a dove from the air. She *liked* dating a reality star. And it seemed in those days that the audiences for the speeches would grow. That a meeting with a producer could turn into a TV hosting gig.

But for Margaret that dream died long ago, and in dying embarrassed her, like he had tricked her into exposing her most secret parts. And he was still giving these speeches.

"This could be an opportunity," he says to her now. "Billy Phillips will be there—"

"Billy Phillips the tech entrepreneur?"

"He was on this past season."

"Why would Billy Phillips do reality television?" she asks, with the disdain she now harbors for the one significant thing in his life.

"I don't know. Because he can? I was thinking—I could hit him up for a job."

"A job?" She looks suspicious. "What kind of job?"

"Any job," Kent says. He hadn't even thought of it before this moment, but it's true. He really could ask Billy Phillips for a job. The man employs hundreds, maybe thousands, and Kent has a way with people. "You know how these things work. Some HR employee gets a résumé forwarded by the CEO. They almost *have* to find something for me."

"Oh, Kent." Margaret takes his hand and kisses his fingers with a tenderness he hasn't felt from her in years, and Kent thinks maybe he can pull magic from the sky.

CHAPTER 2

BECK

I only took the gig on *Surf Dogs* because the prodco offered me show-runner with an EP credit. My work until that point had been teen moms and feuding housewives, emotional stuff, and *Surf Dogs* was exactly as ludicrous it sounds. Dogs were pulled by their owners on surfboards into the sea and then rode back to shore, where they were judged on balance and poise. My dad had thought I'd be a doctor. "We're bringing you in because we're hoping for a more elevated surfing-dog show," the network exec told me in my interview, quite earnestly. In my vanity, I let myself believe him. The show was tucked so high on the cable dial that flipping there too fast could make your ears pop. Still, we had a niche audience of animal fanatics and stoners, and our production crew had the scrappy unity of a high school math team.

Short, slobbery Buster the bulldog was going to be an audience favorite. Between rides, he'd dig holes in the sand and snap his jaws at the sand crabs. But while the show was ostensibly about the dogs, really it was about their owners, and Buster's hairstylist owner Dave was TV gold. He was six foot three with an extra inch of bleached-blond hair. While Buster surfed, Dave patrolled the shore like a jumbo-size bird of paradise, squawking at curious onlookers to keep away from his "hound."

It would have been easy to caricature Dave as a classic stage dad. From the way he name-dropped his salon's clientele—surf royalty I'd never heard of and eighties sitcom actors who'd retired to the shore—I could see in his mind he was basically already a celebrity. There was just the minor fact that he'd never appeared on-screen, and *Surf Dogs* was the very thing to buff out that flaw in the universe. But I wanted to give Dave more than a snarky parody edit. A decade of filming reality television has taught me that within every fussy fame whore lies a telenovela's worth of heartbreak, so I'd scheduled one last day of filming. One last chance to spelunk into Dave's subconscious and discover whatever trauma he was displacing onto his goofy little pet.

My crew set Dave up for an interview with his back to the ocean. Buster was cradled in his arms. The dog's tongue lolled from his mouth as he panted contentedly. It was a hot afternoon in Huntington Beach, the kind of brutal summer day in climate-apocalypse California where the air itself could ignite. Down the coast, tourists swarmed the pier. A little boy was standing on his tiptoes to stare through a rusted-out spyglass. Kids clustered around a kiosk where a hippie sold shark-tooth necklaces, clamoring for a totem of danger in their innocent little lives. My awareness was like a sonar, constantly pinging the world for stories.

"We've been talking for days about Buster," I began. "Let's talk about you. Why did *you* want to be on this show?"

"I'm out here to celebrate Buster and all the surfing dogs who bring joy to the community through their talents!" Dave scratched Buster behind the ears, and the dog snorted happily.

I smiled and nodded. "Did you have any personal reasons for applying?"

"I personally believe so much in these incredible dogs."

I kept smiling. This was the challenge of filming reality TV today. People lived inside a carapace of clichés. They'd read so many hyperbolic articles from entertainment media that their internal headspace was like a breathless headline from People.com. But for the sake of Dave's story, I needed to shuck that shell like an oyster. Let the camera slurp up his salty-sweet humanity. I'd been noticing his accent. You can learn a person's life story from their diphthongs, and Dave's flattened vowels suggested small-town Midwest. I imagined a taciturn farmer dad, a long-suffering mother standing over the stove. And here this bleached-blond man-child was racing across a California beach playing hype monster for a surfing bulldog.

"You're not originally from California, are you?" I asked.

"Iowa, actually."

Nailed it. I feigned surprise. "I'm from Chicago. Look at us, two Midwesterners. What brought you out west?"

"The same thing that brings everyone, I guess."

"Fame?"

He nodded, suddenly wary.

"When I moved here from Chicago, I figured I'd be an Oscar-winning director by now." I shook my head and laughed, though I was never interested in following a script. Reality television lets you tie a bow out of the tangled ribbon of life.

"I wanted to be an actor," Dave said.

"Let me guess. You were a high school theater star who moved to Hollywood?"

He shifted on the sand and ran his fingers through his spiky hair.

"You can imagine how my doctor dad feels about reality TV," I said. "My mom—she passed away. Aneurysm. When I was four."

Sharing your tragedies is a tactic. You make the subject comfortable by showing that you're vulnerable too. The trick is that you have to show real feeling, because people have sensitive barometers for BS. I pictured the tickle of my mother's hair falling on my face as she read to me in bed. The rough corduroy of her skirt in my hand as I hid behind her legs. I had to come at it sideways–fragments, discrete sense memories–or I'd lose it for real. A lone tear slid from the corner of my eye. I could see the sympathy well up in him.

"I was the same. A . . . disappointment," Dave said tentatively, not performing anymore but genuinely sharing. I had him. "I thought if I made it big, I could show everybody back home."

Normal producers would end the conversation there. I was sure Dave would give me more. I said nothing and let the silence build. Silence exerts its own pressure. It demands to be filled.

At last Dave whispered, "If I can give Buster his moment in the spotlight, maybe I didn't fail."

If my cameraman wasn't zooming in on Dave's face, I'd have to strangle him to death later.

I AM A REALITY TELEVISION PRODUCER. FOR OVER A DECADE, I'VE walked through people's private worlds, my camera crews recording the vulnerable details that my subjects wouldn't share with their most intimate friends. After we film a hundred hours of chaotic real life, I edit the story into a tight forty-two minutes of television. People's long-shot dreams turn into victories. Their tragedies are mere setups for healing and growth.

That's the promise of reality TV. That's what drew me to the medium. I was a lonely kid, but in high school I'd come home and watch *The Real World* and feel like I was hanging out with my own best friends. We'd go on adventures, start businesses, have fights that we'd resolve by hugging it out after a boozy night. In college I started to see that reality television could be even more. While my roommates were out partying, I watched people have life epiphanies on *16 and Pregnant* and *Celebrity Rehab with Dr. Drew.* They realized they'd never faced their traumas. They'd been offloading their pain onto sex and drugs.

I wanted to gift people that kind of closure. I couldn't believe when I got my first job logging tapes on *The Bachelor.* I spent late nights and weekends in my cubicle scrubbing through the raw footage, watching people confess their deepest desires. I felt like I'd gained private access to the universe's hidden secrets. Even the contestants who didn't get a rose learned valuable truths about themselves. In the process, we all caught a glimpse of our shared humanity.

"You can fix a joint," I told my dad when I got my first job as a story producer. "But I can fix a life."

Dad was an orthopedic surgeon. He snorted in derision.

Still I believe that every beat-down, cynical adult was once a wide-eyed child who deserves more from this meat-grinder world. If they open up, I can give it to them.

Everyone gets the story arc they deserve.

BY THE TIME MY INTERVIEW WITH DAVE WAS OVER, THE WIND WAS shivering down the shoreline, and parents were bundling their kids into towels. Somehow it had turned cold.

"Should we call it?" Conrad, my cameraman, had been stealing glances at his watch.

I looked out across the sea. It was the golden hour, that moment before dusk when the sun's angle scatters the harsh blue light and suffuses the earth with reds and oranges. The kind of light that renders our transient and flawed world into something mystical and serene on camera. I could imagine Buster's perfect ride set against Dave's heartfelt confessional. The little dog fulfilling Dave's displaced dreams.

"I want to shoot one last ride," I said.

Disappointment etched Conrad's face.

"You guys go home, though."

"I don't mind hanging out," Conrad said, clearly not meaning it.

I shooed him away. Conrad had a two-hour drive in traffic back to his family in Santa Monica. I was living out of a suitcase in the Surf On Inn.

"Take care of my baby." He handed me the Sony FX9. With its thick black carapace and distended eye, it evoked a giant mechanical bug. "And get him to admit that he named the dog after the Dave and Buster's arcades, okay?"

My crew walked away down the beach, and I beckoned Dave toward the ocean. He saw the perfect light and hurried to slip Buster's life jacket over the dog's head. His fingers fumbled as he buckled the straps. He positioned Buster on the surfboard and pushed the dog into the water. A few gawkers gathered to watch the local legend.

The sun was sinking toward the horizon, and the waves settled into a momentary calm as I set my shot. Buster crouched on the board. He flexed his haunches and leaned forward. Dave let go and ran out of frame.

"Are you getting this?" he shouted. "Are you getting this?"

It really was beautiful, if you could forget the ever-present absurdity that this was a TV show about surfing dogs. The sun saturated the Pacific. Fat little Buster balanced on his board. I felt—a moment of peace. I had my perfect story, neatly framed in the viewfinder.

Then a small wave, barely a ripple, caught the board sideways. Buster wobbled and tipped. Dogs fall off all the time, so I kept filming. His orange life jacket bobbed on the waterline. In my camera, I watched the waves lap against his chin as he paddled toward shore. But the undertow pulled him farther out. Dave was still running toward me, shouting, "Are you getting this?!" I yelled at Dave to turn around, but the wind snagged my voice. Another wave—a much bigger wave—was massing. "Keep rolling," I told myself. It's the number one rule of reality production. If a crisis occurs, find help, but no matter what, keep rolling. *This* was drama. As soon as Dave heard me, he would race into the sea. Dave would save Buster, just like Buster was saving him. I could imagine the clip in the local news, the giddy calls from the network's execs. Could *Surf Dogs* win an Emmy? The whole country witnessing the zigzag ways that people rise above their past failures. Through my viewfinder, Buster's chin was hoisted above the water as his little paws desperately paddled, and in my mind, I was onstage at the Peacock Theater hoisting my statuette. I caught Dad's eye in the audience. *I told you so*, I mouthed to him. The wave crashed down.

A few onlookers on the beach began to shout. I couldn't see Buster anywhere. "Keep rolling," I told myself again. You can hear me on the tape if you watch it back. Millions of people heard it when the network leaked the video. I pressed my eye into the camera and shouted again. Finally, Dave heard. He twisted on his lanky legs, stumbled, righted himself in the sand, and sprinted into the surf. I zoomed in on him. This was a decision the commentariat would notice: that I *zoomed*. Like it was proof of my complicity. Dave splashed into the water. At last the orange life jacket popped above the surface. In the viewfinder, Buster's thick head bobbed on the waterline. His paws weren't paddling anymore.

Dave lurched through the shallows with Buster's body sagging in his arms. The dog's tongue was slack. A crowd gathered as Dave performed canine CPR. "Keep rolling," I whispered, the camera pressed so hard against my eye that my forehead ached. I was nothing more than an eye, nothing more than a lens. A noble bystander shouted, "Stand back, everyone! Stand back!" The crowd gasped when water dribbled from Buster's jaw. But it was too late.

The reds and oranges of the golden hour were bruising into the dark blues of early evening as Dave staggered off the beach with his lifeless dog in his arms. His grief was magisterial. I followed him with my camera in a daze until a bystander swatted at its lens.

"You monster," she hissed. "What's wrong with you?"

That's where the video ends.

CHAPTER 3

KENT

As he walks through the lobby toward the garish hotel bar, Kent wonders if the fans will even recognize him. It's an eighties party, and he's wearing a feathered blond wig and sequined pants. But when he steps into the swirl of pointing fans, of reality stars high-fiving over rounds of shots—"Dude, I loved you on your season!" "I loved you on *your* season!"—the old show pony inside him shakes its mane.

There is an order to this chaos, like the physics of a tropical storm. At the fringes of the party are the casual fans. They shift uncomfortably, not entirely sure why they're here, nudging one another as each passing reality contestant enters the fray. Past them is a circle of superfans. These people show up at every event and have formed a community that exists on top of these events, like bees pollinating a flower bed. Some Kent recognizes from his early days on the circuit. They've come prepared, with high-priced photo gear to capture the evening in HD and push it out across social media. Finally, in the eye of the party, at the bar, is the mass of contestants themselves, feeding off the attention from the fans and each other. For six months while their seasons aired, they were celebrities, and then they weren't.

A tentative fan approaches him. "Excuse me, Kent? Can I get a selfie?"

"Of course!" His mouth smiles into the flashing phone as his eyes scour the crowded bar for Billy Phillips. "Would you ever go on *Endure*?" Kent asks.

"*Me?*" The fan chuckles, delighted with the idea. "I get grouchy when I miss lunch."

"You could do it," Kent says. "If you believe in yourself, you can accomplish anything."

He spies Billy Phillips across the room. He's in a leather vest like Billy Idol, and his hair is dyed blond and spiked. He's chatting with two young women with dark mascara, both dressed in black. They look like the backup dancers in a Robert Palmer video. Kent shoulders his way through the crowd, smiling for selfies.

"Kent!" Billy Phillips screams into his face. "Kent Duvall! The legend!" It's only seven p.m., but Billy Phillips is already wildly drunk.

"Billy. It's such an–"

"You're a beast," Billy says. "Dude, when you– Man, I still remember how– Woooo!" He raises his drink into the sky as if he's clinking glasses with God.

"Sorry to interrupt." Kent is used to the antic energy of reality TV contestants, but Billy Phillips is drawing his power from a purer source. An old photo from Billy's pre-wealth days lives on the internet. Overweight, fully bald at twenty-three. Now he has a personal trainer, a private chef, probably an on-staff hair replacement surgeon personally harvesting follicles from a high school's worth of teenage boys. He looks like a werewolf on the Atkins diet. Kent says, "I wanted to talk to you about–"

"Hold that thought." Billy leans in close and stage-whispers to Kent, "I think I'm going to have a threesome with these girls." The

Robert Palmer girls shift in place. They can clearly hear him but seem not to care.

"I'd love to grab a moment," Kent says. "Just to discuss—"

"I am fucked up, man. But tomorrow. I'm peacing out after the group dinner. But I would be honored. Let's sit together. Dinner with the legend. I can't believe it. Dude. You are a *beast.*" Billy fist-bumps Kent, hugs him, looks him in the eyes, and fist-bumps him again.

"I'll be there," Kent says. "And, listen, a word of advice."

"Hit me."

"Don't hook up with fans. It's taboo."

"I think you may not have heard me," Billy says. "I said *threesome.*"

"Think about it. You sleep with a fan, and that's going to be on every chat board on the internet."

"So what?" Billy asks.

Kent has no answer for that. So what? There was a code. It just wasn't done. So what? It was so obviously bad that it didn't bear explaining. So what? Kent twists his wedding ring and walks away.

He sits down at a table with a group of former contestants—a gravedigger, an astronaut, a school bus driver, and a Roller Derby girl.

"Well, well," the gravedigger says. "Look who's come out of retirement."

"Doing some pregaming for the new show?" asks the astronaut.

"They're doing another *All Stars*?" Kent asks.

"Oh ho, Mr. Coy." The Roller Derby girl smiles. "Not an *All Stars.* Some spin-off. They're looking for legends like *myself* to help launch it."

"First round of calls went out last week," says the school bus driver.

"Is there going to be a second round?" Kent asks.

"Smile for a picture," shouts a fan. With barely a ripple, the five pivot, smile, and turn back to each other.

"I'll make a pregame deal," says the Roller Derby girl. "But I already have a side deal with Carl."

"Carl?" says the astronaut. "There's no way they'll cast Carl. His confessionals are shit."

"Fans *love* Carl," says the Roller Derby girl. She points across the room, where a mob has surrounded a six-foot-four Goliath in full camouflage, with a huge tangled beard that looks like it might be the winter home to a family of woodland creatures. "What a slut," says the Roller Derby girl.

The subject of going back on television makes the show pony tug against its bit. It worries Kent that he hasn't heard anything. No early calls, no rumors. Not that he would even want to do TV again, he thinks. These people spend their lives waiting to redeem their past failures on another season, but he hadn't done anything wrong. He'd won.

Still, the idea that they would cast *Carl.*

And what would going back on TV even do to his legacy? When the fans look at him, they see that slow-motion shot of him beating his chest, his hair feathering around him in the sun. Could forty-four-year-old Kent—balding, sagging Kent—ever live up to that? But what if he could? What a story that would be. And think of the fans. Not that he needs the attention, but it could be great for his speeches. He could sell out auditoriums again. . . .

No. Because ten years from now, he'd be right back here, with even less hair. Margaret's right, he thinks. These events are all the same. But Kent has dinner tomorrow with Billy Phillips. He's a *beast.* He's a *legend.* He'll redeem all that wasted time. He texts Margaret: *spoke to billy, getting dinner tomorrow.* She sends him back three hearts. *My babe*, she writes. *I'm proud of you.*

He heads to the bar for a drink. A cute blonde is standing next to him. He's noticed her eyeing him all evening. Ashley something. She was the first person off the show this season—a beverage marketer or pharmaceutical sales representative. She had volunteered for her team in the gross insects challenge, he remembers, and then panicked when they poured tarantulas on her. Was a tarantula even an insect? There'd been an on-screen chyron, #TarantulaFreakout. Now she's looking around the room with that familiar first boot expression, desperate to be recognized and certain that she doesn't deserve to be.

"Hi," he says. "Ashley, right?"

"Oh my god, you know who I am. Kent Duvall knows who I am!" Ashley's wearing a spandex leotard with pink wristbands. She looks like she just stepped off the cover of a Jazzercise VHS. "I am literally dying right now. I'm such a fan!"

"Don't say that. You're one of *us* now."

"I remember watching you win when I was eight years old!"

Kent refuses to do the math.

A thin man with a skin disorder wearing a Megadeth T-shirt is standing a few feet away taking pictures of them on his Nikon and smiling secretively to himself. It's not clear if the T-shirt is part of a costume or if the man simply hasn't bothered to change clothes since 1988.

"Smile for the camera!" Kent says. He grips Ashley by the shoulder and gives a loopy, exaggerated grin. The fan takes the smile as an invitation and closes the distance.

"I want to shake your hand," he says to Kent, barely registering Ashley.

"You can do that." Kent offers his right hand, keeping the left one around Ashley's shoulder. Hanging loosely. Casually. Two pals. Kent's never cheated on Margaret, but he has enjoyed the occasional innocent flirtation. It's as if by his physical proximity to Ashley he's maintaining—not a set of options, exactly, but a set of possibilities.

"Man, when you—when you caught that shark with a spear," the fan says. "I couldn't believe it. I said to my wife, someday I'm going to meet him and shake his hand."

"Dreams really do come true," Kent says. He never caught a shark with a spear. He killed a boar, and the man was either misremembering that or confusing him with some other contestant, possibly from some other show.

"Sure enough," says the man. "I'm Travis."

"I'm Kent. This is Ashley."

"I know who you are!" Megadeth says to Kent. He hardly glances at Ashley. "I'd like to buy you a shot, Kent."

"Only if you buy Ashley one too."

Megadeth leans in to the bartender and orders three lemon drops.

"Lemon drops?" Kent asks. "Are we sorority girls?"

Megadeth stammers a response, and Kent's heart squeezes in pity. "Just kidding," he says. This is how he is supposed to feel. In control. Extending pity. Bestowing grace.

"What should we toast to?" Kent asks.

Megadeth is speechless, still flushed with embarrassment over the lemon drop debacle.

"How about to sharks?" Kent offers. "Because they don't stop moving till—"

"Till Kent kills 'em!" Megadeth exclaims. "To sharks!" The three clink glasses and down the shots. The sweet and sour liquid puckers Kent's mouth.

"It was great meeting you," he says to Megadeth, and with a firm handshake he ends the conversation. Megadeth walks away, and Kent whispers to Ashley, "Should we get a non-sorority-girl drink?"

The night speeds up. He's signing autographs, posing with groups of other contestants. There are more shots. A shy fan approaches and asks him to autograph a photo, and he autographs her forehead. He performs karaoke with the survivalist from *Naked and Afraid*, belting out "We Are the Champions" in a trilling falsetto as he struts across the stage.

He is walking outside with Ashley to the hotel pool. The air smells of chlorine, and the sliver of moon at the pool bottom looks like he could scoop it up into his hands. Ashley leads him to the far end, away from the crowd. They sit on the diving board. She's asking him about the other contestants she's met that night, and Kent is eviscerating them one by one. He's so drunk that his guilt at this series of small betrayals is far down inside him, like the pulse of his heart in his toe. The Roller Derby girl buys her Instagram followers. The astronaut tried to kill himself. Carl's only a millionaire if you're counting STDs.

"You know what I hate the most?" Kent's face is numb from the booze. It's like speaking through an ice-cream cake shaped in his image. "People make these judgments based on this edited show. But that's not the *real me*. Sometimes I feel like the fans just expect so much—and I hate that I'm letting them down."

"You? You're *Kent Duvall*," Ashley breathes. "I was only out there for four days. I was barely even on the show. Nobody here knows who I am. When the fans do talk to me, it's almost, like, out of pity."

"Hey. Those first four days are the *hardest*. You were there as much as anybody. You starved. You slept in the dirt. You shivered in the cold."

"I'm not even scared of tarantulas," she says, as if picking up an argument that was already in progress, one that has been in progress for many months. "It was that coffin. It was so *hot*. You lose control for one second, and then for the rest of your life, you're hashtag tarantula freakout."

"Nobody thinks that about you," he says, though in fact that is exactly what he remembers about her. The show did a slow-motion zoom on her face, frozen in Pompeian terror. Kent wasn't sure if the high-pitched shrieks were hers or a sound effect added in post.

"I'm *not* one of these ditzy girls," Ashley is saying. "I grew up on a ranch. Did you know I built our shelter? Me. A girl. But they didn't show *that*. If you're blond and you freak out, then . . ." Ashley shakes her head and looks up at Kent. "If I ever get a second chance, I've been practicing."

"Practicing?" A ranch girl. He notes the muscles in her forearms that definitely aren't from spin class or cardio boot camp.

"With the tarantulas. I go down to the pet store. The owner's a friend. He lets them crawl on my face." She shudders, despite her practice. "Do you think they'd call me for an *All Stars*? Or this new show? People say I'm a memorable first boot. I heard they might do a season that's all first boots."

"You'd be a *lock*," he says. "You're exactly who they want. Someone who has a big story inside them, who just needs a second chance."

The way she gazes at him reminds him of the way girls used to look at him, when his season first aired. Before *Endure*, he'd been average Kent, a normal guy who blended into the background in a crowded sports bar. And then, at his viewing party for the show's premiere, a superfan tipsily asked if he wanted to fuck her in the men's room. She had sandy hair in a ponytail and a look of worry around her eyes that suggested in her sober hours she was somebody's mom. Kent was twenty-nine and had only had sex with five people. Now suddenly women were texting him unsolicited naked pics. The veterinarian from *Endure*'s first season messaged him on Facebook saying she heard a spoiler he'd done well, and did he want to party?

The most puzzling part was why. It wasn't like he was on *Top Chef* or *Project Runway*, shows that demonstrated how he could fricassee a chicken or create haute couture from a pile of garbage bags—skills that could theoretically at least be applied in real life. On *Endure* he'd made fire and shat outside. And so the only explanation was that it was the very fact of being on television that somehow made Kent appealing, the very fact that high-definition images of him under a soaring orchestral score were broadcast via cable to households nationwide.

He met Margaret at one of those viewing parties. She was out at the same bar with her friends. "Who are *you*?" she asked, in a *Why should I give a shit?* way. At the time he found her irresistibly alluring, a cold breeze as he was swaddled in his blanket of praise. She saw his inner undeserving self, the disappointing muck he knew was at the core of his being, but she stayed with him anyway. But Margaret's chill wind kept blowing even as his blanket frayed. At a certain point their relationship became a mystery to them both. They were still together simply because they had been together, because they both secretly believed they didn't deserve more. She doesn't really have to drink day-old coffee, he thinks now. She's punishing herself. To punish him.

"Do you want to see my boobs?" Ashley asks.

Suddenly Kent feels old and paternal. Is this what the young people do now? Just show their breasts? *Oh, Ashley*, he thinks. *You do not want to show me your boobs.* But he can see the neediness blaring from her eyes. She needs validation—*Kent Duvall's* validation. If he refuses, she'll feel rejected. How could he do that to poor Ashley? Really the only decent thing for him to do is to look at her boobs.

"It's a hard offer to turn down." Nobody can accuse him of *asking*. He's simply not *refusing*.

Ashley pulls down her top, and there are her breasts.

"Very nice," he says, trying to maintain eye contact.

"That's all?" she asks.

No. That's not all. They are gorgeous breasts. Is there such a thing as the reverse of a memento mori? Something that makes you believe in possibilities that transcend time? That no matter how much his own skin sags, no matter how far his hairline recedes, somewhere in the world there will be perfect breasts like Ashley's? He realizes he is staring, and just to relieve the awkwardness of the moment—just for Ashley's sake, really—Kent leans down and kisses her.

CHAPTER 4

The pounding that he thought was coming from his skull is in fact coming from his hotel door. Kent staggers across the room. Standing in the hallway is a small woman with pancake makeup and a bouffant hairdo.

"We're all *waiting.*"

He recognizes that cowbell.

"Waiting for me?" Kent is struggling to get his bearings. Last night is a series of disconnected images, like a flip-book out of order.

"On the bus. The reason you're here?" Gita Seuss leans in close. "The reason I am paying you fifteen hundred dollars instead of donating that to the *children*?"

"Children?" A clue. Okay. So the charity has something to do with children.

"Let's go."

"Could I have a moment of privacy?"

"Now."

He's still wearing his sequined pants. Gita Seuss stands there watching while he slips on a T-shirt from his duffel. His mouth tastes of dead weasel, and he makes a lunge to grab his toothbrush, but she thrusts herself into the open bathroom doorway.

"*Now,*" she says again.

He opens the minibar and takes a tiny bottle of vodka.

"You're going to pay for that," Gita says, with genuine loathing.

"I know." He chugs the vodka and tosses the empty bottle into the trash.

Gita Seuss grabs his hand and pulls him shuffling out of the hotel toward a yellow school bus that is idling in the parking lot. "I don't know why it's so difficult for you people," she says. "I work so hard to do a little good, but give someone an ounce of fame, and suddenly they're better than everyone else." The bus smells of exhaust and vinyl seating. They're all sitting there, crammed into the tiny benches: fifty-seven glaring, hungover former reality television contestants. At the back of the bus, Billy Phillips is chattering to the Roller Derby girl, as high-octane as a revving motorcycle. Ashley scoots to the side of her bench, making room, but Kent can't even look at her.

"Plant your ass," Gita Seuss says, and he sits down in the open seat.

"Hey," Ashley says.

"Hey." Kent angles his feet away from her, into the aisle. The seat in front of him is ripped, exposing tufts of foam, yellow as an aging cheese. He deserves to feel like shit, he thinks. This is his penance. As the bus pulls out of the parking lot, Kent forces himself to think of Margaret. The time they went sledding at India Point Park, cramming onto one child-size plastic orange disk. On their first run, they hit a bump sideways and flipped, tumbling down the icy hill. Kent panicked as he pulled her from a snowdrift. Would she be injured? Or worse, furious? But when she surfaced, Margaret was laughing so hard that he couldn't tell her tears from the melting snow.

He learned there was nothing Margaret found funnier than wipeouts. "Diggers," she called them. He's seen her contorted over a YouTube video of people falling off rope swings. Ski fails, inner tube flips. Margaret was a connoisseur. And when it was herself taking a digger, that was funniest of all. But the first time Kent saw her overcome with glee was in that snowbank, and he forces himself to think about her laughing, crying face.

As the bus's diesel engine throbs beneath him, however, the blurry mental Polaroids of last night start to saturate. And as Kent is dragging the sled up the hill for their second run, Margaret heckling the other sledders, there's the slalom of Ashley's hip. And as Kent tries to steer back toward the same bump, hoping to wipe out in the same way, there's Ashley on the edge of the hotel bed, wearing only one sock and both pink wristbands. And a new feeling starts to surge upward, much, much worse than the guilt. Kent starts to feel aroused. He focuses on the rip in the seat in front of him, forcing the foam back inside with his fingers.

The bus takes them to an outdoor mall that borders a man-made lake, where volunteers herd the contestants toward three rows of long tables. Kent's grateful just to be led, to be liberated for a moment from the weight of his consciousness. In front of each seat is a placard with the contestant's name, their reality show, and how well they did. It must be a thousand degrees. Heat warps the air. In the distance, a line of fans stretches into infinity. Each has paid thirty dollars or fifty dollars to receive a poster with pictures of the different contestants. They will progress through the gauntlet of tables collecting autographs. Kent can hardly believe anyone would wait for two hours in this obscene heat to receive scribbled names on commemorative posters. He wishes he cared about anything as much as these people care about former reality TV contestants.

Gita Seuss blows a whistle, and the press of fans files in. The contestants are arranged in order of their show's season, so Kent is near the front. Fans approach the table and hand him their posters, and he scrawls *Kent Duvall, winner*, above his face. The picture is the same shot of him smiling into the starry future that is framed in the Memorabilia Room. Some of the fans want a selfie. They lean across the table, and he puts his hand around their shoulders and smiles into their phones. He can feel them shaking beneath his hand like frightened rabbits. "Would you ever do the show?" he asks. "*Me?*" They chuckle. "I get grouchy when I miss lunch!"

An hour into the event, and the line of fans still blurs into the horizon. Kent's head is pounding when a man thrusts the poster into his hands and says, "Can you sign it 'To sharks'?"

The phrase is vaguely familiar, like a jingle from a long-ago commercial. Kent looks up. Standing above him is a man in a Megadeth T-shirt. Oh yes. This guy.

"To sharks," the man says again, like it's their private joke.

"Oh, hey," Kent says. "To sharks."

"That was a fun night," Megadeth says.

"Hell yeah."

"Check out these pics. You're in a bunch of them."

Megadeth leans over the table and presents Kent with his Nikon's LCD screen. He clicks through a re-creation of Kent's previous evening. "There's you and Ashley at the bar. That's you singing karaoke. That's you signing an autograph. That's you and Ashley at the pool. That's another of you at the pool." Kent's breath catches in his chest. You can clearly see in the second picture that Ashley's top is pulled down. In the next, their foreheads are almost pressed together. "Here's you and Ashley kissing." Megadeth keeps narrating as if these pictures that could destroy Kent's life are of purely anthropological interest. "That's you and Ashley leaving the bar." There's no menace in the man's voice. Just description.

Kent can sense the line shifting behind Megadeth, annoyed fans jostling in the heat.

"Wait. Go back." Kent's voice is hoarse.

"Go back?" Megadeth asks.

"Scroll back," Kent says, but what he really means is *go back* in time, flip backward through the camera's pictures so that the night can end in that first loopy grin.

"Sir, there is a *line*," the woman behind Megadeth says.

"I paid my thirty dollars," Megadeth says to the woman. "I'm going to take my turn."

"I paid my thirty dollars just like you," the woman says. "Your turn doesn't get to last all day."

"Sorry, ma'am." Kent grabs Megadeth and pulls him away from the tables, toward the artificial lake. The stagnant water stinks. Green algae scums its surface. The lake is clogged with discarded debris from the mall patrons—a Starbucks cup, food wrappers, the plastic packaging from a Barbie.

"I'm going to lose my place," Megadeth objects. "I want to get Carl—"

"I need you to delete those pictures."

Megadeth takes a step back in horror. "Delete them? I can't do that."

"Why not?"

"I've got to upload them. The whole reason I come to these events is to document them for my followers."

Kent feels his headache pushing out from the center of his skull. Little black specks polka-dot his vision. "I'll pay you back your entrance fee. How much was it? Thirty dollars? I'll pay you a hundred dollars. I'll pay you five hundred dollars."

"It's not about *money*." Megadeth looks offended. "My followers count on me."

"Okay, not all the pictures. Just delete the ones of me and Ashley." Kent leans in close and holds up his ring finger with its scratched gold band. "I have a wife."

"I have a Facebook," Megadeth counters. "My followers expect me to document this event. Who would I be if I deleted these because it's inconvenient for you?"

Kent stares at Megadeth. In his hangover, he must be missing something. "Are you fucking with me?"

"Can I tell you why I like *Endure*?" Megadeth asks. "Because it's pure. No tricks. No compromises. Man against the wild."

Wonderful. He's being held hostage by a lunatic. Kent isn't a romantic person, but romantic notions are flowing out of him. "Please. My wife—Margaret—she's the best thing that ever happened to me. My whole life has been looking for people to *like* me, but Margaret, she *loves* me." Is it true? It could be true. "Even in spite of—me. That's why I'm here, to—"

Megadeth is unmoved.

"Is there anything I can do?" Kent begs. "What if we—trade?"

Megadeth takes a deep breath, as though the prospect that something might weigh against his fidelity to his Facebook page has never occurred to him. "Wow. A trade."

"Yes! A trade. You'd be giving me the photos, and in exchange, I'd be doing something for you. A trade."

Back at the tables, Kent sees the woman from the line talking to Gita Seuss.

"Well, the kiddos are big fans," Megadeth says. "Not of you. You're before their time. But of the show. You could come to dinner at my house tonight."

"Tonight?" Tonight is dinner with Billy Phillips. "Tonight's no good. Tomorrow?" His mind is spinning. He can reschedule his flight. It's not like he has work. He'll make up some excuse to tell Margaret—

"Nuh-uh," Megadeth says. "First it's tomorrow. Then tomorrow something comes up, and it's next week, and by the time you finally come over, none of my followers will even care about the pictures anymore."

Gita Seuss is storming toward him.

"Okay," Kent says, the show pony spooking and rearing. "Tonight."

CHAPTER 5

The Megadeth household is shockingly normal. Family photos are taped to the refrigerator. Inspirational slogans are carved on wood blocks. BLESS THIS HOUSE WITH LOVE AND LAUGHTER. A PERFECT MARRIAGE IS TWO IMPERFECT PEOPLE WHO REFUSE TO GIVE UP ON EACH OTHER. Mrs. Megadeth—a careworn mom of two—bustles around the kitchen preparing roast chicken. What does this woman think of her husband spending his nights playing paparazzi with reality contestants? A towheaded boy sets the table. A little girl peeks shyly from behind a door. Kent swanned in here like an honored guest, but this is a functioning family he could only dream of.

At dinner, Megadeth peppers Kent with questions about the shark he killed. Kent doesn't want to correct a man in front of his wife and kids. So he makes up a story. He was wading into the water to spearfish when a dorsal fin cut through the waves. It was giant—not a great white, but close. The creature was swimming straight for him. He raised his spear into the air and—

"No," Megadeth says. "That's not how I remember it."

"It was edited differently on TV," Kent says. "Trust me."

"Don't tell me what I saw with my own two eyes."

Kent shrugs. He doesn't care what Megadeth believes. All he cares about is salvaging his marriage and, if he hustles, making his dinner with Billy Phillips.

"This was delicious. But I really should be heading—"

"You know what the kiddos would love?" Megadeth says. "For us to face off mano a mano."

"You want to . . . fight?"

The entire family cracks up. "Not *real* fighting," Megadeth says. "Wii boxing."

"Sounds fun, but I have to go," Kent insists, but Megadeth's look says *Remember our deal.* And so Kent follows the family to their sixty-five-inch flat-screen, where the game is already loaded. Megadeth hands him the Wii's plastic remote. Kent throws a tentative jab and watches his digital avatar swing its fist into a digital Megadeth.

"Ya got me!" Megadeth says. "You ready?"

They fight. Kent jabs with his left arm, shifts his hips for right crosses, and pivots for hooks. He connects with a few good punches, but Megadeth maneuvers his controller with the precise tiny motions needed for maximum impact. Before long, Kent's avatar is KO'd.

"You did it, baby!" shouts Mrs. Megadeth. "You KO'd Kent Duvall!"

"You can do better than that," Megadeth says. "Rematch."

"I really should be getting back," Kent says. It's seven thirty. His window of opportunity is closing.

"Best of three," Megadeth insists.

Kent glances at his phone. There's a text from Margaret: *How's dinner with Billy?* she wants to know. *An unexpected struggle*, he writes back. He takes up the Wii boxing remote. The announcer shouts, "Fight!" This time Kent doesn't even try to dodge or counterpunch. He takes a dive. He lets Megadeth e-pummel him. Within seconds, his avatar is on the mat.

"There it is. You won," Kent says. "Thank you again so much for—"

"You can't just get KO'd in ten seconds," says the wife. "You killed a shark."

"Don't be such a lump," says the little boy.

"Lump!" repeats the little girl, giggling.

"You said best of three," Kent says. "You won. I'm going back to the hotel."

"You have to *try*," Megadeth says. "Now it's best of five."

The next round, Kent is angry. He made one stupid mistake, and now he's trapped here for eternity? Watching his one shot at a decent life slip away? Rage fills him, and he flails and jabs with his whole body. To his amazement, it works. Megadeth is on the ropes. The digital crowd goes wild.

"Beat his ass!" Mrs. Megadeth laughs.

Kent dances across the living room as though it is the arena of his life, punching and dodging. Yes, he is going to e-fight his way out of here. He is going to knock out Megadeth and storm out the door. He's taken by a wild physical joy. He will meet Billy Phillips, he will get a job in sales, he will go home to his wife. He made a mistake, but he's learned from it, and isn't that all you can ask? Megadeth's health meter is heading to zero. One more good punch and he'll be finished.

But as Kent winds up a haymaker, Megadeth flicks his wrist. The man has only been toying with him. A massive uppercut sends Kent's digitized head thudding to the mat.

BY THE TIME KENT'S TAXI ARRIVES BACK AT THE HOTEL, IT'S TEN P.M. and he's drenched in sweat. Megadeth went six undefeated rounds, and this pummeling was followed by Mrs. Megadeth and both children.

"*There* you are," Gita Seuss hisses. She's standing by the hotel entrance, as if she's been peering into the night for hours waiting to accost him. "*Everyone's* been asking about you."

"Have you seen Billy?" Kent asks. "Billy Phillips?"

She squints at him like he's covered in open sores. "Billy left hours ago, and you could benefit from learning a few—"

Kent walks past her, toward the bar.

"This is your last year!" she shouts after him. "You're not welcome again!"

He laughs at the absurdity of her threat. He's failed at the main goal of this now lost weekend, but at least he's salvaged his marriage. He sits at the bar and orders a Jack neat. Next to him is a professional poker player, and as Kent drinks the whiskey, to take the edge off, she explains to him why chemtrails are a government plot to control the weather. He's comforted by the familiar lunacy. He will stay here for hours, he decides, having ridiculous conversations, and tomorrow he will gratefully return to his normal life.

"Have you seen this?"

Ashley is standing behind him, brandishing her phone inches from his face. Her browser is open to a Reddit thread: "Did Kent Duvall and Ashley Collins hook up at the Alabama event?" He grabs her phone. There's a zoomed-in picture of him and Ashley on the diving board. The image is grainy, but it's clearly them. Ashley's top is pulled down. Did Megadeth upload the photo? No, that would go against the man's insane moral code. And the pictures are far too low-res for Megadeth's pricey Nikon.

"Who took this?" he rasps.

Ashley shrugs and gestures around the bar. There are hundreds of fans who have uploaded thousands of pictures over the last two days. Among those thousands, some enterprising sleuth has zoomed in on the extreme background of just one.

"Can you believe someone made a thread about us?" Ashley's concern can't disguise her delight. "Does Casting look at this stuff?"

In the picture, Ashley gazes past his shoulder right into the crowd. *She knew.* His phone buzzes in his pocket. He orders a shot of Jack, but the phone is buzzing; it won't stop buzzing.

"Hello?" He's in a toilet stall, whispering.

"I'm so fucking *embarrassed*," Margaret says. "Three friends of ours have already sent me the link to your little escapade."

"I didn't ask her to. She just–"

"The worst part is, I thought better of you. Not that you wouldn't cheat. I'm not that naive. But I figured if you did, you'd show a little fucking discretion. On a diving board, Kent? Why not yell *cannonball* and motorboat her midair?"

"I didn't see the cameras."

"You didn't see the cameras?" She laughs, a short, staccato stab. "*You* didn't see the cameras?"

She's still laughing when she hangs up, will laugh all evening at the sublime digger of their marriage. Kent staggers back to the bar, his empty shot glass in his hand. *Did* he know? He can't even consider the possibility. Tomorrow he will reckon with his life choices, but tomorrow is a lifetime away. For now, he is slamming shots. The bar smells of beer and sweat. He is making alliances with the Roller Derby girl, and the gravedigger, and the astronaut, and Carl. Now he is signing autographs, clinking glasses. The lights in the room are far too bright. Ashley is chattering to him about *All Stars*, but Ashley was yesterday's adventure. Now he is taking a selfie with a group of fans. On the screen he sees a forty-four-year-old bald man with a paunch, nose crimson, dark bags hanging under his bloodshot eyes as he presses a flushed cheek against a giddy teen. "That is me," he whispers. He spots one of the Robert Palmer girls, and now he is buying her a drink.

CHAPTER 6

BECK

In the video on my laptop, my mother was crouched beside me, holding a small pink ceramic cup, dropping in marshmallows one by one.

"Okay." My dad's voice from off camera. *"Rebecca's first-ever hot chocolate."*

It was snowing outside. Through the back door, the whole yard was white.

"Am I going to like it?" I asked in my toddler voice. I was wearing my favorite bunny pajamas.

"You're going to love it." Mom lifted the cup to my lips. I took a tentative sip.

"Mmm!" I held up my elephant stuffie. *"Can Ellie taste too?"*

She laughed, looking to where my father must have been. I paused the video. Her face was frozen in joy. She had a lopsided smile, the left side higher than the right, which dimpled her left cheek. There was an arch in one eyebrow, like she and my father were sharing a private joke. It was the week before she died.

I'd returned to the Surf On Inn to email the production company and network. *One of the surf dogs drowned. What do I do?* My inbox was open, waiting for a ping. I rewound to the moment Mom lifted the cup to my lips. In my mind's eye I saw Buster, his little paws paddling. "You're going to love it," Mom said. She looked exactly like me. The same sharp nose and red hair. *"Mmm! Can Ellie taste too?"* The image was grainy, and our voices were staticky with distortion. By the time I'd digitized the VHS, the magnetic tape had degraded from overuse. That was how I remembered her voice now. How I heard her in my dreams. I paused and rewound again. *"You're going to love it."* I never watched the video straight through. Some days I barely watched it at all, just paused and rewound. Paused and rewound. I was completely in control. My mother dropped marshmallows into the cup. The laugh formed on her face. Pause. Rewind. Play.

The phone rang.

"Rebecca?" It was Jeremy Englander from the network. I'd met him at the show's launch, a suave little man in a tight blazer, looking aggressively corporate among the "social influencers in the pet space" who cooed over one another at the craft services table. I felt a wash of relief. Someone with expensive clothes was here to help. "What happened?" he asked.

I tried to put it into words. The calm ocean. The freak wave. I left out the part where I daydreamed about an Emmy. "I—have it on camera."

"Thank God. Which dog?"

"Buster."

"Is that the golden retriever?"

"No—the other Buster. The bulldog. What should I do?"

"First, upload your footage," he said. "Second, don't do anything. If you get any calls, refer them to me. We're pulling together a release."

Release. What a lovely word. All I wanted was release. I uploaded my memory card and lay down on the bed's scratchy quilt with my laptop, where I paused and replayed my mother's smiling face until my mind flickered to a blank like the end of a reel.

I woke the next morning to my phone vibrating with news alerts.

First, I saw the BuzzFeed post: "Did TV's Buster Have to Die?"

CNN.com listed "9 Times Reality TV Exploited Pets" and provided steps for how you could help animals in your local community.

Fox News explained, "Why Beck Bermann Is the Worst Person in the World."

Each article recycled the same story. The sea was rough. I'd forced Buster into the waves. Catastrophe was inevitable. They all featured the same file photo of me staring wide-eyed into the camera, a dopey smile that came off as both oblivious and cruel. I was sure the picture had been photoshopped to make my skin paler, my hair even redder, my nose more hawkish, all the features I'd inherited from Mom warped so that I looked like an exotic bird of prey.

No, I argued with the articles. The sea had been calm. I'd only wanted to film a lovely ride, to give Dave his displaced moment in the sunlight. It was a freak accident.

But then, wasn't it a freak accident that I secretly wanted to happen, because it could win me awards?

Of *course* I recognized the moment's drama. How could I not? That didn't mean I caused it! Reality producers can't control the tides. Not yet anyway.

Or maybe, my most vicious inner critic argued, in a deep yet nasally voice that sounded startlingly like my dad's, you were willing to let a dog die to prove a point, and anything else is a lie while you blind yourself–

I turned back to my laptop. My mom and I were in the living room now. I was belting out "The Itsy-Bitsy Spider" while she performed the hand gestures. Down came the rain to wash the spider out. My phone pinged. A Twitter DM. "You're an evil bitch. I hope you get raped and killed." The user's profile pic was a blurry photo of a man with a backward cap. "An average guy. All about positivity," his bio read. I paused and rewound. The itsy-bitsy spider climbed up the waterspout.

Friends texted. *Are you okay?* I clicked on the television. "In local news, a beloved legend—" I clicked it off. My father called.

"Dad?" I answered.

"Rebecca, I just got a call about you. Some . . . dog has died?"

"He— Buster. I'm filming this reality show, *Surf Dogs*, and a wave— He drowned, Dad."

There was a long pause. I was desperate for something, I couldn't say what—some kind of consolation that would make it all feel better.

"Dogs don't have souls, you know."

I shut my eyes tight. Of course Dad would have no clue what to say. The injuries he treated could be clicked neatly back into place.

"This could be an opportunity," he continued. "To shift away from TV. It's too late for you to go to medical school, but the front desk at my office—"

I hung up the phone. I had six texts waiting for me. *Beck are you okay?* a colleague wrote, with a link to the press release. The network apologized to their viewers and all those who loved Buster. No words could express their sorrow that a show meant to celebrate his unique life had resulted in this tragedy. A funeral would be held on Huntington Beach that afternoon. The network disavowed the horrific actions of one reckless producer who no longer worked for the show.

I was fired. Attached to the release was a clip of the monster wave crashing down and Dave racing into the surf. "*Keep rolling*," you could hear me say.

My phone was pinging with a seizure of DMs. "I hope you die." "YOU should be drowned."

Of course you keep rolling, that's the whole job! I'm not a lifeguard, I'm a TV producer.

"Die in a fire." "Someone should kill you. Maybe I'll do it."

I couldn't stop reading the messages. It seemed unsafe *not* to read them. I checked the time. I could just make the funeral. Dave knew what had happened. He could tell the world it wasn't my fault.

He could prove it to me.

I ran down the beach, veering past rollerbladers and strolling tourists. With my red hair and freckles, I would stand out anywhere other than an Irish Spring commercial. I put on my sunglasses and kept my head down.

Dave stood on the shore, dressed in a midnight-blue tuxedo that looked like it had been banging on his closet door for an occasion to be worn. Buster's urn was cradled under his arm. A small crowd of dogs from the show lined up to pay their last respects. I'd filmed every one of them. There was Poochini the rottweiler, who'd whip himself in zoomy circles after a good ride, and Stella the poodle, who looked nervously over her shoulder when she peed. Curious onlookers swelled the throng–dropouts and searchers, conscientious objectors to the corporate system, gluten-free ingredients in that California salad that mixes sun-soaked pleasure seekers and rapacious fame hunters. A TV news crew from the local Fox affiliate was covering the event. Dave stared into the sea like a Roman bronze while the audio tech ran the lavalier mike up his shirt.

I pushed toward him through the crowd.

"You!" a woman with a nose ring said as I passed, loud enough for people to hear.

"Hey," I said quietly. She was dog mom to Buster the golden. She was teaching her Buster to surf to help move past the loss of her brother. Everyone in the world, working through our grief in the most desperate ways.

"You've got a lot of nerve–"

But just then, Dave started to speak.

"We are gathered here today to celebrate," he began, like he was officiating a wedding. He stopped short, choked up, and hoisted the urn into the sky. "Buster!" At the sound of his name, Buster the golden perked his ears and wagged his tail. "A dog who became one with the waves. Who loved everyone, the sand crabs most of all. Buster!" Buster the golden whined. Throughout Dave's sobbing speech, whenever this second Buster heard his name, he strained against his leash. At the end, Dave reached into the urn and heaved out Buster's ashes in big handfuls. "Buster! Take your last ride upon the heavenly surf! Buster!" The golden retriever panted and barked. The woman with the nose ring tried to soothe him. There was no wind, and Dave's throwing technique was poor, so Buster's ashes fluttered to the ground. Dave became frustrated and then furious that the ashes weren't making it into the surf, and he ran into the water and dumped the urn upside down. "Buster! Buster! Buster!" he shouted. The golden retriever broke free from his owner's grip, raced into the waves to lick Dave's face, and started licking up Buster's ashes as they floated away. The woman with the nose ring ran and yanked her Buster up the sand.

This was my moment. The eulogy was over, but the cameras were still rolling. "Dave!" I shouted, and wove through the crowd.

When he saw me, Dave drew himself up to his full height, his wet tux hanging off his frame. Beneath the camera-ready makeup, his eyes were red and puffy. "Oh god, Dave, I'm so sorry—"

"How dare *you* be sorry!" He gestured to the crowd with a sweep of his arm. "This is *her*." A few onlookers took out their phones to record.

"I only wanted to give you a beautiful moment," I pressed on. "Please, tell them. The sea was calm. It wasn't my fault."

"Buster's dead! Is *this* your beautiful moment?"

Buster the golden began to bark, feeding off the crowd's hostile energy. The sand beneath my feet started to feel wobbly, my inner world heaving.

"I wanted what you wanted. You trained Buster to surf."

"Not in a monsoon!"

"Monster," someone hissed. Stella the poodle and Poochini the rottweiler started barking too. These dogs had licked my hand and taken my treats. Now they were here to judge me. I stepped backward, looking for solid footing, but the entire world was spinning.

"Please." I turned to the crowd. "The sea was calm."

"Dog killer!" someone said. Stella the poodle ran yapping at my feet. I staggered back, but she wove between my legs, and I bumped into her with my knee.

"Save Stella!" someone shouted.

"You've killed your last dog!" Dave closed the distance and pushed me hard. I toppled backward onto the sand. All the dogs were barking now. A red-faced Dave loomed over me. A cell phone was thrust in my face. Maybe it really was my fault. They all seemed so sure. I had forced Buster into the violent seas. Through a dark subconscious urge, I'd deluded myself that I was making a sweet story about a man and his dog, while really I'd instigated disaster. The sand felt like it was swallowing me, and in that moment I wished it would.

Then I saw a tiny movement from the corner of Dave's eyes. He'd glanced at a camera. He was performing.

The world snapped into focus. "No!" I shouted. "It was calm!"

I got to my feet and faced all of them, the barking dogs and the furious people and the cameras.

"It was calm!" I shouted again, and then the pressure became too much and I ran, away from the dogs and the crowd, off the sand and onto asphalt, toward the safety of the Surf On Inn. My phone was ringing. It was a string of unfamiliar digits. I naively hoped it would be Jeremy Englander, telling me the network had reviewed the footage and would stand behind me, that it was a producer from the Fox affiliate who believed my story and wanted to share it with the world, or—in a fit of delusion—that it was my mom, calling to tell me it would all be okay.

I answered.

CHAPTER 7

KENT

Kent Duvall is sitting in the Stratus conference room of the Kimpton Hotel Santa Monica. The room smells faintly of Xerox toner and ancient lunch meats. It comforts Kent to be in a place where official business is conducted by authoritative people. His life for the past three months has been a maelstrom of guilt and recrimination, but sitting here, he can practically hear the confident voices of senior vice presidents. At the laminate tabletops around him sit twenty former reality TV contestants and TV hopefuls. Twenty aspirants competing for eight spots. The Roller Derby girl is here. They pass covert smiles. Carl hunches over his forms, the tiny plastic pen ridiculous in his sledgehammer hand, like a grizzly bear's working a desk job at the DMV.

The room is a Noah's ark of archetypes, assembled to take the Minnesota Multiphasic Personality Inventory. There's a bespectacled nerd girl, a blond-haired bro who looks about fifteen, pimple-faced and dewy-eyed. Ostensibly the test tracks whether they are psychologically fit to be cast. The actual goal, Kent suspects, is to share their deepest subconscious urges with the Casting team to determine who best can be exploited for TV drama. A young woman traumatized by an authority figure will be cast beside a drill sergeant. Two people with a pathological compulsion to be leader will be forced to compete for dominance of a bamboo hut.

Even knowing this, Kent feels a sense of competence as he ticks his way down the bubbles. His public speaking career is a joke. His wife is furious at him. But he can complete this form with aplomb. He could answer questions about himself all day.

False/True: I think I would enjoy the work of a librarian.

Would he? Kent's not much of a reader, but he imagines spending his days in a cool, dark room where smiling children pluck picture books off the shelves. True, he ticks.

False/True: I have no fear of spiders.

True.

False/True: I do not have a great fear of snakes.

Kent doesn't like snakes. There's something revolting about a land animal with no legs. He shivers in his chair from the image—muscles pulsing up wormy bodies. But he doesn't want to be cut for being a coward. And he *definitely* doesn't want to be thrown into a snake pit for drama. True, he ticks.

False/True: I often hear voices without knowing where they come from.

False, though right now he is hearing a voice. The woman sitting next to him has been muttering to herself since the test started. *She* is hearing voices all right. She's one of the few non-white people in the room. She's mid-fifties, in a trucker hat and tank top. A giant crucifix is inked across her leathery deltoid, little red dots where Jesus has been nailed. A Christian mom–blue collar minority. Like a marketing consultant dropped profiling sheets into a blender. She's definitely getting cast if she can pass the psych test, but from the way she's muttering to herself, scratching her head, popping her dentures out and sucking them back onto her gums, that may be an impossible hurdle. *Godspeed, you oddball chimera*, he thinks.

False/True: I would like to be a singer.

False.

False/True: Someone has been trying to rob me.

False.

False/True: Evil spirits possess me at times.

Do they want to determine that you're not crazy, or that you're not too sane? They want you crazy enough to act out, to stir up conflict, to fight and bicker, but not *so* crazy that you'll run amok with a machete after three days without food or sleep. Just crazy enough to sign up for the show at all. False.

False/True: I have never been in trouble because of my sexual behavior.

Kent looks across the room. Ashley's by herself at a first-row table by the podium. The other applicants have been trading sly, alliance-building smiles. Ashley hasn't looked up once. When Kent walked in, he wasn't even sure it was her. From the back, with her hair in a ponytail and wearing a strappy top, she could be any number of young blond women from *Endure*'s past—the PR rep who won season seven, the hairstylist who was medevacked from season thirteen for "severe gastrointestinal distress" after bingeing on unripe coconuts. But then he caught her profile, and guilt washed over him. He promised Margaret she wouldn't be here.

False, he ticks.

False/True: I have not lived the right kind of life.

True.

False/True: In most marriages one or both partners are unhappy.

True.

False/True: I often feel guilty because I pretend to feel more sorry about something than I really do.

Okay, test. This is getting personal.

WHEN KENT ARRIVED HOME FROM THE ALABAMA EVENT, HE BROUGHT with him a bouquet of roses from TF Green Airport. Margaret was in their bedroom stoned and watching *House Hunters* on her laptop. "Yell at me," he said, bouquet extended. "Punish me."

"Why don't you get your stuff and leave?" Her words sounded crisped from the weed.

Kent begged her for another chance. He felt frantic, like he was scrambling on the floor to pick up the jagged pieces of a shattered family heirloom. He practically pulled her out of the house, pleading with her to berate him. It was the only path to healing.

But as they walked around Providence, Margaret sounded almost bored as she told him that he was feckless and lazy. "You're selfish," she said, in a distracted, offhand way. "You're insecure."

The terse response terrified him. Her angular face, the severe nose and chin, Margaret's whole body down to her knobby knuckles seemed fashioned for elbowing her way through an unforgiving universe. She saw *everything* as a playground for her razor wit, and while the stream of ridicule could become too much, he'd never seen her not care. When they walked across the new pedestrian bridge over the Providence River, and she said in a flat tone that he was an asshole, he got down on his knees and clutched her legs. "Please," he said.

As she looked down at this abject performance, the cool plaster of Margaret's facade cracked open to reveal a chasm of hurt. She reamed him out. Being on television had made him believe he was *special*, she said. But just because a paid team of producers hung on his every word during interviews, that didn't mean he had a single interesting thing to say. And "fame"—he could hear the air quotes in her voice—"fame" had warped him into a selfish, insecure shell of a man, desperate for validation, who had no identity outside of a DVD box set. In the real world, *special* was an adjective you earned, a label you wore yourself to the bone for. And *special* was something he'd never be.

Even Margaret was taken aback by her rage. Strolling couples gave them a wide berth as she shouted, like all the frustrations and failures of the past years—all the lost promise they had papered over with comfortable routines, in-jokes, and shared memories—were crashing in on her at once. He clutched her skinny legs, and she belittled him, while somewhere inside he thought—*This is not Kent Duvall. This is not who he is supposed to be.* And yet there he was—craving this abasement—

begging for it—and that disjunction—the feeling that his true self and his actual self were irreconcilably sundered—made him weep.

Back at their apartment, Kent moved his things into their second bedroom, a tiny dormer where the roof sheered at such an aggressive slant that Kent once suffered a minor concussion from standing up too fast. When they'd moved in, Kent had pictured a child's room. "I can't support *two* children," Margaret had said with a laugh. Kent had always wanted to be a dad, but he'd tried to laugh too as he said goodbye to his daydreamed future. Now he gave Margaret his email password as a pledge of his fidelity. They fell into a routine. At night, Kent would cook dinner, and she confronted him with flirty emails with other women from the early days of their relationship—*before they had agreed to be monogamous*, he thought but didn't say.

Two weeks ago, she woke him up. "Kent?" The clock read five a.m. "Kent, is Ashley going to be there?"

Predawn light was filtering through the dormer window, so that the room was gray and half-formed. "Where?" he asked, confused.

She held up her phone. His vision was blurry, but he made out an email. From Casting. Inviting him to a session in LA.

His adrenaline kicked in, like a jolt of caffeine.

"No, Ashley's not going to be there," he said, trying to keep his voice steady. "Nobody remembers Ashley. She's completely unmemorable."

"Do you promise?" Margaret asked. Her eyes were puffy, and her hair stuck out like a hedgehog's.

"I promise."

"Kent," she said, and Kent clenched, bracing. "Kent, am I lovable?"

Sitting in the Kimpton Hotel Santa Monica, the sincerity of the question flays his heart. It was the kind of vulnerability you could only reach in the middle of the night, when your daytime defenses were lulled. Margaret lay down in the narrow twin bed and he moved to spoon her. "Margaret, you are lovable," he said. "I am the fuckup. Me."

They lay that way for a few more moments, her breath warm against his arm, feeling an intimacy that hadn't emerged in years.

False, he tells the test. He isn't pretending to be guilty. Hurting Margaret is the worst thing he's ever done in his selfish, feckless life.

CALLIE THE CASTING DIRECTOR IS SEATED IN A DESK CHAIR IN ROOM 237 of the Kimpton Hotel Santa Monica. The room smells like cigarettes and the chemical floral notes of cheap room spray. She gestures Kent toward the bed, and he perches on its edge. The mattress is too soft, forcing him to hunch forward to avoid sinking into the cushion. It's all jujitsu, he thinks. Every bit of this interview is destabilizing theater. He half believes that Casting requested an extra-squishy mattress, that they deliberately pumped the room full of nauseating spray.

"Kent." Callie looks skeptically down at the chart in her hands and back up at him, like she's received a knockoff of an item she ordered online. "It's been a long time."

"Look at you," he says. Fifteen years ago when Callie recruited him at a bar, he wondered why this bubbly teen was hitting on him. Even when she explained that she was casting for *Endure*, he still thought it had to be an intern's embarrassing mistake. Now she's running Casting. She's had an entire career while Kent's been stuck in place.

"This new show is going to be a little more bare-bones than *Endure*," Callie says. "Have you figured out why we want you? First, our fans remember you as—a dominant outdoorsman."

"You sound skeptical."

Callie looks back at her clipboard. "You'd enjoy the work of a—librarian?" She says it like she's giving him a terminal diagnosis.

He sits up straighter, but the bed sags beneath him, forcing him to hunch forward again, pushing his gut over his thighs. "Can't a dominant outdoorsman like books?" he tries to quip.

"Seriously, Kent. What's this librarian shit? The staff psychologist says your profile is meek and fearful."

It's like a vortex has opened in the mattress. Meek and fearful? He said he wasn't afraid of snakes or spiders! But then who knew the hidden subtext of a question like "False/True: I am easily awakened by noise." Even worse than Callie's skeptical gaze is the possibility—what if the staff psychologist is right? What if Kent *is* meek and fearful?

"And the second reason you wanted me?" he asks.

"Why don't you guess?"

"Ashley. From last season. She's here."

"Smart boy. We're betting there's sexual chemistry."

"You don't care that I've got a wife?"

"Not on TV. Our viewers don't need to know."

Kent feels the overwhelming guilt return. Margaret would be furious that Ashley was even in the same building. Imagine her response if the two of them were stranded on a tropical beach, hand-selected for a romance storyline.

"Would you pick me without Ashley?"

"This isn't an à la carte casting menu."

"When do you need an answer? Can I talk to my wife?"

"Once again, we're making a TV show, not offering vacation packages," Callie says. "If you're not all in, we'll go with someone else."

There's nothing to consider. Kent heaves himself off the mattress. For the first time in months he's taking control of his life. He sees

Callie's disbelief as he walks out of the room, the door slamming behind him.

Waiting in the hallway is the Roller Derby girl. The way she leans against the wall makes standing in a hotel corridor appear sultry and glamorous. "Gotta admit, I'm a little surprised to see you," she says. "I thought you were ancient history."

"I *am* ancient history." He's a little short of breath. "I told them no." No. He said *no*. For the past fifteen years he's been nurturing the idea that someday he would go back on television. But he said no.

"Wow. Respect." The Roller Derby girl gives him a high five. Her real name is Kelly-Anne Nguyen, but it's hard to stop picturing people as their chyron. She has a reputation as a major flirt, but to Kent all the lip puckering and theatrical winking seem cartoonish. "People always say they'll turn it down, but I figure that's so they won't be embarrassed when they're not cast."

"I need to work on my relationship."

"Because of the Ashley thing?"

The casual way she says it, like it's common knowledge, not even worth discretion, makes Kent stare at his feet. He feels embarrassed for himself, but furious for Margaret. What does Kelly-Anne know about his wife, other than that he cheated on her?

"Yeah."

Kelly-Anne touches his arm. "Hey. Everybody fucks up. Believe me, I have." For the first time since he's known her, it's like she's not doing a shtick.

"*Kelly-Anne, let's go*," comes a shout from inside the room.

"Now if you'll excuse me, I've got a TV show to get on. At least one of us will have the opportunity of a lifetime, a second time." She puckers her lips and gives him a wink, and she's slipped right back into her persona and is gone.

As Kent leaves the hotel, he calls Margaret to tell her that he gave up his shot. For *her.*

"Was Ashley there?" Margaret asks before he can say hello.

His first instinct is to lie, but he's promised he'll be radically honest. She'll find out from Reddit anyway. "She was," he admits. "And because of that, I told them—"

"You said there's no way Ashley would be there."

"I told them no. I told them I wouldn't do the show."

"You promised me Ashley wouldn't be there. You fucking *promised.*"

"I didn't lie," he begs. "I had no idea."

"I can't do this anymore. How do we ever move on if you can't stop lying? I'm moving out."

"I told them I wouldn't go." He hears her hang up, but he keeps shouting. "I told them I wouldn't go!"

Kent stands alone in the parking lot watching cars zoom past on the freeway. Thousands of people, off to their destinations, while he has quite literally nowhere to go, because he hadn't arranged a car to the airport before storming out. He opens a rideshare app. The tiny gray vehicles blink across the screen, circling a blue dot. The ride will cost him $47.63.

That's $47.63 he doesn't have, $47.63 he'd have to ask Margaret for. He believes her, that she's leaving him. Her voice sounded dead, like even the hurt was gone. What will he do when he gets back? Being married to Margaret was who he *was.* They called each other "Mouse" and "Moose." They got high and made Kit Kat s'mores over the gas burner and critiqued the dishes on *Top Chef.* She had a cat when they met, and for their fifth anniversary, Kent had a portrait of him painted as a seafaring admiral. They wept together when the admiral died. It wasn't the life he imagined, but it's all he has. And those memories—what do they mean without her? The tiny blue dot blinks on his phone. That's me, he thinks. He used to be on television. Now he can fit in a pocket.

He sprints across the parking lot, through the revolving doors of the Kimpton Hotel Santa Monica, back to the chemical florals of Room 237, back to Callie. He bangs on the door. Nobody answers. The bolt on the door has been thrown to keep it propped open, and he pushes inside. Ashley is sitting on the bed, her shoulders hunched into her chest. "I'm more than a flirt," she's begging. "I'm a country girl. I'm a provider. I promise you, I can be amazing television, even without—"

Kent gets on his knees in front of her. "I'll do it," he says. "Whatever you want. I have so much sexual chemistry with . . . her." He shudders, so slightly he hopes Callie doesn't notice.

"Oh my god. Kent. He is so hot," Ashley says with a flood of relief. Kent knows he looks sweaty and pathetic. Ashley gets on the floor beside him. "I can't wait to make out on some sexy beach."

Callie observes them with a mixture of fascination and pity. But he couldn't care less. None of *this* matters. None of this will be on television. He can't *wait* to be on an island with Ashley, he promises. It is going to be *so* hot and heavy. Once he's out there, they can't force him to do anything. Once he's on the island, he won't be the guy who cheated on his wife. He can be the person he is meant to be. He clasps Ashley's hand, and she cuddles into him as they plead together. *This* isn't even real, he thinks. Right now, he can promise them anything.

CHAPTER 8

BECK

"Beck Bermann?" The man's voice was muffled and staticky, like he was calling from a Styrofoam cup on a string.

"Who's this?"

"Beck? Hi, this is Jacob Malibu. The reality producer."

I was confused. Jacob Malibu was a legend in the reality business, if the reality business could be said to have legends. He created the kinds of shows that talk news and the gossip blogs loved to loathe—*Extreme Pregnancy* and *America's Favorite Murderer*—the shows that formed the lens through which society judged all other reality shows. Why was he calling me?

Maybe he was producing a clip show about the world's greatest on-camera fuckups. Or a docuseries on animal killers.

"I'm putting together a new show," he said. "We're calling it *Escape*. Or maybe it's *Escape!* with an exclamation point. The network's marketing team is still debating that one. Some corporate goon says the exclamation point 'communicates excitement.' I'm just happy not to be in those meetings. Basically it's a wilderness show. You know, eight strangers living in the jungle. We're using some reality has-beens from that show *Endure* to launch it. Our twist is that it's all about them trying to get *off* the island, rather than stay on it. So they have to *escape*—get it? Or they have to *ESCAAAAAAPE!* We're currently on location, and filming starts in two weeks, but I lost one of my producers. Nothing major. A staph infection in his right thigh. He needs surgery, and nobody feels good about the local hospital. I'm pretty sure their motto is 'We'll try!' Anyway, we're flying him home, and we're looking for a pro who can step in, fast. I saw you might be available."

"Me?" was all I could think to say.

"You."

"I mean—*why* me?" I could still hear barking from the beach. "I was just—fired."

"That's why I called so fast. We need an ace, and I've heard you're the best."

I snorted. "Come on. Beck Bermann, dog murderer? Don't produce a producer."

"Okay, you're not my first call. To be perfectly honest, all the non-dog-murdering pros are staffed up on other shows. But you have a great reputation, minus this one blip. They say you're unmatched at coaxing real moments out of tough subjects."

I admired how quickly he recalibrated his conversational strategy, from flattery to the brutal honesty I craved. I'd always imagined Jacob Malibu as a hotshot bro, the type of guy who put on his sunglasses like he was being filmed in slow motion. And no way Malibu was his given name. But the voice on the phone sounded both clever and kind. My favorite type of person.

"So I'm good enough," I said.

"Don't sell yourself short. You're good enough and available."

"I should put that on my résumé. Maybe my online dating profile. You're not worried that I'm an—animal murderer?"

"Please. Stop. I watched the clip. You did everything right."

I felt a lightness in my chest. The world was calling me a monster.

My friends texted, *You didn't do anything wrong.* This was the first time anybody said I'd done things right.

"You called for help but kept filming. I'd much rather hire a producer who holds on to her camera when the seas get rough. Metaphorically speaking and, I guess in your case, literally speaking. From my perspective, you're getting a Bad Edit."

I laughed. The "Edit" is shorthand for the story that a TV show tells about a character. When we reduce the messy chaos of life to a narrative arc, our job is to simplify and clarify. Reality shows film with multiple cameras for days at a time but air only forty-two minutes a week. A single episode might have to select from over three hundred hours of footage, so producers choose their moments wisely. Some people get a Hero Edit or a Winner's Edit. The show highlights their best moments and layers a soaring orchestral score beneath every action. Then there's the Bad Edit or the Loser Edit or the Crazy Edit. You see only the awkward moments, the petulant asides, a person's hidden lunacy underscored by dopey music or cymbal crashes. I wanted to believe him. I was receiving a society-wide Bad Edit.

"Okay. That's why me. But why you? I mean, why this show? From what I know, you're not a wilderness series type of guy. It doesn't seem . . ." I struggled for the right words, then laughed awkwardly. "Outrageous enough?"

Jacob laughed. "You're right, I'm the outrage guy. But we're living in a *world* of outrage. My last few shows haven't exactly lit up the Nielsens. When I call the networks, I'm transferred to assistants who weren't even born when I launched my first show. What viewers want today is simplicity. Something inspirational, to remind us who we are. As people. As Americans. So I'm going back to basics. Eight contestants in the wild. We're filming on a little island in the Pacific in the heart of the Bermuda Triangle."

"Isn't the Bermuda Triangle in the Atlantic? By . . . Bermuda?"

"Yes. Of course. Some other triangle, then. The point is—a spooky polygon. Lightning crashes in the opening titles. Look, America has changed, and I need to change with it. I *need* this show to succeed. Losing a producer two weeks before we shoot is basically the worst-case scenario. This is my chance for redemption. Why don't you make it your redemption arc too?"

I told Jacob that I needed time to think about it. He said he'd send over the show bible, but he wanted a decision soon, because if it wasn't me—and he hoped it would be me—he had to find a replacement fast.

But I knew I couldn't accept. I was raw and confused. I'd never worked on a wilderness show before. I'd barely been camping. How could I trust myself in the jungle, with eight desperate, malnourished contestants, when I couldn't film a dog in a life jacket?

CHAPTER 9

The first jungle reality show to capture the American public's imagination was *Survivor* in 2000. Sixteen strangers were stranded in Borneo to live off the elements while they formed alliances, competed in obstacle courses, and backstabbed one another out of the game. One hundred twenty-five million people—almost half the country—tuned in for the first season's final episode. Watching corporate consultant Richard Hatch beat rafting guide Kelly Wiglesworth for the million-dollar prize and the title of Sole Survivor is the Gen X equivalent of the moon landing.

These days, survivalist shows have amped up their bare-bones intensity. *Naked and Afraid* literally strips its contestants nude before stranding them in the African veldt. *Alone*'s survivalists live in complete solitude while they're stalked by wolves and bears. *Castaways, Survivorman*, *Remote Survival*, *Dual Survival*, *Extreme Survival*, *Ultimate Survival*, *Survive This*, *Fight to Survive*, and *Stranded with a Million Dollars*—America has gone gaga for survivalism. Maybe it's because we're so cosseted, because our home lives are so comfortable, because our only connection to our hunter-gatherer forebears is the anxious decision of which avocado to buy at Whole Foods. Or maybe it's because in a world of viral pandemics and environmental collapse, it's comforting to be transported back to the raw elemental struggle of man versus wild. (*Man vs. Wild*, also a reality series.) Maybe it's both, that sandwiched between our numb personal lives and the overwhelming scope of global apocalypse, the idea of foraging for food and building shelter evokes a personal agency that, somewhere along the way, we've fundamentally lost.

I wasn't going to do Jacob's show, but I was curious about what his twist on the genre would be, so I sat down at my hotel room's tiny desk, cued up the plastic drip machine, and, as it wheezed out its watery coffee, read the story bible.

ESCAPE!

THE PREMISE

In this groundbreaking new wilderness competition series, contestants will be struggling to get *off* the island rather than stay on it.

For two decades we've watched people *survive*. Sometimes they're naked, sometimes afraid. Sometimes alone, sometimes together. But until now, their number one mission has always been to stay *on* the island. Ask any *real* castaway, however, or even anybody who's seen the Tom Hanks movie *Castaway*. The true struggle is to get *off* the island.

To escape!

Escape! (exclamation point TBD), the thrilling new reality competition series from legendary producer Jacob Malibu, will push the jungle survival genre beyond what we've ever seen. Eight survivalists and renowned TV icons will be stranded on a remote tropical island. They'll have nothing but the clothes on their backs and one survival item each. The challenge? To reach an offshore islet where a treasure chest is buried with a million dollars inside.

But there's a twist. The cash won't be there all at once. Every day more money will be added to the pot. How long will the contestants wait? Will they brave the hazards of the wild jungle—as well as the twists and turns of the game—as they try to maximize their moolah? Or will a devious player build a raft and snag a chunk of treasure early—eliminating themselves from the game but taking a huge wad of cash? Whatever they choose, they'll first have to win grueling physical and mental challenges to earn a key to even open the treasure chest—or ally with someone who can.

Will our contestants betray one another or work together in their quest to escape the island and win the prize? What *really* happens when people are stranded together in the jungle? What is the true nature of humanity?

With *Escape!*, we'll soon find out.

THE LEGENDS OF *ENDURE*

We're casting four reality legends from *Endure* to drive tune-in—and show these newbies how it's done.

Kent, the Faded Hero: For years, fans have been clamoring to see the return of Kent Duvall, the alpha male who made TV history when he hunted a boar, won six challenges, and earned the $100,000 prize on the third season of *Endure*. He's the guy who women want, and men want to be. But the question for Kent is—can he live up to the man he once was?

Ashley, the Beauty: This blond-haired, blue-eyed knockout is your classic beach babe—and she's back for revenge. Ashley was the first person off her season, and now *nothing's* gonna stop her. Nothing, that is, except romance! This spicy single has hookup history with Kent. Will love—or sex—keep her from the big bucks?

Kelly-Anne, the Praying Mantis: You may remember this Roller Derby girl from *Endure: The Jungle Strikes Back*, where she killed a python and then sliced the throats of her male allies. (Don't worry—only figuratively!) Kelly-Anne made national news when she stripped down naked to slither out of the locked-box challenge. But for all her wiles, she still couldn't clinch that win. This time, can she scheme her way to success?

Carl, the Fan Favorite: With his distinctive camo gear and bushy beard, Carl's roar resounds in the hallowed halls of *Endure* legend. This massive (in every sense of the word!) fan favorite has electrified the hearts of TV viewers. But will his wilderness savvy help him outfox his new competition?

THE NEWBIES

These four new players are hungry to prove their mettle against the epic survivalists of yore.

Ruddy, the Preppy: Alec "Ruddy" Rutledge is the character that fans will love to hate. Ruddy's the silver spoon kid who doesn't even need the money. He just wants to win, and he doesn't care who he has to cross to do it.

Barb, the Mom: This tough southern mama's a school janitor from Tennessee who's lived her whole life hunting and fishing. But Barb's got a secret—she lost a kid to cancer! Will that crazy tragedy haunt her journey? Or will she overcome her trauma and wheel and deal her way to victory? Barb's down-home Christianity is sure to connect with Middle America.

> **Bartolo, the Grouch:** You're just going to have to trust us on this: Robert Bartolo is TV gold. He's a dance instructor in a strip mall in Pawtucket, Rhode Island, but if you hear him tell it, he's also an army veteran, a champion swimmer—and a lothario. We'll see if this potbellied polymath is truly all he claims to be.
>
> **Miriam, the Nerd:** This brainy scientist has never even been to the outdoors. We wonder if she's ever been kissed! Miriam's spent her whole life in the science lab hunched over her test tubes. We'll laugh along as our Girl Gilligan stumbles her way across the island, trying—and failing—to stay out of trouble.

I smiled. Every show promised to push the genre beyond what anybody had ever seen. I flipped through the episode synopses. You can't control everything that happens on a reality show—not yet anyway—but production companies will give sample breakdowns to help the network understand what might happen. What's *supposed* to happen.

> **EPISODE 1**
>
> We start with eight contestants, on a boat, journeying into the unknown. Each of them has one piece of survival equipment. They're about to be stranded on a remote tropical island. The question is—can they get off?
>
> We'll meet our leading characters. Kent, the Faded Hero. He's older now than the last time he was on television, but he naturally steps into a leadership role, immediately building a fire and discovering a nearby food source.
>
> Then there's Ashley, the sexpot. The sexual tension between these two is crackling! Ashley follows Kent around camp, but the savvy older woodsman doesn't want to become an early target. They know they need to keep their romance a secret.

We'll follow fan favorite Carl and the old grouch Bartolo. A rivalry naturally springs up between these two old-timers, as they compete in small contests of one-upmanship to be the better senior survivalist.

Meanwhile Ruddy, the villain, is already up to no good. While the rest of the contestants build shelter, Ruddy builds alliances. Just minutes into the game and he's scheming! Will he break off with his own group and abandon the others?

While seven of our hardy adventurers get to work at surviving and strategizing, we'll watch as Miriam, the nerd, falls on her face—literally! Miriam face-plants into the waves simply getting off the boat! Set against the life-and-death struggle to survive, Miriam's hilarious bungling is a welcome comic moment in this otherwise deadly serious show.

Poor Miriam, I thought. Doomed to fail, and she hasn't even left her house. I flipped to her full write-up in the dossier. Twenty-nine years old. A chemist at a pharmaceutical startup in New York. Originally from Bemidji, Minnesota, population 15,279. That's where they'd list her hometown in the credits, to make the show seem regionally diverse. Another nice Midwestern girl making it work in the big city. I could've sat next to her on the subway. In her photo, she was wearing a lab coat and awkwardly smiling, the tips of her fingers slightly blurred as she fumbled with a button. She was nice-looking, I thought. Geeky, sure. Thick-framed glasses. Curly hair in chaotic strands that were all wandering off on their own individual unkempt journeys. A gap in her front teeth. But with strong cheekbones. Not the rom-com girl where you take off her spectacles, give her a blowout, and suddenly she's a ten. But—big, wide eyes. Shy smile. The girl you were happy to bring home for Passover. Was I crazy to think she looked like me? Not the hair or the eyes, none of the marquee features, but—the lines that ran from her nose to her mouth. The arch in her eyebrow. Maybe it was simply her expression, like she was trying hard to put on a brave face. The rest of the contestants leered out of their photos with all their ego and attitude. Ruddy the preppy smirked like he'd just dosed his first roofie. Kelly-Anne the Praying Mantis vamped with a kiss.

Why was this brainy scientist headed to the jungle? Maybe she needed money. To fund cancer research. Maybe she was the wallflower who simply wanted an adventure.

I skimmed through more episodes to see how her arc was supposed to play out.

EPISODE 2

Alliances are starting to form. Kent and Ashley are an obvious pair—they tried to keep their romance a secret, but they've been caught canoodling under the stars. People keep going into the jungle in groups of two or three. Will they build a raft to take what they can early? Or will they tough it out? But here comes Miriam! Nobody wants to ally with her, especially after she comes in last at the first challenge! We'll have a montage of our silly scientist awkwardly trying to talk to the other players. This brainiac just can't fit in.

EPISODE 3

Miriam tries to make a fire—and almost burns down the camp!

EPISODE 4

Miriam gets a bug bite on her face. It seems small but soon swells up so big it almost smothers her! Our on-staff medic

> **races to the scene. While we chuckle at our Daffy Doc, it's another reminder of how very real the . . .**

I was growing hot from the unfairness of it all, with the indistinct sense that it was myself I was indignant for, that it was me the story bible was plotting to humiliate. We really were so similar. Social pariahs because of how we seemed rather than who we were—the "awkward scientist" and the "manipulative producer." Where had the story bible even gotten its ideas about nerds? The document read like the plot of an eighties teen movie, with its pratfalls and embarrassments. Weren't today's tech titans all former geeks? But then cable TV lives and dies on how it connects with viewers' deepest biases. Maybe a mass audience show like *Survivor* would cheer on a scientist. But a cable survivalist show was always meant to celebrate the survivalists. The nerd was comic relief.

Parents died when she was nineteen, the staff psychologist wrote in Miriam's psych assessment. *Never felt secure since. Deep fear of missing out on her own unexplored potential, but fundamentally lacks direction in life. No romantic involvements. INTP on the Myers-Briggs, meaning introverted and logical, with a deep sense of wonder. Innate need to please authority.*

What if I could give Miriam a different story? I thought. Sure, she could start out awkward and clumsy. Give the execs what they'd been pitched. But then, little by little, you see her develop wilderness skills. Miriam learning how to use a machete. Miriam making fire. Miriam building a raft out of salvaged junk. Miriam sailing solo to the million-dollar prize. A growth arc. The cast-out pariah becomes the hero. And as I plotted her storyline in my mind, I felt that delicious shiver that I sometimes got, where it seemed like *I* would be using a machete, *I'd* be sailing the raft to victory, my mirror neurons firing like I was reading a book, but so much more intense. In my mind, I wasn't only saving Miriam. I was saving myself.

CHAPTER 10

I had a meeting at the network office in Times Square, where I waited for an hour in a conference room with sweeping windows overlooking the Hudson. Across the city I could see the Manhattan Cruise Terminal. A massive ship was docked, hundreds of feet high, its white panels shimmering in the afternoon light. I imagined the giddy elderly couples stepping up the gangway and was filled with yearning. *I* wanted the shuffleboard, the two-bit magician, the detailed itineraries outlining every excursion to shore. That was how the tropics were meant to be experienced, from a protective cocoon with a seafood buffet. Not getting drenched by a superstorm on an abandoned island in the Satanic Rhombus.

A harried-looking executive in a pantsuit swept into the room and handed me a business card. Senior so-and-so of such and such division. I felt her size me up. She threw out a few enthusiastic remarks about the show that sounded lifted from a press release and pushed a massive contract across the table. It was as thick as a nineteenth-century Russian novel and just as full of catastrophe. I would release the network from liability if I died from natural disaster or animal attack or infectious disease or global terror. I swore I wouldn't reveal any of the network's secrets on pain of an elite squad of lawyers redlining me to death. "You don't have to read every word," the executive said, vibrating with impatience. "It's fairly standard."

She sent me to a doctor, who pumped me full of antibodies and began to explain, in his dispassionate doctor voice, the region's dangers. I cut him off. I'd already googled the area's perils. I knew there'd be venomous creepy-crawlies: the snakes, the spiders, the scorpions. I knew about the disease vectors: rats and mosquitoes that carried malaria, yellow fever, dengue, typhoid, and who knew what unimaginable hemorrhagic fever that lay lurking in the deep jungle. None of it mattered. Jacob was gifting me the chance to move past my national embarrassment, and I couldn't screw it up. Second acts, American lives, et cetera.

On the long-haul flight across the Pacific, I watched a video interview with Jacob from the early 2000s. A bespectacled journalist asked pointed questions about the societal significance of reality programming, while Jacob smirked and gave glib answers. He must have been in his late twenties, his ripped-up jeans a stylistic *Eff you* to the journalist's gray suit. I transferred in Bangkok's Suvarnabhumi Airport to a tin-can puddle jumper, then spent a restless night in Mud Town, which was the juvenile, borderline offensive nickname the network brass transliterated from the name of the small city on the mainland's tip. It was your classic regional port, tuk-tuks circling a marble plaza and careening onto cracked side streets. The road from the airport was crowded with billboards for mobile phone plans and the local beer. In the hotel lobby, I ordered a ham sandwich and bottled water. There was one other patron, a large, sweaty man reading an English-language newspaper and drinking an espresso.

"American?" he asked after he heard me order. He looked like he might eat me alive just to taste the lingering Western Hemisphere on my skin. I took the wobbly plastic chair across from him. The man wanted to talk, and despite my jet lag, I always love to listen. He was a contractor from Sydney who "wanted to get away from it all." I guessed from the gaps in his story—the pauses and ums—that he had found a too-young local bride. Tale as old as time. The novelty of marriage to an impressionable teen had worn off, but he was still stuck here, starving for English conversation. "And where are you headed? We don't see many Americans here."

I told him about the production job on the island, careful with what I revealed, thinking about that squad of redlining lawyers.

"Oh yes. I've heard about that. It's a big scandal here. The locals believe the island to be cursed." He spoke with the mixture of condescension and insight common to white men in the developing world, relishing their access to regional lore even as they imagine themselves above it.

"Why do they believe that?" I took a sip of my water. It tasted metallic.

"Who knows? Local legend. An ancient disaster ingrained into collective memory. They say the place was a monkish religious retreat a hundred years ago or a thousand. An evil animal spirit haunts the place." He gave me a theatrical wink. "Some enterprising soul built a hotel there and—disappeared. Now there's nothing."

"I think that's the point."

FOUR HOURS LATER, I WAS STRAPPED INTO A HELICOPTER, CLUTCHING the door handle as we buzzed over the ocean.

"You want to know how long a chopper can stay aloft after flying into clouds?" The pilot's voice snapped over the headset in his thick Aussie accent. He was a heavyset man in his mid-fifties whose face was obscured behind his aviator sunglasses and massive beard. He reeked of body spray.

"I'm pretty sure I don't," I said.

"Six seconds, give or take. You lose track of what's up and what's down in a cloud. Wild, right? We assume our instincts can tell our up from our down, but as soon as you lose visibility, you keep your orientation for about six seconds max. Then—" The pilot made a spinning motion with two fingers, spiraling them down to the control panel, where he simulated an explosion with his fist.

"Let's stay out of the clouds, then, okay?"

"Too late!" He banked hard into a white swirl. "Start counting!" I shouted *"one, one thousand—two, one thousand"* over the headset before we emerged into clear skies. The pilot's staticky laughter echoed in my earpiece.

There is no worse blight on the planet than funny pilots.

"There she is," the pilot said.

On the horizon, a green hump shrugged off the surrounding sea. At this distance, the island looked hazy, like I was viewing it through a blurred lens. I could make out an emerald curtain of jungle and a mountain whose sheer pink cliff jutted from the coast like an upraised hand. A small river curved from the mountain base toward a beach. As we approached, I saw that the blurriness was caused by a shroud of smoke, which billowed from the treetops and twisted around the cliff face.

"Is it on fire?" I shouted.

"Fire?" The pilot laughed. "That's mist! Beautiful, right? But don't let her good looks fool you. She's a mercurial bitch. Weather out here gets wild."

We descended into a small clearing on the island's northeast edge, where a brush-cleared dirt circle marked a makeshift helipad. A trash bag rigged to a stake served as a windsock. Below us, beside a concrete hut, stood a half dozen people. One of them was waving into the sky.

"I'm not going to shut her down," the pilot said. The people by the hut were shielding their eyes against the dust storm kicked up by the rotors. "When we land and I say go, you take off your headset, open the door, and run. Remember to duck. My last passenger forgot and–" He sliced his hand across his neck. The helicopter's skids kissed the ground. The pilot gestured to the door. "Remember to duck!"

I pulled off my headset, grabbed my bag, and bolted out the door in a crouch, repeating "duck duck duck duck." Six men waited by the hut, watching me squat-shuffle across the field: five locals dressed in dark green military fatigues, assault rifles dangling from slings across their chests, and one man in a plain white shirt with cuffs rolled to his elbows. As I avoided decapitation, the man in the white shirt almost bounced across the distance and welcomed me in an enormous hug. I expected a backslapping bro-ish greeting and was surprised to be enveloped in a sincere embrace, the kind that lingered at peak clench. When he let go, he shouted a few words, but they were lost beneath the bellow of the helicopter's blades. The pilot circled the clearing until we were all adequately coated with dust. Then he turned east, away from the setting sun, and shot back toward the mainland. I watched him go, wishing a silent farewell to my only way off this place.

The sound of the chopper faded. The man turned to me with a big smile. "Welcome to the island! I'm Jacob."

CHAPTER 11

Jacob Malibu was well past forty. His hairline was receding at the temples, silver flecked his dark beard, and he had bags under his eyes. But these minor signs of age and wear were swept aside by an overall impression of boyish enthusiasm, by his wide, eager gaze, and by the slight part to his lips that made it seem as if he was always ready to exclaim in wonder or delight. A radio clipped to his belt chattered constantly, but as he took me in with those hazel eyes—almost green, they channeled the brightness of the jungle—the thousand ancillary details of production were meaningless. All his attention was focused on me.

"I can't tell you how thrilled we are to have you here," he said.

"I can't believe I'm actually here!" I meant it literally. The island was too bright, too loud, too hot. The temperature hovered between a steam bath and a crematorium, and ecosystems of sweat were already developing under my arms. A pervasive chittering pulsed in my eardrums. "What's that noise?"

"Cicadas," Jacob said. "They're all over this part of the island. It's much more tolerable near the City."

"We're going to a city?"

"That's what we call our production HQ. Come on, we'll talk in the van."

Jacob picked up my bag, and I followed him across the scrubby clearing. A city in the jungle! Who knew what small luxuries had sprung up out here. Out of habit I checked my phone and found that I had no reception. No calls. No texts. No DMs. None of the anonymous threats could reach me, and I felt so free that for a moment it was like I was floating through the jungle.

"By the way, what did you think of our pilot, Benjamin?" Jacob asked. "He's a character, isn't he?"

I couldn't tell Jacob what I really thought: another wannabe cowboy with a pilot's license. "He got me here," I said. "No higher compliment."

Jacob's smile wavered. "You can't brush people off out here, Beck. In the jungle, we're all in it together. Out here, we're a family."

"Roger that. Won't happen again."

I'd been here five minutes, and I'd already disappointed Jacob. He patted me on the shoulder. "You're going to do great," he said. Still my momentary euphoria soured. Social media wasn't the problem. I was the problem.

At the edge of the clearing sat three vans, gray slabs shaped like bread loaves with wheels. Jacob threw my bag into the back of the nearest one and slid open the rear door with a slight bow. I squeezed inside. The seats were jammed against one another, forcing me to contort my legs to enter the vehicle, let alone sit down. The ceiling was padded with yellow foam. I fingered the cushioning.

"That's for your head," Jacob said as he climbed into the front passenger seat. "The UAZ-452s were built by the Russian military to handle any and all terrain, and they work great out here on these chewed-up dirt paths. But they were not designed for human comfort. I'm pretty sure the engineers never heard of shock absorbers."

I nodded, trying to seem tough.

In the driver's seat with his feet on the dashboard was a small man in fatigues. Jacob introduced him as production's local fixer and head of security, Million. "Like rich," Million said. He rubbed his fingers together as though he were shuffling bank notes.

"Million's real name is difficult for us Westerners to pronounce," Jacob said. "He's chosen his own nickname."

Million turned the key, the van jolted alive, and within seconds branches scraped the window as the trees closed around us, while the old Soviet van shuddered at every dip and bulge in the road.

"Any questions?" Jacob asked.

"Just one," I said. "Tomorrow, eight people arrive on the beach. We tell them there's a treasure chest a couple miles out in the ocean. What happens if, the instant someone wins the first key, they join forces to build a raft and end the show in under a week?"

"That's a *great* question," he said, and I flushed with foolish pride, like a second grader getting a gold star. "First of all, the prize increases the longer they're here, meaning they're going to *want* to stay. These people are hungry for money. They're not going to split a hundred thousand dollars eight ways, when they can take a million dollars for themselves. Second, we haven't exactly cast a crack squad of survivalists. We've got one or two at the most who could make a fire, let alone build a raft, and the journey won't be easy. Bad currents and bad weather. No to mention the sharks—"

"Of course there are sharks."

"Little reef sharks. Scare-you sharks, not eat-you sharks. Still, they'll need the raft supplies we eventually give them. But most of all, we'll be relying on you and Erika, our other story producer, to ensure contestants hold out till the end."

"So in a show titled *Escape!*, you want us to stop them from escaping."

"More like delay."

"Got it. Distract them with their local squabbles, alliances, and journeys of self-discovery."

"Exactly," he said. "Produce them."

The van was heaving with exhaustion by the time the rutted path opened into a clearing. Sunlight streamed through the windows. Around us surged the familiar chaos of TV production. PAs hauled gear. Two carpenters with chainsaws were hewing rough shapes out of thick pine logs. At the center of the hubbub hunched a squat two-story cinder-block structure.

"Here we are," Jacob said. "Home sweet home."

The "City" was more survivalist's bunker than luxury resort. Wood scaffolding and iron poles poked out of the top story like quills, and a generator rumbled in the yard. I knew Jacob could read my disappointment in the tilt of my eyebrows and the slight gape of my mouth. Reality producers are trained to analyze a subject's microgestural cues. I strained for something positive to say.

"What's this place even doing out here?" I managed.

"It was some Russian oligarch's bright idea." He generously ignored my distress. "He dreamed of a fantasy hotel at the end of the world, but he abandoned the plan when he discovered that the end of the world is a quagmire of mosquitoes and snakes. Even if you're looking to get away from it all, this is too far away from it all. He could barely contain his relief when we came along. He cleared out so fast, he left the building half-finished."

"I heard he disappeared." I rolled my eyes at the stupidity of local gossip, but I was relieved there was a more mundane explanation.

"Oh yes, disappeared back to his palace on the Black Sea."

The lobby was decorated in the tropical international style you can find in any postcolonial village. Rugs, rattan settees. A wooden slab covered in bottles marked out a small bar area. A ceiling fan spun slowly, conjuring a breeze that was just cooling enough to remind me how hot I was. Jacob led me up a stairway and into a conference room that had been converted into a production office. Screens lined a wall. A table covered with computers ran down the side of the room. A giant whiteboard was scribbled over with red marker. *SUNRISE 05:35 / SUNSET 18:21. LOW TIDE 12:48. HIGH TIDE 21:12 BREAKFAST 05:00 TO 09:00. LUNCH 12:00 TO 14:30. ~~FIVE~~ FOUR DAYS UNTIL NEXT MAINLAND RUN.*

The core crew was clustered around a table, poring over plans for the first day of filming. They looked up when we walked in. Jacob rattled off names and job descriptions—two cameras, two boom mikes, production management, Art Department, our challenge head. They were mostly men, all in some state of unshaven ruggedness. They wore cargo shorts whose pockets were bursting with gear and T-shirts in moisture-wicking fabrics. I felt like a gangly transfer student on the first day of class. Even so, I pushed through my fear and gave each new colleague a big smile and a firm handshake. I was a professional, here to do a job.

"Nice to meet you, Killer." I froze mid-handshake with the room's only other woman. She was small, her wiry body like an adolescent boy's under her khakis and baggy tank top, and her mouth twisted to the side, so it was impossible to tell if she was insulting me or joking, though I would soon learn that with Erika Huizenga, there was little difference. Life was all one big insult-joke. The ambient chatter dropped, and my creeping shame crawled along my skin. How naive I'd been to think that the island would be a place where I could escape judgment. These people, my colleagues, would be the ones to judge me more than anybody. Then Jacob laughed as though it was good-spirited fun. Erika would be the other story producer on the beach, he explained.

The crew ran through an overview of how the show would open. There would be little fanfare. The contestants would arrive on the island and decide for themselves their next steps. Would they build one shelter and live together? Would they splinter into groups and adventure off into the jungle?

"With two cameramen and two producers with handhelds, that's four cameras. What's the plan if all eight contestants head off in separate directions?" I asked. "Do we have additional coverage?"

"It's a judgment call," Jacob said. "Follow who you think is best for your story. We've got robocams rigged up at key spots, and Ralph, our PA, here"—a hairy twentysomething who resembled an otter waved a hand—"operates a drone. But people tend to congregate."

"And who's with them overnight?"

"They're by themselves. Though you're welcome to sleep out there if you want!"

The crew laughed.

"We give them a radio, and our medic is on hand, obviously." Erika rolled her eyes. "This isn't like your *pet* shows. We keep our contestants alive."

"Everybody will be fine," Jacob said, putting a restraining hand on Erika's shoulder. "Million's a snake wrangler, and our security guards patrol the perimeter. Though we don't tell the contestants that. Or the press. Keep them away from the heart of the jungle. But nobody's going there anyway."

"'Heart of the jungle.' That's ominous." I was trying to sound glib, but I was used to filming in "fancy Japanese restaurant" and "Italianate mansion." How had I wound up in a world where there was an actual location named "heart of the jungle"?

"It's what we've been calling the island's deep interior," Jacob said. "Just colorful language. We commissioned a risk assessment from an outside company. All clear."

From the little I knew, these risk assessment companies could be a couple of small-time insurance agents doing a glorified Google search. An uninhabited island might not trigger any warning signs because the dangers were still hidden.

After the production meeting, Jacob walked me down the beach. Along the shore a row of bungalows housed the overflow production team. Most of the senior staff had rooms in the hotel, but the producer I had replaced apparently liked to be alone. I was now the victim of his solitary temperament, stuck in the farthest bungalow at the very edge of the jungle.

The day was turning to dusk, and in the dimming light the trees were like a black screen on which were projected all my fears and anxieties. I wasn't prepared for how loud the jungle could be: the whoops of the tree frogs and trills from night birds and the cicadas' chittering. Even the night air was sticky with humidity. Sweat beaded my scalp and the back of my neck.

"How are you holding up?" Jacob asked.

"I'm good. This is all so exciting." It sounded like the lie it was.

"The first day is always a doozy. Don't worry about Erika. She's a great producer and is a softy at heart."

At heart. I'd always hated that expression. I'd filmed enough well-meaning jerks to see the way people rationalize their bad behavior. What matters is how you treat people, not whether beneath your carapace of cruelty you're hiding good intentions.

My bungalow was a lopsided wooden cabin with a thatched roof that slumped to one side like a bad toupee. Jacob unlocked the door with a small key, which he handed to me. He flipped the light switch. I could almost hear the generator groan. A single bulb stuttered to life. The inside was just large enough for a bed, a small dresser, and an old cooler with a spigot above a porcelain bowl. A knotted mosquito net hung from the ceiling. The windows were latched, but the wood had swollen so they couldn't fully close. I could already see—or I imagined I saw—a battalion of insects marching around the edges.

"Where do I—pee?"

"There are porta-bins down the beach next to the guard hut. You can also use the hotel facilities. And no judgment if you pop a squat in the woods. Oh, and there's a tokay gecko living in your rafters."

"A gecko? Like a lizard."

"A bit bigger than that." He held his hands out the length of a small dog. "The locals claim it's a good omen. They bring luck and prosperity."

"Can we get the gecko out of my rafters? I'd prefer less luck if it means I don't have to cohabitate with a dragon."

"It was her home before it was yours. We have to coexist with nature out here. But so you know—they have a vicious bite. It shouldn't be a problem, just don't get into a tussle with her."

"Roger that. No gecko fighting. Not the first time I've gotten that note."

"Ha. Now, rest up. Tomorrow filming begins." He patted me on the back. Somehow that simple gesture communicated an entire philosophy of understanding and support. He walked back to the hotel, and I watched his dwindling form disappear into the night. Then I was alone in the dark, my only company the chugging diesel engines of the fishing trawlers, looking for the last catch of the day, and an invisible gecko.

Suddenly, I was overcome by exhaustion. I untied the mosquito net and spread it across the mattress. The filthy polyester sagged and bunched, and as I lay down on the rock-hard bed, it draped over me like a shroud. I picked up the show's story bible and reread the episode synopses. I studied Miriam's photo. Her blurred fingers. The lines running from her nose to her mouth. The deep sense of wonder in her eyes.

Tomorrow the contestants would arrive. Tomorrow I would once again be the storyteller. Tomorrow I would stop feeling like a character out of control.

ACT TWO
PRODUCTION

CHAPTER 12

KENT

DAY 1

As the bright yellow Zodiac shivers across the choppy waves, Kent's already thinking about how he'll describe it in his interviews. *I was like an explorer*, he'll say. *Adventuring into an uncharted world.* The island beckons to him, a tropical paradise, palm trees belly dancing at the edge of a white sand beach straight from a Corona ad. Two cameramen race up and down the shore, their rigs gripped against their shoulders. Two sound engineers balance their boom mikes on their heads. A drone swoops through the air. He feels like he's rocketing into a myth, like he's writing himself into the pages of *Treasure Island*. The spray is in his face. He shakes his machete into the sky and lets out a giant whoop, which is echoed by the scream of a red-and-green bird that flashes upward from the jungle.

There are nine of them clutching the Zodiac's rubber edge, speeding toward the show. Eight contestants and Erika, a skinny producer with the look of a furious terrier glaring at them from a handbag. The boat's driver, a bearded maniac who reeks of body spray, whoops as he steers into the swells, launching them skyward and crashing back. Ashley's next to him, dolled up in a red wrap mini that's breathtakingly, spectacularly impractical for the outdoors. Across the boat, a young guy with thin lips and a sweater tied around his shoulders leans back and splays his legs. He looks like the asshole boyfriend from every teen movie. The older lady who was muttering to herself in casting is there. A nerd girl with Coke-bottle lenses pulls her lab coat close. The sexpot. The villain. The battle-ax. The nerd. And here's Kent Duvall. The alpha male.

He never thought of himself as an archetype before his first season on *Endure*. He was Kent. He worked construction. He went out with the guys. Dated a bit, but never a ladies' man. He waited until he was eighteen to lose his virginity because he wanted to find the right girl. Kind of a screwup at times. He'd once been detained by the police when he and some buddies drunkenly sprayed fire extinguishers across the thirty-third floor of a Vegas hotel. An average guy, he figured. Then fifteen years ago, he was walking through the hallways of the Kimpton Hotel Santa Monica, paired with two other broad-shouldered, rough-handed men as they moved between meetings with casting associates and network execs. The three of them sat side by side outside hotel room doors waiting to be interviewed, forbidden from speaking, clearly competing for the same spot. They weren't the only group. Three leathery older women stalked through the halls. There were three nerds, in different varieties of nerdiness—a skinny nerd with glasses, a chubby nerd with a Captain America T-shirt, and a biker with pierced eyebrows and a tattoo sleeve, who would gaze at Kent's trio with yearning every time they passed in the hallways, like somehow he got misfiled into the wrong group.

At first Kent hated how quickly he'd been reduced to a tick on a demographic survey. Like finding out you're a clone, you start to wonder which parts of yourself are authentically *you* and which parts have been mass-imprinted by the social machinery. The trio would use the hotel gym at the same time, each guy adding another couple of plates to the bench press when it was his turn. At some point the third guy wasn't there. Then Kent was the only one. He was the alpha male of alpha males. This morning, when Erika gave each contestant a single survival item, he got the machete.

He leaps off the boat before it even stops moving, holding the blade aloft like a flag. He's wearing a lavalier mike disguised as a beaded necklace—they all are—but the necklaces are supposedly waterproof, and the transmitters are in small waterproof pouches clipped to their underwear. Behind him the boat motors to a stop. The wind stills. The heat presses in, warping the air. The other contestants climb off the Zodiac and follow him toward shore. Kelly-Anne sashays up the beach in full-on vamp, like she's on a *Sports Illustrated* photo shoot. An older man, aggressively spray-tanned with a pronounced gut and dyed black hair that's swept backward along his neck, looks like he might be carried away by the tide. Carl roars again and again as he splashes in, like a children's toy with only one button.

They gather on the shore and give each other excited hugs. The last one off the boat is the nerd. They all watch as she hesitates on the gunwale. "You can do it, Glasses!" shouts Ashley. The girl takes a tentative step forward, stumbles, and face-plants into the waves. The group exchanges little looks. Kent can practically hear the clown music. "I hope they let us vote people off," says the bro. Kent starts to laugh but glances quickly at the cameras. He doesn't want to be the bully.

When the sopping girl has joined them on the beach, one of the producers separates from the huddle of production personnel. "Welcome to *Escape!*," he says.

The contestants applaud.

"Are you the host?" asks the bro.

"I'm Jacob, the executive producer," the man says. "That means I personally handpicked each of you over thousands of other people to be here. This game is going to test your bodies and your souls in a way you have never been tested before. But before I let you loose on this island, I need to lay down the guidelines. You all know the basic premise, and hopefully you've read your contracts. Look out into the ocean. See that little islet? You can just make out the tips of three palm trees? There's a treasure chest buried there. By day fifty, there's going to be one million dollars in that chest. Whoever gets there holding a key can unlock the treasure and divide up the loot. If the eight of you work together, that's a hundred and twenty-five thousand dollars each. If two of you make it, that's five hundred thousand dollars each. And if it's only one of you—well, I think you guys can do that math yourselves. But here's the first twist. All that money isn't there at once. Starting today, we'll be adding twenty thousand dollars into the treasure chest each morning. If you or your ally has a key, and you decide you're better served to build a raft and snag some of that money for yourself, rather than wait until the end? Go for it. You get to scoop up what's there. But as soon as you touch Treasure Island, your story ends—and the game moves forward without you."

"How do we win the keys?" Kent asks.

Jacob smiles. "You'll find out."

"Who's the host?" the bro asks.

"I'll be the one explaining how games work and handing you rewards," Jacob says. "But we don't have our own Ryan Seacrest or Jeff Probst, if that's what you're asking. There's no host and no rules. Go anywhere. Do anything. It's you eight and the island."

"And all these cameras," the bro says. With his salmon shorts and brown boating shoes, he looks like he's arriving at a frat party booze cruise rather than a jungle survival show. Production chose his outfit, Kent knows, a wardrobe consultant's outdated idea of what a preppy wears. But nobody forced him to pop that collar.

"Okay, one rule," Jacob says. "No talk about production. The TV audience at home doesn't want to hear about the cameras or the crew. They don't want to hear anything that takes away from the story of you eight facing off against this island and each other. Oh, and obviously you can't hurt each other. So, two rules. Now, why don't you guys introduce yourselves."

Jacob disappears back into the production huddle, and the overtanned older man draws himself up. "As the elder statesman of our company, I should begin the introductions. I am Dr. Bartolo. I want to say what a profound honor it is to share this experience with such a distinguished group of explorers." Bartolo bows in the direction of the cameras, and the contestants applaud, which Bartolo acknowledges with a small inclination of his head.

Following Bartolo's model, the other seven introduce themselves. The bro, Ruddy, just graduated college in Austin. "I've got a silver tongue, so I know I would ace it in sales," he says, "but the plan is to see where this whole deal takes me. Maybe after this I'll never have to work again."

"One million dollars isn't exactly retire-at-twenty-two money," Kelly-Anne says.

"Haven't you ever heard the first million is the hardest?" Ruddy says.

"After taxes it's only six hundred thousand dollars. And split eight ways—"

"Who says we're splitting it?" Ruddy asks. The other contestants laugh, but Kent's not so sure he's joking. "But let's all agree—we all stay on this rock for the full fifty. Nobody goes rogue and steals the loot."

They stick their hands in the middle and do an eight-way pinky swear. "Anyway, it's not really about the money," Kelly-Anne says. "It's about the exposure."

"You can have all the exposure you want," says the older woman.

"I could use that cash." Barbara, but call her Barb, is a school janitor. That money would do a mess of good, but no matter what she walks away with, she plans to give half to charity.

"You're the mom, right?" Ruddy says.

"The mom?" Barb asks.

"The mom character," Ruddy says. "Every show has a mom character."

"I'm not *your* mom," Barb says. "Don't expect me to do your cooking and cleaning, if that's what you're asking."

The group laughs again.

A cameraman approaches. "Can you guys open this circle up? You're bunching. We want to see all your pretty faces, not a row of backs."

They spread out in a semicircle, and the cameraman takes a knee.

"This is so cool," Ruddy says.

Barb turns to the nerdy girl in the lab coat. "I can guess from that coat what your job is. Looks like we got two doctors."

"I'm in—chemistry," the girl says. "Miriam. I work in a pharmaceuticals lab in New York."

"Pharmaceuticals! This is the girl I need to meet," Ruddy says. "Make sure to give me your number when we're out of here, Miriam from New York."

"Not *that* kind of pharmaceuticals," Miriam says. "My company makes skin care products."

"So I'm the one who should be getting that number," says Kelly-Anne.

"Me too," Barb says, and when everyone starts to laugh, she looks around with mock indignation. "What's so funny?"

As the group chatters, Kent can't shake the sense that he's in the imitation of an imitation, like they're all moving through the expected beats of a scene they've watched many times before. He looks over at Ashley and Kelly-Anne and Carl to see if they're thinking it too, but they're laughing along with the rest of them. *Am I a jaded old man?* He remembers his first show. The giddy introductions, the excitement that it was *these* fifteen people with whom you'd be boiling water and foraging for berries and gathering wood. The production activity was a blur, like watching a video in fast-forward, so much happening that you couldn't identify any one thing. And even as you began to plot and form alliances, still there was the camaraderie that it was *these* fifteen people whose hopes and dreams you'd be dashing out. What Kent didn't realize then, what over a decade has taught him, is that the experience lasts a couple of weeks. The money lasts a couple of years. The TV show is forever. Kent's not here for the cash, or the plotting and scheming, or the banter. He's here to slip into the old costume, which has started to sag and tear. He's here to *be* Kent Duvall.

"Okay, guys," Barb says. "We're in a survival situation, so let's take an inventory of the gear the producers gave us."

"Remember our rule," Jacob shouts. "No talk about 'producers.' You need to say *you* brought those items to the beach."

"Can we get an inventory of all the items *we* brought?" Barb casts a meaningful look at Jacob. He gives her a thumbs-up. "This is *my* tarp."

They lay out their equipment on the tarp. There's a hatchet, a small knife, a coil of rope, a bottle of iodine, and a blue enamel pot with a loop handle. On the boat ride over, these items seemed magical. These would be their tools as they plunged into the wild! Now the tiny glass iodine bottle and the fraying rope look trivial against the enormous backdrop of the jungle. Kent hesitates with his machete. As long as it's in his hand, he has control. He can sever himself from the group and survive alone. He can build his own raft and paddle solo to the island. He can win the game and the million dollars by himself.

"Put that down with the rest," Barb tells him. "We've got to share everything if we're going to make a real go of it here."

Kent looks over at Jacob. "*Do* we need to share?"

"I already told you." Jacob smiles. "Two rules."

Kent feels like he's calculating an entire season of content within a few dense seconds. If he goes off by himself, is he the lone adventurer surviving on his wits? Or is he the arrogant meathead who dooms everyone? He forgot this aspect of television—the million split-second decisions. Trying to balance what you want to do, what the other players want you to do, what the producers want you to do, and what's going to look good to viewers. He wishes he had the chance to talk things through in an interview and check in with the producers.

Barb puts a hand on his shoulder. "Don't worry, hon, you can pick that up again in two minutes. Let's figure out what all we've got before we start charging into the woods. You know as well as I do that no piece of gear is more important than a solid plan."

He lays the machete on the tarp. The loopy, muttering woman from casting has become the most practical force on the beach. Really, he thinks, the iodine will make drinking water a lot safer, and the rope will come in handy. And he shouldn't make any big moves until he knows *how* they win keys. It could be physical challenges, but it could just as easily be a vote or popularity contest.

"That's it?" Barb asks. "This is what all we've got for our little camping trip?"

"That's only seven things. There are eight of us," Kelly-Anne says.

"It was here a minute ago." Miriam is searching the pockets of her lab coat.

"You're kidding," Kent says, grateful the attention is off him.

"It was *here*," Miriam says. "I put it in this pocket on the boat."

"What was it?" asks Barb. "Maybe we can get along without it."

"It was a little metal rod—about two inches long. It can't have been important—"

"A ferro rod?" Kent shouts. "You lost *the fire starter*?"

"It—must have slipped out of my pocket when I fell into the water."

"Fire will be vital here," Dr. Bartolo intones.

"No shit," Kent snaps. No fire means no food. No fire means no *heat.* But most of all, no fire means they're going to look like idiots on TV.

CHAPTER 13

They search the shallows for over an hour, feeling their way among thick clusters of seaweed, avoiding the jagged whorls of coral. Kent can't stop glaring at Miriam. Even on the plane ride from the States, and the brief glimpses through hotel room doors while they were in transit, she struck Kent as comically miscast, pale and awkward, with thick-lensed glasses that made her big brown eyes look watery and confused. *This* was who he would be surviving in the jungle with? Now stripped down for the search—they all stripped to only their underwear and their lavalier necklaces—she's got the milky softness of a veal calf. Even her hair is exasperatingly impractical, a mass of curls that in the island humidity has sprouted with frizz, like an overgrown topiary. She looks like someone you might stumble over in a bookstore.

He knows exactly how this will play on television. They'll cut to a close-up of the ferro rod, bobbing jauntily on the tide. Then back to the eight of them, splashing around like toddlers, missing it by inches. The audience will wonder how *anybody* could be so stupid. He looks straight into a camera. If he's staring into the cameras, they'll focus on someone else.

As he splashes waist-deep through the water, a horrible thought flickers into his mind. What if it's all a setup? There was a show years ago, *Joe Millionaire*, where the contestants thought they were competing to marry a multimillionaire. Only in the finale did the "winning" woman discover he was broke. *Gotcha! We've destroyed your life!* On the *Joe Schmo Show*, and later on *Jury Duty*, all the contestants but one were paid actors. What if the whole premise of *Escape!* is to watch his unraveling? Here's Ashley, the girl who publicly humiliated you and caused the breakup of your marriage. Here's Kelly-Anne, perfectly cast to give withering asides to our at-home audience. Here are the clowns, Bartolo and Carl. And now here's Miriam, who's going to bungle everything. Let's all laugh it up at this middle-aged loser. It's not impossible. There are always two games. The one you're playing against the other contestants, and the one the producers are playing against you.

Even if it is a "real" reality show—whatever that means—what kind of show *is* it? The production crew has twenty people at most. Two camera guys, two sound engineers, two producers. A handful of miscellaneous staff. But that's it. Walking into *Endure* fifteen years ago was like entering a movie set. There were a hundred people running around, cameras mounted on cranes, a helicopter swooping overhead. Divers with underwater cameras just to catch the foam churning around their feet. The jungle itself had looked groomed and manicured, like every snake or rat had been shampooed by a team of wildlife professionals, each tropical bird color-coordinated to match their outfits. You would stumble on a trove of coconuts when you were at your hungriest, or find bamboo logs lying in the bushes that were the perfect size and shape for shelter building.

But the jungle here looks fungal, like an overgrown petri dish. The trees have twisted trunks and swollen limbs. The entire island seems to writhe. At the edge of the tree line, a single palm juts onto the shore, its trunk crooked like a beckoning finger. Clustered on the beach, the tiny crew looks like a missionary sect about to be swallowed by the wilderness. For a brief moment Kent is afraid. He was so desperate to go back on TV, he didn't even think to ask what sort of program he was stepping into.

"Not the best beginning," Ashley says to him, dunking down into the water to feel along the silt.

"That's quite a dress they've got you in," he says.

"Don't start. I told Callie there's no way in hell I'm wearing that into the jungle. She said I'm free to wear whatever I want . . . in the comfort of my living room."

"*No talk about production*," someone shouts from the shore.

People always wondered why anybody would set off on a jungle adventure dressed in blue jeans, but they didn't realize many contestants never had a choice. Months before filming, the wardrobe team asked for three options, and they would reliably pick the worst one. Kent only sent in a T-shirt and a pair of pants that he'd coated beforehand in a clear silicone water-resistant spray. Someone like Ashley would follow the rules because she didn't know how to break them. He remembers her poolside in Alabama, desperate to prove herself. *"I'm* not *one of these ditzy girls. I grew up on a ranch."* She's the opposite of Miriam, he thinks. She's clearly been preparing. Muscles pop around her traps and abs. He looks away. Even a single glance can be slowed down and zoomed in or looped a dozen different times to seem flirty or horny or pervy. Put one lusty look above a sultry saxophone, and the audience is spoon-fed an entire storyline. And it's not only the narrative Kent's worried about. Being physically near Ashley still feels wrong, like even though Margaret moved out and won't take his calls, he's somehow still betraying her.

"Listen," he says to Ashley.

At the same time, she says, "I'm so glad I have a chance—"

They both laugh.

"You first," she says.

Kent lowers his voice. "About what we said in casting—"

"*No talk about production!*" The shout is louder, more annoyed, and they veer apart. He hopes she doesn't think he's proposing anything. The last thing Kent wants is a showmance. There was a time when showmances were celebrated in competition shows. Boston Rob Mariano and Amber Brkich found love backstabbing their way through *Survivor: All Stars*. The audience swooned. CBS televised their wedding. Now viewers think differently. If two contestants are canoodling, they've lost sight of the game. The relationship isn't going to last. They're making themselves a target. They're there for the wrong reasons.

Barb proposes that they sweep the coast in case the ferro rod washed ashore. They walk up and down in an ordered line. But the scorching sun burns off any last vapor of good humor, so that even walking through sand feels exhausting. Finally, Ruddy complains, "This is ridiculous. That fire starter could be halfway to China."

"China's actually not particularly far from here," Dr. Bartolo says sagely.

"Can we have another one?" Barb shouts over to the producers.

The production group is silent.

"She lost it before the show even started, so technically it's not like she lost it 'on' the show."

No response.

"Well, shit," Barb says. "Does anybody know how to make a fire *without* a fire starter?"

"Glasses," Kent calls to Miriam. "Are you nearsighted or farsighted?"

Miriam touches her hand to her frames, like she's worried he'll try to snatch them off her face. "Nearsighted. Why?"

"Damn. We can't use your lenses."

"Didn't you make a bow drill fire on *Endure*?" Kelly-Anne asks him.

"That was fifteen years ago," Kent says.

"Could you at least try?" Barb asks, a touch of desperation in her voice.

It feels like the entire island is staring at him. Even the trees crowd together in expectation. He looks around at the group, at Dr. Bartolo nervously twisting his fingers, at Carl in his camouflage outfit trying to disappear into the tangles of his beard. This is the standout moment Kent was hoping for. But now that it's here, he's terrified.

Before *Endure*, Kent spent months reading survival guides. He learned how to make friction boards and bow drills. He practiced tying knots. He even went into the woods outside Providence and built a debris shelter. He slept on the dirt in a rainstorm.

But this time he'd been lazy. There was the move out of his apartment, and finding a new place to live, and simply trying to make sense of life without Margaret. Really, those were excuses. The truth is, he was counting on circumstances to magically work out, for his old inner hero to smash through his torpor like the Kool-Aid Man bursting through a wall. As the afternoon sunlight unravels into dusk, he realizes how idiotic that was. Now he has no choice *but* to try to make this bow drill. And if he fails, he knows that the show will open with a montage of him and Miriam, a duo of idiots, set to a custom score of clown music.

"Okay–someone get tinder," he says. "Dried grasses, twigs, that kind of thing. We're also going to need bigger wood. Logs, dried driftwood. Anything that'll burn. Glasses!" he shouts at Miriam as she goes running off down the shore. "You need to keep looking in the water. That ferro rod didn't vanish."

"Sorry," Miriam calls back. She's tall, maybe five foot ten, but so hunched into herself that she seems a half foot shorter.

"You don't need to be sorry. You need to keep looking."

Kent unspools a length of rope from the coiled bundle, severs the end with the hatchet, and ties it to a supple branch, making a bow. He picks up the machete, feeling the comfortable weight in his hand. Using its tip, he notches a flat piece of driftwood to serve as a fireboard, carves another piece of wood into a spindle, and twists the spindle into the bowstring. He places the end of his spindle into the notch on the fireboard.

"It's been a long time since I've done this," he says again, really to the cameras. The bow squeaks as he saws back and forth in slow strokes. The contestants huddle over him with handfuls of dry grass, small branches, and midsize logs. The cameras focus in.

A small pile of dust builds in the fireboard. Kent saws faster. Fans pick who to root for in the first episode and stick with that contestant the entire show. You have one chance to be a hero. A finger of smoke trails up from the point of friction. He saws faster and faster. For one brief moment, Kent isn't thinking about the contestants, or the cameras, or his edit, or the fans. It's just the squeaking rope, the back-and-forth sawing of the bow. Lactic burn laces his forearms.

The darkness is coming down onto the beach when he sees it. An ember no bigger than a pinprick. "Omigod," someone whispers. "Not in the clear yet," Kent says. He moves the ember to a coil of dried grass and blows a stream of air. The smoke thickens. A red blaze blooms. He cradles the flaming pile of tinder in his hands and pushes it under a teepee of small sticks. A twig catches with a snap.

They have fire.

Kelly-Anne and Carl hug. Ruddy howls at the sky, and Bartolo does a jig, kicking sand into the air. "Oh, Kent!" Ashley says, and it sounds almost romantic. The fire licks up.

As the flames beat back the quickly falling dusk, Kent's barely aware of a splashing from the waterline. It's Miriam. Still wading through the ocean, still looking for the lost ferro rod. It's starting to get cold, quickly. She must be freezing. One of the producers, a woman with red hair, is filming her. In the dusk, Miriam's eyes look big and wet and mournful.

Kent turns away and stokes the flame.

He built it.

Kent Duvall.

CHAPTER 14

BECK

NIGHT 1

I made it a point to ride back to the City with Jacob, crowding into his van with a group of PAs and a stocky man with a shaved head named Brian, who was in charge of the show's production management, and who everybody called Logistics Brian, although there was no other Brian. Logistics Brian put forth a truly prodigious quantity of sweat, and over the course of the ride, his shirt became increasingly soaked until it was barely more than a damp rag dripping off his shoulders, and the entire van reeked of his BO.

"What did you think?" Jacob asked when the door slammed shut and we were bumping along the jungle path. "I thought it went well. Do you think it went well? Who do you think has a good story?"

He looked like an actor who'd just stepped offstage, jumpy with nervous energy, thrilled by a job well done yet still craving the audience's approval. I was touched by that neediness—and comforted by it. Every reality show I ever worked on started this way, with that drive back from set, debriefing about what happened and plotting what was to come.

"It went great," I assured him. "Kent's a star. That trick with the fire was spectacular. And Bartolo is gold. All that stuff about 'this distinguished group of adventurers.' Is he really a doctor? I don't remember that from his dossier."

"It didn't show up in his background check," Logistics Brian said from his puddle of sweat. "He runs a dance studio in a strip mall."

"That's definitely an angle," Jacob said. "What kind of 'doctor' is he? What about Kelly-Anne?"

"She's obviously got a big personality," I said. The van hit a bump and our heads bounced into the padded roof. "And she's got those wide-set eyes and sharp cheekbones that pop on TV. But did you notice she kept looking at the cameras? I'm always leery of the ones who are meme-ing."

"True, but she knows how to deliver drama," he said. "What about Miriam?"

Jacob gave me a strange look, and I felt for a moment like an oyster being pried open with a knife. It was hard to believe Miriam had fallen off the Zodiac, exactly as the story bible predicted. After that, I'd kept my viewfinder focused on her, maybe to—protect her, I thought. At the very least, to honor her suffering. As she waded through the cold shallows looking for the ferro rod, I didn't say anything to her. I *couldn't* say anything. But I tried my best to radiate sympathy, while I filmed her humiliation.

"She's definitely going to struggle out here," I said brusquely.

"One small thing. I saw you wipe sunscreen off her shoulder."

"Yeah, I didn't want a white glob to ruin the shot. I swear, some people don't know how to blend."

"I know that's normal on most shows. But this is a competition series. You can't touch the contestants, ever. FCC rules. It could be seen as interference. It's called crossing the line. Think of it like an invisible line between us and them."

"Roger that. Sorry."

"You didn't know. Now you do. What do you think of Barb?"

"I like her. Kooky, but smart."

"Too smart. She was more of a nut in casting. But you can never tell who someone really is until the cameras start rolling."

BACK IN THE CITY, I WROTE UP MY HOT SHEET OVERVIEW OF THE DAY'S events. Night brought a cool breeze, but sitting in my bungalow still felt like being trapped forever in the last ten minutes of spin class. Something skittered down my back, and I couldn't tell if it was sweat or bugs.

The hot sheets were how we communicated the key plot points of the stories we were tracking to the network and the editing team. Obviously, I had to write about Miriam's fall and her loss of the ferro rod. But I didn't want to lock her into the story bible's comedy of degradation. I couldn't claim she was some hero-in-waiting. That didn't pass the sniff test, and the hot sheet had to offer realistic guidance to postproduction. But Miriam . . . persevered. She stayed out in the waves, searching. Doing her best. That was who she was. Someone who tried hard, never quit. I could work with that.

By the time I finished my notes, the crew was celebrating the first day of filming with a beach barbecue. From down the shore came the screams of the junior staff, leaping in and out of the surf. Production teams on location are like pirate crews, or at least we tell ourselves that, though from my limited knowledge, burgers and volleyball weren't huge among the Caribbean freebooters. I walked along the sand in search of a hot dog. A few of the PAs were smoking cigars and playing poker. Afa, one of the sound engineers, was pacing up and down with his boom mike over the sand. Listening to the sand fleas, he explained with a dismissive wave of his hand, as though it were obvious. The idea that he was appreciating a hidden sonic universe open only to him was a bit affected, but I suppose we all imagine we have unique access to something.

By the grill, in the light from the embers, I saw Erika and Jacob huddled together. I watched them for a moment from the safety of the darkness. Erika was showing Jacob something in her hand and laughing. Her eyes caught the firelight, and they were animated with giddiness. Then she turned and saw me, and her expression curdled.

"Are you spying on us?" She pocketed whatever she was showing Jacob.

"Don't put it away," Jacob said. "Show her."

"Are you sure?"

"Of course."

"Show me or don't show me," I said. "I don't really care." The most frustrating part of Erika's psychology was that it was so transparent—the whole *I'm threatened by the new girl* routine that petty coworkers have been playing out for millennia. But what could I say? When I was a teenager dealing with the mean girls who mocked me for my hawk nose or the shapeless dresses that Dad bought, Dad would tell me to "talk to them like an adult." At the time the advice was transparently ridiculous, and I longed for that future grown-up day when problems could be resolved through conversation. Now, twenty years later, even the thought of talking things out with Erika intimidated me. "Like an adult" was such an oxymoron. Adults played out their junior high insecurities for eternity.

Erika reached into her pocket again and opened her hand. In her palm sat a small metal cylinder about two inches in length. The ferro rod.

"You're joking."

Her whole face expanded into a mocking smile. "It fell out of her coat when she tripped off the boat. I simply—" She mimed snatching it up from the water. "They might not have seen it anyway."

"But they might have seen it. The group searched everywhere. Miriam was in the water for hours. And now she's—"

"Do you have a crush?" Erika asked. "Don't get attached. She won't be here long."

"I don't get it. Jacob, you told me I couldn't wipe sunscreen off a contestant."

"Did I touch her?" Erika asked. "She already dropped it. I simply . . . helped fate along. And plus, I didn't do it on camera. Where's the evidence?"

"The evidence is right here!" I picked the ferro rod up from her palm. Stealing a vital tool that the group was relying on to survive in the jungle seemed beyond production's usual tricks, especially because all the blame fell on one person. I'd seen the other contestants' looks, heard them whispering over the mikes. Miriam was isolated before the show started, for something she didn't even do. And even as I knew it was crazy, I felt like *I* was the victim.

"Hardships push people past their limits," Jacob said. "Look what happened. Kent stepped up. Even he didn't think he could make that fire, and now we have the start of a phenomenal episode. If you guys see an opportunity to drive story, you have to take it." Erika looked like she was about to ascend to heaven. "And, Beck, I saw you shooting Miriam in the water. That's going to be the perfect counterpoint to Kent's heroism. The faded hero recovering his glory, while the nerd watches awkwardly from the waves."

"It doesn't seem . . . *fair*," I said, knowing I sounded like an indignant child.

"There's no such thing as fair," Erika said. "Only good television. That girl was born to be comic relief."

"That's bullshit!" I was surprised at my vehemence, but I could see that in Erika's mind, Miriam's whole story had already been written, a string of humiliations. "Jacob, you told me that America wants something inspirational. Why not—a journey of growth. From the girl who was scrambling in her underwear for the fire starter on day one to the woman who—well, she doesn't have to win. She just needs a big redemption moment."

"That's a nice fairy tale." Erika smirked. "But Miriam's only big moment is going to be if she's medically evacuated in a machete accident."

A sound squealed through the air, and something exploded overhead. I flinched and pivoted. A moment later the sky filled with brilliant green spangles. Another whistle of air, another pop, and a red chrysanthemum bloomed overhead. Down the beach, the junior staff were cheering. Ralph, the skinny PA, was launching fireworks from a steel tube at the water's edge.

Something burned my shoulder. A fleck of ash. Another hit my neck. Flakes of burning ash from the fireworks rained onto my arm and below my eye, as above us materialized purple and orange and pink anemones.

"Watch out from above!" Ralph called out. Another mortar whistled into the air and burst into a rash of blue pinpricks. The PAs cheered.

"Shit!" Erika cursed. "My hair's going to catch fire!" She ran toward the safety of the hotel.

Jacob and I exchanged a look. He had a way of making it seem like the rest of the world was a private joke. In his khakis and rumpled linen shirt, with the slight outline of a paunch and the worry lines of fatigue, he seemed more like a harried father of three kids on safari than a television impresario masterminding his new show. I had the sense that part of his awareness was always looking over his shoulder to make sure that none of the other children were fighting, that nobody had been eaten by an animal. But somehow, his gaze never left mine.

"We should go too, before *we* catch fire," he said. "I'm actually glad to get a moment to talk with just you."

Even his voice reminded me of a dad—*my* dad. Not the distracted, hollow man who emerged after my mom died. The dad from my video, whose voice you could hear the delight in, even though he was off-screen. I put the ferro rod in my pocket, not sure what else to do with it, and let him lead me across the sand into the hotel. The lobby was deserted. The only sound was the thrum of the fan and a faint thump. A congregation of moths was circling the fluorescent lights, bumping one by one into the glow. I followed Jacob up the stairs, through the dining room, and into a dark kitchen. When he flicked on a light switch, I saw or imagined I saw dark shapes evaporating into the shadows. Dirty pots and plates covered a stainless steel countertop. Scraps of lettuce and meat were everywhere. An oversize refrigerator hummed in the corner.

"I was *hoping* to finally see the kitchen," I said.

"Hold on." Jacob opened the fridge. It was crowded with plastic bags, translucent from the condensed air. He snaked his arm past containers of chicken carcasses, ground meat, and orange and yellow vegetables and emerged with a miniature bottle, green glass topped by gold foil.

"Champagne?" I asked.

"I think you deserve a little celebration. But this has to be our secret."

"Pinky swear." I caught his pinky in my own, mirroring the contestants from earlier, and was immediately aware of how long it had been since I showered.

"Are you okay meeting in my room?" he asked. "It's hard to find a quiet place to catch up."

A champagne toast in the boss's hotel room was a violation of every workplace handbook. But even in the day I'd been here, whenever I tried to have a conversation with Jacob, a PA would pop in with a question about batteries, or Logistics Brian would come running waving a spreadsheet. The whole island was jockeying for his attention. I didn't want to miss my moment. And really, I told myself, he was nothing like the hotshot wunderkind in ripped jeans whose old interview I'd watched. He was a kind, middle-aged man who overfilled the pockets in his cargo pants. Life wears down even the sharpest edges.

"Lead the way," I said.

He motioned me out of the kitchen, up two flights of stairs, and down a concrete hallway. His room was barely large enough for a sagging queen bed covered in crisp white sheets, tucked at their corners. An ancient cathode-ray television sat on an unvarnished wooden dresser, its cord tied neatly with a rubber band. On a folding table by the window were piles of papers, smartly arranged at right angles, but a little breeze that pushed in around the cracks kept threatening to blow the piles askew. The only other piece of furniture was a bedside table, which was covered in books. I looked at the titles as I sat down at the edge of the bed. There was *The Beach* by Alex Garland and *State of Wonder* by Ann Patchett and *Lord of the Flies* by William Golding and Shakespeare's *The Tempest*, all stories of urbanites facing off against the wild.

"You have a television?" I asked.

"A television that only picks up static." He pulled over a chair. "I'm not even sure why these things are in here. It's like someone knew a hotel room was supposed to have a TV but never considered how it would work a hundred miles from the nearest broadcast tower."

The small champagne bottle was sweating in the still night air. Jacob peeled off the gold foil and, his grip firm on the cork, popped it open and poured champagne into two plastic cups.

"Sorry about that outburst back there," I said. "That's not who—"

"Hold on. We'll get to that. But first, I want to thank you. I know how hard this must be for you," Jacob said. "Starting any new job is difficult, and it must be especially tough with a close-knit crew like ours. Thank you for taking the risk. We literally could not do this without you. You're saving my butt."

"It's me who needs to thank *you*. Without this job, I'd be unemployable. Maybe forever."

"To saving each other, then." He clinked his plastic cup against mine, and we drank. I always loved the luxurious feeling of champagne fizz sliding down my throat. Jacob leaned back in his chair, so at ease, so open, and it made me aware that my arms were crossed over my chest and my fingers were interlaced around my cup. I forced myself to relax.

"I have a lot of faith in you, Beck," he said. "How are you doing, with all your—you know?"

"My you know?"

"With any baggage. From Buster."

"So it's going to be one of those conversations."

"You only have to tell me as much as you want." His eyebrows were raised, and his head was tilted to the side.

"I definitely came out here a little rattled," I said. "To be honest—it gives me sympathy for the contestants."

"And one contestant in particular."

"About Miriam. I see your point that we need to drive story. But I still think—" I took a breath to gather my thoughts. From outside I could hear the fireworks igniting into the sky and the shouts of the staff. A dog was barking somewhere, though I didn't remember having seen a dog. "I get that this is a cable wilderness show. I know that the core demo is guys who build bunkers in their backyards and hunt elk with hand-carved bows. They'll love Kent. And Carl of course. Maybe

Barb. But there's lots of viewers out there at comfortable desk jobs. People who feel stuck and numb. They're bored. They're starving for . . . *something*. Miriam can be the person they tune in for."

Jacob nodded as I spoke. "I absolutely agree," he said. "Is Miriam going to win this game? It's a long shot, though the one thing I've learned in my two decades doing this is that people will surprise you. But Miriam's got the potential to be a great character. And in the end, you can't have a great story without great characters."

"I think we could go even further," I said. "Look, I haven't totally formulated this, so I'm sure it's going to sound like a jumble. But what if we created something—different? Like you said, inspiring. Everything these days is so manipulated. What if we made a reality competition that doesn't feel like a dirty trick? That's not all about—backstabbing and lying. Something—I don't know—slower. Kinder. What if we focused on—friendship. How meaningful it feels to stare at a stream." I laughed at how stupid I knew it sounded. "That Buster stuff really did a number on me, didn't it."

"No. Don't say that." I'd been looking at the floor while I talked, and when I looked up, he was staring at me intently. "That was beautiful."

"I can only imagine Erika's response."

"One of the reasons I hired you is because you're *not* Erika. Erika can see everybody's weaknesses. I get the sense that you can see their strengths. This show needs both. You made me actually care about surfing dogs. I can't promise this whole series is going to be about staring at a stream. But I'm not opposed to a little stream content. Let's see where it goes. Tomorrow, some of the stronger contestants are going to abandon the weak ones."

"What? Since when?" So much for my beautiful fable, I thought.

"It happened an hour ago. Ralph saw Kelly-Anne and Ruddy plotting on one of the infrared cams. But Kent doesn't know about it yet.

Wouldn't it be great if somehow the camp's best provider stayed on Miriam's side? Then you'd have the space to pull your story together."

"So you want me to convince Kent to—"

"What I want is for you to trust your instincts," he said meaningfully.

Higher-ups on reality shows will often blind themselves to what they're asking their story producers to do. But Jacob was giving me room to play, and if we were going to put our fingers on the scale, I was grateful that it could help Miriam.

"Let's drink to that," I said. "To trusting our instincts." Though as we tapped our cups together, my gut clenched like I was about to swear to a lie. How could I trust my instincts when they had led me to national embarrassment and a dead dog? Still, for Jacob's sake, I drank.

As my eyes tilted up, I noticed the one decoration on the room's bare walls. It was a small gilt frame hanging above the television, filled with pinned and labeled butterflies.

"Creepy." I gestured toward the frame. "Do all the rooms have dead bugs?"

"That's actually mine. I brought it with me."

"You're joking."

"People think that butterfly collecting is cruel, but for centuries, it was a way to do just what you were talking about—encourage appreciation of the natural world."

"By killing things?" I asked.

"A lot more butterflies die from climate change than middle-aged men with nets."

I walked over to the board, trying to see it through the lens of his enthusiasm. There were maybe twenty specimens. Below each was a small label that displayed in neat script a scientific classification and then a more evocative informal name.

"I like this one," I said, pointing to a large butterfly whose brown wings looked covered by an iridescent purple-blue sheen. *Apatura iris.* The Purple Emperor.

"You have a good eye." Jacob came up behind me. Again I noticed my arms were crossed. What was wrong with me? "They're very rare now and hard to catch because they fly in the canopy. I got him when he came lower to feed."

"What's *your* favorite?"

He looked embarrassed but gestured to the top right corner. All the other butterflies were displayed with only their backs toward the glass, but for that one, he had two samples, so you could see both its back and its stomach.

"She always reminds me of what I love about reality TV," Jacob said. "You look at her from the back, she's gorgeous." The dorsal specimen showed brilliant orange wings with dark Rorschach markings that faded to midnight blue. "But if you turn her over—" Its stomach side, the ventral side, looked cracked and brown like a dead leaf. "She's all dried up. Scripted shows tell you who to root for, who to hate. Who's the hero, who's the villain. But in a show like ours? It's like what you were saying about Miriam. Everyone sees themselves in someone different. And that means everyone is watching a different story."

I leaned a little closer to make out the faded label, centered carefully beneath the butterfly's brilliant wings. *Polygonia interrogationis.*

The Question Mark.

CHAPTER 15
KENT

DAY 2

It's dark. He's been lying there for hours, shifting his aching joints on the hard-packed sand. His clothes are damp from the salt spray, his mouth is dry, and a dehydration headache pulses at his temples. Kent forgot how physically uncomfortable the outdoors is. It's not merely the cold or the wet or the bugs. It's the impossibility of ever finding a good position. Nothing about the jungle is ergonomic.

The other contestants are asleep, sprawled around the fire, which has faded to orange embers. Barb is snoring, an arm draped protectively across Miriam. Bartolo makes small jerks, like a dog dreaming. Ashley looks angelic, a little drool glistening along her chin.

With no producers around, it's the perfect chance to talk to her privately. The crew will see their conversation when they watch the footage from the infrared cameras, and maybe he'll get a lecture about talking off camera. But he needs to have this chat now. He has to let her down, but delicately. He can't risk breaking her heart and making an enemy so early in the game.

He pushes himself up and taps her on the shoulder.

"Mwhhh?"

He puts his finger over his lips and gestures down the beach. She follows him to the water's edge. The wind is freezing, and the wet sand soaks his socks. The dark here is complete, dark like you never see at home, dark so total that even the stars are mere pinpricks in the black fabric of night. She's looking up at him, shivering in her red mini, her legs totally exposed, her face all anxious anticipation.

"Listen," Kent says, feeling terrible. She probably thinks this star-lit chat is going to be the epic start of their TV romance. "You seem like an awesome girl. And I know what we agreed in casting. But I don't think we should—"

"Oh god. Yes. One hundred percent. Thank god." Ashley gives him a quick hug she's so overjoyed. "What a relief. I thought you might actually want a showmance. Thank god."

"Ha. No. No way. Never." He's taken aback by the intensity of her response. "I mean—it wouldn't be *that* awful, though, right?"

"Noooo. Of course. You are so sweet. And cute. Obviously. I just—I can't be *that* girl. You know? I can't be hashtag freak-out on my first season and then hashtag showmance on my second. Especially with a—no offense—gentleman in his . . . later days. Then it's hashtag inappropriate. I need to have a chance to show people who *I* am."

"Right. Totally. Phew. I'm glad we're on the same page," he says. "Let's go back before anybody thinks we're strategizing—or doing something more. Ha ha ha."

She leans in and at first Kent thinks she's going for his lips, and in spite of himself he turns toward it, but she gives him a peck on the cheek and a pat on the arm and leads him back to the fire, where they lie down on opposite ends of the group, so there won't be any footage of them spooning. *Perfect*, Kent thinks. *Great. Couldn't have gone better.*

Still.

Did she have to be *so* excited? And what did she mean, "later days"? Surely a showmance with Kent Duvall would elevate *her*. He's a legend. He made fire. She's . . . nobody. Plus who exactly was "inappropriate" with whom? She was the one who seduced him.

And really—later days?

He falls asleep trying to remember the look on her face of lust and anticipation as she gazed up at him from the Alabama hotel bed.

When he wakes again, there's a camera in his face.

The redheaded producer, Beck, is hovering over him.

"Kent, do you want to go exploring for food and water?"

He grabs the machete and walks up the beach toward the tree line. Yes. Already they're helping craft him into the person he is meant to be. This is the storyline he craves.

CROSSING THE THRESHOLD FROM THE BEACH TO THE JUNGLE IS LIKE stepping into a Jurassic world. The humidity spikes. The trees close in. The air practically vibrates with insectoid buzzing. The island's jungle is nothing like the straight pine forests of America, neat and redolent of fresh spring. Here, palms and strangling figs and the giant banyans twist and claw over one another toward the canopy, the entire jungle locked in a life-or-death struggle for the light.

"Tell me what you're doing." Beck trails him, filming with her handheld camera.

"I'm exploring. Looking for food and water for the group."

He plays up the bushwhacker routine, creeping forward, edging cautiously around lianas. He waits for Beck get into position to film him from the front and then swaggers boldly past. It's easy to imagine the scene on television, the brave explorer striding forth. Clouds of mosquitoes eddy and swirl, but he ignores their high-pitched whines. Beck for her part moves in frantic and sudden ways—her wrist snapping at horseflies, her entire torso pivoting when a branch catches her shirt—but somehow she keeps her camera steady.

A short ways inland, Kent notices the ground getting damp. Soon he hears running water. He quickens his pace. "Water," he whispers to the camera. "But we have to be careful, in case there's predators. Water sources bring animals." It sounds like it could be true. He slinks forward until, as he pushes past a cluster of ferns, the canopy curls back into a sun-dappled glade. A stream runs through the center, and beside it is a small grove of succulents. Bright red fruit dangles from their fleshy leaves.

"Food!" he breathes. "And water. Food and water! I've found food and water!" He whoops into the air, and for a moment, he is twenty-nine again, and the show pony is galloping around the clearing bucking and neighing.

"How do you feel?" Beck circles to capture his face. "Tell me what you're thinking!"

"I feel—excited, woo! I found food and water. We're going to survive!"

"Give me another whoop!" Beck shouts.

He whoops into the sky.

He made fire. He found water. He found food! It's day two, and his résumé is already packed. He plucks a fruit off a tree. It has a red rind with what looks like flames licking up its skin. The rind is tough. He cuts it in half with the machete. Inside the fruit is white with black seeds. He sniffs it. It smells sweet. He rubs it on his forearm. No reaction. He knows he should wait a few minutes to see if a rash develops, but he's hungry, and really, if it were poisonous, Beck would stop him. He reaches into the flesh with two dirty fingers and pinches out a bite. The texture is crunchy, like an underripe pear. The sugar rush hits his bloodstream.

He holds the fruit out to Beck, feeling loopy and loose. "Want some?"

"Definitely not," she says.

"Come on. Try it."

He breaks her off a small piece, and she tentatively sticks it into her mouth and spits it out.

He laughs. "Your first time in the jungle?"

"Is it that obvious? Hold on. *Go for Beck,*" she says into the radio, cocking her head to listen.

The first thing Kent noticed about Beck the day before was her shoes, pink-soled Pumas that looked so clean you could almost smell their new-shoe tang. He found himself inexplicably moved. There was something not just naive but wildly optimistic about wearing such footwear into the jungle. The other producers wear boots. They're as tan and leathery as dried fruit. Beck's as white as vanilla ice cream. Since they've been walking through the jungle, she's been constantly turning her head to the side, holding her finger to her earpiece. Something about her feels—more human than the typical jaded reality producer. More genuine. He takes another bite of the fruit.

"They're doing it now?" she's saying. *"Yeah, I'm with him. Okay. We'll be back in a beat. I just need a quick on-the-fly."*

"What's going on?" Kent asks.

"Production stuff. Nothing important. But we absolutely *have* to capture this awesome moment. So. Describe for me what's happened."

He nods. Every survival show starts with the giddy discovery of food and water. Thanks to Beck waking him up, *he* is the one who found this clearing. They want this story for *him*. Ashley's going to wish she'd fought for their showmance. Beck makes a fist next to the side of her handheld to indicate where he should talk.

"I was adventuring through the jungle and discovered food and water for the group." He holds out the red fruit for the camera.

"Wow, you're really trying to provide for people out here, aren't you?" She smiles at him, that big producer smile that you know is phony, you know they're using it with everybody, but still you can't help but be warmed by all that wattage. And with Beck, it feels almost sincere.

"I'm helping for now. At some point, when I've got my key, I'll make my escape and—"

"Let's not talk about escaping yet. Don't even think about it. You've got a huge game ahead of you. I'm much more interested in *why* you're helping. Would you say it's because you're a real hero?"

"Oh, I wouldn't say I'm a hero. I'm just a guy, doing my best to—"

"But for someone watching at home, they might think you're the hero?"

"Well, okay. I could see someone thinking that."

"Thinking what? Come on, Kent! You're a pro. Give me complete sentences."

"I could see . . ." If he claims outright to be a hero, he might be setting himself up as the blowhard and for an eventual comeuppance. But he's not saying *he* thinks he's a hero. He's merely open to the idea that a viewer could believe it. "Somebody might assume I'm a hero out here." Merely saying the words, he can imagine the audience leaning forward on their couches. Choosing him.

"Go for Beck." She places her hand on her earpiece again and holds up a finger. *"Yes. Yes. We're almost ready. I only need one more— Yes. We'll be right back."*

"Everything okay?" Kent asks, feeling annoyed. What could possibly be more important than the hero discovering food and water? Something about the way she's talking worries him. Something in the tone of her voice. The way her thumb taps a staccato down each of the fingers on her left hand, like she's trying to figure out the beat to a new song. Then she takes a breath, lifts the camera, and smiles.

"Production stuff. We should head back soon. I only have a few more questions. Kent, what do you think of Miriam?"

"Miriam?"

"Don't you think there's something inspiring about her being out here?"

"You're asking me if this person who keeps falling face-first is inspiring?" What does Miriam have to do with Kent Duvall, legend, providing for the group? "A cancer patient is inspiring. A firefighter is inspiring." *I am inspiring.* "This girl shouldn't be here. We're surviving in the jungle, and that's why I was so excited to find—"

"But wouldn't you say, if you're a hero, you should help the people who need help most?"

Kent nods. Okay, he's starting to see where she's leading him. "Let me rephrase." This was exactly the guidance he was craving. Someone telling him what to do, how to be. "I do think there's something inspiring about Miriam. Sure, dropping the ferro rod was a big setback. But now we have fire and food"—*he made fire, he found food*—"and out here, the jungle tests every one of us—"

"And wouldn't you say being a hero means putting yourself on the line for someone in need? Even when it might hurt?"

"On the line?" He's losing the thread.

"Sure. If you're a hero," Beck insists, "doesn't that mean—you have to save someone?"

"I would say that—say that being a hero means you have to save someone."

"Okay, let's go back to camp."

He takes off his shirt and makes a sack to gather a bundle of fruit. Even a day of starvation has pulled in his gut, so that he can already imagine the faint outline of abs. What did Beck mean, *putting himself on the line*? Something to worry about later. Right now, he is walking back to camp with food. He imagines the moment when he steps onto the beach, the other contestants crowding around as fruit spills from his hands. He can see the look on Ashley's face. Admiration. Awe. Every two weeks, Margaret would show him her pay stub when she deposited her check into their shared account. Now he's feeding the entire tribe. And this is only the beginning, he thinks. First fruit—next meat. Spearing a boar on *Endure* was the moment that made him legendary, and there must be a pig or a boar in this jungle. The show pony is prancing as Kent high-steps over dead logs. He'll follow the boar's tracks deep into the jungle dark. Could he even follow a track? Why not? He sees a desperate chase, the choppy edits and jump cuts. The bloody end.

When he steps across the threshold of palm trees back onto the sand, he's holding one of the fruit aloft like a trophy. The sea breeze wicks away the sweat from his forehead, and for a brief instant he feels cool.

"Kent, thank god." Bartolo comes running up the beach, his hands flapping like the wings of a flightless bird. "I told them—I said, you can't go without *us*. Without Kent and Bartolo, the two—why we together have—is this food?" Bartolo takes the red fruit out of Kent's stunned hand and holds it aloft. "Food! Look, Kelly-Anne. Look, Ruddy. Kent and I found food!" He takes a bite of the rind. "A bit rubbery," he says aside to Kent.

Kent tries to take in the chaos on the beach, but too much is happening. Contestants are running around in groups of two and three, cameras and boom mikes zipping after. On the shore, where the firm sand of the beach becomes wet and unstable, Barb stands with her protective arm around Miriam, in the exact same posture that they slept in, like fallen figurines that've been plucked upright. A camera crew hovers over them, getting in close. Defiance in Barb's face. Shame in Miriam's.

Kent plows forward, trying to rescue the moment.

"*I* found fruit!" He flicks a glance at Beck's camera. "A few minutes' walk from here, there's a—"

"Kent, we're leaving." Kelly-Anne elbows Bartolo aside. She's giddy with the news. "Ruddy and I talked it over last night. This is a game for a million dollars. We shouldn't be dragging along the deadweight."

It takes Kent a moment to process what Kelly-Anne's saying, because his first reaction is annoyance. He got up early. He found food and water. Now if it makes air at all, it'll just be a setup to his stepping out of the trees and gawking in confusion. "What do you mean—leaving?"

"Exactly like it sounds, babe. Into the jungle. *Without* the old and infirm. We're ditching Mom, Gramps, and Glasses. We're going to strike out, set up camp somewhere else, and wait for these losers to quit. You should come."

"Go on," Barb shouts from the shore. "Get. We don't need you."

It's a brilliant move for Kelly-Anne, Kent thinks. The villain teams with the diabolical bro to abandon the weak. Instantly she's a huge character. He can imagine her whispering into Ruddy's ear while they cuddled by the fire, Kelly-Anne observing, *Wouldn't it be funny if we just . . . left?* He can see the flirtatious twist of her lips. There's no way Ruddy came up with this scheme. He reads to Kent like one of those collegiate douches who are experts at the pile-on: a real scientist of kicking a person when they're down, but not the instigator to take a first swing. Not the person to stab you, but the one to twist the knife—though maybe Kent's reading too much into the popped collar and the salmon shorts. Either way, he's the perfect partner. Kent feels a pang of jealousy. It's not sexual jealousy, really. More like—alliance jealousy.

Ashley and Ruddy join them, and they form a tight circle. Bartolo peers over their shoulders. A cameraman takes a knee in the sand. A boom dips down into the circle's center. Kent can feel the moment's TV significance. They're all wearing their lavalier mikes, but for this conversation, production wants the best audio.

"Ashley—you too?"

"I'm here to win." She won't meet his eyes.

"You're taking Carl?" Kent looks across the beach, where Carl is shaking the pot into the sky and roaring.

(Truly, Kent cannot understand it. Why cast Carl?)

And that's when it hits him. The pot. Why is Carl holding the pot? Ruddy's got the tarp bundled under his arm. Ashley's holding the rope. Kelly-Anne has the hatchet.

They have everything. Every single item except the machete in his hand.

"You can't take *all* the gear," Kent says. "That's not fair."

"Actually," Kelly-Anne says, "as you specifically clarified yesterday—we can."

This isn't abandonment. This is ruination. Without any gear, the group left behind will quit in a handful of days. Less if there's rain. Ashley's right. If he wants to win, he *has* to leave with them. If he stays, he'll be a noble idiot, dragged under by the deadweight.

But if he goes, he's not only a villain—he's a follower of villains. A *henchman*. His entire persona is ruined. He wonders if this is part of Kelly-Anne's plan. Maybe she waited for him to leave camp before pulling together her plot precisely *because* he stood out as the dominant character. The role she wants for herself. There was a rumor about her circulating in the reality TV community, that she gave a blow job to a cameraman on *Endure* in exchange for a protein bar. Who knows for sure, but he can believe it. There were times toward the end of his season, those starvation days when he'd black out for a few seconds merely from standing up, when he'd happily have traded BJs for snacks. Protein two ways. Of course, these are the sorts of rumors that get started about girls like Kelly-Anne, but true or not, he feels it captures something essential about her. She'll do whatever it takes to get ahead.

Now he either goes along with her plan or dooms himself to failure.

Or maybe, he thinks, what if there's another way? What if he's the hero who can hold everything together and convince the Deserters to stay?

"Everyone—hold up," he says, trying to access the deeper registers of his voice. He straightens his posture and sucks in his gut. "We were stranded on this beach for a reason. If we're going to last the full fifty days and win the million dollars, we'll need food. I found fruit, not far from here. Production obviously wants us—"

"No talk about production!"

He looks over at the knot of crew, but all he sees is a phalanx of Ray-Bans and camera gear. How can he make his case if he can't argue the actual points? "They put us— We find ourselves—" He takes a breath. He can thread this needle. "There's a water source nearby. And food. If you leave, with no idea where you're going—"

"If you found fruit in ten minutes by yourself, I'm sure we can find something else in a couple hours tops," Ruddy says.

"That's not how this works." Kent looks at Kelly-Anne. Surely, she understands.

"We're going to survive in the jungle, we're going to last the full fifty, and we're going to look awesome doing it," Ruddy says. "If you come with us—it's a done deal. Game over."

"Yes, yes! Let's all go together." Bartolo grabs at the hem of Kent's shirt from outside their circle. "They *have* to take me if you make them. You and I—what a pair—why—together we found fruit. And yesterday we made fire—"

"What *about* fire?" Kent shakes Bartolo off and turns to Kelly-Anne. "How are you going to make fire?"

"We were just getting to that." With the blade of the hatchet, she scoops the embers from last night and dumps them into Carl's blue pot, then picks up the bow drill that's still sitting by the fireside.

"Do you even know how to use that?" There's a petulant edge to his voice that he hates.

"We'll see. Either way—now *they* can't."

"It's not immoral," Ashley says. "It's a game."

"Come with us," Kelly-Anne urges.

Kent's not sure if Kelly-Anne's talking to him or to the machete, the only tool they don't have. Barb and Miriam stand mutely on the shore. Nearby, a seagull is marching up and down the sand, cocking its head like a little Napoleon.

He looks over at the producers, wondering what to do. Erika is nodding her head, *yes, go*, but Beck is shaking hers, *no, stay. Now* he understands what she was trying to tell him. *To be a hero, you have to save someone.* Does he want to win the money? Or does he want to *be* the hero he's always imagined himself as, even if it costs him the game?

"I won't abandon them," he says, looking right at Beck. "It's not right."

"Well, with or without you—we're off," Kelly-Anne says.

Bartolo lets go of Kent's shirt and grabs Ruddy by the arm. "Please. I could be extremely useful. In my day, I was—"

"I don't know about your day." Ruddy pulls away. "But today, you're not coming."

"I'll follow. You can't stop me. I . . . I have panic attacks," Bartolo says in a small voice. The thatch of dyed black hair at the crown of his head is trembling. "I won't last out here."

"That's the point," Kelly-Anne says.

Carl roars, and the Deserters walk up the beach and into the jungle. Kent can't escape the feeling that he's been replaced. Those are *his* friends—or if not exactly friends, at least *his* group of screwy narcissistic oddballs, the post-*Endure* reality community that *he* is at the top of. How has he gotten on this side of the divide? As the group disappears past the curtain of the palms, Ashley gives him one last look. *Good luck*, she mouths. Bartolo collapses at the tree line. "I can be of so much service!" he calls. But they're gone.

"Thank you," Miriam says. He looks over at her and her ridiculous hair and oversize glasses, at the way this five-foot-ten girl with the frame of a warrior hunches into herself like a prey animal doing a bad job of making itself invisible. He looks at Barb in her posture of impotent defiance, her turkey neck and crow's-feet and bat wings, the whole menagerie of feebleness. Bartolo lies prone in the sand. This is his tribe now. The heat of the jungle feels like it's expanding past the trees and onto the beach and closing around him. The air is filled with insects. And there in the production huddle is Beck. She's beaming at him, but something about her gaze. It's too intense. Almost—possessive.

All the cameras are trained on him. The sand fleas are eating him alive. He feels like a small child wearing an oversize costume. The sun is beating down, too hot, too intense, reflecting off the brilliant sand. He runs down the shore and dives into the water so that the cameras can't capture his scream.

At the line of the jungle, the fruits have fallen from his shirt and lie scattered along the beach.

CHAPTER 16

BECK

NIGHT 3

"I want you to think about how much we're consuming on this tiny island in the middle of nowhere."

The senior crew was gathered in the dining room for our production meeting. There was me and Erika and Jacob and Callahan, the show doctor. Million jangled a massive ring of keys, like the housekeeper for a Victorian mansion, silently mouthing each one's purpose before flicking to the next. Logistics Brian held the floor. In his hand he held a spreadsheet that tallied the show's expenses, and he was waving it around like an apocalyptic prophecy.

"I don't think I need to remind you that driving three vans back and forth through the jungle every day costs fuel, and that shipping fuel isn't cheap. I don't think I need to remind you that we have to pay our local staff—our security staff, our cleaning staff, our kitchen staff." He gestured grandly to the kitchen crew that was wiping down tables and dumping out tins of overcooked chicken thighs after the dinner rush. "I don't think I need to remind you that feeding our crew requires cases of food from the mainland. That hydrating our crew means fresh, filtered water, and that coffee doesn't grow on trees. Well, it does. But not local trees."

Logistics Brian was always reminding us about things he didn't think we needed to be reminded about. He lived in a world measured by consumption, the human being reduced to charts, but I didn't know if even he could say what those charts were supposed to accomplish. No matter what he said, we would keep driving to camp. No matter how many times he said it, we would drink our morning coffee. Still, Jacob was taking notes on a yellow legal pad in his neat script, and so I pretended to pay attention as well.

The production meetings were our chance to get on the same page about the stories we were tracking, to bounce ideas off each other, and, really, to get Jacob's approval. Of course, you could never know exactly what stories you were telling until the show was finished. You couldn't narrate the beginning before you knew the end.

When Logistics Brian had appropriately warned us of the dangers of fuel and filtered water, it was Erika's turn. She leaned forward with a secretive smile, like she was telling a ghost story around a campfire, and described what happened after her group abandoned the drop-off site.

"Okay, so. Imagine. The Deserters tramp out of alpha camp, through the jungle, and onto the headland. They're tired. They're hungry. But most of all—this is *fun*. *We* are the top dogs. *We* made a Big Move. Those losers are goners already. They tromp through the jungle. Then, look, a clearing. It's beta camp. Scoop the ashes out of the pot. There's still a little smoke in the embers. Ashley breathes it into a fire. Big moment. Ashley and Kelly-Anne run into the surf for a celebratory skinny-dip."

I sighed internally. Of course Erika had the hot girls skinny-dipping. It wasn't too hard to guess where they'd got the idea.

"But as soon as the group wakes up the next day. Boom. Conflict.

Ashley and Carl are at each other over how to build the shelter. Ashley wants a lean-to. 'I grew up on a ranch!' she says. About fifteen times. But Carl starts stacking stones. 'We need a hut from rawks!'" Erika mimicked his roar. "'A house of rawks!' Like a three little pig." As Erika talked, she looked at each of us—even me—her eyes flickering with glee. In spite of myself, my skin prickled.

"Ashley and Carl are building shelter, but Kelly-Anne and Ruddy are building *an alliance*. They sneak off into the jungle. Ruddy's got the idea—what if we get Carl to quit? Ruddy's *drunk* on this whole getting-people-to-quit thing. 'Carl?' says Kelly-Anne. Carl's her friend. 'No way. Carl's strong. He's here for his kids. He'll never give up. How about Ashley? It'd be funny to get another tarantula freakout.' But Ruddy doesn't bite. 'His kids?' Ruddy says. Close-up on an evil smile. Cut to—Ruddy that night, around the campfire. 'Carl, did you say you were from Wyoming? How close are you to that child predator? . . . I heard a story about how this one babysitter left a kid alone in a bathtub and . . .' Zoom in. We've got infrared footage of Carl's eyes, big wet tears dripping into his beard."

As Erika narrated, I kept looking over at Jacob. He was transfixed. Even if he theoretically liked my idea about a different, kinder show, that all went out the window when the footage hit the editing bay. By the time Erika finished, Million was smiling as he thumbed through his keys, and the kitchen staff had gathered around the table to listen.

"Great job," Jacob said. "Sounds like you've got everything well in hand. Beck?"

God, how could I follow that? Cut from Ashley splashing naked to Bartolo's wrinkled butt?

I took a breath and plowed ahead. "Well, it's not the flashy theatrics that Erika's tracking, but I think there's a lot of story with this group. They know they're the underdogs, and, sure, maybe they're a little depressed about it, but they're soldiering on. Kent made another bow drill and a fire. They go to the stream. Without a pot or the iodine, they can't disinfect the water. So they drink it, hoping it's clean."

As I was filming it, the moment had seemed fraught and tense. Kent, Bartolo, Miriam, and Barb were bleary with dehydration, but the muddy stream could have bacteria and parasites. The water was their salvation, but it could also be their downfall. Should they drink? This was exactly the kind of intense human moment I loved. But now, as I narrated it at the table, it was pathetically bland. Erika had fights and alliances and boobs. I had—people drinking water? I was boring myself.

"Then they built a shelter," I pushed on. "Your standard lean-to. Not too much drama there for us, sadly." I looked around the table, hoping for a titter. Only Jacob smiled back, encouragingly. "Let's talk about storylines. What Kent really wants to do is hunt. He killed this boar on *Endure*, and he thinks that killing one here is going to recapture his former glory. He goes into the jungle every day with the machete. So far, he hasn't caught anything, but that's a story too. Does the wannabe hunter finally catch something? Or does he fail?" I knew *that* was a good storyline, so why did I sound so tentative? I'd always believed that an audience would care about my subjects' small hopes and dreams, because *I* cared. But then, I'd been making a cable show about surfing dogs. Which I'd been fired from in disgrace. The kitchen staff was drifting back to their cleanup. "Okay. I think even more interesting is this developing bond between Miriam and Barb. Barb's really taken Miriam under her wing. You have this young scientist, and the experienced country woman—"

"Miriam and *Barb*?" Erika interrupted. "You've got our leading man on your beach and you're going to sideline him for a friendship between the comic relief and the crazy old lady?"

"I'm not 'sidelining' anybody." I flicked my eyes to Jacob. "I just told you, Kent's got a story. And Miriam's more than comic relief.

Plus Barb is definitely not 'crazy.' It's two women, working together. There's something beautiful here. This morning, they were watching the sunrise." I realized how lame that sounded. "'Ain't we so blessed to be here, Marian?'" I tried to do Barb's voice but only managed a mangled country twang. "Anyway I think this unlikely duo's a better story for today than focusing on Mr. Chest-Thumping Alpha Male. Plus it's happening organically—"

"Happening *organically*?" Erika's mouth drooped open. "Who gives a shit what's happening organically? Produce them."

Logistics Brian looked down at his spreadsheets. Million was squinting at his keys. *Bungalow six*, he mouthed, and flicked to the next one. *Dining room*.

"You focus on your storylines," I said. "I'll focus on mine."

"*Your* storylines are part of *our* TV show. 'Watching the sunrise.' Good lord. I don't know how it works with surfing dogs, but with people, we try to—"

Jacob put a hand on Erika's shoulder. "Here's the thing." He said it gently, but his kindness, like he was explaining the facts of life to a small child, cut far more deeply than Erika's cruelty. "I love Barb. Barb is a great character. But she's a *character*. She's a B storyline at best. I hear you. We're in a new world, and there are shows out there celebrating different types of heroes. But we're on cable. Our audience *wants* their—chest-thumping alpha male. Chest-thumping alpha males *work*. And for better or worse, that's the show we pitched the network."

"Kent's a has-been," I said, feeling hot and indignant. "Maybe he was a hero once, but—"

"And that's exactly who our audience wants to see. Think of those guys who used to play high school football, who want to believe they're ready to step out on the field again, they only need to be called. That's who's watching this show. So if you want Miriam to have a big story—and I think we *both* want that—why not do it through the lens of Kent? It doesn't have to be sexual—"

"But it should be," Erika said.

"They could be friends," Jacob said. "It could be a—mentorship. Kent takes Miriam under his wing, teaches her how to survive. Isn't that the reason you got him to stay? Which you did absolutely brilliantly. Now, what's going on in your world, Callahan?"

Callahan gave his update about the contestants' health—all limbs presently attached. I barely heard what he was saying. I could only focus on the twist of Erika's mouth, like she was smiling and grimacing and puckering her lips all at once.

After the meeting, I walked down the beach with Callahan. He was the only other senior staffer in a bungalow. I was too embarrassed to even speak, and I kept hoping he would say something to break the awkwardness, but he walked along silently, looking out to sea at the fishing trawlers. Something in the forlorn sound of their chugging diesel engines evoked a memory, or really the awareness of a memory I couldn't quite access, of my mother, by a lake or near the sea, somewhere close to water, and I felt a vertiginous grief, like my entire life was carried aimlessly by the currents of longing and loss.

"So is Erika always—so vigorous?" I asked, when the silence became too much to bear.

"She's one fantastic producer," Callahan said.

God, this cult. Couldn't people gossip about each other like respectable humans? "I'm not used to getting so many . . . opinions on the stories I'm tracking."

"Oh, that's Erika. Don't take it too much to heart." He was a short man with a big belly who looked like he could play Santa Claus at a discount department store, and as he talked his fleshy jowls jiggled. "Jacob's so kind and supportive. I think Erika considers it her job to say the tough things. Be the bad cop."

That made me feel even worse, that Jacob had been coddling me and unleashed Erika to give me the hard truths. I changed the subject. "I still can't get over that you actually chose to be in one of these shacks."

"Oh, I love it. The jungle is where I was meant to be. Medicine was a trade, never a calling. I figured with a doctor's license, I could hang a shingle anywhere. Now I've gone so far there's nowhere to hang it. Maybe on a tree branch. Look at this magnificence. How do you beat that?"

He spread his arms wide as if to embrace the horizon. Sunset had marbled the night sky with veins of purple and orange and crimson. It looked painted, like a movie backdrop. The air smelled of salt and clay, but beneath it, at the back of my throat, I could almost taste the rotting fish.

"It's beautiful," I admitted. "But I'd trade it all for a can of Raid."

"You don't mean that."

"I never liked the outdoors," I told him. "When I was growing up, my dad said that the entire point of civilization was *not* having to sleep outside."

I had the impression that most of the crew were like Callahan—Boy Scouts who grew up into wilderness junkies. Meanwhile I was the only idiot here wearing new sneakers. Even as a kid I never liked those books about children surviving in the woods—*Little House on the Prairie*, *Hatchet*. I preferred Jane Austen, nineteenth-century drawing rooms and scandalous breaches of etiquette. I had a boyfriend in college, Jeff, an American Studies major who was obsessed with "narratives of transgression" and made me watch a half dozen Werner Herzog movies about wild-eyed men trying to tame the wilderness. The protagonists always seemed so arrogant, forcing their will onto the alien landscape.

"That's what's so compelling," Jeff had insisted. *"It's a phallic viola-*

tion. The male is thrusting his penis into the literally virgin depths of the feminine forest."

Jeff and I didn't make it very far. I eventually got exhausted with reassuring him that doggy style didn't reify any oppressive systems. Now as I walked down the shore with Callahan, beside the massive jungle teeming with chattering creatures I couldn't even name, I didn't feel like a phallic aggressor. I felt exhausted and embarrassed.

"I know it can be a lot at first," Callahan said. "But the jungle has rules, like a city. You don't cross the street without looking both ways. And if that stick on the ground starts slithering, don't step on it."

"Is that what happened to the producer I'm replacing? Crossed the wrong street and stepped on the wrong stick?"

Callahan looked uncomfortable and turned away, so I couldn't quite read his face. "They shuttled Stellan out of here so fast, I barely saw him."

"Stellan? Not Swedish Stellan. With a scar on one cheek."

"He's the one. You know him?"

"I've met him a few times, at industry parties." I thought of the tall blond man, angular and severe in the classic Nordic mold. "I always found him to be . . . atypical for a producer. Stoic. Most producers are a little gushier."

"That's what worked about him," Callahan said. "You need a certain toughness out here."

"I'd hardly call myself tough."

"You? You watched a dog drown and kept filming. You're a legend," Callahan exclaimed, and trotted off to his cabin.

Alone in my bungalow under the flickering bulb, I experienced a muddle of pride and shame. I never imagined my nationally televised fuckup might be a badge of honor. And when I thought of Buster's little paws paddling as the water lapped over his chin, I wasn't sure I wanted it to be.

I was uncoiling my mosquito net when I noticed dark pellets on my sheets. They were about the size of peanut M&M's, and I had a passing thrill that the cleaning crew left me chocolates until I picked one up and held it to my nose. It stank of scat.

I looked frantically toward the ceiling and the corners of the cabin, not sure if I even wanted to see it. It had to be the tokay gecko Jacob mentioned. The creature must be as big as my arm to leave droppings that size. I wanted to run outside, down the beach, and away—away from Erika and her twisted smile, away from Kent Duvall and his action-hero narrative, away from whatever tropical monster was shitting down on me from the rafters.

Away from my only chance to salvage my career.

Instead, I lay down and pulled the netting close, hoping it could serve as a thin shield against the jungle's horrors, and tried to imagine how I could build a storyline between Miriam and Kent. Kent *had* to be the hero. Miriam *had* to be the nerd. Barb *had* to be the kook. I'd arrived too late, and the roles were already cast. Beside me on my bedside table, Miriam's ferro rod mocked me with lost possibilities.

"I have a lot of faith in you," Jacob said. I could feel him standing behind me as we looked at the butterfly case in his bedroom.

Polygonia interrogationis. The Question Mark.

On the dorsal side, vivid orange. On the ventral side, a dead leaf.

I didn't have to warp reality. I only needed to flip its wings.

CHAPTER 17

DAY 4

"You want me to sit here? On this stump?"

"That's the spot."

"Where do I look?" Miriam asked.

"Look at me," I said.

"Not at the camera."

"Right—look at me. We're just two friends having a conversation."

"A conversation that'll be broadcast to millions of people."

"That's the deal you signed up for."

"In a moment of extreme stupidity."

We were sitting in a clearing a few minutes' walk from camp. Afa, my Samoan audio tech, braced the boom mike against his massive right thigh. Crouching next to him, Mario, the wiry local teen who was my assistant camera, angled the bounce, the metallic disk that reflected sunlight to illuminate our subject. My cameraman, Friedman, a brawny Brooklynite, framed his shot so that on-screen, it would look like we were surrounded by jungle foliage instead of AV equipment. The footage would be color-corrected in post to be even greener and lusher.

At the center of the shot, twisted awkwardly on a tree stump, was Miriam, wearing her lab coat, squinting as the glare from the bounce sheered into her eyes. Only four days in, and she was already covered in a film of dirt. She stank of sweat and woodsmoke. My poor plucky scientist, so used to her immaculate labs and sterile test tubes. She looked like I felt. Grimy, tired, twisted into uncomfortable positions, and with outrageously filthy hair.

"Remember," I said, "the audience will only hear your answers to my questions, but they won't hear the questions themselves. So try to repeat back my context. Like if I say, 'How's the water?' you don't say, 'Warm.' You say, 'The water is warm.' Makes sense? And try to use people's names. It's much easier to follow a story about *Bartolo* and *Kent* and *Barb* than *he* and *him* and *her.* You're a scientist, so feel free to use science terms." Miriam shifted on the stump, like she was sitting on a knotty bole. "And finally, always use present tense. It may sound silly, but it makes the action more vivid. Like it's all happening in real time. I know that's a lot to remember, but it's an edited interview. We can retake things."

"Hold for sound," Afa said.

"What?" Miriam asked.

"Hang tight for a few seconds so we can record the background noise," I said. "We'd call it room tone, if we were in a room. Your necklace mikes are fine for daily capture, but for our interviews we bring in the big guns."

"This is all a bit overwhelming," she said.

I put a finger to my lips, and we sat quietly for a minute, listening to—what? Leaves rustling. Birds chirping. The honks, whistles, and pings of the tree frogs. If the jungle was supposed to be a city, it was one where they spoke an incomprehensible language and drove on the wrong side of the road, and all the citizens wanted to eat me. Ostensibly this interview was my chance to get Miriam's perspective on the past three days, so that as we edited the season together, we could intersperse her commentary and insight. But what I really needed to do was to shape that perspective. Produce her. This morning, when I arrived at camp, Miriam and Barb were bobbing together in the shallows scrubbing silt on each other's faces. *That's it, Marian. Like a mud mask. Get in there, girly.* Barb in her sports bra, Miriam wearing her white blouse. It wasn't skinny-dipping, but it was intimate. Kind. And Jacob wanted none of it. If I wanted Miriam to be a big character on this show, I had to show her that she *needed* Kent.

The very thought made me want to throw up in my mouth.

Afa gave me the thumbs-up.

"So. Not the easiest first few days," I said. My pen was poised above my notebook, to jot down story arcs and key quotes. "Let's start with first impressions of the other contestants. What do you think of Kent?"

"He's—fine, I guess." She shook her head and laughed at her own inarticulateness.

"Don't be nervous." I gave her a smile like a preschool teacher urging along a faltering child. "Just be true to your experience. That's all we can ask."

"Okay," Miriam said. "I guess I'm—not a fan? He seems . . . cocky. Arrogant. And I know we're obviously starving, but the whole hunting-a-boar thing is getting a little obsessive—"

I crossed my arms and leaned back and let out a sigh. The micro-gestural markers of approval and disapproval—the smile, the frown, leaning in, and leaning away—guide the contestants so subtly they don't even know it's happening, like that feeling you get at the tip of your spine when someone's bored at a dinner party. On set, it's magnified. The producers are the only friendly faces the contestants see. You give approval, they lap it up. You take it away, they become frantic to get it back.

"Did I say something wrong?" She looked genuinely worried.

"There's no right or wrong, only what's true for you. But wouldn't you say when Kent made the fire that first day—that he saved you? And when he decided to stay after the rest of the vets left. Wouldn't you say Kent saved you again?"

"I'm—conflicted," Miriam said. "That fire saved us, for sure. But I don't buy that—savior thing for Kent. Like, great, he decided to stick around after his friends left. And he *was* a big help with the shelter. But ever since, he's been in the jungle. Really, it's Barb who's—"

"*Barb?*" I sighed and shook my head. "The Barb who can't even get your name right? The Barb who's always ordering you around? 'Put yer shoes on, Marian. Keep your feet clean, Marian! Be mah pet, Marian.'"

Miriam laughed. "Okay, but she's been looking out for me—"

"And wouldn't you say there's something fake about her? What's with her 'Ain't we so lucky to be here' shtick? You've been out here three days and she's already gazing at the sunrise and feeling hashtag blessed?"

Miriam shifted again on the stump and pulled at one of the buttons on her lab coat. "I thought that was sweet."

"You looked pretty uncomfortable from where I was standing. And wouldn't you say there was something—performative about it?" Part of me hated what I was doing. I hated chipping away at this developing bond, and especially hated that it was Erika setting the beats for my stories. At the same time, I felt the deep satisfaction that comes with expertise. My self-doubt from the dining room was gone. This was the game of reality producing, and I was good at it. If Miriam said something negative about Barb and something positive about Kent, even if she didn't believe it now, she would start to think it was true. "Maybe Barb's angling for a career as a motivational speaker. Or, I don't know, a social media influencer."

"Barb? An influencer? I really don't . . . Is that what you think?"

"It's not about what I think. I'm just asking questions. But wouldn't you say that Barb's a little bit phony?"

"I . . . don't want to say anything mean. Barb's the only person out here who's nice to me."

I felt her resistance swell. There was a point where you pushed too hard, and the contestants dug in their heels. I took a breath. Honestly, I was touched by Miriam's devotion. They'd only known each other three days.

"I respect that. You don't want to insult Barb. I'll let it go. One last question about her and we'll move on. Have you ever noticed her snoring?"

She smiled. I had her.

"Hard to miss, right?" I asked.

"Okay, I can admit she snores."

"And how would you describe her snoring? Wouldn't you say"—I grinned like we were two girlfriends about to share a devilish secret—"that her snoring sounds like a malfunctioning chainsaw?"

"A . . . chainsaw? Maybe?"

"So say that, then."

"You want me to repeat what you just said?"

"Only if you feel it's true for your experience."

"Okay," Miriam said. "Barb's snoring sounds like a . . . chainsaw."

"A malfunctioning chainsaw," I said.

"A malfunctioning chainsaw," Miriam revised.

"The whole sentence."

"Barb's snoring sounds like a malfunctioning chainsaw."

I leaned back and laughed, as though she'd just come up with this off-the-cuff observation, and she flushed with the rush of my approval. A gift from me to the sadists in post. Now whenever Barb was on-screen, they could layer in a chainsaw grumbling in the audio bed.

I walked her through the other contestants. We laughed about Bartolo, the way he loomed over every conversation, offering up his "expertise." Expertise in fire making! Expertise in shelter building! But god forbid he should lift a log with his dainty, expert hands. Then there were Kelly-Anne and Ruddy, running off into the woods with their grand schemes. They were probably half starved to death by now. I leaned forward, my eyebrows hiked and my mouth open just a touch, like I couldn't *wait* to hear her thoughts. Suddenly she was the wittiest guest at this cocktail party. What about the bombshell, Ashley? What idiot came into the jungle in a dress? My pen danced across my notebook as I nodded and laughed. Sitting here, surrounded by all this production equipment whose entire subtextual message was that she was worth miking and worth videotaping, that she was worth spending tens of thousands of dollars to record, Miriam started to untwist on the stump, not just that she was sitting up straighter, but as though her entire spine was expanding.

"I *like* this character we're making!" I exclaimed. "Sure, you're having a tough time. But you're the storyteller, you're the one we go to for your snarky, funny, sharp-eyed observations!" She beamed in delight. I doubted if Miriam had ever been the narrator. I got the sense that she was usually the one on the outside listening. Now I could weave it all together. "One last thing. And this is going to be a little uncomfortable. Those first few seconds as you stepped off the boat. You fell face-first into the water."

All the mirth drained from her face. "I've been wanting to talk to someone about that, but—I didn't know what to say." She stared off, out of the clearing and into the chattering jungle. In the distance, a tree frog honked out its call, whether of mating or of warning I couldn't tell. "I know it looked like I tripped. I didn't. Erika pushed me."

I exhaled sharply. I knew it. It had been too convenient for her to fall off the boat exactly as the story bible predicted. "Are you—sure?"

"I was the last one on the boat. Everybody else was jumping into the water, like they'd spent their whole lives jumping onto reality shows. I guess a couple have. But I was nervous. Erika put her hand on my back. I thought she was being supportive. But then there was more support, and then a little more support, and finally too much support, until—"

God, Erika amazed me. She was like a caricature of the manipulative reality producer, shoving contestants off boats, stealing supplies. Maybe that was simply business as usual on a jungle show. There were no retakes. You did what you had to. But to what end? This was the dark side of power, using it to humiliate rather than to lift someone up. "Until she pushed you face-first into the water," I finished.

"No talk about production," Afa said.

I looked up in surprise. Afa was expressionless behind his Ray-Bans. The camera crew wasn't supposed to talk during interviews. They were supposed to be invisible as the foliage, human room tone, so they didn't distract from the bond between the producer and the contestant. Afa wasn't telling Miriam. His message was for me. I felt like I'd been rapped on the knuckles by my teacher for running in the halls. But he was right. If I wanted to save Miriam, I couldn't have her worrying about the manipulative crew.

"Let's forget Erika," I said, swallowing my outrage and leaning forward with a sympathetic smile. "Think about it this way. What the cameras saw was you tripping over the edge of the boat. That moment is definitely going to make the show. Not because I want it there, but because it's an important moment. We're going to have interviews with the other contestants saying how they cringed for you or were angry at you. I want to give you the chance to say something about yourself. But if you talk about production, it will never make air."

"If I can't tell the truth, what can I possibly say?"

"You can tell *your* truth. How did it feel to be you in that moment?"

Miriam sat silent, pulling so hard at the button on her coat that the threads snapped and the button popped off, and she held it there, staring at it, like it might contain some secret, before letting it drop to the ground. "I felt . . . bad," she said at last. The sun passed behind a cloud, and her face was dappled in shadow. "I felt embarrassed. Once again, there's Miriam, failing even before she starts." Her lower lip started to tremble. She bit down hard to keep it still.

"And then you lost the ferro rod. How did that happen?"

"I guess I dropped it when I . . . fell."

"I need you to use its proper name. You dropped what?"

"The ferro rod. I dropped the ferro rod." She was crying now, her cheeks scrunched into her eyes, the tears mingling with the sweat. I'd seen it many times. Talking about the moment can be more emotional than even experiencing the moment. It's like the camera does more than record. It leeches feelings to the surface. "I still can't believe it. Why am I such a—such a fuckup?"

I knew that feeling so well. The shame. Shrinking from the world in a spiral of self-doubt. I wanted so badly to tell her about the story bible. Even if the show demanded that we go along with this fiction, at least underneath, in her heart, she'd know it wasn't her fault. That she'd done everything right.

But if I told Miriam the truth, she could quit, walk off in a fury, refuse to be interviewed. The show could face a lawsuit. My job wasn't to free her from her shame. It was to transform that shame. To use it as a motivating force. "We're only on day four," I said in half a whisper. "You can *change*. I really think you can be the hero of this show. People *love* an underdog story. By the end, the entire country could be cheering you on."

She shook her head and rubbed her eyes. Her cheeks were smudged with dirt. "Even if I make it to day fifty, they'll still build a raft and leave me behind."

"Nobody's building a raft yet. Nobody even has a key. You need someone you can learn from, someone you can rely on, before you even *think* about a raft. Tell me again about when Kent made that fire. Think back to *being* there. You're in the water. It's cold. You're looking for the ferro rod, even though you *know* it's already floated out to sea. And there on the shore—the fire—"

She looked down at her hands. I could see her thinking back. The water was freezing around her thighs, and the wind bit into her neck. And then—Kent's blaze leaped into the sky, like her own position in the game flickering back to life.

"They all hated me. But when Kent made the fire—nobody cared anymore that I'd lost the fire starter. I was—forgotten. And I could go back onto the beach and be warm." She looked up at me, as if she was coming to an epiphany. "Kent—he may be kind of a jerk, but—he saved me."

I was smiling so hard that the muscles around my mouth hurt.

I FOLLOWED HER BACK TO CAMP. BARTOLO WAS DOZING IN THE SHELter's shade, and Barb was scrubbing her teeth with the broken-off end of a stick. Ralph the PA was standing under the crooked palm, barely bothering to film, though as soon as he saw us cross onto the beach he stared intently through his viewfinder. My crew set up and sent him off to the production tent for snacks.

"How was your first big chat?" Barb asked Miriam.

"It was fine."

Barb glanced over, sensing something was off. "You missed one hell of a mud mask."

Miriam couldn't meet her gaze.

"Look what I found on the beach." Bartolo held up a chipped and dirty glass Coke bottle.

"I'm not going to drink out of that," Miriam said.

"It's not to drink out of. We can use it as a symbol of leadership. Whoever holds the Coke bottle is . . ."

Bartolo rambled on about the importance of symbols and leadership, while Miriam fed the fire.

"Well, well, well," Barb said. "Look who's showed up with our machete."

Kent was walking down the beach from the jungle, looking ragged and sweat-stained.

"There's something out there," he said. "I know it. Something big—"

"Oh really, there's an animal in the jungle? And what?" Barb propped herself up on one elbow. "You're going to chase it down and chop its head off?"

God, I loved her. What were Jacob and Erika thinking? Kent looked down at the machete in his hand and back at the woods, like he never considered that part of the equation.

"You can't run off after imaginary monsters," Barb said. "If we're going to be here for fifty days, we need to build out this camp—"

"If we're going to be here for fifty days, we need *meat*," Kent says. "If you want to build camp, go ahead and build. I'm not stopping you."

"Except that you seem to be superglued to our only piece of gear." Barb turned to Miriam for support, but Miriam kept staring into the fire. There *was* something like a broken-down power tool about Barb, wasn't there? I felt like I could see Miriam's thoughts, because I'd placed them there.

"Our only gear, because I'm the only one who didn't hand everything over to the Deserters. Thank god I came back when I did. You'd have helped them cart off the driftwood," Kent said. "Good lord. First, I built fire. Then I found the fruit and the stream. And now you're on me to—"

"You *found* the fruit and the stream? Well, shit, I didn't know I was in the presence of Kent Columbus. I thought that fruit and that stream were about ten feet from where we got left off."

Kent glanced at the cameras, looked wildly around the camp, and then huffed back up the beach and through the curtain of palms.

"Off again to measure his dick against the jungle," Barb said. "Marian, let's you and me get some lunch." She gestured for Miriam, who hesitated a moment and then followed her. I trailed them with my handheld. They walked toward the path that led into the fruit grove, Barb talking again about the beauty of the natural world, how the jungle was an intertwined living system, how every mosquito was proof of a divine plan. "Watch your feet," Barb interrupted herself. "You bang up your feet out here, and your goose is cooked. Mmm—cooked goose. I could go for a cooked goose or ten."

Miriam was silent.

"Say." Barb looked at her slyly. "Kent's in the jungle chasing vapors. Barty's back at camp humping that bottle. What say you and me get into a little trouble?"

She veered off their normal route, up a sandy bank strewn with pine needles, and pushed through the trees until she came to a dense copse. She leaned down into the overgrown bushes and dragged out a few sad pieces of driftwood lashed together with vines.

It was the cobbled-together beginnings of a raft.

"It's not much to look at now, but it's a start. If us girls work together, we can build something respectable and get the jump on the rest of these goobers. As soon as either of us gets a key—we vamoose. My hope is for day twelve. That's two hundred and forty thousand smackers."

"Day twelve is kind of random," Miriam said.

Barb shifted uncomfortably, like she didn't want to answer. "That's right. Nobody will know it's coming. But we need to see how this key thing shakes out. We'll scoop up what we can, when we can. You look about as excited as a cow on the conveyor belt."

"Oh–I'm just–I'm not sure we should betray Kent. I mean–he did build fire for us. Twice. And he *did* find the fruit. I don't want to steal money–"

"It's not *stealing*. It's going on our terms. Those others sure as shit ain't taking us along for the ride on day fifty."

"I–don't think I can betray him."

"Oh." Barb sucked on her dentures, vacuuming her lips inward.

"What if we all worked on the raft? Together?"

"This is *my* raft," Barb said. "You don't want a seat on the Barbtown Express, that's your call. But I'm not waiting on ol' Kent Crusoe, and you sure as sugar don't get to tell me what to do." She kicked the raft with her boot, and one of the sad logs cracked. "I thought we had a good thing going, the two of us."

"I wasn't trying to–no. You're right. I'm sorry. I just–I don't think I can commit to this."

"We all make choices. That's fine," Barb said. She turned away from Miriam, away from my camera. For the first time, I noticed how Barb's tired flesh sagged and puddled down her back. "That's fine," she said again.

CHAPTER 18

KENT

DAY 6

Kent Duvall is face-down in a wash of mud studying markings in the dirt. He's holding the spear he carved from a sturdy branch, its sharpened tip white and smooth against the dark and knobby haft. *Excalibur*, he has dubbed it. He's pushing through jungle foliage. Low light filters through the canopy. A sullen cameraman lags behind. Kent's nose is inches from the ground as he follows animal tracks up the streambed.

At least, Kent thinks they're animal tracks. He hopes they are tracks! If he's being honest, tracking was never really his skill set. On *Endure*, Kent was a challenge beast. He could float across a balance beam and skitter over the rope bridge. Then one day out hiking, he came on a boar in a clearing. It was the size of a large dog with batlike ears that twitched in the breeze. Its brown hair was perfectly silhouetted against the jungle's bright green ferns. He hurried back to camp to get the spear they'd won in a reward challenge. When he returned, like a miracle, the animal was still there. It merely looked at him, as though it had been waiting. Kent inched toward it, his spear held high. It blinked softly, like they were both in a dream. He raised the spear, brought it down, and—he was transformed. He wasn't only the challenge guy. He was the *hunter*. That moment was part of the winner montage they showed in the finale. It was what he flashed back to when he thought about that pure sense of purpose that reality TV had gifted him, the sense that life could truly be a storybook adventure.

Now, though, with his tribe of misfits counting on him, it's clear to Kent that he doesn't actually know how to hunt. The crisscross of indentations in the mud could be made by an animal, or debris, or just the wind, the random forces of chaos that pockmark the jungle. What Kent wouldn't give for a pile of scat. The unmistakable proof of animal life!

It's day six, and the fruit grove—Miriam informed them it's dragon fruit, which sounds a lot more exciting than it tastes—is already looking emptier. Only a few rare coconuts fall from the palms. Without a pot they can't make seaweed soup. But Kent has a bigger problem than hunger. There's an enormous sunk cost of footage. After days of hunting with no success, after a half dozen scratch-faced interviews about his plans to be the Provider, to bring Meat to the Women, he's narratively committed. The longer he goes *without* spearing an animal, the more his storyline narrows to failure, especially with Barb's relentless withering insults every time he comes back empty-handed. Kent keeps jerking awake at night in a panic, his heart revving like a race car that's about to skid into a wall, the tires frictionless against the asphalt, the driver struggling to regain control, unsure if he should accelerate or brake, certain that it's too late, that his reputation and his edit are already a montage of smoldering wreckage, scored to loopy circus music. Yes, he made fire. Yes, he found food. But what has he done to be Kent Duvall lately?

He needs to find an animal, and he needs to kill it.

Kent follows the stream, feet sucking into the muck at the water's edge. In the distance, birds are screaming. It's the bird alarm. He's seen it on other shows, *Alone* season two, when one of the survivalists used the hysterical squawkings to track game. You knew there was an animal lurking nearby by the tone of the birds' freakout. And while Kent himself does not actually know the meaning of the tones, he is aware of it in a TV-friendly way. Enough to make air.

"That's the bird alarm." He gives the cameraman a three-quarters profile. "Means there's game. Close."

The cameraman smiles. It's not a smile Kent likes.

It's a new cameraman today. At first it was Beck following him, asking breathless questions about his heroism. Then Friedman took over, looking like heavy infantry but almost acrobatic in his camera-work, shooting downward from the crook of a tree with his colossal Sony to get the angle of the sun just right. Now it's Ralph, a weasel-faced PA with a plastic-looking contraption that might have come from a toy store. Kent can feel his story arc slipping down the rungs of HD, from 4K to 1080p to standard. He wonders if that spit-and-paste camera can even handle the jungle's low light, or if this whole search will be a grainy blur, as delusional as Bigfoot footage.

He pushes on. Whenever he gets discouraged, he visualizes himself walking back to camp, a massive boar slung over his shoulder. In his mind's eye it's not only Barb and Bartolo and Miriam waiting by the fire, but Kelly-Anne is there, gazing at him in adoration. Ashley is giving him sex eyes like when they first met. In this daydream, even Margaret is at the edge of the fire, her knobby knees pulled into her chest, staring ecstatically into the wilderness as he struts home. And the thing is, if he catches this thing—this boar or beast or whatever it is that he can hear panting at the fringe of his consciousness—she *will* be there, at least virtually. She'll see him doing it on TV. They all will.

There's a rustling in the underbrush. His adrenaline spikes. Could it be his boar? He grips Excalibur tight. His palm is sweaty.

He sees the pink of her shoes first. "We need to get you back to camp." Beck pushes through the underbrush. "There's about to be a twist in the game."

THEY HERD THE CONTESTANTS DOWN A NARROW PATH THROUGH THE jungle that Kent has never seen before, and into the back of a gray van. Nobody tells them where they're going. Nobody answers when they ask. It must have to do with the keys, he theorizes, but he can't be sure. The four Deserters are already inside the van, their legs crammed into the seats, their heads jammed into the ceiling's foam padding. "No talking," Ralph the PA says when they step inside. The back was designed for six people, and they are eight large adults. Kent squeezes beside Ashley, their shoulders shoved tight, their thighs wedged together. She gives him a kind smile. Last time he was seated next to her was on the bus at the Alabama event, where she was the desperate first boot and he the returning legend. Now she's the one extending grace to the poor sap who'll be lucky to eke out a few more humiliating days. Ralph slams the door. The van's windows are blacked out, and there's a cardboard divider between the front and back seats, so the only light is a thin halo around the blackout tape's edges. The car is steaming hot. A plastic hose has been jerry-rigged to vent air from the front window into their little chamber so they don't asphyxiate. Kent glares at Ashley, at Kelly-Anne, even at Carl, trying to impress on them the full weight of his hurt and betrayal, but with the door closed, the light is too dim for anybody to be struck low by his mighty judgment. The engine turns, the van jerks forward, and the contestants give a collective "oof" as their heads bang into the ceiling.

"How's it going at Camp Loser?" Ruddy asks as the van bumps along, taking them who knows where. "Or is it Camp Failure? We can't decide what to call y'all."

"No talking," Ralph the PA says from the front.

"We can't talk about *anything*?" Ruddy asks.

"Nothing," Ralph says. "What if you talk about something important? What if you talk about the game and we don't have it on camera?" He leaves *that* dire implication hanging in the air.

"What about pizza?" Ruddy says. "We can't even talk about pizza?"

"*No. Thing.* What if you start fighting about pizza?"

"You think we're going to have a fight about pizza?"

"Come on, it's just pizza," Kelly-Anne chimes in. "You can't expect us to sit back here and not say a word."

"Okay, fine," Ralph concedes. "You can talk about pizza."

"Man, imagine all the pizza the four of us at Camp Awesome are going to eat when we get on the raft together and win the game," Ruddy says.

"Oh my god." Kent hears the slap as Ralph puts his head in his hands. "No more talking. About anything. Not pizza, not cookies, not pocket lint."

"Man, imagine all the pocket lint the four of us at Camp Awesome are going to eat when we get on the raft together and win the game," Ruddy whispers.

What feels like hours later, but who knows, it might be twenty minutes, the van stops, Ralph slides open the door, and Kent is blinded by sunlight. They step shakily into a clearing. Every joint feels like it's been through a rock tumbler. At Ralph's instruction they face the van while he places thick black blindfolds over their eyes. Kent's always a little surprised by how eight people selected for the show because they are erratic and volatile can so quickly become muted and docile, like their made-for-TV personalities hibernate when the cameras turn off. When everyone is blindfolded, Ralph snaps his fingers in their faces to see if they flinch. He lines them up single file, each person's hand on the shoulder of the person in front of them, and they stumble forward down a narrow dirt path. "Bump," says Ralph, and it travels person-to-person down the line. "Tree roots. Step high." What is the purpose of the blindfolds? Kent has always wondered. Are the producers worried that by seeing a road or a patch of familiar trees, they'll have enough local knowledge to escape into the jungle and run to freedom? The confusion itself is the point, he thinks. The disorientation of never knowing where you are. It makes you compliant, willing to be dragged from place to place on a moment's whim.

When Ralph lets them take off their blindfolds, they're standing outside a canvas tent. He shuttles them inside and closes the flap. They wait in the dirt. Barb sprawls out her legs. Inside the tent is hotter than outside, like they're being baked alive in a kelly-green kiln. Again, time seems to stretch, every moment an eternity, or maybe it's an eternity and it feels like just a few moments. Even sitting is painful on the hard turf. Ralph's radio chatters at his hip. He escorts them one by one out of the tent, where a doctor is crouched over a three-legged stool. "All good?" the man asks. Kent gives him a thumbs-up. "Keep at it, then." He's sent back inside. An audio tech comes into the tent to adjust their mike packs and change the batteries. He Purells his hands each time after he touches one of their filthy bodies. This is the part of the show that nobody knows about. The waiting. The boredom. Kent's stomach aches with curdled adrenaline. This twist may upend his entire life, and all he can do is sit silently. "Can somebody please tell us why we're here?" Ruddy asks. Nobody answers. "I said please," Ruddy says, like he's already far exceeded what could possibly be asked of him. They're all peevish, tired, uncomfortable, and excited. If the goal is to win a key, it could be anything. An endurance challenge, like hanging from wooden beams until their limbs go numb and they drop to the dirt. Or their loved ones are here to compete in pairs, flown by the production company across the world for a few fleeting moments of dramatic heartbreak. Carl's daughters will push past Kent to leap into their father's hairy hands while Margaret scowls at him from across a clearing. Or maybe this is when they drop the mask and reveal that the whole show has been a setup to humiliate him. All possibilities are equally likely. He glances at Ralph's watch to see what time it is, but it says 4:23 a.m. All the producers' watches are set to random times. More tricks to disorient them.

"Okay," Ralph says. "Let's go." Outside the tent, he lines them up in height order, short, stocky Barb at the front, Kent second to last, right in front of Carl. "When I give you the signal, you walk down this path," Ralph tells Barb. They wait. The show pony stamps its hooves.

"Hit it," Ralph says.

They walk down the scrubby path, through a copse of twisted trees, and around a curve. They turn the corner, and Kent's heart leaps. He feels like prancing, like whooping into the sky, like doing an Irish jig down the dusty path toward the waiting red mat. Before them, a cool breeze gusts off a brilliant aquamarine cove. The sun winks off the placid water, and small ripples roll into the beach.

Looming over the landscape like a cathedral is a massive multistage obstacle course.

"WELCOME TO YOUR FIRST CHALLENGE!" JACOB MALIBU SAYS. A SHIVER runs through Kent's prostate, like right before he orgasms. In front of him, there are eight rows of wooden hurdles, eight giant brick walls, eight human-size hamster wheels, eight differently colored buoys out at sea, eight balance beams, eight puzzle stations, eight slingshots, and, at the very end, eight two-foot-tall figurines. The camera crews stand ready at the sidelines. Every stage looks holy. Every step along that balance beam is another chance for redemption. "This is your opportunity to take control of this game," Jacob says. "Whoever wins this challenge will win the very first key, which will unlock the chest on Treasure Island. Maybe even more importantly"—chuckle—"you're competing for food." Kent's stomach growls in anticipation.

The contestants follow Jacob as he walks the course. "First you clear these hurdles, then you have to find a way to punch and kick through this brick wall." Nothing with Jacob will make air. A gravelly voice-over will explain the challenge to the viewers at home. "On the other side of the wall, you step into that hamster wheel and race down the sand to the water, where you'll swim out to a buoy and dive down to release a bag containing puzzle pieces. Bring back your puzzle pieces with you, spin around five times with your head on this baseball bat, then cross over the balance beam, complete the puzzle, and run up that ramp to the slingshot. Hit your target right in the center with the red paintball and you win."

"Wait a second—are these—figurines of us?" Kelly-Anne asks.

"That's right," Jacob says.

The effigies are about a third their height, made of wicker branches and twigs, with straw hair hanging limply off the women. They look like voodoo dolls, dressed in scarecrow versions of their clothes. Kent's figurine is clad in a sackcloth T-shirt and blue slacks.

"The goal of this challenge is to . . . shoot ourselves in the heart?" Miriam asks.

"It means you win." Jacob sounds annoyed at having to defend the imagistic muddle. "It means—your heart's pumping reddest of all!"

Back at the mat, Kent strips to his underwear. He doesn't want any drag for the swim. Every challenge can be optimized. Seeing him, Ashley strips down too. He feels a twinge looking at her abs, even more chiseled by a week of starvation, at the swell of her breasts in her dirt-smeared bra. More than her body, he's struck by her face. She has an almost feral intensity, like a jaguar ready to pounce. Barb's snapping her dentures. Ruddy's collar is full sail to the wind. They are eight race cars, revving their engines. Eight titans, ready to storm Olympus. This is where gods are born. The warm sun caresses his scalp. It feels like new hair is about to sprout from his skull.

"Ready!" Jacob says. Carl roars and shakes his arms into the sky. "Set!" A peal of thunder booms. Suddenly, it's raining. Seconds before, the skies were a clear blue swath of brutal heat. Now cold rain pours down. It's hard in moments like this not to think that production timed it to cinematic perfection, that Jacob Malibu consulted a team of meteorologists or has a mad scientist on staff pointing his weather machine into the sky.

"Go!"

The first thing Kent sees, before the impulse even makes its way down to his muscles, is Ruddy shooting across the field like a snapped rubber band, high-stepping through the mud, and leaping headfirst over the hurdles. Then Kent is off. The thick mud grabs at his heels, and the rain is freezing on his skin. He vaults over the hurdles, swinging his legs into the sky, and *CHOO-CHOO!* goes crashing right into the brick wall, which meets him—*boom*—like a steel slab. It is quite solid, this brick wall. Somehow Ruddy is through it and racing toward the water. Kent tries shoving, but the wall shoves back. He slams his fist into a brick. His knuckles bleed, but the brick barely budges. Beside him Ashley is knocking down bricks with precise roundhouse kicks. *Note to self: Do not get into a physical altercation with Ashley.* But a good strategy. He heaves his leg. His toes ache at the smash, but a brick dislodges. He kicks again and again, feeling like he's snapping a toe joint with every impact. Carl steamrolls straight through his wall, roaring.

By the time Kent knocks over his wall, he is in fourth place. No worries. The challenge is long. He'll pass them all on the balance beam. He steps into his human-size hamster wheel and gives a tentative shove. The wheel teeters, but as long as he keeps his weight centered, it balances surprisingly well. He pushes again. The wheel inches forward. In front of him Carl's wheel totters and crashes sideways, but Kent finds the rhythm, the perfect lean that keeps the wheel balanced and rotating, and now he is all movement, cruising over the sand toward the water. These are the show's most blissful moments, he has thought at other times. Not the thrills of victory, not the wild celebrations after eking out a long-shot triumph, but becoming pure action, pure movement, pure rotating hamster wheel. The sublime beauty of the human body diving into the sea and stroking through freezing seawater toward a buoy, pulling yourself down along its tethered cord and unclipping a carabiner to watch your bag of puzzle pieces pop to the surface, and swimming back to shore, only registering Ruddy as a blur in your wake, held back by his soggy polo shirt. On the beach Kent is in second place. Only Ashley is in front of him, and even in his competitive heat, he feels a moment of grace. *Good for you*, he thinks as he sprints to the balance beam. She places her head on the baseball bat, spins around in a circle five times, woozily veers to the side, but then, slowly, one foot in front of the other, her toes angled in, strides across the balance beam toward the puzzle.

Kent places his head on the bat, spins, and the world goes blurry. He wobbles a few steps, shakes it off, runs to the balance beam, and promptly falls off. He laughs, goes back to the start of the beam, and tries again. He can't put any pressure on his swollen toes, and his feet immediately slip off the rain-slick wood. Not a problem. It happens. Ruddy is crossing the beam now, arms spread wide like a pelican riding the breeze. Carl is there, plodding across with giant bear feet—and then Kent's in fourth place again. It's fine. He takes a breath. The balance beam is about four inches across, painted red with black-and-yellow markings down its side. On his next attempt he gets halfway before his foot slips, and he bangs his shin. Kelly-Anne is making her slow way across. She does it smoothly on her second try. He starts to panic. The obstacle course is his *thing*. The rain is freezing. His body is shivering wildly. He takes one step onto the slippery wood, and he's down, feet in the muck, toes throbbing. To his right, Barb goes slipping past, followed by Bartolo, whose precise steps are shockingly elegant, as dainty as a ballerina's. He tries walking across the beam sideways and falls again. He's starting to hyperventilate. There are spots in his eyes and a taste in his mouth like he's regurgitating dirt. He's not only squandering his present reputation, he thinks, he is destroying his past self. The internet trolls will be all over this. Maybe *Endure* was a fluke, they'll say. He got lucky. Kent Duvall was always a clumsy mess.

Now even Miriam is on the beam, wobbling like a foal. She teeters, falls, and splashes into the mud. Oh god, he's going to be passed by Miriam. He tries again, slips, and is down in the mud too. She's up before he is. There's something dogged about her that he can't help but admire. It's not Ashley's ferocity, but beneath the absurd chaotic hair and the watery soft eyes, her jaw is jutting forward, and he remembers how on day one she kept looking for the lost ferro rod in the freezing surf long after he made fire. It's a quality he's always both admired and looked down on, the ant drones of the world who tunnel-vision their path forward. He never had that quality, that stick-to-itiveness. After her third failure, Miriam lies stomach-down on the beam and pulls herself forward, her feet awkwardly thrust in the air to avoid scraping the ground. How humiliating, Kent thinks. Scraping your face over the muddy beam like a worm. But then, inch by inch, she pulls herself over the balance beam, and now Kent is in last place, left in the dust by that worm.

It's over, he thinks. Even if he makes it to the puzzle, he can't possibly catch Ruddy or Ashley. *Spare yourself, don't let your final humiliation be a GIF of you wriggling on your fat belly, eating mud.* He's freezing cold, and the ache from his toes is radiating up and out along his entire body. Strangely, right in the middle of his despair, he feels a wild elation. Ever since he was a kid, even the things he excelled at, the Little League games where he was shortstop, the youth soccer where he played center midfielder, his father shouting from the sidelines, he always felt that it could all crumble, that a throw to first base would go wildly awry and bean someone in the bleachers. Now that it's happening, he feels light and giddy. His whole self is raw and exposed. Kent's been whispering to the universe for decades that he was no good. Now it's decisively true. Margaret has left him. The fans at home are laughing. And the only single person in the world who ever really loved him, the way everyone deserves to be loved, purely and without reservation, is long dead. What he wouldn't give for a hug from his mommy. After every Little League home run, he would sprint to the first row of the bleachers, and she would scoop him into her arms and squeeze. "What are you *doing*?" his dad would shout. "Show some respect!" and his mom would drop him to the ground like they'd both been chastised, which they had. But now all he remembers is the ache of her arms squeezing his ribs. Thank god it's raining. Nobody can see his tears. How long is it going to take them to finish this damn puzzle, he thinks, so they can leave? The wood of the balance beam is swelling, and the red paint is smearing down its sides.

And suddenly he is with Beck, earlier that day, walking from his failed boar hunt back to camp. She was prattling on. "Kent, did you ever notice in the puzzles on *Endure*, when you looked at how the pieces connected, you could see little paint flecks from the neighboring pieces?" He thought she was rambling, the erratic producer filling time by chatting about behind-the-scenes production dirt. "I think it's sloppiness from the Art Department. The pieces scrape against each other when they're painting, and then don't fully dry before we test them. So each piece has little color swatches from their neighboring pieces."

Now he wonders, was it a hint? At the time, he didn't even know there would be puzzles on this show. And really, why did Beck come into the jungle and bring him back to camp herself, when she could have radioed Ralph to bring him in? He unlashes the bag of puzzle pieces and peeks inside. There, along the edge of a purple triangle, are flecks of orange paint.

His heart starts to race. You can't trust the producers. They aren't helping *you*. They're helping themselves. A producer could give you a hint that destroys your game, because that's better television. But still there in the near distance he can see Ruddy's soggy polo shirt and Ashley's muscled back. All seven of them are still struggling at the puzzle. What if he has secret information that nobody else possesses? Kent Duvall lies face flat on the beam. His forehead is pressed on the filthy wood for balance, and his hands are raw as he scrapes his stomach forward, until finally, he is across.

He dumps his pieces on his solving platform. Beside him, Kelly-Anne is arranging and rearranging the multicolored triangles and parallelograms. It's a twenty-piece tangram, impossibly complicated. "Is this some kind of prank?" Ruddy shouts at the cameras. Kent picks out the purple triangle and places it on the puzzle base, then lines up the orange square, which has yellow paint, so after that he grabs a yellow rectangle. He follows the path of the scuffed paint. "Check!" he shouts into the sky.

"What the actual fuck?" Kelly-Anne says beside him.

"Kent's good!" Jacob shouts from the sidelines. The seven other contestants are staring in shock. He pushes the pieces off his board so nobody can copy him and runs to the slingshot. He only needs to hit his effigy in the circled target at its heart and victory is his. He pulls back the band. His first shot is wide. Right now, there is nothing more important in his life than this carnival game. The second ball is high, snapping the branches at the effigy's neck, leaving flecks of paint running down the wicker man. Little Kent's head sags to the side. The third ball flies true. Even before it hits, as the paintball careens through the air but before the red paint spatters across the effigy's sackcloth shirt and runs down its legs, before mini-Kent collapses inward at his caved-in center, Kent Duvall knows that he is slingshotting his way into immortality.

"KENT, YOU'RE ABOUT TO GO ON AN INCREDIBLE REWARD, WHERE you'll gain your key and power in this game. But first, you have a decision. Choose one person to join you," Jacob Malibu says.

The rain has slacked to a drizzle, as though, the challenge now over, the weather scientists switched off the storm. The seven other contestants stand before him shivering in their misery and disappointment. They were agog when he won. "That was the greatest come-from-behind victory in reality TV history," Ruddy said, mouth agape, and Kelly-Anne hugged him extra close. "I can't believe I flubbed that," she said. "*I'm* supposed to be the puzzle person." His abject failure is transformed into shocking success–somehow even better *because* he stumbled so badly on the balance beam, his win even more dramatic. He can imagine the raucous huzzah erupting at Moonshine Alley in Providence six months from now at his viewing party.

But only because of Beck. Not himself. No hidden resource within that was called out in a moment of adversity. He won because he had a cheat code that nobody else must have had.

Why him?

The other contestants are giving him little smiles and winks, hoping to be chosen. Kelly-Anne puckers her lips. Bartolo points ostentatiously at himself. Even Ashley is giving him sly looks. She's obviously not worried anymore about a showmance with the old guy.

"Think carefully about who you choose," Jacob says. "Not only will you be sharing a feast–but you will be sharing power in this game."

Sharing power. It could mean anything. Kent doesn't even want to look at Beck, because he dreads what he might see. What signal she'll give him. Who *she* wants him to take. When he does glance over–truly, only for a second, he can't help himself–she is making circles with her fingers over her eyes. Glasses. Miriam.

It's exactly what he feared, the same perverse fixation he saw when she pressured him to stay behind at the desertion. Choosing Miriam would be the worst possible strategic play. She's the only contestant *not* gesturing at him. She's hunched into herself, shivering. Why take someone who doesn't even want to be taken? The smart move would be to bring Kelly-Anne and make inroads with the other team. But there are good reasons to pick almost any of the other contestants. Build a Bros Alliance with Ruddy. Bring Barb to mend their relationship, and maybe get her to stop taking constant swipes at his manhood. Take Carl for . . . whatever it is that Carl does. *He could take Ashley.* He can imagine them sitting side by side at the feast. Maybe there would be wine. Her hand would find his. The challenge winner and the runner-up. What if they let their showmance happen? Kissing Ashley on camera has become conflated in his mind with spearing a boar, the pure sign of the narrative he was meant for.

Miriam offers him nothing. Less than nothing, because she's a squandered opportunity. He looks over at Beck again. Again she makes the glasses sign.

He can pretend not to have seen. Not to realize that she helped him win.

But *she* knows. And something about her frightens him. It's the same human quality that initially was appealing. Most of these producers leer down on you from their pillars of greatness as they move you across their chessboards. But that kind of person is comforting. That relationship is unambiguously transactional. The way Beck is looking at him, it's too intense, too personal. And even against the looming backdrop of the jungle, the dirty cove, the stormy sea, and the array of cameras there to capture it all, that flagrant human need is the most terrifying thing of all. Because just like she's helping him now—she can destroy him.

"I'll take Miriam," he says, watching the frustration spread out across Kelly-Anne and Bartolo and Barb, Ruddy kicking the ground, a slight thrill as Ashley crumples in disappointment, seeing a murmur ripple among the crew, even the audio guys look shocked at his choice, and nobody more surprised than Miriam herself, neither of them knowing or understanding the plan, yet having no choice but to follow it.

CHAPTER 19

The hairy Australian with aviator sunglasses is launching them out of the cove, but the chop feels like nothing on the pontoon's cushioned seat. Kent's stinky and starving, he's bruised and mud streaked, but soon he will have food. Soon he will have the game's only key. The pain in his toes recedes. The boat driver's wearing his heavy body spray, and Kent basks in the synthetic cedar scent.

Winning a challenge is the opposite of sitting in the pre-challenge tent. Suddenly the whole world feels open and expansive. The sun is shining. The ocean breeze is crisp and cool. Even the production team is nice to you. The driver, Benjamin, turns back and smiles, the sunlight reflecting a supernova in his aviators, his mouth stuffed full of oversize teeth. "Congrats, mates! Our champions!"

"One champion," Miriam says, looking embarrassed. "I'm a passenger here."

"Hey, I'd still be back on that balance beam if I hadn't seen you do it." Kent can afford to be generous and self-deprecating, since they're not being filmed. He's still annoyed that it's Miriam sitting next to him, but in the ecstasy of the moment, it's hard to feel mad about anything.

The boat zooms along the coast, and the island's sandstone wall roars upward into a sheer pink cliff that looks like a hand beckoning them onward to a brighter future. For a few blissful moments they're tourists on a pleasure cruise, gazing out at the horizon, a paradise of turquoise seas and palm-flecked emerald islets they never would have glimpsed if not for the globe-spanning miracle of reality television. They pass along a mangrove swamp, the skinny trees with their twisted, multi-limbed roots like a herd of undiscovered cryptids striding through the brack, and there, tucked into the foliage on the edge of the swamp, where the coast rises and the muddy earth solidifies into tangled thickets, a brightly painted stilt house stands in the water. The awning is brilliant red, and the sides are a green so vivid and minty Kent can almost smell it. Standing on the dock, Beck and Friedman are flipping them off exuberantly.

The Australian cuts the motor. They coast in. The pontoon thunks against a railing, and Friedman leans down a brawny arm to help them up the rickety wooden ladder.

At the end of the dock, before the entrance to the wooden longhouse, are three villagers dressed in crimson sarongs and intricately beaded black-and-gold shirts. While Friedman films, Kent and Miriam walk slowly toward them down the wet planks. A bureaucrat in a suit, probably a local tourism official here to check in on the production, watches from the side.

"Welcome to our home," the villager in the center says, like she is sounding out the syllables. Her hair is gray, and her silver earrings clink gently together.

"Thank you." Kent bows stiffly.

"It's an—honor to be here," Miriam says.

"Before you feast, we invite you to drink our ceremonial tea."

The two men on either side of the elder hold out ceramic bowls, and Kent and Miriam accept them with solemnity. Kent takes a sip. The tea is cloudy and bitter, but he feels pure physical bliss to taste anything other than water or dragon fruit. He swirls it in his mouth and savors the pleasant burn down the back of his throat.

"Cut!" Friedman shouts.

"Did we—do it wrong?" Miriam asks.

"We need more angles. Let's run it back."

Friedman resets his camera, this time behind the villagers, and Kent and Miriam walk back to the end of the dock. The three villagers stand placidly, like every day they film multiple takes greeting filthy, stinking reality TV contestants. Friedman gives the thumbs-up. Again Kent and Miriam walk down the plank bridge.

"Welcome to our home," the elder says again.

Kent feels like he can refine his greeting. "Thank you so much for your generous hospitality." He bows low.

"We are deeply honored to be here," Miriam says, bowing too.

"Before you feast, we invite you to drink our ceremonial tea."

Again they accept the bowls. Kent drinks deep.

They shoot the scene three more times, and each time their flourishes becomes grander, their greetings more profuse, until by the final take Kent sweeps his arm beneath his torso like an opera tenor accepting roses and pretends to gulp down the now-empty bowl in a single swig. The villagers lead them inside the longhouse, which is empty except for an ornate carved rosewood table, surrounded by cameras and klieg lights. On the table is a ceramic bowl of rice, the buttery steam oozing upward. Any lingering concerns for the decorum of the moment dissipate, and he and Miriam grab the tiny stools and start scooping hot rice with their hands.

"Oh my god," Miriam says. "I never thought rice could taste so delicious."

"Don't fill up before the good stuff comes," Kent says, but his fingers are in there too, shoveling dirty handfuls.

The villagers soon return with plates of steaming whitefish, a glazed blue bowl filled with a green curry of shrimp and lemongrass and shredded vegetables, rice cakes wrapped in jasmine-scented leaves, ceramic ramekins with orange and purple pastes, and a fried dish wrapped in banana leaves that looks vaguely like sushi but smells like meat.

"I don't even know what this is," Kent says, "but I'm eating it."

"I'm already full," Miriam says.

"Push through," Kent says.

"Oh, I'm pushing."

For the next few moments it's just sounds—satisfied umms and ughs as they force the food into their shrunken bellies. Kent's focus collapses. If the villagers are there, if production is still filming, the duo doesn't notice. It's him and Miriam, their hunger and the feast, and the rest of the world is a blurry haze at the margins.

"I think this is the best meal I've had in my life," Miriam says. "Truly—thank you. For whatever reason you picked me—"

"You deserve it," Kent says, squinting at another of those fried sushi meat things, debating whether to force it down his gullet or go instead for more curry. His stomach real estate is becoming precious.

"Do I?" Miriam laughs. "I feel like this whole experience has been a days-long face-plant. But you—you keep saving me. Again and again."

A warmth ripples outward from Kent's core. His taste buds are tingling. His belly is full. His toes are healed. Strongest of all is the feeling that he finally can relax into being Kent Duvall, hero and savior. The fact that he needed Beck's help to achieve it is the whine of a tiny insect he can barely hear.

"I have to ask," Miriam says, "why on earth would you choose to do this a second time?"

"I can think of a million reasons." He opts for the sushi, tossing it into his mouth.

"So you're not going to make your escape tomorrow with your new key?" Miriam asks.

"Didn't we pinky swear that we'd all stay for the full fifty?"

"I had no idea pinky swears were so sacred," Miriam says.

"I'd never break a pinky swear," Kent says with mock gravity. "But also, I'm not willing to leave money on the table."

"I've basically given up the idea that I might win any money."

"You never know." But of course, Kent already knows. "If you believe in yourself–"

"At this point I believe more in Santa Claus." Miriam wipes away sweat with her sleeve. A few strands of hair stick to her forehead. "Is it hot? Holy cow."

"Better question, why did *you* choose to be here?" Kent asks. "You're not the–typical type."

"I'm not a strapping handsome woodsman?"

Kent blushes. Is that what he is? Is Miriam–flirting with him? His head is spinning a little, but pleasantly. In the cozy warmth, there *is* something sexy about her. She's not Ashley, but there's–an intensity beneath her bushy brown eyebrows. Something erotic about the slight gap between her two front teeth. She reminds him of the studious girls in high school who always had their hands raised. God, how he envied and disdained those girls. "There's not a ton of chemists on reality TV," he says.

"Chemists." Miriam pauses with a forkful of fish half-raised to her mouth and stares at it like she's waiting for the buttery flesh to speak. "Can I tell you a secret?"

Kent leans in, maybe too close, he can't tell.

"I'm not really a chemist."

Panic grips his heart. The walls of the longhouse blur. Here it comes, he thinks. Right when he was comfortable. She's an actor. He's the patsy, and everyone else is in on the–

"I do work for a chemistry company. A startup. Ellis Pharmaceuticals. But I work in PR and marketing. I—write press releases."

"You've been lying to us?" Honestly he's more relieved than anything, but his head is spinning, and he's worried that he's missing an important clue.

"No. I didn't lie. I just . . . didn't tell the truth." Miriam squirms on the stool. "I don't know why I'm saying all this to you. I—when Callie—she recruited me in line at a Starbucks." She glances up at him with a half smile like it's the punch line of a joke, and then her gaze falls to the dregs of her curry. "The glasses, they're mine. I was on my way to a sales meeting where my boss wanted me to *pretend* to be a scientist, which was why I was wearing a lab coat. We were pitching our debut product. Fog. 'Blur your lines away, like you're looking in a foggy mirror.' I wrote that. Why not bring an actual scientist, you ask. Because I could be trusted to 'stay on message.' What every girl dreams, right?" She's staring down so intently that Kent has the vague instinct she might tip forward onto the table, until she snaps up straight. "Anyway, Callie saw me in line and we started talking, or I guess she started talking to me, and she said, 'You're a scientist?' and I laughed and said no. But it was like she was telling me, not asking."

Kent's surroundings are zooming in and out of focus. Why hasn't Beck stopped them? How has nobody shouted *Don't talk about production*? The world appears both too close and too far, like he's looking through a fish-eye lens. "Anything to get on television, right?" His mouth is weirdly dry. "Well, you're here now, so—"

"No! It wasn't like that at all. I'd never once dreamed about being on a reality show. At first I said no way. But the way she was pitching it, it was like I'd be going on this . . . grand adventure. I assumed I'd come out into the wild and—" Miriam makes little grasping gestures. "I thought there would be—more. You know? You watch these jungle shows, and everyone is always having these great revelations. 'I hadn't realized how much I love my family.' 'I'm quitting my finance job to bake cupcakes.' I thought my own experience would be just as profound. Do you hate me?"

"God no." Kent's unexpectedly teary. He picks up a fishy napkin and dabs his eyes. He's seen it so many times. New contestants, opening themselves to the wilderness, desperate to receive a message. Then the producers tell them who they are. Turn them into a cartoon. And they spend the rest of their lives playing a part. Like Kelly-Anne and her puckered lips. Like Carl and his stupid roar. Like . . . so many others. Lost in a role. "You're doing your best. You don't have to be a person you're not. You can be yourself."

"But I don't even know what my self is!" Miriam exclaims. "That's the whole problem. My whole life I've bounced from job to job. I worked in local government. I did freelance copywriting. Then PR. Now this startup. And I'm only twenty-nine. I know it's stupid, but I imagined I'd come out here and, like, build a shelter. Find food in the jungle. Not be 'Kent Duvall' obviously, but—be *someone.* I wanted to—to touch something real. On a reality show. Hah. And instead I'm cold and hungry and in the worst part of high school."

"It's hard enough for me to be Kent Duvall, and I am Kent Duvall," he says, instantly proud of the line. "That thing you're talking about? Being hungry and cold, that *is* the thing. You struggle. You overcome. You learn how much you can take." Kent's aware that he's parroting a motivational poster, but in the moment, it feels profound and true. "What's more real than that?"

"I didn't want to lie to anybody. But after I . . . fell in the water—everyone seemed so excited that I had a skill, other than my actual skill of making PowerPoints. I really did love chemistry as a kid. But—look—" She holds up a wobbling spoonful of curry until soup spills over the sides. "Can you imagine these hands filling a beaker? I'm much better with words than anything physical. So I wound up in the same place as everyone who loves words. In a tiny cubicle under a fluorescent light. Good lord, why can't I shut up?"

Has Kent ever really *seen* someone else's hands? he wonders. Like really *looked*? She has long fingers, slender and elegant, shimmering in the light, but the edges of her cuticles are raw from gnawing, and her nails are caked with dirt. Dirt from hauling wood. Dirt from tending the fire. She works so hard around camp. He's been unfair to her. Sure, this isn't her natural environment–but she's trying. He wants to reach out and straighten her hunched posture. *You're an Amazon*, he wants to say. Instead he takes her hand, encircles those elegant fingers with his own rough paw, and gives her a squeeze. Maybe they have more in common than he knew. He loved chemistry too, Kent remembers. What year was it? Tenth grade? Old Mr. Pascal drawing the atomic structure of a carbon molecule in red marker, and Kent looking down at his hands and thinking, *None of this is real.* The more he learned about atoms and electrons, the more the visible world started to seem as thin and glossy as a postcard. Matter was mostly empty space. His desk, the crooked elm outside–the entire world of appearances was all masks. Reality–real reality–was deep and invisible.

God, he thinks, what happened to the sensitive kid who wanted to dive into an atom's invisible depths? The world happened. His father happened. Kent Duvall Senior, a larger-than-life character who manned the grill at every barbecue, who told the best blue jokes at a dinner party, but saved all his charm for friends and neighbors, a hustler on the street and a tyrant at home, berating his mom in the kitchen. Kent hated him, but now, as the old man's gray head swims up in his mind's eye with Kent's same hairline, and Kent's ears that stick out a little more than they should, his heart lurches in unexpected sympathy. It couldn't have been easy in Providence back then, being a French-origin Duvall in the Italian world of Christofaros and DeAngelos. He had to have worked so hard to be that joke-slinging charmer. Could that be why Kent married Margaret? Someone who could stand up to him? Someone he couldn't overpower? Oh god, Kent thinks–

"But you're *not* your father," Miriam is saying. "You didn't have a kid. You messed up, once, and you're taking accountability. People screw up."

They've been having a conversation? Kent looks down to see that they're still holding hands. It's like he's surfaced from a pool, and the blurry world has snapped into focus. Suddenly, his surroundings look fake. The longhouse walls are thin plank cutouts like the phony buildings on a Disney ride. The red and green paint is too fresh. If this is a real home, where's the laundry hanging out to dry? Why is there no fishing gear? They're on a set, he thinks. Who even are these villagers? Actors who production dredged up from the mainland's theater scene. He's sweating, and his mouth tastes vile from the backwash of fish and tea. *The tea.* What was in the tea? A local psychoactive ceremonial herb? Did production *want* them high and loopy, confessing their deepest selves? It's possible. It happens on other shows. It's legal because it's not illegal. He can't stop jabbering, both of them are jabbering.

"I can see you're a good person, a good man," Miriam says. "You don't need to prove yourself anymore. And your father isn't–" He's back at his dad's funeral, carrying the coffin down the gravel path, his sweaty hand clenched around the iron handle. He couldn't believe how heavy the casket was, it kept tipping him sideways, and when they lowered it to the ground his grip gave way, and he stumbled in the dirt. He can still smell that earth, fresh and alive. "What's the matter with you?" said his uncle next to him. "I'm an orphan," he's saying to Miriam. "A forty-four-year-old orphan." "I'm an orphan too." Miriam is crying. Her nose is sculptural, he's never seen such a beautiful nose. "Ever since my parents died, I've been lost too," she's saying. "Do you want to know how I even got my job?" She met her boss at a bar. He said he was working at a "pharmaceutical startup" and needed a brilliant mind to write their marketing collateral. She could have eight percent of the equity for her efforts. Eight percent! Startups were worth billions, or at least millions. She could pay off her student loans. She could finally write that novel. She quit her PR job and bought a pantsuit she couldn't afford. When she showed up to sign, the contract said 0.08 percent. "*Eight percent?*" Her boss scoffed. He must have misspoken. Of course he hadn't meant *eight percent.* What could she do? She'd moved to the city because there was nothing left for her in Bemidji, and she had no cushion. In their cramped coworking space, Miriam quickly learned that her boss often "misspoke." He spent his days on the phone, pale fingers twirling in the air, his dirty sneakers propped on his desk smudging the press releases she'd written for his review, while he chatted with VC funds and tech press. On one call she overheard him tout hundreds of thousands of sales. "Hundreds *of* thousands?" He looked surprised when she called him on it. "I meant hundreds *or* thousands," he said with a baffled smile, bouncing from foot to foot. Miriam won the English prize at the University of Minnesota. She'd stood for Phi Beta Kappa. Once in a Shakespeare seminar, Professor Pollack-Pelzner offhandedly called her a "genius," though largely, Miriam suspected, because she quoted liberally from his books in her essays. She'd just assumed that, by virtue of her glasses and her pale skin, of the wild tangle of hair that in her mind was a kudzu that would overrun her body unless she gardened it obsessively, of how diligently she applied herself to every task, that *specialness* would somehow envelop her. It wasn't like Miriam believed the universe owed her for working hard, but—didn't it? "I want something I do to feel like it's—on purpose," she says. "My choice."

Kent finally reaches over and adjusts her posture, tilting her shoulders up. "You're an Amazon," he says. "You're going to win that million dollars. I promise you. That's on purpose. That's not an accident."

She leans into him, so that their foreheads are touching. "And you can be free from trying to be Kent Duvall," she says. "I promise you." He jerks away. What has he said to prompt that? It's too intimate, like she's secretly been watching him on the toilet and now has stepped into the stall to tell him he's doing it wrong. He opens his mouth to explain that, no, actually, being Kent Duvall is *all* he wants, but right then the village elder comes back into the room and bows, the silver circlets along her ears gently chiming, and leads them out of the longhouse to a rickety bridge that you might find at a miniature golf course. On the shore, more "villagers" are gathered, the entire Mud Town performing arts department, all in their beaded shirts and spangled headdresses, and they lead Kent and Miriam in a synchronized dance that Kent's fairly sure he saw on YouTube. As they turn in the circle, their arms around each other's shoulders, their legs kicking, laughing and crying, the elder gives him a golden key, three inches long and coiled into a crown at its bow, and presents each of them with an oar, tools, she explains like she's reading a script, that only they will be allowed to use. Now they have power in this game, the elder explains. The power to escape it all.

CHAPTER 20

NIGHT 6

Kent's lying asleep in the shelter when a noise jerks him awake. His head is swimming with the comedown from whatever drug he was dosed with, and the shelter looks fragmented, its beams zigzagging from disconnected planes like a cubist painting. He sits up, his skin prickling. "Miriam." His voice is hoarse, like in a nightmare. "Barb." The women are dead asleep. The fire has burned down almost to its embers, and the small orange and blue flames cast terrifying shapes among the shadows.

He waits for what feels like a long time. The only sounds are the waves and the wind rattling through the dried-out palm fronds that line their shelter roof. He must have dreamed it. The night vision camera is perched on its tripod close to the shelter, its glowing red light a comforting reminder of the multimillion-dollar production that protects him. He gives it a little salute and heads out to take a leak. The alpha predator marking his territory, he thinks, as he sprays a wide arc. Nothing to be scared of here but him.

He is patting his belly, which is still achingly full from the feast, when he hears it again. A rustling at the trees' edge, like a large animal. His stomach gurgles, a mixture of anticipation and fear. Something big is moving along the edge of the jungle. He has the uncanny certainty that it's his boar, coming to him, waiting to be hunted by him, their two destinies drawing close. Margaret ridiculed him for this kind of thinking, but in his more mystical moments he truly believes that on reality TV, in the crucible of man against nature, you could catch a glimpse of the universe's hidden patterns and manifest your will upon the world. He thinks of the boar he speared on *Endure*, the way it stood in the glade waiting, like the strands of fate were twining together. Or maybe it's Beck leading a pig to him on a rope as payment for taking Miriam on reward. Who cares what's knotting together his storyline, whether it's the producers or the jungle gods? He readies himself to meet his destiny.

Then the animal roars and four shadows burst from the jungle and pound down the beach. The two smaller shadows race to the firepit, kicking it in with sand. The largest one roars again.

"Shut the fuck up, Carl!"

Carl roars again.

"It's supposed to be a *sneak* attack, idiot."

"I've got the bow drill."

"Get the machete."

"It's pitch-black. Where is it?"

"What's going on?" Barb calls sleepily from the shelter.

Kent drops to his hands and knees on the sand, sweeping his arms in wide arcs. Normally they leave the machete at the fire's edge. A moonbeam catches the metal. Kent dives, but a shadow grabs it first. He hurls himself after, eating sand but seizing an ankle. He yanks hard. The form crashes to the ground, and Kent's on top, pressing down on the man's shoulders.

"Get off!" Ruddy shouts.

"Give it!" Kent scrabbles at Ruddy's arms.

"Get off! It's against the rules."

He pries at Ruddy's fingers. The blade presses between their chests.

"You're not allowed to wrestle me. I'll tell Jacob!"

The shadows stretch Ruddy's mouth into a jagged maw. Kent pulls back his fist. He can almost feel the satisfying crunch.

"Go on," Ruddy whimpers. "Don't be a pussy." He scrunches up his face, half bravado and half terror. He's looking at something off to the side. Turning, Kent sees the red camera light. It's all on tape. Ruddy will get a black eye, and Kent will be pulled from the show. He rolls off Ruddy into the sand, his limbs heavy as adrenaline leaks from his body.

"Loser." Ruddy picks himself up and runs up the beach, followed by Carl with the oars and the two women. Kent forces himself up. If he can follow them to their camp, he can raid their gear right back. But his skull is pounding, his stomach is overfull, and his limbs feel like heavy sandbags. By the time he gets to the jungle, they're gray outlines amid the trees.

"You can't take the oars! It's against the rules!" he shouts, knowing how pathetic it sounds. They clatter to the ground, and the Deserters disappear.

Now he has no fire, no tools, and—his stomach surges through his throat, and he vomits into the dirt. He doesn't think he can make another bow drill without a knife to carve the spindle and notch the fireboard. All that's left is Excalibur the spear, a sad gnarled stick lying ignored in the dirt. How could Kelly-Anne do this to him? How could *Ashley*? There's no reason to be so cruel. A cold drizzle patters on the leaves. Of course it's raining. An hour ago he was the challenge hero. Why, as soon as he achieves anything, does it feel like it's already slipping away? It's the edit, he thinks, looming over him like the Day of Judgment. The edit, which can warp even your triumphs into failures, then expand those outward into your identity. The air reeks, his bile saturating the beach, permeating the entire world.

There's a hand on his back.

"Looked a lot better going down than coming up," Miriam says.

He hacks out an angry laugh. "They took everything."

"Let's get back to the shelter. We'll figure it out tomorrow."

"Figure what out? We don't have fire. We're going to freeze to death."

"We'll figure something out," Miriam says. "We have oars. You have a key."

"How are we going to build a raft with zero tools?"

"The Deserters didn't vanish. They're out there somewhere."

"They could be *any*where."

"They did this because they're scared. They were counting on us to quit, but we didn't. You won that challenge. And now they're desperate."

"*They're* desperate?" Kent scoffs. Even so, her words make him feel slightly better. Yes, his come-from-behind victory was more than they could take. He sees Miriam on the balance beam, her jaw jutted forward, refusing to give up.

"Let's get back to the shelter." She takes his hand and gently tugs. "It's cold." He allows himself to be led. Margaret never comforted him when he was low. She saw his moments of neediness as opportunities to lecture him about the world's tough truths. If he wanted more speaking gigs, he should write better speeches. If he didn't like the Reddit thread about how Kent Duvall was overrated, don't read Reddit.

"How's your head?" he asks her.

"Throbbing."

"Mine too. I think there was something in that tea."

"File that under things I didn't expect would happen on reality television."

They look at each other with a shrug as they pass the med box, a gray-green tub hidden in the foliage with plastic baggies that hold their pre-approved medications. He tells Miriam he forgot to take his malaria pill, which is true, but really, he needs a moment to himself. He almost *punched* Ruddy. He's not a violent person. It scares him, how quickly the urge boiled up. It scares him too, how much he still wishes he'd done it.

Riffling through the med box for his slim sandwich bag, he looks covetously at the other contestants' sacks. Bartolo and Barb have gallon-size Ziplocs that bulge with orange cylinders. If he had something extra, a pick-me-up or a painkiller that could clear his dull and achy brain, he could think his way out of this mess, but all that's inside his baggie are the rust-colored nodules of Malarone and a white vial of Propecia, one last forlorn rearguard action against baldness. He palms Barb's bag, not quite willing to unzip it. He pushes the vials up against the bag's plastic skin and, squinting, reads their names in the moonlight. Tramadol, metformin, rosuvastatin, prednisone. A jigsaw of meaningless syllables. He picks up Bartolo's bag. Mydayis, clonidine, gabapentin. He stops himself from peeking into Miriam's, feeling noble at his discretion. He should've been more strategic with his scripts. With the right doctors' notes you can titrate a medically approved performance-enhancing cocktail. Adderall for focus. Zoloft to calm your nerves. Kent knows for a fact that the only two-time winner of *Endure* popped ADHD pills before each challenge.

He forces his malaria pill down his throat.

Back in the shelter, rain drips like icicles onto his spine, and a freezing wind blows off the sea. Without the fire, they're all shivering. Kent's body, seemingly acting on its own, spoons Miriam. His chest presses into her back. His arm wraps around her rib cage. It's not sexual, he thinks, as he cuddles close. It's *animal.* Miriam's warm beside him. That's all.

It has nothing to do with the calming pressure of her hand.

Nothing to do with the small dark hairs along her upper lip that he finds oddly attractive, unlike Margaret, who was so depilated and lasered that naked she looked like an action figure.

He turned down a showmance with Ashley. He's certainly not going to have one with Miriam. Anyway, they're doomed. They won't last long enough for a showmance even if he wants one, he tells himself as he pulls her shivering body tighter into his.

CHAPTER 21
MIRIAM

NIGHT 6

She never knew it was possible to be so cold, and it's not even snowing. In New York, she could put on a coat. Have a hot cup of coffee. Even on those blizzardy days when she trekked to the subway like a polar explorer in Canada Goose, Miriam knew she'd thaw in the steamy station. Here all she can do is shiver. Her fingertips are pruning from the damp. When Kent wraps his arm around her, and the heat from his chest pours into her back, Miriam's first thought is how the unrelenting cold has turned her into a desperate animal and erased her body shame.

Her second thought is body shame. Her hair must reek. It's been a week since she washed it, and the bushy mass is right in his face. Slowly so as not to disturb him, she twists the kudzu over her shoulder, which bares the nape of her neck to his breath, which tickles, but in a good way, hot and wet against the freezing night. Kent's arm pulls tighter around her stomach. Should she suck in? And if she sucks in now, will he know she's sucking in? And how many more days of starvation will it be before she doesn't have to suck in at all, she's wondering, when she feels his dick twitch in the crack of her ass.

A strange feeling uncoils inside her, half embarrassment and half arousal.

It twitches again.

She holds every muscle taut. She has to make certain that the jolts are beginning with him, and not—god forbid—that her own body is initiating the movement, that *her* hips are bucking backward accidentally and rubbing against it. Kent's breathing is deep and steady. Is he asleep? Lying there not daring to move while her shoulder goes numb beneath her is like sitting at a high school party next to the cute popular guy and wondering if your arms touching was deliberate, and debating both if he wants you and also what that might mean for your own place in the social hierarchy, except here Miriam's asking herself—did Kent bounce his penis on purpose, and does that mean he'll share his key?

Kent's not her usual type, but she's also never met a person who talked earnestly and desperately about spearing a boar. Miriam's exhausted by the New York dating app men. There was Brett the Squarespace project manager with plaid flannels and glasses as thick as hers that he didn't actually need. Or Bryce the MTV marketing associate in a button-down white oxford with paisley patterning on the collar and sleeves, just the right amount of flair to show his peers he's quirky but his bosses he's serious. They all went to Film Forum, played board games, and recommended the latest buzzy book. They always knew the coolest dark-lit bar with amber bottles of small-batch whiskey. At first, she was dazzled by them, how confident they seemed, how they shared so many of her interests. But there was always something missing, or that's what she told herself when they stopped responding to her messages. They didn't *really* care about films or literature or even games. (Though they did care sincerely about drinking.) They had put on a costume of what it meant to be young in New York and were biding their time until they cast off their flannels, donated *Settlers of*

Catan, and became middle-aged junior executives at suburban barbecues surrounded by picket fences and Peloton bikes.

As she drifts asleep, Miriam feels like she's entered a magical wild space where you can connect with a human soul beneath all those signifiers, and the very fact of not being able to articulate why she's bonded with Kent, what qualities he possesses or interests they share, makes that bond feel even purer.

CHAPTER 22

Over the next three days they search for the Deserters' camp. They follow the creek upstream to its source at the mountain's base. They pick their way past massive ferns that are taller than she is, around acid-green lotus pods with plum-colored seeds. One day they see a curl of smoke over the canopy, but they get lost winding through the trees and end up at the edge of a mangrove swamp, blocked by the channels of murky water and tightly knotted roots.

As they trudge through the jungle, Miriam can sense Kent's irritated heat. She feels like it's directed at her, like somehow this is her fault. Her fault that he's at her camp instead of theirs. Her fault for giving him hope after the camp raid. What did she expect, that they'd discover a wooden arrow pointing down a path, DESERTERS' CAMP 5 MILES? They're in the freaking jungle. Their real hope, she knows, is that the game itself will change. A challenge, a twist. The gods descending from the sky.

Every day the dragon fruit grove is emptier. They institute rations, one fruit per person per day, but on day nine they find Bartolo slumped against a bush surrounded by a week's worth of red rinds, guilty tears running down his cheeks. Without a knife, they have to rip the rough hide with their fingers. Every day they are a little leaner, a little sharper with one another.

The best part of Miriam's days are her interviews with Beck. The producer giggles like a sidekick from a rom-com while Miriam recounts her jungle treks. "Would you say you and Kent are really vibing?"

"I *would* say we're vibing." Miriam nods. Are they, though? At night she feels his dick leap and shimmy, but every morning is like waking from a sex dream, where the hazy erotic charge quickly fades to the sharp contours of grim reality. She feels like she's living a double life, their intimate nights and their tetchy, irritated, exhausted days.

"Would you say your nerdiness is being stripped away?" Beck asks, as though tramping through the mosquito-infested woods is an exercise DVD, like if she just grinds out her daily fifty minutes, her flab will melt away to reveal the warrior-Miriam with rock-hard abs beneath.

"I *would* say my nerdiness is being stripped away," she agrees more enthusiastically. Change—it's why she's here. *"Oh, Miri,"* her mother used to say when young Miriam proclaimed that some experience had irrevocably altered her. *"Don't you know I love you just the way you are?"* That sounded to her teenage ears like her mother's love was so enormous it could tolerate even Miriam's awful flaws. It made her even more certain she needed to fix them.

Then her father would pop his head into the room and croon, *"I love you just the way you are,"* in his awful Billy Joel impression.

But she *is* changing. She's started to notice how if the clouds turn left as they scud over the mountaintop they're doomed for rain, but if they turn right the storm will pass. She can tell a log that's been hollowed out by termites, its bark sloughing off its skin. It's not the total transformation she daydreamed about. She's still hopelessly awkward. This is more like—new growth.

FOR THEIR SECOND CHALLENGE, THE CONTESTANTS ARE DRIVEN TO the edge of the island, to a sandstone wall that plunges thirty feet into the sea. The Deserters arrive in a separate van, presumably to prevent them from discussing pizza or pocket lint. They line up on the side of the cliff while Jacob explains the challenge. They have to jump off the ledge into the water, swim to a cave, and as a team carry a massive stone statue up a winding path to a platform where one person will solve a slide puzzle. The puzzle solver will win a key, while the whole winning team earns comfort. "Pillows. Blankets. Enough to turn surviving into thriving," Jacob says, walking up and down the contestants' line in carnival barker majesty. "Oh—and pastries. Coffee cake. Crullers. Croissants." The contestants rub their stomachs and pull O-faces at the idea of these soggy pastries, mirroring the reaction shots they've seen from other contestants on previous shows. All but Kent, who glowers at the Deserters.

Never in her life did Miriam Bloom imagine she would jump off a cliff. And yet, she's here, staring down at the chop. The cameras are filming. She has no choice but to jump. The contestants strip to their underwear, and the producers strap GoPro cameras to their chests.

"The plan was to have you choose teams, but you've beaten us to it. If anyone wants to change squads, speak now," Jacob offers.

Miriam looks down the line, at Ashley's muscled arms and Carl's bulk, at Ruddy and his captain-of-the-baseball-team vibes, at Kelly-Anne, who knows yoga poses she's never imagined. Her own group is exhausted, skinny, malnourished, and depleted. But she'd rather be swallowed by the rock than request new teams.

"Perhaps we should consider—for the sake of fairness—" Bartolo says.

"Shut your trap." Barb elbows him. "We're good."

"Good?" scoffs Ruddy. "That's a stretch."

"Ruddy, you sound skeptical," Jacob says. "Care to elaborate?"

"They're *terrible*. We have a fire, a huge shelter, more food than we can eat. These guys look like they've washed up on the beach after a storm. When I was a kid, I looked up to Kent Duvall. And now"—he gestures dismissively—"it's sad."

"Kent, wow, some strong words," Jacob says. "Any response?"

Kent looks stricken. "Oh, I've got a response," he says, and trails off. Miriam knows that he's worried the back-and-forth will make air. That he's overwhelmed by the pressure to say the perfect thing that will please Jacob, cow Ruddy into submission, and redeem himself to the audience at home. She can see him cycling retorts, rage and indignation and hurt and maybe some positive affirmation to blanket over the pain.

"Kent *won* the last challenge," she interjects, surprised at her own boldness. It's not like her to speak up without being called on. "Ruddy can steal our supplies at night. But Kent's the only one here with a key."

"Not for long," Ruddy says.

"Well, we are about to find out," Jacob says. "Escapers, take your spots."

They shuffle to the very edge of the precipice.

Thank you, Kent mouths to her.

"We've got this," she whispers back, although looking into the water thirty feet below, Miriam's fairly certain she's about to leap to her death. Jacob blows the air horn. Kent whoops into the sky. And then Miriam is plummeting down, her first thought how it can't be her jumping off this cliff, Miriam Bloom would never do anything so reckless, giving way to the wild adrenaline rush, until the crash into the cold surf shunts all thoughts from her mind.

IT TURNS OUT THEY DON'T HAVE IT. THEY STRUGGLE AGAINST THE CURrents on the swim, and by the time they make it into the cave, the Deserters are already charging up the path with their statue. Ruddy solves the puzzle and earns a key, and in the postgame debrief, he dangles it mockingly in Kent's face. "Not the only one with a key anymore," he says, laughing, as the Deserters march out in triumph.

The return drive to camp is gloomy and sweaty. The blacked-out van's AC vent coughs its pathetic stream of cool air into the sweltering back.

"We're doomed," Kent says. "We'll never win a challenge. We'll never build a raft."

"Save it for the cameras," Ralph the PA says from the front.

"Save *what*? We're finished."

"Save this."

"I'm sure it's fantastic content," Kent says acidly.

They sit in silence. Miriam takes Kent's hand and squeezes. Here in the dark of the blacked-out van, it's like a borderland between their nighttime intimacy and their daytime misery. He squeezes back and they sit with their hands together, feeling the sticky heat between their palms. She hates that he's saved her over and over, and now he's being mocked and belittled. She hates that the thing she said about his key further set up his humiliation. She hates that once again she's Miriam Bloom, the useless sidekick. Her freshman year in college, she would follow her roommate, Penelope, a breathtaking blond girl who now works on-air for Fox News, to dorm mixers and frat parties. Once Penelope drunkenly accosted her while she stood awkwardly by the drink table. "What are you for?"

"For?" Miriam asked.

"Like, what do you bring to the table?"

At the time she looked confusedly at the folding table with its array of empty beer cans. She hadn't brought anything. And that, she realized miserably, was exactly Penelope's point. Now she ransacks her brain for something, anything, she can say to make Kent feel better, to solve things, to be useful, when suddenly it hits her. Honestly, she's surprised she didn't think of it sooner. She leans in close to his ear and whispers in her smallest voice, so nobody else in the van can hear: "Barb–she's built a raft."

"*What?*" Kent loudly whispers back.

She puts her finger to his lips and waits impatiently as they drive back, and production films their miserable walk into camp, and Bartolo heads for the fruit, and Barb lies down in the shelter. Then Miriam giddily leads Kent up the sandy bank and into the dense copse where Barb showed her the raft. Beck follows, recording. Miriam pulls back the thicket with a flourish to reveal a sturdy raft of seven logs lashed tight with vines.

"How long have you known about this?" Kent asks.

"Barb showed me a week ago, but honestly, I forgot."

"You forgot someone was building a raft."

"The last time I saw this, it was a few branches. I'm amazed she's done this much work. I can't believe she left it here in the same spot she showed me."

He nods. "She didn't think you'd betray her."

Betray. The word shocks her, and the fun curdles. That's exactly what she's doing. She is *betraying* Barb. She never imagined she would betray anybody. It simply wasn't something that happened in marketing. Kent crouches down and starts jimmying out a crossbeam.

"Wait–what are you doing?"

"Destroying it," he says, as though it's obvious.

"I thought we would use it to escape."

"We can't leave now. It's day ten."

"Aren't we . . . starving? And no tools?" She must be missing something.

"There's only two hundred thousand dollars in that pot."

"That's a lot. Split three ways, it's—"

"Three ways?"

"I was thinking—we could bring Barb. So we're not . . ." She looks at Beck's camera. *Betraying her*, she doesn't say.

"We get sixty-five thousand dollars each?" He pauses his destruction. "After forty percent taxes on contest winnings, that's forty thousand dollars."

"Forty thousand dollars is a lot."

"Not against a million bucks."

"You were just saying we're doomed!"

"We *are* doomed," Kent says. "But if we sail off in episode two? Nobody remembers who we were by the finale. And Ruddy and Kelly-Anne get to be the stars? Earn hundreds of thousands of dollars? I'd rather they drag me out of here as a withered corpse. Then at least I can get cast on *The Traitors*. That could be a hundred thousand dollars right there in appearance fees."

Miriam's vision blurs, like she's looking through the lens of a camera that's zooming too quickly and she can't tell if it's zooming in or zooming out. Seconds ago she was betraying her friend to give hope to the man she was falling for. Now he's talking about tax rates and appearance fees?

"Ruddy's got a key now," she says. "Aren't you worried the Deserters could build a raft?"

"They're not going to leave all that money on the table either. Ruddy's the one who made us all pinky swear."

"Of course. The inviolable pinky swear." Miriam turns to Beck, desperate for a way out. "Are we even allowed to destroy it?"

"Jacob told you at the start," Beck says. "Anything goes as long as you're not physically harming each other."

"At least let's save it," Miriam pleads with Kent. "Barb can't even use it herself. She doesn't have a key."

"She might," Kent says. "These games always have another layer. She could have a secret treasure map and sail off in the night, and we'd look like idiots."

Miriam stares at the sun-bleached driftwood. The vines that lash the base are brown and dried, but the ties that secure the crossbeams are brighter, some so plump and green that Barb might have been here working on this yesterday.

"What if we . . . let her go?" Miriam says quietly.

Kent squints at her like she's gone mad.

"Let her have her raft. Maybe she gets some money, but the show keeps going. You get to starve to death, and maybe they'll cast your corpse on *The Traitors*." She tries to keep the bitter edge from her voice.

"You want to gift her two hundred thousand dollars? It's a game. That money could be ours."

In spite of her guilt, a pleasurable shiver runs down Miriam's spine. *Ours.*

"And it's not only about *The Traitors*," he says. "I'm—not ready to say goodbye."

Her heart accelerates. Feeling impossibly bold for the second time that day, she takes his hand. They've never held hands in full daylight. "It won't be goodbye. You live three hours from me on Amtrak."

Kent flinches when she picks up his hand, but he lets it happen. He can feel the pressure of Beck's zoom. But maybe that's—okay? These last days with Miriam, he's felt more at peace than ever before in his adult life. Even with the frustrations of looking endlessly for the Deserters' camp, somehow it was okay, because it was with her. With Margaret, it felt like he was constantly struggling not to fuck up. Or maybe that he'd already fucked up irrevocably, some time at the start of their relationship, and so he was constantly working to repair an indefinable crack. In his mind, that's what a relationship was, struggle. But what if you could simply—exist with someone? What if they could transplant the peaceful companionship they have out here to home?

But Kent's been doing this way too long to be so naive. He knows that as soon as you leave the show, even the strongest bond starts to loosen. The connections, the friendships, the loves—they're real, while you're out here. The myth exists as long as you can sustain this artificial world. Then the show ends. You go back to your friends and family, your life as it existed before. The network shuts you out. The legend you told about yourself smolders and dims until it's barely an ember. Even the skateboarder, his runner-up on *Endure* who he thought would be his best bro forever—now they exchange text messages on each other's birthdays. Most years. That's why he's not worried about the Deserters making their escape. They know it too.

And to be honest, he didn't even really mean that he isn't ready to say goodbye to *her*. Kent's not ready to say goodbye to all of it. To the show. To the boar he's been imagining for ten days, that he's certain is out there for him. Goodbye to Kent Duvall.

He turns from her and yanks a beam roughly from the raft. A vine snaps. An ooze of sap drools down its side. She gasps. "It's a game," he says again, not daring to look at her face.

She watches in horror as he pulls at the vines and tosses pieces of wood like he's disemboweling an animal with his hands. This is her fault, Miriam thinks. But isn't he right? *It's a game.* They all signed up knowing that. She picks up a gray piece of driftwood and hurls it into the underbrush. *We're playing a game.* It's not like all of Barb's hopes and dreams, that the first thing she wants to do with her cash is treat herself to a steak dinner at the Ruth's Chris in Asheville, could be contained in this heap of splintered wood and stringy vines. Barb's plan to give half her money to the sick children at St. Jude's? None of it is real. It's a TV show. And their nightly spoon sessions—that's part of the game too, right? Kent yanks apart the raft with his hands, and she hurls the scattered driftwood into the jungle, feeling a rage she can't understand, as the sticky sap from the vines stains her fingertips.

On the walk back to camp, Kent keeps passing her looks, but she fixes her eyes on the ground. The thin crust of sand crumples at her footsteps. Her body feels weak and jellied. Around her, she sees as if for the first time all the trash that the tide has washed ashore. There are cartons of old cigarettes and beer bottles, the usual detritus, but they also walk by a toilet seat, a Nerf gun, and a coil of netting. The litter spreads down the beach and penetrates the jungle. An umbrella lies stripped of its webbing, a few flaps of faded red fabric cloaking the skeleton of its spines. A plastic baby doll is missing an arm and an eye.

It's been here for the past ten days, she knows, but somehow she never noticed it before, against the backdrop of the massive jungle, against the sweep of the horizon. The garbage shunted into the oceans and circulated across the world by the currents. The entire world connected in a global web of trash.

They're passing by a tall tree with thick branches when Kent pauses, reaches into the leaves, and plucks a small green fruit. "Oh my god," Kent says. "Food! Should we eat this?" He's smiling at her solicitously, and she feels guilty and ashamed. He's not the one behaving irrationally. He's doing the correct thing, playing the game to maximize his upside, stopping his competition from escaping. It's *her* emotions that are spiking. And yet—selfish Miriam—she's put him in the position of having to placate her.

"Is it safe?" she asks, forcing herself to engage. The fruit is hard and furred, about the size of a shriveled peach, with a seam that runs along its edge and wrinkles at the base of its stem.

"You're the scientist," he teases. "You tell me."

Miriam takes the fruit and turns it over in her hands. She presses her thumbnail into the flesh, and the juice oozes onto her fingertip. She looks at it with what she imagines is a piercing, scientific gaze. It all feels so impossibly fake.

"You're the hunter, you tell me."

"I'm not a *fruit* hunter."

"It seems like you're not much of an *anything* hunter," she says, but immediately sees from his hurt look that she's misjudged her snark, and with an upswell of guilt, she sticks the fruit in her mouth, shocking them both.

"My tongue ith numb," Miriam says, spitting it back into her hand.

Kent grabs the fruit and hurls it into the trees. "That means it's poisonous."

"Poison?" The pure idiocy of what she's done strikes her. Her tongue is *numb.*

"You're an absolute maniac. Now you've got to pull the trigger."

"The—trigger?"

"You've got to get it out of your system. You've never forced yourself to puke?"

"I mean, no?"

"There's a button in the back of your throat. The little flappy thing."

"The uvula?" She reaches a finger tentatively back and gags. Her heart is pounding. Anxiety or poison? "I can't— Can you? Push the trigger for me?" She opens her mouth to him.

"You want me to—"

"Just do it!"

Kent takes Miriam by the head and forces one of his dirty fingers down her throat. His finger is thick, and her throat feels full, too full and gaping, and the tip of it curves to tickle the very back of her until all of a sudden she starts dry-heaving around his hand, and a dark green stream of vomit jets out of her mouth. Kent starts whooping and laughing. Miriam falls to the ground, bracing herself on her hands and knees, puking into the grass. "Looked a lot better going down than coming up," Kent gasps, as Miriam, on all fours, struggles to breathe. She's laughing too now, laughing and moaning as she spits the last traces of vomit onto the dirt. He wipes his wet finger on a fat green leaf. He's having trouble breathing he's laughing so hard. Around her the trees shimmer, everything outlined in a thin margin of brilliant light, haloed and holy, and as stupid as she was, she also thrills at her own wildness, her daring. This *is* real. It is life-and-death real.

And there too, as she pants and spits vomit, she sees Beck, outlined in her own small halo. Beck who has been following them, Beck who filmed them destroying the raft, Beck who's been there like a guardian angel every step of her journey. The game is real and the competitions are real and the show is real and the experience is real. It's all real, and it's all hers, and she's glad she destroyed the raft because she wants more of it. And she doesn't consider at all—not yet—that the producer she was counting on to be her friend and guide in the treacherous jungle stood beside her as she put a poisonous fruit into her mouth, filming.

CHAPTER 23

BECK

DAY 11

I was getting used to existing in a constant state of dampness. I was learning to accept the sunburn that singed my pale skin. My storyline with Miriam and Kent was taking off. For all its rugged misery, the island was starting to feel like home. In a fit of optimism, I even asked Erika to have breakfast with me. I wanted to get to know her, I said, what she was really like beneath her veneer of evil. (That last part I kept to myself.) She looked at me skeptically over dry eggs and burnt pancakes while we traded stories. She'd been a PA on Jacob's first show, *Extreme Pregnancy*, and stayed with him ever since. Yes, she'd been there for that quadruplets episode. Yes, she'd been the one to hose down the host of *House of Felons* when season three's arsonist ignited the man's toupee. It was touching the way she recounted these tales I'd never heard of as though they were industry legends. Here among Jacob's crew, they probably *were* legends, and Erika's presence at these historic milestones sanctified her. She was dressed as always in an oversize T-shirt and billowing khakis, the brim of her gray baseball cap pulled so low I could barely make out her thick eyebrows. The way her loose clothes draped her boyish, shapeless body ignited a flicker of compassion in me. Even as her oversize personality demanded that the world take notice, she hid away her physical self. She gestured with her fork like it was a conductor's baton, a strand of soggy bacon dangling off its tines. When it was my turn, I told her about my dating life, focusing on the disappointments. Build empathy with my captor. About how my long-term boyfriend broke up with me one night at a karaoke bar right after he'd finished "Eye of the Tiger." "You know boys and their anthems," I said. The line reliably got a laugh, but Erika looked like she was gritting her teeth through a medical procedure. Then, out of nowhere, a sardonic smile lit her face.

"Oh my god," she hissed. "His fucking shark story."

"Shark story?" I whispered, a little giddy at the sudden relief from her scowl.

She shushed me and gestured to the next table, where Friedman was regaling a pretty young PA with a ponytail. "Its teeth were a foot long and covered in blood," he growled. "And when it swam by the cage, it looked dead into my eyes. The beast and I saw each other. Two predators, facing off."

Erika leaned into me and, in perfect unison with Friedman, whispered, "I can't tell you what was going through that prehistoric monster's tiny brain, but the only thought in my tiny brain [self-satisfied chuckle] was—I may die, but I will get this shot."

"Let me guess," I said. "He showed up on set, was lowered into the water in a cage, then given a sack lunch and a juice box."

She snorted. "And Mommy wiped his ass when he got home."

I laughed, as much from the release of tension as from amusement. It felt good to be included in her ridicule of someone else. It showed that I wasn't her exclusive victim. Maybe this was simply how she was, an insult comic, and I'd been taking it personally. She was squinting at me, like she was seeing me in a new light just as I was seeing her.

"Tell me about when Barb found her raft," she said. "Afa says it was quite a scene."

"That *scream*." I rolled my eyes though it had actually been heart-rending. Barb had gone to work on her raft in the late afternoon and discovered its wreckage. Friedman and Afa recorded while I listened over the radio. "You could hear it across the jungle. I'm surprised you didn't hear it at beta camp." It wasn't the indignant cry of someone who's been tricked, but a wail of disbelief like a parent who's lost a child. "Aaaaaaah," I mimicked it, suppressing my guilt about mocking such deep human pain. I was being given a chance to prove to Erika that I was in on the universal joke, and I didn't want to fail my test.

"Aaaaaah!" Erika echoed in delight.

"What are you girls screaming about?" Friedman asked from the next table.

"We're doing Barb's scream when she discovered her broken-up raft," Erika said.

"That's not right at all. I was there. It was more–'WAAAAUGH.'"

"Awwooooagh." The ponytailed PA added her own riff.

"No, no." Ralph ran over. "I just logged that footage. It was higher pitched. 'AIEEEE.'"

"AWWOOO," cried Benjamin the pilot from across the dining room. "AYYAHH!" shouted Afa. The whole crew was doing it. "RAWOO!" "HIEEE!" I'd watched the scene back that morning. Barb collapsed on her knees. Friedman zoomed in on her exhausted, wrinkled face. Tears streaked her dirt-covered cheeks. Yet as the crew clustered close, my heart was pounding dizzily like I'd stepped on-stage for my first open mike night, and I was killing.

"Barb reels into camp and goes straight to Miriam. 'Yew lying, thieving, two-faced harlot. It was yew! Admit it was yew.'" I did a horrifically mangled Tennessee accent. "'Ah worked so hard. And yew destroyed—David!'"

"David?" Erika asked, relishing the detail.

"That was everyone's question," I said. "'Your raft had a name?' Kent asked.

"'Most great ships have names,' Bartolo says." I made my voice deep and grumbly to mimic him. "'There's the *Queen Mary*. The *Titanic*, of course.'

"'Whore of Babylon!'" I did Barb.

"'The USS *Arizona*.'" Grumbly Bartolo. "'Which the Japanese bombed on December 7, 1941. Pearl Harbor Day.'

"Then Kent steps in to save the day. 'I destroyed your raft.'" I gave him a resonant Superman voice. "'Miriam had nothing to do with it.'

"'Yew never would've known there even *was* a raft if this harlot hadn't led yew to it!'"

"Why *did* she name the raft David?" Erika asked.

"That was the name of her son," I said quietly. "Who died."

Erika sucked in her breath. A pall fell over the laughing crowd.

"Wow," Erika said. "Your stories are nastier than mine."

I wasn't sure if that was criticism or, coming from her, the highest praise. The crew dispersed back to their tables and their jobs. *It was a raft*, I wanted to say. *It wasn't actually her son.* I picked up my plastic tray and dumped the remains of my breakfast into the trash.

At camp, my exhausted, malnourished contestants lazed in their shelter. The sky was the color of asphalt, a long gray road stretching nowhere. Barb wasn't speaking to any of them, but then, nobody was talking. On television, you see the chaos and the drama, but the bulk of any reality producer's work lies like an iceberg below the surface in a glacial mass of boredom. Hours dragged like eons as we filmed the contestants doing nothing.

Standing there sipping water from my CamelBak, I replayed the conversation with Erika. Had she set me up from the start, convinced me to share this vicious story so that she could deflate me? Or was it real praise? I assumed she'd orchestrated the Deserters' camp raid, that she was the reason my contestants were irritable and desperate, listless, turning on one another. She was everything I disliked about the way reality producers could be. So why did I feel compelled to seek her approval?

THAT NIGHT I WAS LYING IN BED BENEATH THE SHROUD OF MY MOSquito net when I heard the muffled sound of talking outside.

"I still can't believe we have *her* instead of Stellan." Erika's voice.

"I thought you guys had a moment at breakfast." Jacob. "Anyway, you know why."

"Stellan pissed ice water. Not this constant . . ." A mumbled word I couldn't hear.

"Shh. That's her cabin."

The voices hushed. I lifted my head to the window, close enough to peek out, but not so close I'd be assaulted by the beetles that had colonized the gaps around my window frame. Silhouetted in the moonlight, Erika and Jacob walked down the sand, away from the hotel.

I don't know why I followed them. I told myself I needed to hear more. Why *had* they hired me? The dog killer? The Stellan question nagged at me too. Callahan said he'd barely looked at the guy. Why would you send a senior producer back to the States without a once-over by the show's medic? I had the vague impulse I'd confront them. But if that was my goal, why did I slip on my shoes so quietly? Why was I so careful as I closed my cabin door?

Outside, the full moon silvered the sand. I held back so they wouldn't see me, but the diesel growl from the fishing scows in the bay muffled their voices. The air stank of exhaust mingled with sea spray. Down the beach, they stopped at the wooden guard hut. Laughter. Then they walked to the headland where the shore ended in a black jag of volcanic rock and gave way to the jungle.

I held my breath as I approached the guard hut, praying the guards wouldn't call out. The three men were sprawled on woven mats around a silver radio the size of a toaster oven. An announcer chattered urgently in what I assumed was a sports game. One of them held its bent antenna pointed at an angle to keep the signal. They didn't even glance up as I passed.

Inside the jungle, the darkness was pristine. The shrieks and hoots were louder at night, and my skin prickled with the awareness that an invisible claw or fang could strike at any moment. Nighttime was when predators hunted. Through a gap in the canopy I could see the moon, and looking up, I had the uncanny sense that the dark world around me was a solid black bottle I was trapped inside, that the tiny yellow circle was the light I could see through its neck, and if I could only break out of this dark cage the entire universe would be radiant and bright. Soon my eyes adjusted, and I saw the wavering halo of Jacob's flashlight. I followed carefully through the underbrush. They were talking about camera positions for the next challenge. Jacob was complaining about the network's meddling. Logistics. Meanwhile if I tripped or sneezed, they would turn and see me acting like a lunatic.

"Ask me a sound," Jacob said.

"A sound?"

"Describe a sound, and I'll tell you what animal's making it." They both seemed completely at ease.

"Okay–" Erika paused, listening to the cacophony. "What's the one that's like a squeegee across a windshield?"

"Brown tree frog," Jacob said quickly.

"That's quite a party trick."

"Ask me another."

"What's the pinging?" Erika said. "Like—a smoke detector with a low battery?"

"Cinnamon tree frog."

"You're making these up."

"Million's been giving me lessons. Try again."

Here I was slinking through the pitch-black jungle, and he was IDing frogs. *Talk about Stellan*, I wanted to shout. *Talk about me.*

"What's the one that sounds like a duck?"

"Golden tree frog."

"Is everything out here a fucking frog?" Erika asked.

"Most animals aren't so loud. I think it's romantic. Blaring their desires into the world, damn the consequences."

"The whole jungle wants to eat them, but these idiots won't shut up about love. Reminds me of Beck."

I froze.

"You talk about Beck more than Friedman talks about sharks," Jacob said. Their bodies got close. I was too far away to make out what they were doing. "I know you don't like her. But we need her."

"I don't like anybody. I don't *trust* Beck. She's—chaotic. Worse, she doesn't know she's chaotic. I'm here to make the best TV show I can and go the fuck home. If she needs to work through her demons, she should go on reality TV, not produce it."

"You don't have to trust her. Trust me. She's the perfect person." Jacob placed a hand on Erika's back and kept it there—too long. They probably fucked. There wasn't anything to do on location but drink and fuck.

"You come up with these plans, but I'm the one who cleans up the mess," Erika said. "Remember that arsonist on *House of Felons*?"

"You were clutch then, and I know you'll be clutch now. Ask me another sound."

"Ugh. Fine. What's the one that's like an alarm bell? Like—a prisoner escaped from lockdown and now the guards are out to get him?"

He cocked his head, and together we all listened to the distant blaring, the way the alarm gathered in intensity and halted, gathered and halted. "I don't know."

"Wow," Erika said. "So there are some things even Jacob Malibu doesn't know."

What did Jacob mean I was the "perfect person"? It sounded nefarious, but then I was a reality television producer. I saw storylines everywhere. Maybe Jacob was simply giving me a compliment. But then what did Erika mean by his "plans"? My heart was racing, and as we walked deeper into the jungle, and the strangling figs clustered thick, I felt as vulnerable and afraid as a lost child. Around me I could hear the pinging cinnamon frog, the quacking golden frog, and the squeaking brown frog, but all my fears centered on the nameless alarm frog, the way its anxious blare wavered wildly from frantic to unsure.

"Holy shit." Jacob pointed his flashlight up. Spread before us, an interlocked network of thousands of spiderwebs reached for yards across the trees. Silver webbing spiraled over twisted banyans and across the straight spines of taraw palms. Jacob's flashlight panned the scene, refracting into rainbows across webs that were wheels and helixes, webs that sagged like cast fishing nets, webs that exploded outward like sunbursts.

"Are you fucking kidding me? You've taken me to see spiders?" Erika said.

Jacob brushed a hand up the back of her neck. She screamed and hit him in the shoulder.

"*Asshole,*" she said.

"There must be thousands of them. Million said it was amazing, but words don't do it justice. Look." Jacob shined his flashlight at a flickering in one perfect web. I could barely make it out, a light pulsing on the silver strands, like a sigh or a breath of wind.

"A blue pansy," Jacob said.

A butterfly was trapped.

"It looks like it's covered in eyes," Erika whispered.

"A defense against predators. Isn't nature marvelous? Every tiny insect is part of a story millions of years in the making. I'm going to catch it."

"You're kidding."

Jacob reached into one of his overstuffed pockets and pulled out a white plastic bag.

"Even after all these years, you still surprise me," Erika said.

Jacob opened the mouth of his bag wide. The butterfly was barely moving. He brushed aside the strands and scooped it into his bag. Silver webbing floated to the ground as the spiderweb listed to the side. "Oh," Jacob said. "That alarm bell sound–it's the frilled tree frog." *The frilled tree frog.* Nothing special. Nothing to be scared of. Yet one more irrelevant voice in the jungle chorus. I laughed at myself, for what I'd been imagining. He was here for spiders and butterflies. Nothing malevolent about that. Right? Jacob twisted the bag's neck. The plastic rustled as the butterfly beat its wings. A few moments later it was still.

CHAPTER 24

KENT

DAY 13

The first thing Kent's going to eat when he gets home is an entire bowl of chocolate chip cookie dough. Miriam misses sushi, which they tease her about, because—well, it's raw fish. Dream bigger. They take turns planning Thanksgiving dinner. Everybody gets to bring a course, except Barb, who sits beside them in the shelter in silent anger. Is it lame to bring salad? Miriam asks. Yes, the group confirms. It is lame. Bartolo is on the mains. Turkey and stuffing and candied yams. Also grilled cheese. For Thanksgiving? Why not? He wants a grilled cheese. And a cheeseburger. A cheeseburger inside two grilled cheeses instead of buns. They goggle their eyes. Bartolo's blown open the culinary universe. A cheeseburger inside two pizzas with Oreo cookies instead of pepperonis. For dessert, pecan pie on top of a pumpkin pie, all baked within a chocolate cake. Topped with cookie dough. Barb hates it, she mutters. Talking about food makes her hungrier. But for Kent, merely saying the words evokes the flavors, like the syllables in "chocolate chip cookie dough" contain all that is desirable in the universe.

So when Beck approaches them on day thirteen and tells them

that at sundown, each group will vote one player to face off in a duel and the victor wins food for their team, their first question is what kind of food.

"Cookie dough?" Kent asks.

"Grilled cheese?" Bartolo says.

"Sushi?" suggests Miriam. The others groan.

"You'll find out when you get there," Beck says. "Oh, and one more thing—the loser of the duel will be immediately eliminated from the game."

"What kind of duel?" Kent asks.

"Something else you'll learn when you arrive."

"So we vote someone in without knowing what we're voting them to do?" Miriam asks.

"That's the fun," Beck says.

"Whatever the task, I know you will prevail," Bartolo says to Kent. "Of course I could acquit myself magnificently, but given our dire need for sustenance, I will defer to—"

"We don't have to pick someone to *win*," Kent says, with a resigned sigh.

The group looks at him in confusion.

"They're definitely going to vote Carl, right? He's the strongest person here. He's got twenty pounds on me." Say what you will about his terrible confessionals, his nonexistent strategy, or his noxious breath, but Carl is unmatchable when it comes to raw force. Meanwhile Kent's so worn-out, he wouldn't prevail against a strong wind. It's galling for Kent to admit defeat before the contest has even started. But he *is* defeated. Ruddy was right. "We're going to lose, so we may as well vote someone who we want to eliminate."

"You want to throw a game?" Barb asks, the first time she's engaged with them in days. "That doesn't sit right. We need food."

"It's not throwing a game." Kent enunciates for the cameras. "It's playing the actual game, which is *Escape!* You want to volunteer? Go ahead."

"Well, if we're fixing to send a lamb to the slaughter, I got a good idea who *I* want slaughtered." Barb glares at Miriam with all her hurt and rage.

"I think we should have those discussions privately," Kent says.

He stands and offers Miriam his hand.

HE'S WALKING WITH MIRIAM INTO THE JUNGLE TOWARD THE STREAM. Mario the camera assistant is pulling Friedman backward by his belt, so the cameraman can film their faces as they strategize.

Fifteen years ago on *Endure*, Kent looked down on the game's strategy. Of course he made alliances. But he was the challenge guy. There was something unsavory about the weaselly schemers who invented obscure maneuvers that contorted the game's rules. Now after a decade and a half in the reality TV circus, of going on podcasts and being asked to analyze big moves, of those very same weasels being celebrated by the fans as strategic titans, the lying and the scheming are comfortable grooves, and the spike of adrenaline as he scrambles into the jungle plotting the demise of his enemies feels like the welcome return of an old drug. He may not be able to face down Carl, but at least he can do this.

"Barb hates you and wants you gone," Kent says, "so let's vote her out."

"I can't." Miriam winces in anguish. "I can't—betray her twice."

"Better to betray one person twice than two people once."

"That sounds like a mistranslation from *The Art of War*. But really, I—I can't."

He feels a flash of annoyance, but Miriam looks miserable. "We won't do anything you don't want. I guess that means Bartolo. Unless we vote *you* in," he teases.

"You wouldn't dare. What would you do without your fruit tester?"

They reach the clearing and kneel to sip from the stream. Lowering his weak, starving body to the ground feels like the last creaky gasps of an ancient machine. The rivulet is swollen with rain, and the ripples push fast and cold against his lips.

"I'll try to convince Barb to vote with us," he says. "You blow smoke with Bartolo."

"I should—lie to his face?"

"Pretend to ask what he wants to do. Unless you want to be the one talking to Barb."

"I probably shouldn't be alone in the woods with her."

"And that was the last time they ever saw Miriam Bloom."

She splashes his face. "Something to remember me by."

He splashes back, harder. "Don't start something you can't finish."

"Oh, I can finish." She scoops her arm deep into the water and sends a torrent splashing toward him, leaving him sputtering. For a few minutes he's not even thinking of the cameras or his starving belly or the game. They pound their fists into the cold stream, splashing each other, as silly as kids, until they're both drenched.

"Well, that was extremely dumb," she says, water running down her smiling face.

"Nobody I'd rather die of hypothermia with," he says, and oddly it feels true.

They walk back to camp, silent, the two of them simply existing together in perfect quiet and intimacy, without posturing or plotting. Kent has the sense that there's another version of himself starting to form, still barely a shadow, like he's at the intersection between two paths, and down one, the Kent he's been chasing is calling him onward, and down the other there's Miriam, her head turned, reaching backward with her hand. He's always had a sense that there was a version of his life that should've worked out differently. If he studied harder, or made better choices, or—let's be honest, never met Margaret. But he never knew who that person was. Now he can see a world where he's funny, noble in small ways, patient, and encouraging. He's wondering if Miriam's feeling anything similar when she blurts out, "I hate this. I hate us choosing whose dreams we're going to destroy."

He's brought abruptly back to the game. "Better their dreams than ours."

And the truth is that Kent loves this. Last year he was a sad middle-aged man waiting in a freezing bus station. Today he's a warrior calculating whose neck the ax will sever.

HE'S LYING IN THE SHELTER WITH BARB WHILE CLOUDS OF BUGS DANCE around them.

"It's got to be Bartolo tonight," he tells her. Sabotaging the raft has actually improved Kent's relationship with Barb, as her ire is now exclusively focused on Miriam.

"So you and—that one—decided our fate, huh?"

"He doesn't do anything around camp. He stole rations!"

"At least he's not destroying rafts."

Kent sighs. "It's over. It happened. Let's move on," he says for the hundredth time.

"I'd 'move on' if I was on Treasure Island with two hundred thousand dollars, not lying here with your stinky ass."

"Should we have sat politely on the beach and watched you escape? Waved goodbye from shore? If we have any chance of lasting the full fifty days—"

"Then I'd be a fool to let Barty go. Because what happens next time we've got to cull a lamb? Who gets the ax then? I see you two canoodling."

She's right, he thinks in surprise. It would be terrible strategy for her to vote Bartolo. He can't believe he's being outmaneuvered by the crazy lady from casting.

"We're voting Miriam," she says. "If you vote Barty, I guess we'll see what happens in a tie. Could be random. Could be you going in. Wouldn't that be stupid. Risk your neck and all that money to save the backstabber girly. You watch your ass with that one. She'll come for you too."

"BARB'S SET ON VOTING YOU," HE TELLS MIRIAM. THEY'RE IN THE grove eating their daily dragon fruit. The trees are almost barren now. A few withered red fruits still cling to the branches, but most have been plucked clean. "What did Barty say?"

"'Each man must resolve according to the honor of his own heart and soul.'"

"I guess his honorable soul is accounted for."

"So we're voting Bartolo, and they're voting me," Miriam says. "What happens in a tie?"

"It could be anything. Some shows, it's the people who don't get votes who are at risk."

This was supposed to be easy. Kent Duvall the strategic powerhouse effortlessly corralling the numbers. He's the only experienced player in a group of newbies. He should be running circles around these people.

"Wait up. What if—" Miriam pauses with her hand on a tree. "Okay. Brainstorm. If we know Barb is definitely voting for me—what if we get Bartolo to vote for you?"

"I'm going to be honest. That idea doesn't immediately jump out to me."

"No, seriously. Do the math. Barb votes me. Bartolo votes you. We vote Bartolo–"

Kent follows on his fingers. "And our two votes are enough to win out. You're a genius."

"Not just a pretty face." Miriam's cheeks flush, and Kent feels an upswell of pride. In two weeks she's gone from the awkward pariah to a savvy gamer. It's not *all* thanks to him, but–it is remarkable how a little boost of confidence, of somebody believing in you, can help. Maybe he's not the strategy guy or the challenge guy. Maybe that's not his story. Maybe he's the mentor, the coach, the elder statesman who brings out the best in the people around him.

"But how do we get him to vote for me?" Kent asks.

"What if you tell him–you *want* to go in. You think you can take Carl."

"I like it. But Barb can't switch her vote, because then we're back to a tie. I'll pull him right before the sun sets, so he won't have time to say anything. Hey–great job."

She gives his fingers a squeeze, which has become their small gesture of affection, the tiny flicker of physical intimacy that damps down the jungle noise.

HE'S TREADING WATER WHILE BARTOLO TAKES AN AQUADUMP. THE clouds are staining red. It's their last chance to talk, so of course Bartolo chose this moment to "use the commode." They're close enough for their voices to carry, but far enough–Kent hopes–that no feces will float to him.

"Do you need to film this?" he shouts to Friedman on the shore.

"Believe me, brother, this is not what I want to be doing," the cameraman shouts back.

Kent prays the edit will show that he is a man who will do whatever it takes.

"Here's the deal," Kent says. "You should vote for me tonight."

"For you?" Bartolo wrinkles his brow and purses his lips, and Kent hopes he's only thinking intensely. "It's reached my ears that you've been trying to eliminate—myself."

"It's a crazy game. Everybody's name came up at one point. But I know we can't afford to lose you. You're our team's anchor." He means it literally, the thing dragging them down. "I want to face off against Carl. I think I can win."

"An honorable ambition. Of course, I considered it myself." Bartolo scoops a handful of silt from the seabed and scrubs his palms. "Out of respect, I will defer to you."

"Only—don't tell Barb," he says. "I want it to be a surprise. You know how she's been riding my ass since day one. I want to show her on camera I can step up."

The sun is dipping below the horizon as they walk from the sea. The producers will lock it down any second. *He did it.* Kent and Miriam split the vote—her idea, his execution. But as soon as they're back at camp, Bartolo goes straight to Barb and bends down beside her ear. The boom mike lowers to their mouths. You know people are plotting when you see the boom get close. Kent goes to join them, when Beck says, "Time's up. Lock it down."

"Wait," Kent says. "I need one quick chat with—"

"Lock. It. Down," Beck says. "No more talking."

The four contestants sit silently on the edge of the shelter while the camera team preps the shot of their walk from camp. *What just happened?* Did Bartolo tell Barb to vote for him? Is he going to be eliminated? The producers stop conversation when they have a result they like, so what happened in that ten-second chat to cause Beck to lock it down? He *can't* go home. Not now. He needs to figure out what's going on, immediately, but the contestants normally sleep at sundown, so anything after dark feels groggy and half-real.

He excuses himself to go to the bathroom. "It's urgent," he explains. Instead he walks to the med box, opens its lid, and roots around inside until he finds Barb's baggie. It's crazy at this point not to try something. His fate in the game is on the line. He needs to *think*. He unzips the baggie, takes out a vial, and squints at its warning label, trying to gauge what the medicine does. *Tramadol*, he reads. *May cause drowsiness or dizziness.*

He replaces it and takes out the next one. *Metformin. Take with food to reduce upset stomach. May cause nausea or diarrhea.* No, thank you.

Rosuvastatin. Avoid drinking large amounts of grapefruit juice. Avoiding grapefruit juice won't be a problem, but it also doesn't give any indication what the drug does.

Prednisone. May cause increased appetite. That's the last thing he needs.

He puts Barb's baggie back into the box. He peers through the trees toward the beach to see if anybody's coming to get him. Camp is obscured. He takes out Bartolo's baggie.

Clonidine. May cause drowsiness.

Gabapentin. May cause drowsiness or dizziness.

No wonder everyone in camp is catatonic. There's one vial left, then he has to consider Miriam's baggie. Please, you beautiful plastic bottle, save him from this moral test he's pretty sure he'll fail.

Mydayis. Mixed Salts of a Single-Entity Amphetamine Product.

Mixed salts of a single-entity amphetamine product! He would shout it from the rooftops if there were rooftops. Amphetamines are stimulants, which means sharper thinking. *May cause increased heart rate, blood pressure, and anxiety*, and that's exactly what he needs, a way to turn the dial on his central nervous system to FAST. He twists the cap and slides the white pill roughly down his dry throat and goes back to the shelter to wait. "There you are," Beck says. She leads them to the blacked-out van.

They're bouncing down the road when he feels the almost physical sensation of his brain sliding into its groove with a thunk. Could it possibly work that quickly? Does your brain thunk? But his mind suddenly feels like a motorcycle ready to peel out. So. Let's think. Why wouldn't Beck give him thirty seconds to talk to Barb?

The producers want the most epic challenge. That would be him against Carl. If Bartolo told Barb his plan, that would still be a tie. Unless . . . Miriam's in on it. Kent squirms in his wet clothes. She wouldn't do that—would she? *"You watch your ass with that one,"* Barb said. He squints at Miriam in the blackness like he can peer into her soul. She takes his fingertips and squeezes. No. She wouldn't. He squeezes back. But then, how many times has he seen lovesick contestants blindsided, their beloved waving goodbye in their farewell confessional—"Sorry about this. I do care for you. See you on the other side." His racing brain shapes the day's scenes into a jigsaw of betrayal. Miriam's silly splashing. Barb's feigned outrage. Oh god, was Bartolo's aquadump all theater to humiliate him?

It can't end like this. The patsy. The rube. There has to be a way out. The car hits a bump, and his head smashes into the padded ceiling. *What if—he volunteers?* Before they vote. He'll deprive them of their blindside. There's a chance he can beat Carl. It's not like the challenge will be sumo wrestling. There could be a puzzle. Maybe they'll have to stand very still on a pole, and Carl's weight will work against him. All day he's been locked into the idea that only a madman would take on Carl, but—he could?

The van stops. Ralph leads them to the pre-challenge tent. It's too dark to bother blindfolding them. A camp lantern hangs from the crossbars, casting a wobbly orange light. A green bottle of bug spray sits in a corner. They spritz themselves. He tastes the tang of citrus and deet in the back of his throat. His mind is sprinting up and down the tent's small patch of dirt. The moment before they vote, he'll stand up and say, *Stop!* Ralph guides them to a torchlit trail. There's a drumbeat playing. He's not sure if it's piped in from speakers or the blood beating in his ears. They follow the path to a clearing, where Jacob Malibu stands beside a carved urn. There are four logs where they're clearly meant to sit. Voting into an urn, a total *Survivor* rip-off. Wild that the most crucial decisions in your life could be defined by a lazy intern in the Art Department. But before they sit down on their stool-logs, Miriam puts a hand in the air like she's answering a question and says, "Hold up." The group pivots to her in surprise. "We don't need to vote. I volunteer."

"What–no. What are you doing?" Kent whispers.

She puts a hand on his waist. "I saw that crazy look in your eyes. You were about to do something noble again–to save me. But it's time I saved myself."

"No, wait–what?" Something isn't adding up. He's just uncovered their plan.

"I'm not going to let you sacrifice your game for me," Miriam says. "You want to be here so much. Let me step up. I could win." She laughs nervously. "Maybe the challenge is sudoku."

"Does anybody object?" Jacob asks the group.

"Hell no," Barb says.

"I honor the lady's request," Bartolo says.

"Wait–I object," Kent says. Things are moving too fast. *Keep up, super-brain!*

"That's three to one," Jacob says. "Miriam, looks like you're the tribe hero."

Kent flinches at the word.

They follow another path deeper into the jungle. The torchlight casts wild shadows that dance along the grass. Miriam is sacrificing herself for him, which is beautiful and also means she wasn't going to betray him. But—she stole his moment. Through the trees is another torchlit path, the dark outlines of the Deserters bobbing forward toward their rendezvous, and he has the delusion that there are torchlit paths everywhere branching through the jungle, and if he could only step onto the right one it would lead him deeper into the twisting vines, away from this emotional stew and into an enchanted jungle kingdom where he could live forever.

Then they're in the next clearing, a hard dirt circle. Carl comes stomping in at the Deserters' head. Miriam looks stoic, her jaw set. At the center of the clearing are two large rectangular holes. Inside each is a coffin. Standing on a table is a platter of fish on ice. Not cookie dough. Not even burgers. Basically sushi.

"Carl, Miriam," Jacob announces, "prepare yourselves to be buried alive."

CHAPTER 25

MIRIAM

NIGHT 13

She descends into the hole. It's only three feet deep, but every step feels like she's walking into her grave. The coffin is a simple rectangle of blond planks as thin and cheap as a plywood crate. There are cameras and microphones at the four corners and a small pillow for her head. It's an endurance competition, Jacob explains. Whoever can last longer buried alive wins a fish feast, a bundle of strong cordage—and a key. He hands them each a walkie-talkie to radio when they're ready to quit or in case of emergencies. "Quit?!" Carl bellows from his hole. *What kind of emergencies?* Miriam wants to ask, but she doesn't dare show weakness. This is for television. They've probably done this a thousand times. There's an entire department whose whole job is burying contestants alive. Carl roars. She should roar too. "Roar!" she says, and the crowd above them laughs. She steps into the coffin and lies down. It's tight. Her elbows chafe against the splintery sides. They're going to have to scrape Carl in with a spatula. That could be an advantage. The pillow scratches her neck. She locks eyes with Kent, who's gazing down at her from above. It feels like he's building to say something, a declaration or pronouncement, and she feels a gush of anticipation and embarrassment. "The brain can only go five minutes without oxygen!" Ruddy shouts. Jacob slams the coffin lid, and she's met by the blast of her own breath, hot and wet around her as it recoils off the casket walls.

At first, the gloom is broken by slats of light that slant through cracks in the cheap wood. She can see the outline of the box's sides and make out the shadowy knobs of her knees. From above, the chip of the spade. Dirt patters down, and she coughs and sputters as it pours through the cracks into her mouth. She clutches the radio. The spade chips again. She closes her mouth and eyes tight. Dirt rains down, pebbles skittering along the box's sides with a hollow echo, like the rattle of small bones. Her thumb caresses the call button. Every part of her wants to end this now. *No,* she tells herself. Let this be a defining personal moment. She'll come out of this casket and emerge into her new self. *"Oh, Miri, you and your transformational moments,"* she hears her mother say. The reality of those big moments—the teen tour hiking through the French Alps, or the first time she read Plath—was that nothing ever changed. She was always the same on the other side. And yet, this one, stepping out of a literal casket. Seems like it could be big. Another spadeful, and she is surrounded by absolute dark. The voices and footsteps from above are muffled like they're underwater. Soon even the shovel becomes faint. Then it's all gone. The world is sealed in silence. She waits for her vision to adjust, but there's nothing for her eyes to adjust to, only the pitch blackness of the grave. She can *feel* the pressure of the dirt above her, hear the tiny creaks of the wood straining against the tons of earth weighing it down. Again her thumb finds the button. She closes her eyes, comforted by her eyelids' familiar blackness. She should test the radio out. But is it an automatic quit as soon as she depresses the button? It's okay if she loses, she thinks. Nobody expects her to win. And that thought—it's all right—she can fail—she can fly back to New York, sit down for brunch with her college roommate Penelope, who will smile at her indulgently and say, *You did your best and we're all so proud of you—* No. She *will* beat Carl.

From the other box, she hears the muffled, echoing thunder of Carl's ferocious roar.

He's freaking roaring in there? If she can hear it through the earth, even faintly, imagine how loud it must be. God, Miriam thinks, what chance does she have against a legend like *Carl*? Something is tickling her leg. Don't think about it. Find a place for your mind to go. Check in with the senses. Senses registering more tickling bugs. Let's forget the senses. Focus on your breath– Wait, how is she able to breathe? There must be an air hose connected to the box. What if it gets kinked? If she suffocates, will they even see on the monitors? She'll close her eyes, drift to sleep, and– Okay, definitely do not focus on your breath. Think about Penelope's pitying smile. Think of Kent tonight in the shelter when you win, his dick jumping with joyful pride. Think about your first concert. Britney Spears in 2004 on the Onyx Hotel Tour, Britney emerging in a pink-and-gold crop top to sing ". . . Baby One More Time." Except the song had been reworked in a jazz beat, and all Britney's dancers were wearing fedoras, suspenders, and spats. Her mom, who'd been holding her hands over her ears, was ecstatic. She kept leaning to Miriam saying, *"Now, this is my type of music,"* while eight-year-old Miriam was distraught. Still she belted out the lyrics, trying to make the song she knew match the altered music coming from the stage. *"Hit me, baby, one more time, oh hit me hit me one more time."* It felt almost like a betrayal, that the song she'd practiced in her bedroom was so different from what was performed. Barb's scream after they destroyed the raft, her red and furious face. She *deserves* this penance for what she did to Barb. *It's a game. All's fair–* And is this a game too? Something is crawling up her leg–*think of Kent*–and there are more somethings crawling along her neck and under her arms, and she screams, and her thumb depresses the radio button before she can stop it, and for half a second she hears the production chatter. Then it's gone. She wills her thumb away from the buzzer. Did she quit? Did they hear it? Are they rushing to the rescue? *Please no. I have more fight left. It was a moment of weakness.* She slithers her hand down her thigh, snatches the insect, and crunches its carapace in her hand.

She hears the chip of the spade. "No!" she cries out, her voice echoing in her ears. "I wasn't quitting!" The spade gets closer and closer. In spite of her terror that she's lost, that the game is over for her and she'll be whisked away without even a chance to say goodbye to Kent, the prospect of release from this tomb makes her entire body quiver. She pushes hard against the lid. *Don't rescue me but please get me the eff out of this box.* She hears the chip chip chip of the spade. Why is it taking so long? She pushes again on the splintery lid with all her strength, and the spade chips louder and louder, her breath frantic in her chest, until at last the coffin opens, only an inch, and dirt floods into the box on top of her. She forces her way out of the coffin and into the world, covered in earth and muck but who cares, the air is drenched in sweetness, she feels like a new foal blinking alive, all her senses are refreshed, she can hear the night birds and the tree frogs in their brilliant cacophony, she can smell the mineral scent of the stream. Carl is beside her covered in dirt too, and she wants to hug him. They share a bond now, only the two of them, but he is ranting, "God damn you, Ruddy, I'll see you in hell, you rat, you bug." He's shaking and wild, not the same man as before– How long ago was it? Fifteen minutes? Three hours? Forever. He turns to her and his beady eyes are wet with tears. "*Every* day. All *he* talks about–are your girls drowning? What if they're crying missing you, and all Hazel wants is to hold your hand? They need me. I can't suffocate to death in a box!" It's like he's pleading with her to understand, and she feels ashamed that such a big man is looking at her with such desperation. "I'm a warrior!" he cries. "I'm a warrior! I'm a warrior!" Before she can say anything, Jacob comes down into the dirt beside them, presents her with a golden key, and lifts her hand in victory.

CHAPTER 26

BECK

NIGHT 13

The drive back to the City was oddly somber. There was something unsettling about seeing Carl so unhinged. He ranted long after the competition was over, cursing Ruddy's name and calling out to his girls, insisting he was a *warrior* as he shivered and stomped his feet in the open coffin, our cameras drinking it up until he stormed back down the path, not even waiting for his production minders. Now he was the first resident of the Holding Pen, the cabins where the eliminated contestants would stay until the show was over.

"Well, that was fucking stellar," Erika said in our meeting. "And yay for Beck, your pet won a challenge."

"But now what? They won a platter of fish, but they don't have a knife to scale it or a fire to cook it." I was proud of Miriam, yes, but my group would continue to wither if they couldn't eat.

"They could eat it raw?" Erika offered.

"Not if they don't want parasites," Dr. Callahan said. "That ice will last a day. After that they have to chuck it out."

"So they're going to have to watch as the fish rots in front of them," I said.

"What a metaphor," Jacob said.

"A metaphor for what?"

"For—their struggle," he said, annoyed at having to clarify. "The central problem."

"Their central problem is that they're starving." I knew I was being combative, but everything with Jacob felt fraught now. I kept waiting for him to tell me about the "plan," and the longer he didn't, the more agitated I became. "It's not even good television. They're lying around their shelter. Ralph fell asleep yesterday filming them."

"Wilderness shows are *about* four people lying around starving," Jacob said. "Our audience wants to see them suffer. They get to imagine it's themselves out in the elements, rather than sitting on their couches eating Doritos. We do it for an episode or two, then—boom."

"Boom?"

"Boom. A spark. A conflict. A moment of inspiration. Desperation pushes people past their limits."

"The Deserters stole *everything*. And unless you want me to physically lead them to beta camp to get their stuff back," I said carefully, looking for a sign, "there isn't going to be a boom."

"You're not suggesting *manipulating* them?" Erika pretended to wipe away a proud tear.

I rolled my eyes. "Obviously we nudge when we have to. But I think what's beautiful about reality TV is that it's *real*. If you wanted to script it in advance, why not make scripted?"

"Because that's the game," Erika says. "Getting real people to follow our plan."

"I see. The game is for the producers to play, not the contestants." Erika's use of the word "plan" made my skin prickle. I looked over at Jacob, but he had the same patient, encouraging expression as always.

"Aren't you leading your chemist around by the nose?" Erika asked.

"Where did she get the idea that Barb is a—what's the expression?—broken-down power saw?"

"Have you been looking at my *footage*?" I felt weirdly exposed. "And that's something else I've been meaning to bring up. I assume everyone else knew that Miriam isn't actually a chemist?"

"Remind me," Jacob said. "What does she do?"

"She works in marketing."

"Sure, but at a pharma company, right?"

"I'm used to a story bible that exaggerates," I said. "I've seen plenty of so-called venture capitalists who actually run Etsy stores. But the story bible, her dossier, even the laminated contestant cards with her picture all say the same thing. 'Miriam Bloom. Age twenty-nine. Height five ten, weight one forty-five. Chemist.' And she is absolutely not a chemist. They had a whole conversation about it on reward. I didn't make them stop because *I* wanted to hear the truth." I'd been uncomfortable with the idea of the psychoactive tea, but Jacob insisted it was a local custom, and I had to admit it worked incredibly, my two contestants breaking down all their barriers as they confessed themselves to each other in the stilt house.

"Here's my feeling," Jacob said. "Miriam works in pharma. She dresses like a chemist. She looks like a chemist. So to our audience—" He shrugged. "Who do you want to watch more, the nerdy chemist or the nerdy marketing associate? I literally don't even know what marketing is."

"But *I* should know. I have so many interviews where I assume she's a chemist."

"And they'll be better for it. We weren't keeping this from you. Truly, it hadn't crossed my mind. You came into filming so late, and it was irrelevant. Let's focus on the bigger news, which is that the dynamic you're producing between Miriam and Kent is really blossoming. And Miriam winning that challenge against Carl. Wow. This starvation thing is going to work out. Remember. Desperation pushes people past their limits."

I left the meeting feeling jittery and on edge. I hated the idea that Erika was going through my footage. Of course, we all shared notes in our production meetings, and the scenes got logged and made their way into the episodes. But another producer scrubbing through my raw content felt invasive. I couldn't believe Erika told Jacob that I should be on a reality show, when she was the one constantly performing her identity. Outside our meetings, I was cobbling together a picture of her I could empathize with. The sidekick puffing up her résumé. But at the table, she was like the most irritating contestant, delivering nonstop zingers so she'd be brought back for another season.

Some of the staff lingered in the production office, using the Wi-Fi to make calls to their parents and loved ones back home. I yearned to have somebody I could reach out to. But I'd left the dead brick of my phone in my cabin. The only person I could even imagine calling was my dad, who would listen impatiently for a few moments before telling me to come home so that I could get a job filling out paperwork in his office.

That night, the PAs set up a projector on the beach for a film festival. Anyone on the crew could submit a movie they'd made on location. It was something I loved about being a part of a reality crew, that PAs and audio engineers would grab a few moments wherever they could for their art projects. Ralph weaved among the blankets and folding chairs wearing a red-and-white-striped hat, hawking popcorn and beer. I took an empty seat next to Friedman and opened a beer can, trying to unclench the knot inside me. I wanted to celebrate Miriam's win, but I was too worried for my contestants, angry at Erika, suspicious of Jacob, resentful of my dad. Friedman was wildly drunk, but so was everyone. The ponytailed PA was resting her head on his shoulder. Friedman was married, but here on location, the rules dissolved. That's what people told themselves, anyway.

The first movie was from Ralph. It was a dazzling display of drone footage, zipping over the water, hovering above the jungle while a pair of macaws soared by. Brad from the Art Department had quick cuts of his team constructing challenge pieces, dousing each other with cold water in the shower, throwing all-night painting parties. It was like a montage of your best memories from summer camp, if your summer camp had chainsaws. The island *was* like camp, I thought, the way your social world collapsed to thirty random strangers you'd never see again.

The last film was Afa's. It opened in black and white with fluttering drapery like a French art flick. The plot followed a hardworking Samoan immigrant who's in love with a woman named America. Am-Erika. Got it. But this poor immigrant was stuck in a loveless relationship with a shrew named Heck, played by Mario with a red wig.

"Kiss me!" Afa begged the mop that was standing in for America. "Take me away from this terrible marriage!"

Mario burst into the scene.

"Heck!" Afa cried.

"How could you?" Mario wailed. "You destroyed our life, so I will destroy—your dog!" He reached under a bed, pulled out a toy dog, and started ripping out its stuffing.

"Busterrrr!!!" Afa cried. He fell to his knees. Fade to black.

The crowd hooted and cheered and stomped their feet in the sand. I drank from my beer and pretended to laugh too. The joke was on everybody, not only me. The joke was on Erika, whose skinny body was reduced to a mop. The joke was on Afa himself, who everyone knew truly was infatuated with Erika. I was a senior producer. It was only right for the crew to take the piss. At camp my contestants were starving and shivering in the cold. But I was filled with envy for the purity of their experience, the confrontation with the elements instead of this endless interpersonal hell. They could quit at any time. Say the word, and Jacob would wrap them in a warm blanket, hand them a chocolate bar, and tell them how wonderfully they'd done. I envisioned Kent and Miriam spooning, the sweaty warmth at the join of their bodies, his chest pressed into her. I would do anything for them, I thought. They were more vital to me than these howling strangers. The crowd roared around me, and I thought only of being immersed in their heat.

CHAPTER 27

KENT

DAY 14

The morning light blares out as garish as a strip club's signage, and a funky fish smell percolates up from the shore. Kent's head pounds, and his face feels out of whack, like his eyes and nose have all migrated to the wrong places. He barely slept. All night his mind raced from the Mydayis, reliving Miriam's victory. Of course he was happy for her. Thrilled! So proud! But he couldn't quell the nagging thought that the win was supposed to be his. He was supposed to be the provider. He was supposed to kill a boar. Now instead there's hours of footage of his failed hunting trips, and Miriam's the one gifting them food. Even Barb congratulated her after her win, with a slap on the back and an approving *I didn't know you had it in you, girly.*

It's only a pile of raw fish we can't cook, he thinks bitterly. He feels responsible for that, too. He tried to make yet another bow drill, but as he feared, he wasn't a skilled enough woodsman to do it without a knife. Miriam suggested they shatter Bartolo's Coke bottle to use as a sharp edge, but Bartolo clutched it anxiously to his chest, and Barb said she doubted it would be solid enough to carve wood. Kent really didn't want to work with shards of broken glass.

So when Beck arrives and says, "Fuck it, I'm taking you to the Deserters' camp," Kent resolves that this will be his new hero moment. Miriam can *get* the food. But he will be the one to enable them to eat it.

"I believe I may have a plan." Bartolo gestures them close. "We go in disguise. We layer ourselves with foliage so that we become a walking forest, and sneak into their camp."

"I'm not sure a walking forest is going to be able to sneak anywhere," Kent says.

"I was thinking of *Macbeth*," Bartolo says defensively, "when Malcolm's army hides themselves behind the branches of Birnam Wood."

"I'm thinking of reality," Kent insists. "If we're going to be sneaking, it should be one person."

Bartolo grudgingly relents, on the condition that their chosen avatar dons appropriate camouflage. With his splitting headache, Kent's willing to agree to anything, so long as he gets his hero moment. Bartolo and Barb splash his face with mud, lash leaves to his forehead, and insert one large fern into his pants.

"Perfect." Bartolo stands back, admiring.

"I feel ridiculous," he says.

"It's like a ghillie suit," Barb assures him. "You're a tree with legs."

"I wish I had a mirror," he says, though that might be worse. He tries to get a read off Miriam, but she merely gives him a thumbs-up and an awkward grin, her face still covered in dirt.

He adjusts the large palm frond, whose stalk keeps slipping down his leg, and excuses himself to the med kit. As he unzips Bartolo's baggie and uncaps the Mydayis, he tells himself this is the last time. But his brain is killing him, and he can't screw this up, especially not while dressed as a houseplant. The white pill slides down easily, like his throat is expanding to greet it.

BECK LEADS HIM AROUND THE MANGROVE SWAMP AND THROUGH marshy grasses, filming. "What are you thinking?!" she asks as they walk. "What's your plan?"

"I'm thinking I'm going to get our gear back," he says. "My plan is to sneak in there, blending in with the trees." What he's really thinking is that a producer with a bright blue tank top and pink-and-white sneakers does not add to his disguise. His actual plan is to wait for the drug to tell him what to do.

The muddy ground firms. They hike up a rocky headland. The towering mangroves thin to shrubby screw pines and sea almonds plump with yellow-green fruit the size of his palm. Through the trees, he sees their camp. A massive lean-to is bunched with pillows and blankets. The tarp is taut along its roof. The blue enamel pot swings on a gallows over a low fire, simmering with a stew of coconut shards and dragon fruit whose sweetness he can smell from here. Kelly-Anne and Ashley slouch on a low bench, and Ruddy rocks back and forth on a rope swing. They built freaking furniture. The Deserters' cameraman nonchalantly swivels his camera on its tripod toward the trees, pointing right at him. Beck must have radioed. She's disappeared.

He circles the camp, keeping to the tree line. By some miracle, the makeshift ghillie suit is working. Past their camp, a pool of water bubbles up from a crack in the rock. It must be their water source. He leans down to take a sip, and his brain slips into its groove, like a record needle finding its tune. He'll sneak in as far as he can. When they notice him, he'll fake like he's going for the pot and dash for the machete. Secondary objectives are the small knife for scaling the fish and the pot itself for fish stew. He crawls out of the trees, inch by inch, scanning for the blades. There. The machete, the small knife, and the hatchet are all stuck into the side of a tree.

"What the fuck?" Ruddy says, spotting him.

Kent is on his feet and sprinting. He jukes for the pot. Ruddy moves to cut him off. Kent doubles back for the blades. He can scoop them in one motion and be gone. Then who will be pathetic and starving? He reaches for the machete, but the gesture twists the palm frond in his pants. He stumbles, and Ruddy is past him, grabbing the machete, the knife, and the hatchet. Kelly-Anne has the bottle of iodine and the rope. Kent goes for a bow drill, but Ashley snatches it, so that he's standing in the middle of their camp, in his ridiculous disguise, with nothing in his hands and all the cameras focused on him.

"Is it Halloween?" Ruddy asks, panting.

"You stole our tools." Kent tries to reclaim the high ground. "I'm here to get them back." The mud on his face has hardened, and his mouth feels stiff as he talks.

"Looks like you failed."

Kent's mind is racing, but all it's saying are different varieties of what a screwup he is, while it paints fragmented scenes of punching Ruddy's face. "I found your camp. I can come back while you're sleeping. But it doesn't have to be this way. Why don't we trade? We've got twelve fish. We'll give you half, in exchange for half the tools."

"We don't need your fish. We'll sleep with the tools so you can't take them."

Kent struggles to control his frustration. "I'll give you eight." The fish will be rotten by tonight. "For just the machete and one of the bow drills." Which he made with his own hands.

"Fish would be really good," Ashley says.

"The whole plan is to starve them," Ruddy says. "We can't quit when it's working. Plus how funny will it be watching those losers stare at a plate of food they can't eat?"

"Why are you listening to him?" Kent pleads with Ashley. "You don't have to do what he says. How's this going to look on television?"

"It's going to look like we're winning," Ruddy says. Ashley stares at the ground.

Furious and ashamed, Kent grabs the pot handle. The burning metal sears his palms, but he twists it around until the soup dumps onto their fire, dousing the flame. Then the pain is too much. He turns and flees, knowing full well they'll just build another one.

He struggles to catch his breath as he runs through the jungle. He knows jerks like Ruddy, who are happiest when they're humiliating people. What really hurts are Kelly-Anne and Ashley. The two women wouldn't look at him, like they somehow weren't part of Ruddy's cruelty. Isn't Kent still a person they know? He's at the border of the mangrove swamp when he finally can breathe. He wants to go back and slash their shelter to pieces but doesn't even have a tool to do it. His hands are aching and there's a red welt across his palms.

"Let's do a quick on-the-fly," Beck says from behind him, her camera raised, breathless from the sprint. He didn't even know she was there.

"So you can humiliate me even more?" he snaps.

"This is *my* fault?" Beck snaps back. "I'm trying to help. *I* don't want you to starve. But I'm starting to wonder if you're committed to failure."

Normally he assumes everything with the producers is manipulation, but Beck looks genuinely heated, and that combined with his disappointment and hunger overwhelm him. "I've barely eaten in days. I've got nothing left."

"Let's think," she says, softening. "You can't sneak into their camp again. They'll be guarding their tools. How do we get the supplies to come to you?"

He struggles to answer before realizing she's not asking him. She stares into the distance, and Kent considers that Beck really *is* helping, like actually working hard to come up with ideas to advance his position in the game, and whereas before her intensity frightened him, now he feels desperate for it, because he'll take anything.

Beck gasps and leans toward him with an expression of excitement and daring. "Kent, how far would you say you're willing to go to take control of this game?"

AN HOUR LATER, KENT IS BACK AT CAMP, IN THE WATER SCRUBBING his face clean. The others ask what happened, but he only says that the problem should be solved. "When can we cook the fish?" Barb asks. "Soon," he says, and dips his aching hands into the sea.

When the Deserters arrive, holding up the pot and the blades and the tarp like peace offerings, Kent keeps soaking his palms while the rest of the group runs to greet them.

"We have returned," Ruddy announces from the margin of the trees. "Our water supply got poisoned, and apparently this is the only other viable camp on the whole damn island. So here we are. A family reunion. How beautiful."

"Poisoned?" Miriam asks.

"There were these little green fruits in our water source," Kelly-Anne says. "Our cameraman saw them and freaked out."

"Were they furred?" Miriam asks. "The size of my fist?"

"Don't act all innocent," Ruddy says, but he seems oddly blasé. "You guys are playing harder than I thought."

"I don't know anything about little green fruit," Barb says. "But just 'cause you're here doesn't mean we have to let you stay."

"Talk to the bosses." Ruddy gestures at the producers, who merely give tight-lipped nods.

Kent walks up the beach to join the group but can't stand the looks everyone is passing him. They all know it was him. So why is nobody mad? "I'll go clean these fish," he says, taking the small knife from the pot that Kelly-Anne's carrying. "Before they rot." He carries the stainless steel platter down the shore. The ice is fully melted, only a tepid film keeping the fish cool. Beck gets in close as he runs the small knife against their bright blue bodies, the thin scales flicking into the sand.

Miriam comes and crouches beside him. "You *poisoned* them?"

He can't bear to look at her. "I didn't poison anybody. Beck said she'd let production know—"

"No talk about production."

"I . . . figured they would catch it before anybody got hurt. Which is what happened." It pains his heart that she's judging him, but part of him craves it, because he knows he deserves it.

"But what if somebody took a drink before . . . they realized not to?"

"They didn't. And they've been starving us. They smothered our fire. Why does the line stop with me?" He knows he's merely making the counterpoints, saying words he doesn't believe. "They do the most awful things and tell themselves it's only a game."

"Like we did to Barb."

"That was different. That *was* the game." He slices open a fish belly and angrily scoops out the guts with a swipe of his finger.

When they return from the beach, Ashley's built a fire. Ruddy is leaning against the shelter, looking over their camp with an air of casual possession that enrages Kent, but what can he do? This is what he wanted. They spear the fish on sticks and set them to roast. The flames flare up, charring the yellow fins to black. The contestants reach into the steaming bellies, the hot flesh searing their eager fingertips. "Have you dosed these fish too?" Ruddy asks, and then it's moans and sighs as all seven of them marinate in the flavor of the fire-roasted fish, and in that blissful haze they're not competitors or enemies. They're merely desperate hungry people.

"I think I'm going to come," Kelly-Anne says, pulling a fish bone through her teeth.

"Why was Carl acting so bizarre?" Barb asks.

The Deserters exchange glances.

"I guess he wasn't as tough as everyone thought. Anybody else want the heads?" Ruddy pops the eyeballs out of their sockets and grins like a ghoul.

Kent looks at Miriam. She's not looking at him at all.

The shelter was designed for four people, and there are seven of them, so when it's time to sleep, they're crowded tight. The blankets and pillows feel luxuriously soft against the hard shelter beams. "Hey there, handsome, remember me?" Ashley asks, cuddling next to him. She's flirty all of a sudden, the giggly girl from the Alabama event. Didn't she stare at her feet this morning when he begged for help? Isn't she bothered that he *poisoned* them? "Kent, you're so warm. You're like my own special furnace." He has the guilty feeling he used to have in his hookup days when girls would talk dirty or strike porno poses, like he was being performed for in a way that neither of them really wanted.

"What really happened with Carl?" he asks her. "He seemed crazy."

"Oh god, it's been so hard. Ruddy—tortured him. Trying to get him to quit. Out of—meanness, I guess. Ruddy would spin these stories about his kids at home. Every awful thing—drowning, kidnapping. Carl—he's crazy about those girls. In the shelter at night, you know how your mind gets going. Two weeks of that and an hour in that box—well, you saw."

Carl sucks, Kent thinks, but nobody deserves that. "Was Kelly-Anne in on it?"

"She was at first, but I think even she got weirded out. She and Carl are friends. And it was intense. I think she got worried about her . . . brand. The worst was that Erika, our producer, was egging him on. God, Kent. I'm sorry about all this. I couldn't go against Ruddy. That group had everything, and—I *need* to win. But I'm here now. That was a brilliant move with the poison fruit."

His eyes flick to the camera recording in its tripod. This *is* a performance. Yesterday she was probably telling Ruddy that he was brilliant. Now Kent has power, he's shown he's willing to go the furthest, so he's in control. Reality games are all theater, especially for the younger players who grew up watching them. Poisoning their water supply was merely another tactic. And if she believes it, why can't he? It *was* a brilliant move. He did what he had to. Now Ashley the bombshell is grabbing him tight. Plus now that he has food in him, he can hunt the boar that he knows is waiting for him. He'll be the provider, not the poisoner.

"Oh—" Ashley says. "Am I in your spot?"

Miriam is standing at the foot of the shelter. "No, no. I can squeeze in."

She lies down next to Ashley, on the shelter's edge. The group is packed so close that the seven of them can only lie spooned together, overlapping like fish scales, and if one person turns, the rest must turn too. Through the long night, sometimes Kent is spooning Ashley, who's spooning Miriam, and other times they flip so Miriam is the big spoon. She'll come around, Kent thinks. Maybe he should share the Mydayis with her. But what if she looks down on that too? Or worse, what if production overhears? He reaches his hand across Ashley's body, so that his fingertips rest on the outline of Miriam's ribs through her lab coat. *I'm still here for you*, he hopes his fingertips can say. On the next rotation, when they flip again, her fingertips reach out to him and tap along his rib cage to let him know that she's there for him too.

CHAPTER 28

BECK

DAY 15

Filming on the same beach as Erika was less awkward than I'd feared. We were professionals, and we were busy, as the contestants ran off in groups of two or three to strategize and plot. Kelly-Anne and Ashley kept going into the jungle whispering. Ruddy deputized Bartolo as his new chief ally, and Bartolo strutted into camp puffed up with authority. Kent had taken the spear and was spending hours in the jungle looking for his imagined boar. Poor Ralph the PA trailed him, complaining over the radio about the mosquitoes. Barb was glad to have a pot. She wanted a laundry day, and in the late morning she insisted everyone strip to their skivvies and boiled a stew of filthy rags, then wrung out the sopping clothes and set them on branches to dry. With the contestants wearing only their underwear, you could see the bulges of their mike packs and the thin wires that ran from their lav necklaces. But this was a cable reality show. The audience got it.

"Look at Kelly-Anne," Erika said. She was standing next to me, in the shade of a palm, shaking her head. "She *stares* at Ashley. Such a try-hard."

For a second I wasn't sure if she was talking to me, muttering to herself, or giving directions to her cameraman.

"Get close on Bartolo. You see how he clasps his hands behind his back and sticks out his chest? God, check out that mustache on Barb. She looks like Tom Selleck. Hello? Maybe consider personal grooming before going on national TV?"

"You're like a poet of failure," I said. "Isn't there enough story here without a close-up on Barb's lip hairs?"

"This is what worries me about you." She flexed her head to the side like she was trying to work a crick out of her neck. "The lip hairs are *everything.* Tarzan hunting? Zero interesting. An alliance between Bartolo and Ruddy? A little interesting. But get Kelly-Anne laughing about Barb's mustache, and boom."

"What is it with you people and 'boom'?"

"*Boom.* Conflict."

"I'm familiar with conflict. I've done my share of feuding housewife shows. But they're in the *jungle.* Lip hairs feel . . . trivial?"

"It's *because* they're in the jungle that it's hilarious. They're starving to death and still shitting on each other."

I'd known producers like Erika. The work of reality television hardens them. They see so many people suffering so many grand emotions, so many wife swaps and kitchen nightmares, that they become inured to the whole human thing. Their compassion short-circuits, like an oncologist breezing through the cancer ward. They still had wonderfully deep sensitivities, but only for themselves. I refused to let that happen to me. "Maybe I'm naive, but I think we can show them as more than insults and zingers. They're fascinating, complex–"

"Jesus, it's not *Hamlet.* It's *Escape!* With an exclamation point. You think Bartolo has hidden depths, good luck finding them. Although with all this poisoning, maybe it is *Hamlet.*"

I thought I heard a note of jealousy. "Are you mad you didn't come up with the idea?" When I'd brought up the poisoning at our staff meeting, I was sure Jacob and Erika passed each other a look. I felt like one of them was saying *I told you so* to the other, but I couldn't tell who was saying it to whom. Everything now seemed like it might be part of the "plan," and I was never sure if I was going along with it or fighting against it.

"It *is* good drama," Erika admitted. "But I should remind you that our goal here isn't to kill the contestants."

Friedman and Afa were expressionless behind their sunglasses, but I knew they were silently snickering. *Where's Miriam,* I wondered. *I should help her.* She wasn't by the pot, and she wasn't hunting with Kent. I walked away to find her, giving Erika space to be toxic and miserable.

She was on all fours scrounging around the trees, wearing only her underwear, which was streaked brown and black with dirt. The elastic waistband sagged around her small gut. I *was* an empathetic person, I thought, as I raised my handheld and started filming, bearing witness to her humiliation.

"What's going on?" I asked.

"I can't find my pants." She looked up and, seeing my camera, covered her crotch. "Do you have to tape this?"

"It's what you signed up for." It came out more aggressively than I intended, but I knew what Erika could do with this footage. Take this fifteen-second clip and set it to stripper music, the audience in on the joke. "You—lost your pants?"

"I wouldn't say I *lost* them." She turned so I was only getting her profile. "They—disappeared. I hung them here after we did laundry. And now—I think Ruddy hid them. I think he's trying to sabotage me like he got Carl."

"Did you confront him?"

"What's the point? He denies it, and I look even dumber."

"How do you feel right now?"

"Not great. I'm definitely going to suffer without pants. But—I'll find them."

This had to be Erika's doing.

"You're not going to quit, Miriam. Say it with me."

"I'm not going to quit," she said. But I could hear the spike of anxiety in her voice.

"Say it to the camera. Tell the world you're not going to quit."

"No, seriously. I'm not going to quit. I survived that box. I can survive this."

Regardless of her words, there was something else—a smell. All the contestants reeked of sweat and smoke and charred fish. But Miriam had a unique tang. Of panic. Of failure.

And throughout that afternoon, as I filmed the contestants, I saw Ruddy tormenting her.

"Miriam, is that a cut? It kind of looks infected. Have you seen your back? It's covered with—they're like little red boils. I wonder if it's staph. Hey, everyone, look at Miriam's back."

And later:

"God, where's your pants? You must be freezing. That breeze off the water is brutal. My teeth are chattering, and I've got a sweater."

I had to save her.

"WHY ARE *YOU* INTERVIEWING ME?" RUDDY ASKED AS I PULLED OUT my notebook. We had him climb into the crook of a tangled tree, which I thought might suggest the contortions of his nefarious mind. "It's usually Erika."

"I wanted to get to know you. You seem to be at the center of the action."

"That's the goal." Ruddy leaned against the trunk. The weeks of starvation had sharpened his doughy cheeks and spotted him with peach fuzz. He looked like a purebred dog that had turned mangy and wild. "This show is small potatoes. Cable wilderness. How many viewers are you thinking? A couple mil? But if I pop? Maybe my next show is network. Or better yet, get a spot on *The Challenge* and spend the next decade in rotation on MTV."

Normally I had no patience for this type of posturing. My default mode was to dig deeper. Why did he *like* being cruel? Because his father hadn't loved him? But right now, I needed to save Miriam. And also, I had the thought, maybe Erika was right. This wasn't *Hamlet.* Maybe I was delusional and self-aggrandizing to think every subject had hidden depths that only I could uncover. Maybe the very idea of depths, of an "authentic self," was merely another story, buried under layers of stories. Surf-dogging Dave—even what I'd believed was his trauma, that desperate need for success displaced onto Buster, felt like a storyline I'd seen on every episode of *Dance Moms* and *Toddlers & Tiaras*.

Maybe, I thought, the problem was that society had simply exhausted the concept of hidden depths. There were so many TV shows, so many reality series across infinite streaming networks, so much *content*, each narrative delving into secret traumas, that every human complication had become cliché. We were all palimpsests of platitudes. At least Ruddy was hustling up and down the beach, giving us memes and clippable moments. And while I hated his attack on Miriam, still he had a buoyancy, the verve that made movies about Wall Street bloodsuckers so gripping, that they were being creative and Machiavellian as they hornswoggled Grandma out of her retirement account. All the fascination and the terror of a predator that kills for sport.

Maybe the best I could do was give one complex person the arc they deserved. And the rest was footage.

"You're going to be a huge character. The villain of the season. But wouldn't you say it's bad TV to harass Miriam? It's no great achievement to get the out-of-place nerd to quit."

"That's what I said at first. But it's establishing a pattern. Let's say I work on Ashley. She's tough. That could take weeks. But if I get Miriam out, right after Carl—then I've got a storyline."

That's what I said at first. To whom? He had to be repeating Erika's words. He was a kid. The first thing he'd said on the beach was *This is so cool.*

"I totally see your point. But wouldn't you say that networks want *fun* villains? Carl was an All Star. Taking him out is epic. But wouldn't you say nobody likes the guy who picks on the frail girl?"

"She's not that frail. She just won a challenge."

"Only because you did a number on Carl first."

"Fine. Yes." He sounded annoyed, like a petulant teen. "I would say that nobody likes the guy who picks on the frail girl. But who should I go for instead?"

I hadn't thought this through. I'd only planned to redirect him away from Miriam, not serve up someone else. "Who do you think you should go for?"

"What about ol' Barty? That could be funny."

If I got Bartolo to quit, Jacob would never forgive me. "What about—" My stomach dropped. "Barb?"

"I thought nobody likes the villain who picks on the girl?"

"Would you really call Barb a 'girl'? Wouldn't you say Barb's bossy and annoying?" I thought of the tough older woman who came on this adventure to find peace after a life-shattering trauma. To Jacob and Erika, she was the battle-ax knocking down the alpha male. Two sides to the butterfly. But the executive producer only saw one of them. "Viewers will be sick of her. If you manage to get Barb to quit . . ."

"But Barb's tough."

Exactly, I thought. She wouldn't let a twerp like Ruddy bully her. "Sure, Barb's tough on the outside. But haven't you ever felt like there's something inside her that's a little–fragile?"

Ruddy shook his head. "How do you mean?"

"Come on, Ruddy. You're a smart guy. Wouldn't you say her big act has to hide something dark? What was it that took Carl out?"

"The buried alive challenge?"

I couldn't believe I was going to have to spell this out.

"Have you asked her about her family?" I hated myself, yet when his eyes finally lit up with understanding, I felt the familiar thrill of hooking my fish. "Does Barb have any kids?"

CHAPTER 29

That evening was overcast with a low drizzle. The contestants sat close to the fire, trying to stay warm while they waited for this to pass like the other tropical showers. The crew put on our ponchos. Mario covered the camera with its plastic sleeve and blew a gust of compressed air from a canister to clean the lens.

"Catch anything?" Barb asked Kent, as he trudged out of the jungle with his spear.

"Oh Jesus, here we go," Kent said. "Can't I sit down?" Following Miriam's challenge win and the poisoning, he'd spent hours and hours in the jungle looking for his boar, and he looked ragged with exhaustion.

"Don't you take the Lord's name in vain," Barb said. "You need to give up on this hunting thing. Go fishing with that spear."

"You're great at giving orders. You want fish so bad, you get some."

"Maybe I could if you'd ever leave the spear."

"The spear's right there. Take it."

"Not now. It's late," Barb said, faltering. "And raining."

"It's dusk. Fish bite just as well at dusk as they do at dawn. *Espe-*

cially when it's raining." Kent paused for a beat. "I bet you're first in line for ribs when I catch my pig."

"*When* you catch a pig?" Barb laughed. "There's no pigs on this island! Or maybe there are, and they've all outsmarted you!"

"Come on, guys," Miriam said. "You're both–"

The jungle flashed white. Thunder exploded. Kent huffed off to the woodpile and tossed another log onto the fire. But the pace of the rain intensified, too quick to be believed. First there was nothing. Then–a deluge, like somebody upstairs had turned on a tap. The sky was dark and boiling. The contestants moved closer to the flames. The water pounded down. Kent and Ruddy tossed log after log onto the fire. Smoke flooded out of the wet wood as it struggled to catch. Then–the flames roared into a bonfire. Rain pounded against my poncho's thin plastic. I craved the hot ache of that fire. They were standing so close, the smoke must have singed their eyes and burned their throats. Their fingertips must have throbbed from the heat. The sky lit up again. "One, one thousand–two, one thousand," Ashley counted. The sky boomed. The blaze defied the storm. It licked upward in a ragged pillar of red and blue, and the sand flashed silver around them. Steam rose off the contestants' soaked clothes, ascending into the sky in a fine mist. But soon the fire consumed itself. It guttered and spat, and the sky kept pouring down.

The contestants ran to the shelter. It was rain like I'd never seen before, biblical rain that blotted out the stars and churned the earth into mud. The crew struggled to keep the camera lenses clear, to catch a few moments of footage before the shot was impossibly blurred. Water poured through the eaves and onto the contestants' faces. Miriam was curled into her lab coat, still not wearing any pants. *Please don't quit*, I prayed.

"How good would a pizza taste right about now?" Ruddy asked.

None of the others responded. The game wasn't fun right then.

"What are your favorite toppings?"

Silence.

"Mine are green peppers. And sausage. But you know what I'm craving right now? A peanut butter cookie dough chocolate cake pizza. How weird is that?" He was twisting the subtle knife of their misery. My tongue curled around my mouth with taste memories from home. Tandoori chicken. Pad Thai. Chocolate cake.

"What about you?" Ruddy turned to Barb.

"My favorite pizza?" Her teeth were chattering, and she could barely get the words out.

"We don't know *anything* about you," Ruddy said. "Tell us about yourself."

"Now's not the time."

"Am I wrong? She never shares anything."

The rest of the group picked up the thread, happy to have something to focus on that wasn't their suffering. What did they know about Barb? She loved the music of Hall & Oates, and her favorite movie was *Love Actually*. There was something sad about her, some deep wound that she carried inside like a clenched fist.

"Come on," Ruddy said. "What's your deal? Do you have any kids?"

"Friedman, get close on Barb's face," I radioed. *"Afa, give her a haircut."* Afa lowered his boom above her head. Water ran off the microphone's fuzz into her hair.

"Get that thing off me." Barb pushed away the furred bulb. Afa moved it right back.

"Why don't you talk about your kids?" Ruddy asked. "Are they druggies in jail?"

The only sound was the rain against our ponchos. My heart was racing.

"I had—a son," Barb said at last, in a tiny voice. "He died."

"Oh my god," Miriam said.

"Is she crying?" Erika asked. *"I can't tell if she's crying with all this fucking rain."*

"Of course she's crying, you sociopath."

Cancer, Barb explained. Last year. One day he was a beautiful twelve-year-old boy with thick dark hair and a serious expression. The next day there was a golf ball–size lump in his right leg. Her throat was thick with grief. The doctor thought it was a hematoma, a clogged blood vessel. They stuck a syringe inside his calf and tried to drain it. The doctor was wrong. She started to cry. "Let the rain come, Lord. Wash me clean!"

"Oh god," Miriam said. "I—didn't know." She tried to put her arm around Barb, who swatted it away.

"Day twelve—that's why I wanted off this rock on day twelve. For *David*," she shouted at Miriam. "And you stole that from me!"

"I didn't know," Miriam whispered so quietly I could barely hear it in my earpiece. "You didn't have a key."

Kelly-Anne and Ashley reached across the shelter to put their hands on Barb's back, but the squall turned sideways, and rain blew horizontally through the shelter front, drenching them and sending them huddling back into themselves. Barb was weeping. "David. David. David."

"Barb, that's so sad," Ruddy said. "So awful. Tell us more about David."

"He loved to play baseball. He was shortstop."

"An athlete," Bartolo said. "Like myself."

"What else?" Ruddy was smiling.

"He had a—guitar. Damn, he was terrible at that guitar. I'd sit outside his room to listen. Nothing better in my life than hearing that awful twang and his out-of-tune hollering. Oh, David."

Ashley and Miriam were crying too, maybe in sympathy, or maybe because Barb's outpouring triggered all their built-up misery and fatigue.

"Let it all out," Ruddy said.

"Do you have to film this?" Miriam shouted at us. "Can't you give her privacy?"

"*You* don't get to say which part of my story they film!" Barb shouted back. "Oh David, my David!"

We stood there filming until it was too much—the cameras were too drenched, all the footage was a blur anyway, and so after reminding the contestants to radio us in case of an emergency, we hunched into our ponchos and ran down the path to our vans, cranked the heat, and inched along the churned-up mud paths back to the City.

THE NEXT MORNING, THE STORM HAD SLACKED TO A DRIZZLE. THE sand was churned into mud, and the fronds of the crooked palm were ruffled and disarrayed like a rain-stripped pigeon. When our production team arrived, the contestants were staggering from the shelter, puffy-eyed and sunken-cheeked, their sodden clothes clinging to their emaciated bodies.

Ruddy took Barb on a walk down the beach. They gathered coconuts that had been tossed free from the palms. Erika's camera crew followed close. When Barb returned, her arms were filled with coconuts, and a decision had hardened in her eyes.

"I can't do this anymore," she told the group.

"What do you mean?" Miriam asked. The contestants were shivering around the firepit, where Kent struggled to conjure a spark from the soaked wood.

"What do you think that means? I'm done. Vamoose. I'm quitting."

I could imagine the poison that Ruddy had been dripping in

Barb's ear. I thought Barb might distract him for weeks. She would be tough. Ruddy would exhaust himself against her obstinacy. I never imagined it would be so immediate, that as soon as her grief surfaced it would overwhelm her. The storm, I thought. It was the storm's fault.

"What have you been saying to her?" Miriam demanded.

Everyone looked up in surprise. She never spoke so ferociously.

"I've been telling her the truth," Ruddy said. "There's no shame in quitting if she needs to go. We support her."

"This is the guy who harassed Carl out of the game," Miriam said. "Don't give up. We had one bad night. The sun's already coming out."

Barb shook her head. Her eyes were bloodshot, and her cheeks hung slack around her jaw. She'd aged a decade in a night.

"Please," Miriam pleaded. "Try to stay. For—David."

"How *dare* you say his name," Barb snapped. "Don't *you* tell me what's good for David!"

"That's right." Ruddy draped an arm over her shoulders. "Do what you think is best."

"I'm going to grab Barb for a quick on-the-fly," I radioed. Contestants often had low moments after terrible weather. I could provide her support. I could convince her not to quit.

"No need. I already got her," Erika said. *"Very emotional. Powerful stuff. I've also called base camp. The boat's on its way."*

I flashed red with rage.

A few minutes later, the Zodiac sped across the water. Jacob was standing in its bow. The group hugged Barb goodbye, but when Miriam approached, Barb turned her back and walked into the shallows, where she climbed over the side of the boat and into Jacob's waiting blanket. I could see the little smile that Ruddy passed Erika. Then he looked at me and gave me a wink.

I couldn't bear to look at Barb's departing form, so I recorded instead the contestants' wet-eyed gazes as they watched the Zodiac recede. I zoomed in on Miriam. She looked stunned, angry, and ashamed. Exactly like I felt.

"That's it," Miriam said. "We have to get off this island."

The other contestants looked at her in confusion. For weeks we'd been shutting them down when they mentioned escaping. If they couldn't talk about it, they couldn't think about it.

"Let's all build a raft and go together. Right now. The six of us. I've got a key. We make a statement that we're better than this lying, scheming, backstabbing game. We win as one."

"There's only three hundred and twenty thousand dollars in the pot," Kelly-Anne said. "That's just–fifty thousand dollars each."

"If we all go, we're guaranteed money," Miriam said. "Are you sure you'll get anything if you stay?"

They stared at her, with furtive glances at the production team.

"Didn't you apply for this lying, scheming, backstabbing game?" Ruddy asked.

"I didn't apply for *that*. Torturing a woman over her lost son."

"I wasn't the one who destroyed that poor woman's raft."

"I'm about to fix that," Miriam said. "I'm leaving this island, and I'm giving my share to Barb." She picked up the hatchet from where it rested against the shelter and walked down the beach. She kept adjusting her grip, switching the tool from one hand to the other. Down the shore, four skinny palms leaned toward the sea, like watchers looking out across the horizon. Miriam approached the thinnest one. She gripped the hatchet awkwardly with both hands, heaved it back, and swung into the bark. Her stroke nicked the wood and shuddered up her arm. She swung the hatchet again.

No, I thought. This wasn't how I wanted her story to end. In a pointless grand gesture one third of the way through the game. Leaving me alone to focus on—who? I had to pull Miriam for an interview, to remind her of her growth arc. But I couldn't interrupt story, especially not with the whole crew watching.

Her second stroke missed the mark entirely, notching the palm a few inches above the first. Every swing went wide, until she'd scored the tree with a zigzag of disconnected cuts. Her grip was slacking. *Thank god*, I thought, and I let myself pity her.

Still she swung again, harder.

Then Kent walked down the beach with a grim, determined look. He took the hatchet in one hand and with a single stroke, he cut a deep groove. His next swipe hit the same score. Every chop found its mark. Soon he'd cut a wide furrow. He gestured for Miriam to join him, and together they leaned into the trunk and pushed. The tree gave around the groove and collapsed with a crack.

The other contestants stood speechless, like they were watching the violation of an ancient taboo. Miriam and Kent dragged the trunk down the beach toward camp.

"Well if my cuddle buddy's going, I'm in too," Ashley said. She picked up the machete and joined them, hacking off the tree's smaller limbs around its fronds.

Kelly-Anne glanced at Ruddy. "This could be a big TV moment."

"Go. Please," Ruddy said. "You're doing my work for me."

"Come *on*," Kelly-Anne urged. "If we all go, the game's done. They'll have no choice but to turn our sixteen days into a full season."

"Or if I stay, you guys share half a season, and I get the rest. With my good friend Dr. Bartolo here. For as long as he lasts."

"You're going to live alone with Bartolo for a month?" Kelly-Anne asked. "You'll starve."

"There will be difficulties," Ruddy admitted. "But I imagine we'll get rewards."

"Do you even know how to make fire?" Kelly-Anne said. "You're going to *freeze*."

Ruddy looked nervously at Bartolo. "You can make fire, right?"

"I have great expertise in all manner of woodcraft."

"Or build a raft?" Kelly-Anne asked.

"I am an expert seaman," Bartolo assured them.

"Oh hell." Ruddy sighed and went to join the builders, while Kent ran down the beach to chop another tree.

Bartolo stood alone, watching the others work until the pressure of not sharing his expertise became too much, and he trotted over to Ashley to offer minute, exasperating instructions.

And that was it. All of them—on the verge of escaping—on day sixteen. The exact scenario Jacob had warned me to avoid. I imagined him in the Zodiac with Barb, listening to the shit show unfolding on the radio. It seemed too late to stop them, but I had to try.

"Get what you can," I radioed my team. *"I'm going to grab interviews."*

"Don't you want to wait fifty days for the full prize?" I asked Kent.

"I couldn't watch Miriam struggle by herself. I had to help."

I sensed weakness. He realized he'd look like a jerk if he let her flounder. But that didn't mean he wanted to leave.

"You did the noble thing. But are you sure you're ready to go? Right when it seems like you're about to get that boar—"

He glanced to the jungle and back down the beach, where the contestants were hard at work. "I—think I should. I almost hit Ruddy. I *poisoned* them. This is a good end for me. I make a raft. I get out. I win."

I couldn't waste any more time. I let him go and pulled Miriam.

"Wouldn't you say this is dangerous with all those sharks in the water? Can you be sure this raft will even stay afloat?"

"How did Ruddy know to ask about Barb's son?" She looked me right in the eyes.

But she couldn't possibly blame me. She had to understand that I was protecting her.

"It was Erika, wasn't it?" she asked.

"Yes," I whispered. "It was Erika."

"I have to get away from that evil." I stopped the interview so we could both get back to the beach.

It was shocking how quickly it happened when they all worked together, how simply the final hurdle of this challenge could be surmounted. The contestants dragged their exhausted bodies up the shore, and slowly, with palm trunks and driftwood secured by the cordage Miriam had won, pieced together a rudimentary raft.

The show was about to end. And it was all my fault.

CHAPTER 30

DAY 17

The next morning, as the contestants ran down the beach, dragging their raft through the sand and into the surf, whooping with glee, I had the anxious sinking feeling like when I watched the videotape of my mom—like time was churning forward too quickly and I needed to press pause.

Miriam pulled from the front. When the water reached her hips, she heaved herself onto the beams. If only I could rewind back to my interview with Ruddy, who was now flutter-kicking forward with Kent until water sloshed over the raft's sides. They climbed onto the planks and took the oars. Stop myself from saying a damn thing about Barb. I saw the black-tipped dorsal fin of a small reef shark. Ralph's drone zipped overhead.

Jacob had come down to the beach, and he stood between me and Erika as we filmed. He was wearing a cowboy hat, and the morning drizzle speckled his sunglasses. He watched with his hands on his hips, bouncing up and down on the balls of his feet, the overfilled pockets of his cargo pants jangling against his legs, a white smear of zinc oxide down the center of his nose. Friedman was in the ocean in the yellow Zodiac, his heavy camera pressed against his shoulder, bobbing on the tide. Erika's cameraman, Aleister, a former war videographer with a hangdog look and the perpetual stink of too many cigarettes, had set up his tripod in the sand. Jacob fed the crew directions in a low murmur.

"Aleister—get me twos and threes. Friedman, you're on close-ups. Get everybody. We don't know what we'll need. I want hope. I want giddy staring into the distance. And, Ralph, wide shots. Beck and Erika—pick up what you can. Backward glances, last parting looks."

I'd expected Jacob to be furious when I radioed him about the escape plan, but he sounded elated. *"It's about time we had some action!"* I assumed he was being artificially upbeat, not wanting to show concern on the shared production channel, and that evening, as soon as I got back to the City, I sprinted out of the van, up the hotel stairs, and into the production office. He was sitting at a computer, staring at an Excel spreadsheet, and he took off his reading glasses and rubbed his eyes with a look of startled amusement as I rattled off the afternoon's events. I expected him to leap out of his chair and bark orders to head back to camp at once, where we'd talk the contestants in circles. But he was as enthusiastic in person as he'd been over the radio.

"You're not worried this could end the show?" I asked.

"We *want* people breaking open the format. That's the only way viewers will tune in. It's not going to be easy to make it three miles in these currents. How good is that raft? And with six people on board?"

I was certain he was wrong. Three miles was too far to swim in the island's rough currents, but the six contestants working together would reach the islet, and that would be it. We'd have seventeen days of footage to craft a season of content. I knew we could eke out enough drama from the strategy, feuds, and betrayals. An episode on the first day. Another about the desertion. Barb's quit. I'd done more with less. But this wasn't the story I wanted for Miriam. She was supposed to thrive within the show, not to be so disgusted by her experience that she engineered a total shutdown. At least she'd make it to Treasure Island. Her key would unlock the chest. Technically, that was a win. Meanwhile, I'd return home with a solid credit and the drama from Buster behind me. If that was how this tale ended, I could live with that.

I zoomed in on Miriam through my camera's viewfinder. She was seated at the raft's center, squinting as she gazed at the island behind her, and I wondered what she was thinking as she watched it recede—the crooked palm, the lean-to that had been her home, the flooded firepit. To a stranger, it was a heap of branches on a deserted beach, but to her—the crucible where she started to find herself. Was she regretting that she never "touched something real," like she told Kent she wanted on their reward? Or was she simply happy to be part of the escape? She was a frustrating blank, half a story.

I was zooming in on her further, to the point where her features started to blur, when Kelly-Anne shrieked. I swiveled my camera, but my depth of field was off. It was all a pink smear. The contestants' voices came back across the water, pitched and intense.

"Friedman!" Jacob shouted. *"Get Ashley and Kelly-Anne."*

I zoomed out. The girls were flat on their bellies. The beams were drifting apart. They were spread-eagling their arms, struggling to hold the raft together.

Then, like a bottle rocket, one of the logs shot from its lashings. Miriam, straddling the raft's center, dropped into the water with a splash. The ensuing catastrophe was, let's be honest, hilarious. The logs went caroming in every direction. The contestants tottered, arms pinwheeling, then tipped and plunged into the ocean. I was so relieved I started laughing. Jacob had been right. Kelly-Anne shrieked again before face-planting into the waves. Kent dove in and dog-paddled furiously to avoid the freewheeling beams. I could practically hear the antic music in the audio. Then Erika cackled beside me, and I was struck with the very real danger—of sharks, of drowning. I counted off the contestants to make sure they were safe. Ashley was holding on to a beam to stay above the chop. Ruddy had his arms hooked over a plank and was splashing to shore. I could make out most of them. But where was Miriam? I hadn't seen her since she fell.

"Do you see Miriam?" I asked Jacob.

"She's out there somewhere?"

"Anybody see Miriam?" I radioed, but the channel was a cacophony.

"I've got Kelly-Anne," Aleister said. *"In tears."*

"Ashley took a head-first tumble."

"Ralph—get that drone on Bartolo!" Jacob shouted. *"He's like a little rat shivering on that log."*

"Ralph to the rescue!" Ralph called out, as the drone buzzed over the scene.

"Guys—please—can anybody see Miriam?"

My panic spiked. I was back at Huntington Beach, watching catastrophe unfold. There was a shark in the water, for god's sake. People assumed things would work out. Nobody realized disaster could strike at any moment—until it did. And then you were cursed forever. If I'd learned one thing, it was not to hesitate.

I kicked off my shoes and stripped out of my pants.

"Beck?" Jacob said, beside me.

"Not again." I ran into the water.

At first, I didn't notice the cold. I was high on adrenaline, and I swam out strongly. I had a vision of the crew gathering around me to celebrate as I hauled Miriam out of the ocean—alive, but barely. This time the CPR would work. From dog killer to human saver. Redeemed. But the contestants were farther out than I realized. Swells splashed over my head. My eyes stung. I had to keep going—if I was struggling, imagine Miriam, after weeks of starvation. I pistoned my legs to keep my head above the waves. The raft's mangled beams were pulsing toward me and receding, surging in and then pulling back on the tide. A wave was massing. I took short gasps. Friedman was leaning off the Zodiac, filming Bartolo's terrified face as he kept slipping off a log. "Beck, get the fuck out of my shot!" he shouted. I was treading water, counting them–Kent, Kelly-Anne, Ashley. . . . I kept getting four or five or nine. The only thing I was sure of was that I couldn't see Miriam.

I dove. In the murk it was a chaos of limbs and wood. There. The tangled strands of hair, floating at the center of the logs. At best she was unconscious. At worst–I couldn't bear it. I heaved myself over one log and slid under another. A swell caught a beam and bumped it into my head. My temple throbbed. Her limbs were limp, and her face barely broke the surface. I grabbed her torso. She flailed in my arms. A classic sign of drowning. But thank god. Alive.

"I've got you!" I said.

"I'm fine!" Her voice was–strong?

"You're drowning! You weren't breathing." It had to be true.

"I went limp! Like you're supposed to."

The volume on the entire planet muted. The only sound I could hear was a ringing in my ears, and below that a throb, somewhere deep inside my eyeball. The motion of the world slowed to a crawl: the logs surging and receding, the flailing contestants, the remorseless waves, and Miriam's shocked and confused face, all moved in glacial slo-mo. Back on the beach, everyone was staring. The cameras were filming the contestants, but the crew's attention was fixed on me. I wanted to dive beneath the surface and be dragged into the deep. I hadn't merely interrupted the shot. I'd crossed the line. Jacob had chastised me when I wiped sunscreen off Miriam's shoulder. Now I'd gone crashing straight through the fourth wall and onto the show itself.

My clothes were dripping as I came out of the water. Erika gaped.

Speechless at last, I thought grimly. I walked to Jacob. "Tell me I'm fired."

He wrapped his arms around me and pulled me into a hug. "I totally get it." He didn't flinch from the sopping mess of my body as he squeezed me into himself. "You've had a traumatic experience. You were trying to do the right thing." I buried my face in his shirt and was immersed in the detergent tang of the City's industrial laundry soap, which right then smelled like the freshest, most life-affirming scent in the world. "Was this terrible decision-making? Of course. But you know that." He held me tight, and the rest of the crew snapped back into action while the contestants struggled to shore, and I was submerged in my shame, in my enormous gratitude that Miriam was still alive, and in my vicious, selfish wish, like the sharp pang of an insect bite on my eyelid, that she'd actually been dying.

THAT EVENING, I STOOD PAINFULLY IN LINE WITH THE PAs and camera teams waiting to shower, trying to stare straight ahead and ignore the smirks and side-eyes. I felt ashamed even of my white plastic shower caddy, like the travel toothpaste and tiny translucent vial of shampoo secretly revealed my own pathetic smallness.

The three so-called shower stalls were concrete boxes with metal nozzles and the accumulated debris from a staff of thirty filthy people. Clumps of hair; green, brown, and white shards of soap; and strips of mud fringed the lower walls. Turning on the tap summoned a weak stream of tepid water that churned up a chemical froth of shampoos and conditioners, and every time I showered I silently thanked god for the invention of flip-flops. Now as I scrubbed the dirt out of my fingernails and muscled the tangles from my hair, I wondered if I should fly home—make my own escape from the staff's mocking stares and my terrible judgment. But what would I be flying back to? The end of my career? Maybe that would be for the best. Get this madwoman away from these poor contestants.

Erika was standing outside in her robe when I emerged. "Didn't you just have a bath?"

I ignored her.

"You'll appreciate this." She pulled out her phone. "A PA pulled it together."

It was a video mash-up of my dive into the water, set to the Miley Cyrus hit "Wrecking Ball." *"I came in like a wrecking ball . . ."* Miley sang, as I flopped through the water and grabbed a struggling Miriam by the waist. My arms were pale and my shirt clung to my midsection. I imagined the crew, clustered around a monitor, laughing as they made their choice cuts. I thought of Jacob's hug and tried to use the phantom pressure from his arms to tamp down the tears that I could already feel behind my eyes.

Then Friedman came running up. "Beck, we have to go. There's an emergency at camp."

"Hilarious." I wheeled on him. "Is someone drowning?"

But he insisted the contestants were in danger—real danger. A van was idling outside. Callahan was waiting, but they needed a producer. Erika said she was next in line to shower so it was on me. Still suspecting that we'd pull up to camp and the entire crew and all the contestants would burst out of the jungle laughing and pointing, I grabbed clothes from my cabin and ran toward the van outside.

CHAPTER 31
MIRIAM

NIGHT 17

The bitter night wind lashes her soaked clothes. She can't stop shivering. Kent has coaxed the smallest of smoky flames from what little dried wood they could gather, and they huddle around the sad fire, which gives off a flicker of light but no heat, a tiny candle in the engulfing darkness. It's the most physically miserable Miriam's ever been, and the fact that it's all in service of a reality show makes it worse—like the inane final product undermines the scope of her real suffering. Ashley sits with her head between her knees. Kelly-Anne threads a long cord between her hands, and every few minutes she squints at it like she's trying to read the future in its braids. Miriam's feet are swollen and purple. Her legs are dotted with itchy red bites. A crimson line of irritation borders the seam of her underwear. Her teeth are furry from two weeks without a toothbrush. All those discomforts, however, are trivial compared to the hunger, which gnaws at her with such relentlessness that she woke up that morning horny because she'd dreamed of a cupcake. Yet far, far worse even than the hunger, dwarfing it like one of those zoom-out videos that reveal the scale of a grain of sand compared to the solar system, is the weight of abject failure. The broken-down pieces of their raft wash along the dark beach, the shattered wreckage of her plan, and Miriam writhes in agony. It's all her fault.

She's always been her most remorseless critic. As a child, in the warm linoleum-lined cottage in Bemidji, she wielded self-criticism like her superpower. She thoroughly believed that through her intolerance of her own laziness, her refusal to leave belongings scattered around her bedroom, her nonstop drilling of her homework—*Stupid, Miriam, that's not how polynomials work*—she could burnish herself into a flawless gem. Her parents were dazzled by her, but frustratingly, they seemed to love her regardless of how she acted. To be loved unconditionally—it was what everyone craved, right? But having it, she yearned for its opposite. If she was loved simply because of who she was, rather than who she willed herself to be, that meant all her work was meaningless. On rare occasions, she would act out—the time when she was sixteen and drank half a vodka bottle, refilling it with water, or the afternoon she stole a wad of cash from her father's wallet and left it lying on her dresser—attempts to show them the child they might have had, if not for her. But she was invariably met with the same infuriating patience and understanding.

Her parents were in their fifties when she was born. They'd given up on children. Her name meant "wished-for child," her mother told her (although when she later researched it, she discovered the name's primary meanings were "sea of bitterness" and "rebellion"). Her father would sing to her at night and stroke her back. *Miri, Miri, give me your answer do, I'm half-crazy all for the love of you.* His voice was already hoarse with age. Miriam's most vivid memory of her mother is bent over her rosebushes, her curly gray hair matted with sweat, trimming the leaves with rusted shears. She was nineteen when her parents died, within two weeks of each other.

In her most bitter moments, lying in the dark on the Murphy bed of her tiny New York studio, she lashes out at their memories. It's because of *them* that she's so desperate for external validation, *their fault* that she's such an easy mark for every con man and Svengali—all because they provided her with so much unwavering support and failed to give her the guideposts to discover her self-worth. Then she twists and turns with guilt for the sin of condemning her dead parents for being too kind. At other times, she considers her gullibility a form of eternal optimism—her irrational belief that every soul-sucking career move could be the one that fulfills her, that each snake oil salesman's potions might cure her ache.

She daydreamed for years about embarking on an adventure—a journey into the unknown to uncover her true self. But the question was, What sort of adventure should she take? Where was her true self residing? She'd seen way too many photos on her social feeds from prepackaged adventures: colorful spices in market stalls, men posing next to tigers. So many men, so many tigers. And it was obviously problematic to use a foreign culture as an exotic playground for self-discovery. But what was the alternative? Stride into the wilderness with a hatchet and a Bic? She'd seen enough movies to know those crazies starved to death (*Into the Wild*) or were eaten by bears (*Grizzly Man*). She wanted to get outside herself, have a metaphorical rebirth—not literally die. So when Callie the casting agent approached her in line at a Starbucks, she was intrigued by the prospect of a jungle experience that also featured a network's medical chopper ready to whisk you to safety if you severed a tendon.

As she boarded the plane at LAX, it still seemed like an abstract idea. She would venture into the jungle on *reality television*. She would starve and suffer. She'd have deep life epiphanies on a show designed to strip its contestants to their cores. A tropical monsoon would scour away the bullshit of the past ten years, leaving her gleaming and streak-free like a plate plucked from the dishwasher.

Instead, here she is, freezing, soaked, bug-bitten, and, most of all, beset by herself. She moves her numb fingers closer to the tiny flame, and they prickle in the heat, which kindles a momentary whim to throw herself on the fire and be completely warm for a few blessed instants as she self-immolates. But what would happen instead, she thinks, is she'd smother the fire and wind up with a face-ful of ash, with her castmates even more furious at her. Her jaw is chattering. Her socks are waterlogged. Both oars and most of their rope are lost at sea. The challenge of how to escape, which before seemed like only a question of timing, has become potentially insurmountable. There's a chance they will fail. She thought that being buried alive would be her transformational moment. But she'll never transform, will she? She will be stuck as herself for all eternity.

"This is my fault," she whispers to Kent.

"Don't say that," Kent says. "We all made the raft together."

"But it was my idea."

"And it was a great idea. I promise you—this is not your fault."

"I don't believe you. And either way—this sucks."

"Didn't you want to touch something real? Embrace the suck."

He gets up to tend the fire.

Kent's probably right, that suffering is what she came to find. But what could you take home from that? That shivering in misery is ennobling?

Her thoughts turn to Beck. It was Beck who warned her it was too soon to escape. While the other producers stood on the sidelines, Beck leaped into the waves to save her—even if she didn't actually need saving. She watched Beck on the shore afterward, saw the looks from her colleagues. Beck risked her own professional standing for *her*. What if her whole life, all she needed was a Beck—or Beck herself—to guide her, help her, shape her? Even Kent. If Beck hadn't guided her to him, they wouldn't have found each other. She feels warmer merely watching him pacing the fire, shielding it from the wind, dipping to blow it patiently to life. Maybe *he's* what she takes home from this experience, she concludes, with a silly teenage rush.

Though not with Ashley now spooning him in the night. *It's only a question of sleeping arrangements. Ashley happened to take my spot is all.* But Miriam knows that's not true. She's seen how close they spoon. How can dowdy, awkward Miriam possibly measure up against a bombshell? Miriam's treks with Kent, their strategy sessions, their late-night cuddles–his dick jolting against her–are yesterday's storyline. She wishes she'd never said anything about the stupid poisoning. Kent was right. It worked. She just didn't *want* the Deserters at her camp. Didn't want Erika smirking down the beach. She should have told him how much he means to her, the way she feels, and now this brief flicker of possibility is slipping through her fingers because she lacks the courage to speak up.

"Look at this." Kelly-Anne breaks her reverie, holding up the rope she's been scrutinizing. "I got it off one of the logs." Polyps of kelp dangle from the tangled cord.

"Congratulations?" Ruddy says.

"Look at it, dummy. It's split into pieces."

"Okay?"

"Somebody cut it."

The accusation takes a moment to register.

"You're saying–"

"Sabotage?"

"That's dark, man," Ruddy says. "I get that it's a game, but we're all in this together. We're all out here, struggling, building fires, gathering food, keeping each other warm. I honestly thought we were doing something beautiful, rowing out together. I won't accept that any of us is capable of that level of betrayal."

"Okay, that's the most guilty-sounding speech I've heard in my life," Kelly-Anne says. "But I'm not accusing you. It had to be production."

The others stare at her. In the daytime, they're not allowed to mention the producers without getting shushed, and a sense of the subject's sacredness bleeds over into the dark, when the night vision cams relay everything back to HQ. Miriam can still feel the pressure of Erika's hand on her back as she shoved her off the boat. She hasn't spoken of the incident, partially because she's still ashamed, and because she has the vague sense that to raise the issue could invite an even greater retribution, in the same way she clenches whenever she hears a stranger blaspheme God.

But destroying their raft seems a step too far. There's a network behind this show, which is owned by a multinational corporation. The lawyers would never allow it.

"You're being paranoid," Kent says. "How can you be sure a person destroyed that rope? It could have been the rocks or a reef or something."

"Look at the cuts," Kelly-Anne says. "They're clean."

"Perhaps the waves pulled it apart," Bartolo says.

"Waves with knives? Think about it," Kelly-Anne insists. "They don't want us leaving yet. Haven't you noticed that we can't even hint at leaving during our interviews without them shutting us down? Answer me this: Did the producers pull any of you and tell you not to do it?"

The others murmur their assent, leaning closer into the fire. But Beck was *right*, Miriam thinks. The raft *wasn't* ready.

"If our raft was sabotaged, someone sitting at this campfire did it," Miriam says. "Could it be the guy who stole my pants and got Carl and Barb to quit?"

"Interesting accusation from one of the two people with a proven history of boat destruction," Ruddy says.

"Yes, I destroyed Barb's raft, and I feel like shit about it," Miriam says. "I would never do that again."

"'Your Honor, I may have done it once, but my boat-destroying days are over!' A perfect defense. Case dismissed."

"Barb was planning on escaping *by herself,*" Kent says. "She was going to steal over two hundred thousand dollars from the rest of us. And I was the one who talked Miriam into it."

"Plot twist!" Ruddy says. "The guilty party reveals himself."

"I for sure considered Ruddy," Kelly-Anne says, ignoring their back-and-forth. "If it was anyone, my guess would be the asshole who—"

"Asshole? Excuse me? What *happened* to you?" Ruddy says. "You used to be fun. Aren't you supposed to be the villain?"

"Sure, the villain, in the game. Not torturing people."

"Oh please. Showing concern about a friend's departed child is torture?" Ruddy says. "It goes waterboarding, ripping off fingernails, polite conversation. Spare me. We all know what happened. You got scared that looking like a *real* villain would hurt your mindfulness seminars. That's why you jumped at the idea of a kumbaya moment. Now you're what, some kind of raft vigilante?"

"I refuse to bicker over this. It literally couldn't have been you. I was sleeping next to you last night. I don't believe it was any of— Oh!" Kelly-Anne cries out. A length uncoils, bands of yellow against black. Kelly-Anne grips her hand. "Oh no."

Kent leaps to his feet. The machete is in his hand. The snake twists into a figure eight in the dirt, its scales vivid in the firelight. Everyone is backing away, except Kent, who moves closer.

"Oh no," Kelly-Anne says again. She lifts her hand into the firelight. Two red pinpricks score her palm. She turns to Bartolo. "You're a doctor. Can you—"

"I'm not that kind of doctor," Bartolo says.

"You're *some* kind of doctor."

"I'm not *that* kind of doctor!" he shouts.

"What kind of doctor are you?"

"I'm a doctor of dance!" He draws himself up majestically.

"There's two supposed doctors and no actual fucking doctors?!" Kelly-Anne says, her voice pitching higher.

Kent edges even closer to the snake to prod it with the toe of his boot. The snake tenses. Ashley fumbles with the buttons of the emergency walkie-talkie.

"Hello! Is anybody there? We have an—"

"Give me that!" Bartolo snatches the walkie from her trembling hand. *"Emergency! Emergencia! Snake. Kelly-Anne was bit by a snake. El viper!"*

"Wait," a groggy voice says over the radio. A few moments later a man's voice echoes tinnily over the line.

"Snake? What does the fucker look like?"

"What does it look like?" Bartolo repeats.

"It's pitch-black," Kent shouts back. "Tell him it's striped."

"We're on our way." The radio clicks off.

"Ask them what we should do for her in the meantime," Miriam says, but the radio is silent, and Bartolo's attempts to raise a signal go unanswered. Beads of spit ball at the corners of Kelly-Anne's mouth. She stands up, paces, sits down again, then stands up.

"How do you treat a snakebite?" Ruddy asks. "Do you elevate the arm? I think you elevate the arm."

"Stay calm," Miriam says. "The doctor's coming."

"Should I cauterize the wound?" Bartolo asks.

"Nobody is cauterizing anything!" Kelly-Anne shouts, her eyes wide.

Kent circles the snake with the machete. It uncoils and starts to slither away. He lunges, grabbing it by the tail. *What are you doing?*

Miriam thinks. It's both the bravest and most insane thing she's ever seen. The creature slithers along the length of its body, taut as a flexed muscle. Kent swings the machete at its head. It dodges. Recoiling, it strikes back, but Kent uses the flat of the blade to hurl it toward the fire. The snake shrinks from the hot ash, and Kent stamps his boot on its neck.

"Get it, Miriam!" Ashley shouts.

"Get it?" Miriam asks. "I'm not getting anywhere near–"

"Get it!" Ashley says. "With the spear!"

Miriam looks down at her hand, surprised to find that she has somehow picked up the spear. "I don't know–"

"Stab its head!"

Miriam grasps the spear with both hands and thrusts downward at a thick band right beside Kent's boot. Her blood is pounding. She pushes hard into dense muscle. When she pulls the spear out, the tip is wet with red. For a brief, euphoric moment, all her self-doubt and critique are gone. Even the cold and hunger have shriveled to nothing, while her breath fills her lungs like a bellows and she is alive, afire with adrenaline. She screams and stabs the snake again, severing its head, and lifts the spear into the air and howls, like she's seen Kent howl. She chuckles awkwardly at the unnatural sound of her voice, the rush fades, leaking from her body into the puddled darkness, and she feels lightheaded and overwhelmed with a flood of guilt. For the first time in her life she's killed an animal bigger than an insect.

"Holy shit, Miriam!" Ashley says.

The dumb muscle of the snake's headless body continues to writhe in the sand. The tip of its tail thrashes against its severed head, whose jaws snap from instinct. Bayoneted by its own teeth, the frantic tail twists faster to escape, and the jaw clamps down tighter. The snake's furious eyes glare at them, two shards of glass cut from the darkness, until its body slackens.

A production van crashes through the foliage. Friedman jumps out from behind the wheel, and Callahan the show doctor charges out the passenger door, a syringe clutched between his teeth. He shoves Miriam aside and grabs Kelly-Anne's hand.

"Hurry," Beck says, as Friedman sets up his camera. "Okay, Callahan. Tell me what's happening."

Callahan is crouched over Kelly-Anne, the camera's red light glowing along his bald spot. "Kelly-Anne here's been bitten by a snake, and I'm examining the wound. Small puncture in her palm." He holds her hand up to the light. "We need the antivenin fast or Kelly-Anne might not make it."

"Excuse me?" Kelly-Anne says.

"Don't worry," Callahan whispers. "Adding a little color for the cameras. Did anybody catch a good look at the monster?"

"Can you please give me the injection?"

"We need to make sure it's the right antivenin," Callahan says. "Try not to get your blood pressure up. Stress makes the venom work faster."

"Oh god," Kelly-Anne says.

Kent approaches with the snake's limp body.

"You killed the bloody thing? Good work."

"Miriam killed him," Kent says. "I held it down for her."

"Good on you both," Callahan says. "That's a banded krait. One of the region's deadliest monsters. Lucky for Kelly-Anne here, I'm holding the antivenin." Callahan chortles while he stabs the syringe into the lid of the jar. "Thanks to Friedman my old pal for making sure we're fully stocked. Dunno how he knew. My understanding was these snakes nest far from–"

"I'd seen a few when we were location scouting," Friedman says.

"Lucky you did." Callahan rips open an alcohol swab and wipes Kelly-Anne's skin. "This might hurt, but it'll be less painful than getting your hand amputated." He plunges the syringe, and Kelly-Anne winces.

"I hope you're left-handed," he says.

"I'm not." Kelly-Anne is holding back tears. "How can I work without a hand?"

"This is nothing. I once treated a man in Burma whose leg was half-digested by a python. Today he's an accomplished marathon runner. You might have heard of him, but, well, doctor-patient confidentiality. You'll be right as rain in a couple months." He stands back. "Unfortunately, I'm pulling you from the game."

"No," she says. "You *can't.* I can't go out like–"

"If you'd like that hand to heal, you need medical care," Callahan says.

"Please, no. I *need* the money. My stepdad–he lost his job, and the bills– He's given me everything, I need to–"

"It's not up for debate." Callahan leads Kelly-Anne by the elbow to the waiting van. She shuffles through the dirt with hiccupping sobs, cradling her wounded hand.

"Chin up," Callahan says. "We're recording."

"But I almost escaped," Kelly-Anne says. "I almost did it."

The shift happens like the flip of a switch, Miriam thinks. Minutes ago, Kelly-Anne was the savvy, sexy strategist picking apart production's lies. Now, hobbling up the beach, she looks tiny and frail, her clothes hanging from her emaciated frame like a child swaddled in her parent's pajamas.

"Doc!" Kent calls out. "Can we eat it?" He's holding the snake.

"Good for black magic, some say. I'd avoid. Your gut biomes are already pretty compromised."

Kent tosses the snake into the fire. Black tendrils of smoke curl into the air. The van's engine revs as the wheels struggle to gain purchase on the wet sand. Then the van lurches forward and disappears into the jungle.

"Good job," Kent says to Miriam. "You got him." There's a weird tone in his voice that almost sounds like longing.

That night in the shelter, Miriam itches all over from the spent adrenaline. God, how she wants Kent's arm around her, to quiet her body against his, but once again he's holding Ashley. There's more room in the shelter now that they're down to five, but the cold has them cuddling tight. The beams rattle beneath her as her limbs shake.

Maybe *this* is what you take from the jungle, she thinks. You learn what your body can withstand. That you can suffer, that you can be miserable, and starving, and freezing, and almost drown, and kill a snake, and somehow keep moving forward. Absorbing the time, second by second. Maybe what she touched wasn't part of the wilderness but a part of herself after all.

"That's kind of a coincidence, isn't it?" Ruddy says, from the other side of the shelter.

Nobody responds, until Ashley asks, "What do you mean?"

"Kelly-Anne was the one who figured production cut the ropes of the raft. And then a few minutes later . . ."

It's an absurd suspicion. To suggest that the production team has mastery over the wilderness, that they risked Kelly-Anne's life to silence her. More of Ruddy's bullshit. If anything, that paranoia is a fantasy of control. How comforting it would be if there were indeed a connection, if production could summon the beasts of the jungle to do their bidding. The fact is that any one of them could have been bitten by that snake, regardless of what they said or did or thought. They're at the mercy of an irrational universe.

But staring at the scattered and random stars, the absurd suspicions rattle in Miriam's head until, like the constellations above her, they start to take shape.

CHAPTER 32

BECK

DAY 18

When you think of the great medevacs in reality television history, you remember epic scenes of drama and spectacle. The guy on *Survivor* who collapsed from heat exhaustion after pushing himself beyond his limits. The busty *Real World / Road Rules Challenge* girl who tumbled into the water from an aerial obstacle course and burst a breast implant on impact. The three contestants on *Naked and Afraid XL* whose guts erupted when they ate poisonous fruit. An evacuation proves that a show is *really real.* It shocks viewers into a rapid sympathy with the precarious human lives on the other end of the camera.

On the other hand, a medevac cuts a character's story short. A reality show is structured to tell the narrative of why one contestant succeeds while another fails. You tease the arrogance or insecurity in episode one that causes a contestant's downfall in the finale. But how do you tell a story that ends in a moment of randomness? Evacuated contestants are edited into invisibility. Who would read about Captain Ahab if midway into his hunt for the white whale, he sprained his one good ankle and needed to be pulled from the page?

The next morning I had a brief moment of celebrity as everybody wanted to hear about Kelly-Anne's evacuation. Callahan had escorted her to Mud Town for a medical workup, which left me to tell the tale. Everyone seemed to agree that the whole diving-into-the-water thing was not to be mentioned, and was I delusional to hope that some even thought it was noble? At the very least, they could edit around me. Production assistants who'd been side-eyeing me in the shower line now listened rapt at the breakfast table about our race through the jungle. Jacob was giddy. After breakfast he pulled me into the production office to watch the night vision footage from the cams and gauge if we had any clean shots.

"Miriam the snake hunter," I marveled. "Who would have imagined?"

"You're going to *have* to imagine it, because right now it's grainy night cam footage."

I sighed. What did it matter if it happened, if it didn't happen in HD?

"This is a good reminder that anybody can get taken out by an act of God," Jacob said. "You should try to get a few more story beats on this Miriam–Kent thing, in case one of them gets hurt."

"'One of them'?" I arched an eyebrow.

"Well, if I *had* to place odds on the next person to get pulled, I might pick the girl in glasses who doesn't have pants. Give me the beats so far."

"Okay. It starts with a conflict. Episode one: Miriam loses the ferro rod. Kent has to make fire. Immediately one of them is the screwup, the other is the hero. Episode two? The conflict builds. Kent the hero sacrifices himself to stay on the beach, but he can't stand Miriam, and she's only starting to realize how much he saved her. But then—episode three. Kent wins the challenge and takes her on reward. They get close. They destroy Barb's raft. Episode four, Miriam puts herself up for elimination to save Kent—and wins. We edit out some of the sniping along the way, and by the time they watch their story back on television, they'll believe they grew from rivals to best friends. And maybe more."

"I love it," Jacob said. "All you need is a big capstone moment."

"Killing the snake together would've been perfect."

"Have you thought about the mountaintop?" he suggested.

"What mountaintop?"

"The top of the only mountain on this island."

"You can climb that?"

He shrugged. "It's there."

"How extremely male," I said. "I mean—is it safe?"

"Is life safe? It'll be challenging, but it's not Everest. And they've all signed releases."

"I suppose you also want someone filming them."

"You've signed a release too." Jacob smiled. "Don't jump off the edge and you'll be fine. We can ask someone else if you're not up for it." He rubbed the bridge of his nose and suddenly he seemed very tired. He caught me looking, smiled, and made a show of holding his eyes open with his fingers.

"Jacob—" I was going to finally say that if there was a secret plan, he could just tell me. But when he looked up and said, "Yes?" I felt overcome with embarrassment. What a nut I'd look like, admitting I'd followed him in the night. "I'm up for it. So Kent and Miriam climb a mountain and reach the literal pinnacle just as their relationship reaches its peak."

"You got it," Jacob said.

CHAPTER 33

KENT

DAY 18

Kent Duvall is face-first against the sandstone mountain feeling a bit too much like he's halfway through a simile. The sun's glare is in his eyes, his palms still hurt from where he seared them, and his shoulders throb with lactic burn. Yet somehow, step by step, he's pulling himself upward. Is climbing a mountain like being confronted with the weakness of every single joint all at once, or is climbing a mountain like the feeling of overcoming, surmounting, rising up up up in spite of your frail, decaying self? "Describe what you're feeling!" Beck shouts from a few ledges below as she records with her handheld.

"This is the hardest thing I've ever done!" he shouts back. The confessional could use a little color. "Climbing a mountain is like—the movie *Cliffhanger*! You're holding on for dear life, and one tiny slip can mean—!" He's unable to finish the sentence, but still, he thinks, the sudden silence will be a strong end to the byte.

"Miriam?" Beck asks.

"I'm tired, but this is fun!" she says from below, and she sounds like she really means it. That's your twenties for you.

"Isn't it amazing to do this together?" Beck asks. "Would you say you're so happy to be here with each other?"

Kent tries to picture the vantage from Beck's camera and can imagine only the bottoms of his shoes, a twist of his legs, and his foreshortened torso. "Yeah! I would say I'm so happy to be here with Miriam. If there's one person on this island I trust in a dangerous situation, it's Miriam." And as he watches her struggle up the mountain, sees the blotchy red exertion and her gritted look of intense concentration, he realizes it's true.

When Beck suggested the mountain that morning, Kent's immediate response was *fuck yeah.* Climbing a small mountain seemed both manly and achievable. The first few steps were broad flat boulders that circled up the mountainside like a spiral staircase, and he felt gripped by a sense of competency that he hasn't felt since he was in casting. *Climbing a mountain is like ticking your way down the Minnesota Multiphasic Personality Inventory.* He carefully pushed aside the tangled creepers that crowded in from the jungle. But the mountain face soon steepened, and the foliage thinned, and Kent now finds himself delicately planting his feet on dew-slicked stones, gripping for balance at the spindly roots of tiny white-and-purple flowers that sprout from the thin soil. The hike isn't tumble-to-your-death steep, but a bad footstep could still send him slipping down toward a broken limb, which would send him home. The worst part is that he has to be the one leading the way. Miriam and Beck are below him watching his path. Alas, he thinks self-pityingly, the plight of the alpha male.

Climbing a mountain is like asking a girl on a date. Climbing a mountain is like being the quarterback and calling a play. Climbing a mountain is like leading a charge into war.

He grabs a rock and shimmies up, and his vision suddenly blurs. His balance swings out and away, and he has a moment of intense vertigo before he forces his weight back against the rock. He barely slept last night, again. Every day he tells himself it's the last Mydayis, but every following day he needs it. To hunt. For the raft. To climb a mountain! At some point, Bartolo or the producers are going to notice, but it hasn't happened yet. The trade-off is that every night, his mind refuses to settle, and he circles the unfairness, that all down the shelter the rest of them are sighing and snuffling while he—Kent Duvall, who deserves sleep more than anybody—tosses and turns. Occasionally during those interminable hours, he wonders what Margaret is up to. Probably getting railed by a hot doctor. Oddly, it doesn't bother him. It's only been two and a half weeks, yet the only world he knows anymore is this one, and remembering the tiny dormer bedroom in their Providence apartment feels like he's communing with a long-disappeared past self, like a snake mourning its cast-off skin.

The snake. Last night, when he was finally at the border of sleep, the world hazy and the sounds of unreal people whispering in his ear, he plunged awake to the vision of the spear severing the snake head. He *hates* snakes. The thought of that writhing body makes his entire core convulse. But somehow when the banded krait was actually there, he felt like he was moving in a dream, stepping into destiny, puppeteered by his best self in a preordained dance between just them. So why was it Miriam who got the kill?

"Okay, kids. Another on-the-fly." Beck is flushed and panting, and Kent suspects that she's using these interviews as an excuse to rest. She once again unholsters her handheld camera and angles it upward. "How are you feeling?"

"I feel—alive!" he shouts down to the camera lens.

"Miriam?"

"I feel alive too! But in a really precarious, maybe-soon-I-won't-be-so-alive kind of way!"

He loves her nerdy humor, the way she makes herself the butt of the joke. With Margaret, he was the punch line. He likes everything about Miriam, he thinks, not for the first time. His foot stumbles on a loose rock, and he looks down. Amateur mistake. They're higher than he realized. The treetops fan out below them. If he trips and can't stop his slide—what should he do? Spread his arms wide and try to hit the maximum number of branches to slow his descent? Or curl up to protect his internal organs, hoping to shatter only his legs? Maybe he should spend those last few seconds of life without any strategy, searching instead to achieve a final instant of peace. The lines of the jungle below smear together, so that it becomes not many trees but one wide expanse of green, not many things but a single breathing entity, a desperate energy isolated on this island pumping out its ancient life.

But if he plummets he'll go whizzing past Beck's camera, so he'll need to put on one last brave face, shout "Wahoo!" as he rockets to his death, show the world that in his final seconds, the show pony was still a stud.

When he pulls himself over the lip of the rock, he feels dizzy with relief. The plateau spreads before him covered with grasses and clover and thousands of the small white-and-purple flowers. Clouds of blue butterflies dissolve at his approach and re-form in the distance, and he has the vague tickle of a wonderful memory from long ago, something with his mom. Miriam is grunting below him, and he reaches down to pull first her up and then Beck, and they all stand, gasping for air, gazing across the island.

The jungle rolls out like a sea to the thin line of beach where a trail of smoke marks their campfire. To the east there's the tiny outcropping of what must be production HQ. Beyond the island, the ocean expands like burnished steel, scored on its surface by the multicolored flecks of the tiny bobbing fishing scows, and far away at the edge of the horizon, he can just make out the ghostly hulks of container ships, weaving the world together in a web of global trade.

"What's that?" He points toward a deep knot of trees at the island's center. Even from up here, the mass of foliage looks swollen and black, tumorous.

"That must be the heart of the jungle," Beck says. "Jacob said to stay far away."

"The heart of the jungle," Kent repeats. After the stress of the climb, the breeze on his cheek and the breathtaking vista have his soul feeling expansive and free, and he spreads his arms wide to the view like he wants to give it even more space to come surging into him.

"Don't put any ideas into this guy's head," Miriam says.

Beck starts recording as they stand on the edge of the plateau, gazing out at their little world.

"You know," Kent says, "we could live out here forever."

Miriam chuckles. Her face is pale but flushed, and she's still panting hard.

"I'm not joking. Think about what Jacob said. The show doesn't end on day fifty. The money stops *adding*, but the show ends when someone with a key takes the final treasure. What if we leave that cash there and never sail away?" The idea takes shape in his mind as he says it. "We could make a life out here. All of us—well, the five of us left. There's still a little fruit. We could fish. There's *got* to be a pig. Maybe in that heart there."

"It's a beautiful dream," Miriam says.

"I'm serious." Is he serious? Stating it makes it sound real. He thought he was ready to go back—ready to end the show, take what he could, and return home. Save himself from his bad decisions. Stop the endless hours dragging himself into the jungle to hunt. But the night they built the raft, he was once again sleepless from the Mydayis, so he went down to test the rope lashings and make last-minute adjustments. The moon was dim behind the fog, and a chill mist settled on his neck. He was pulling one of the knots tighter, his arms straining against the cord, when suddenly he was overcome with total panic. The raft was solid. He could see them piloting it safely to the islet. Then getting on a plane home, the tiny prepacked airplane meal under a thin plastic wrapper like the pure sign and symbol of his entire life. All this grandeur—slipping away—and he was filled with such a fury that he took the machete and sliced one of the lashings. It was easy to sever the rope, much easier than tightening the bond. He cut another—then another. Not so many that the raft would instantly fall apart, he told himself. Not the total destruction he'd wreaked on Barb's raft. Only enough that there was a chance. He left it to the island gods. Now the gods have weighed in, and they want him here. Looking out across the jungle's multihued green, he sees depths and shades of pine and olive and moss he never imagined, and the shining silver sea stretches into the infinite. "They can't *make* us go back," he says in half a whisper.

"What's so bad about going back?" Miriam asks. "I miss my apartment. In particular, I miss my refrigerator."

"Yeah, but that's—just life. Normal life."

"You think I can stay here forever?" Miriam runs her hand along her torso. "I'm the nerd, remember?"

"You *were* the nerd. A couple more weeks and you'll be the mountain man. Mountain person." Of course *she's* fine going home. She killed a snake. She faced down Carl. What has he done? He made fire—almost three weeks ago. And otherwise, a failed camp raid. A poisoning. He *has* to stay longer, to feed his edit. "You know what I am back home? I'm not even a fake chemist. I'm a—bum. I barely work. When I was a kid I thought maybe I'd be a doctor or a lawyer, something . . . respectable. 'Try to be someone that matters in the world,' my dad always said. But that wasn't the person I turned out to be. Out here—we're living like we're *supposed* to live. Even Kelly-Anne's medevac. It's—the intensity. The emotion. It's . . . *more.*" Whereas real life is getting caught cheating in a drunken hotel fling by a Reddit post.

"Sure, but that only works if there's a medic to evacuate us. Production's not going to stay out here forever. What happens when the next season of *Escape!* films, and we're like—hello!"

The next season. He hasn't even thought about that—how there will be a next cast that will come onto these same beaches, and they'll make fire and find food and glory in their challenge victories. He feels like a punctured balloon, all the heroism leaking from him with a helium whine. Maybe *their* alpha male will find a pig. Maybe *he'll* have a showmance with the hot girl. God, how he prays they'll move the show to a different location, so at least the memories they're making on this beach will be theirs alone. Some series film on the same beaches every season, so that contestants walking down the sand come upon the very trees that their predecessors scored to mark their time in the game, and they see firsthand how they're only shadows, following their preset paces until they fade away to make room for the season that follows.

"I know it's a fantasy," he says. "But we have to try to be more, don't we? To do as much as we can, for as long as we can? Don't we at least have to try?"

He looks at her with a desperate, searching gaze, and she meets his stare with her kind fawn eyes and reaches out and slips her arm through his and squeezes his fingers.

"I hear you, I absolutely do. But—real life can be beautiful too, right? It doesn't all have to be epic. And I'm sort of excited to go home and see"—she looks uncomfortably back at the camera, bites her lip, takes a deep breath, turns to him, and grips both his hands—"what you and I have? Because I do think there's—this . . . connection. You've been sticking up for me since day one. More than anybody else ever has. But it's more than that. I guess I sort of—like you. A lot."

She stares at the ground, and her cheeks are bright with embarrassment, and he realizes with a heart pang that he knows every contour of her face, how her sharp smile lines turn down around her mouth to make her look more worried than she even is, and the way when she opens her mouth, she instinctively covers the gap between her front teeth with her tongue. She's wearing Barb's left-behind khaki pants, which are huge on her, tightened with a twist of rope, and her own filthy button-down shirt that was white once but is now ocher with dirt, and somehow her very awkwardness and dirtiness are the most beautiful things in the world, because they show how hard she's trying, and how somehow she keeps herself grounded and funny and *kind* even as much as she suffers. She glances quickly up at him and back down, waiting. His stomach is churning. Why can't he tell her he likes her too? Or—kiss her. It's the perfect moment, here on this mountaintop, before the whole world and the brilliant sky. Forget about his past self. Take another path. He only has to lean down a little and part his lips, and it can be his.

But Kent knows what will happen if he does that.

Because the Kent she's falling for out here isn't the Kent she'll find when they return home, when she sees him as he really is. A lump.

And that won't even be the worst part. He can live with being a disappointment. Lord knows he's done that with Margaret. But if they go back to real life together—*she* won't be herself on the other side, either. She won't be earnest, kind, hardworking, self-deprecating Miriam Bloom. She'll be Miriam the Chemist from *Escape!* She'll go to bar nights with *Big Brother* contestants and *Bachelor* suitors and check Reddit obsessively and pregame for *All Stars.* At least with someone like Ashley, you knew what you were signing up for. He thinks of Ashley flashing her boobs at the Alabama event, and cuddling theatrically close to him in the shelter. A relationship with Ashley would be transactional, both of them burnishing their little stars. But the thought of going home and trying to find comfortable, loving domesticity with Miriam, and instead she sees the truth of who he really is, while he has to watch all her earnestness get siphoned away, leaving a hollow like an empty mascot costume—he couldn't stand it. No. He knows he needs to cut it off with her decisively, to say or do something that will save them from each other, but he can't manage that either, and he stands there mutely furious at himself, feeling the silence of Beck's camera, the desperate pressure of dead airtime, and Miriam staring at the ground, her anticipation darkening to embarrassment, while overhead clouds blanket the blazing sun and a spurt of rain starts to drizzle on their heads, the weather changing again while he is relentlessly trapped inside himself.

"Okay," Miriam says as the rain begins to fall. "I guess not."

"We should find shelter," he says blandly.

They hurry silently to the far end of the plateau, where a grove of thick, ancient trees sprouts from the rock. It's drier here. The rain patters on the leaves. Deep in the grove, they come on the ruins of a stone hut, with a small doorway leading to a single room beyond.

"Holy wow," Kent whispers. The lintel is carved with smiling faces, their expressions eroded by the rain into a vague mystery.

"It looks like—an ancient temple," Miriam says.

The island gods. He can feel Beck zoom in on his face, overcome with awe, when he's hit with what feels like a small pebble.

"Ow," Miriam says.

"What the hell?" Beck rubs her brow.

Another small pebble hits and then another. He wipes his hand across his face and it comes away smeared and dirty.

"Oh god," Beck says. "Oh no."

High in the branches above them squat a crowd of small monkeys. They've been camouflaged in the foliage, but looking up now he can see their faces, shriveled like newborn children. They're pelting them with feces. They run for safety to the temple door. The air inside is stale and rank, but at least it's safe—but just as Kent's eyes adjust to the gloom, a giant macaque rears up from within the temple and screams, waving its arms, its face pink and its fangs brilliant white. They run out of the grove, back into the open air. The monkeys hurl their scat but don't follow.

"Can you believe that?" Kent asks. It's pouring outside now, the sky roiling with black thunderclouds. "A temple. This must be a holy mountain."

A freezing wind whips over the cliff top, and raindrops explode along the rocky plateau. They don't dare risk the climb down. Beck radios for help, but the signal is weak and staticky. *"Can't fly,"* the garbled voice from the radio shouts. *"Bad storm coming."* Below them, whitecaps thrash the shoreline, and in the fading light Kent watches one of the little fishing boats rise and fall on the swells, until a massive wave brushes it aside and it disappears from sight.

The three of them stand there, alone in the middle of the plateau, nowhere to go and the rain drenching them. Beck films. Miriam's whole jaw is wobbling. Kent tries to look stoic, but misery creases his face. A spear of lightning flashes, and seconds later the sky cracks.

"'Oh, baby, baby, how was I supposed to know?!'" Miriam screams into the storm.

Kent says nothing. She's still shouting, muffled by the thunder. His arms are curled around himself. His teeth are chattering. He is totally exposed, to the elements, to the monkeys, to the island gods.

"'Oh, baby, baby, I shouldn't have let you go!'" Miriam shrieks.

He can't help but laugh. She's screaming ". . . Baby One More

Time" by Britney Spears. He doesn't really know the words, but he joins in and shouts along in tune with the music. And as they cry out the song together, he's not focused on his misery.

"'My loneliness is killing me!'" she sings.

"Yeah yeah, lalala lalalalaaa!" he yells back.

"'When I'm not with you, I lose my mind!'" she cries.

"'Give me a *siiiign*!'" He finally knows a lyric.

"'Hit me, baby, one more time!!'" they scream into the darkness together.

The sky lights up, a thunderclap booms, and they stand there laughing, drenched and miserable, but laughing. And when they finally lie down on the hard earth for the interminably long night, Beck filming it all, they cling together—for body heat and, really, for each other. Maybe he has to end this, he knows, but for tonight he can hold her. He buries his head in her neck. She's crying, little sobs, and he squeezes her as tight as he possibly can, so that he's almost grateful for the rain and the misery and the cold, because for now, for tonight, they have this.

CHAPTER 34

BECK

NIGHT 18

The entire jungle was a massive orifice, dumping on me.

Shit from the gecko. Shit from the monkeys. And now the rain, shitting all over me.

But I had my shot. Kent and Miriam standing on the cliff together. Miriam saying "I really like you." Who cared if he didn't respond? Cut to the two of them on the ground, holding each other so tightly it was impossible to tell where one emaciated heap ended and the other began.

I stood above them filming for an eternity—two hours, four, I had no idea. I'd left my rain gear at base camp, and my clothes were drenched. My whole body was shivering. I could see almost to the mainland, and there was no break in the cloud line, just an angry gray bulging swath. The radio in my ear crackled and moaned. If there were ghosts, I thought, they'd be here. My eyes drifted shut and jerked open.

Looking through the camera provided a little relief. My viewfinder was streaked and blurry, but I could tell myself that this was all a story I was filming. I was barely here—merely an eye. Only a lens. My fingers were numb in the camera strap. Because I wasn't a body at all.

"You must be freezing," Miriam said.

"Get down here with us," Kent said.

"I can't. It's against the rules." My teeth chattered. I couldn't cross the line again. Jacob had been generous once, twice—but three times? I clenched and unclenched my hands, digging my fingernails into my palms, trying to get back sensation.

I can take anything for a minute. I'd heard about this tactic. Patients in recovery or addicts needing their fix would take their suffering one minute at a time. You endure for a minute. Then another minute. And another. Endure the pain of life a few seconds at a time. But I lost track of the seconds. Every time my eyes felt heavy and started to close, I saw the dark shapes of the monkeys massing at the edges of my vision. I was standing alone. They'd get me first.

My body was shaking.

I said a small apology, out loud, though I wasn't sure to whom. Jacob? Myself?

Then I gave up.

I lay down next to Kent. He reeked of sweat and campfire, but I pulled his body tight. "You can't do this," I muttered to myself. I lay there anyway, marinating in his heat, the three of us one tightly squeezed line of flesh, and for a moment I felt what I'd never felt before, the desperate intimacy of the contestants, the pure physical connection, almost bliss, and even though I was the far outside of the spoon, pushed against Kent's hard back, my hand gripped around his stomach, still I imagined what it must be like to be Miriam, wrapped in his arms, his heat pouring into me.

I DIDN'T REALIZE THAT I'D FALLEN ASLEEP UNTIL KENT WOKE ME. Dawn was edging over the mountaintop. Everything was sore. The cracks of blue light, the tiny morsels of warmth, felt holy, and the three of us stood and stretched to the sun. We did jumping jacks to get our stiff limbs moving. Our shadows blurred together on the ground, a three-headed, six-armed monster.

I pulled the contestants for an interview. I was a producer. This was all story. They sat on the edge of the plateau. Somehow they were laughing about the brutal night and how belting out Britney Spears made it bearable. They didn't mention liking each other or nearly kissing. I didn't push it. I had what I needed. I'd done what Jacob asked. I'd built a real relationship from this unlikely duo, and I had my capstone moment. I felt euphoric, closer to these two people than to anybody in my life—anybody since my mother died. They were *my* story. I was a good producer.

"Don't breathe a word about me sleeping next to you last night," I told them. "If anybody found out . . . Nobody will care how much it was raining."

"What was last night?" Miriam looked at me with mock innocence.

Climbing down the mountain, we were like wilderness explorers returning to civilization, exhausted but triumphant. The handholds that were precarious yesterday now were as obvious as a marked path. Kent hopped down swiftly, and even I felt sure-footed, lowering myself along the wet pink boulders and into the steam bath of the jungle. At the base, I radioed camp to let them know we were all right.

"I have incredible news," I said.

"*Tell me,*" Jacob demanded.

But I clicked off my radio. I was going to savor this.

When we could see the shelter, Kent bellowed his arrival. The other contestants ran over. Even Ruddy looked anxious with concern. Ashley gave Kent a huge hug. "I was so scared," she said. "It was raining so hard—and we had no idea—"

And then she kissed him.

He hesitated for a second, surprised, his hands on her waist neither holding her back nor pulling her close. And then he kissed her back.

It was a full-faced, tongue-mashing kiss, the kind of deep, kinetic lip-locking where the kissers' entire bodies are swept up while tiny cherubs serenade them on golden harps. They were kissing? Kent and *Ashley*? My vision narrowed like an iris wipe, when the screen fades inward to black except for a circle of light surrounding the two lovers. I looked over at Miriam, whose face was a muddle of confusion and hurt, and I realized that mine was too. Her jaw sagged open. I forced my mouth closed. Both cameramen, Friedman and Aleister, hurried to film close-ups. In Aleister's shot you'd see her: gazing rapturously up into his face. In Friedman's camera you'd see him: eyes closed, swept up in the moment. My brain felt cobwebbed. Somehow I'd missed something crucial. Ashley? And then, the deep sense of betrayal.

Erika sidled up to me. "Did you have a good night?" I knew how I looked. My clothes were covered in dirt. My face felt bruised and haggard.

"When did . . . this happen?" I was having trouble modulating my voice. I needed to sound curious and disinterested, not frantic and confused.

"I've been producing it for weeks."

"Why didn't . . . anybody tell me?" I asked.

"Tell you? This is literally what we pitched the network in the story bible."

"Of course. But it wasn't—happening. Nobody mentioned it in our meetings—"

"It's not my job to make sure you can see what's right in front of your eyes."

"Yes, it is," I said. "We're supposed to keep each other—"

"Read the hot sheets. It's all there."

"But Miriam and Kent. They—" I gestured vaguely toward the mountaintop.

"Did you have a good hiking trip? We'll probably use a few beats from your footage to set this up."

That was when the full significance of the kiss hit me. My footage. The entire relationship between Kent and Miriam. With only forty-two minutes of TV time a week, there would never be room for that story *and* a Kent–Ashley romance, along with the rest of the show—Barb's quit, Kelly-Anne's evacuation, Ruddy's betrayals. Who cared about two friends going hiking? Their entire relationship would be left on the cutting room floor. Worse, since it was all digital, there'd be no physical remnant at all. The memory cards would be deleted and reused. At best Miriam would be relegated to the awkward sidekick. Even her challenge win would be a blip. All my work irrelevant. Maybe they'd include the clip of her confessing herself to Kent, but only to emphasize how pathetic she was.

Exactly what Erika wanted all along. Maybe this had been Jacob's plan. Following the story bible almost verbatim.

Ashley. Why hadn't I been thinking of Ashley? Of course I knew this was what she'd been cast for. But Kent specifically told her he didn't want a showmance. And she was so—generic. I could have drawn *some* story out of her—her indomitable spirit in lighting the perfect selfie or whatever. But Erika had fixated on her at the beginning. Ashley was the girl Erika visualized as she stared with self-loathing in the mirror every morning. So I happily left them to each other while I focused on the *interesting* contestants.

Now Kent was kissing her?

I could still feel his body heat, could still smell the stink of his sweat on my clothes. Could still feel what I imagined Miriam felt, encircled in his arms. After everything I'd done for him. I hadn't even wanted to. I'd hated him at the start. My mind was numb with exhaustion, but I tried to think, my brain spiraling backward over the past weeks. Of course I knew they slept next to each other, but Kent had barely mentioned Ashley to me. Though had I ever asked?

When we got back to the City, I ran to my bungalow and read through Erika's hot sheets. *Ashley and Kent talked by the water at night. Ashley and Kent spooned.* The details were there, but drained of meaning. There was nothing in these notes that hinted at a budding romance. Had Erika been trying to mislead me? Or had I completely ignored what was right in front of my face?

I skipped dinner and sat in the production office, scrubbing through Erika's footage. I was surrounded by computers and cameras, neatly shelved batteries and a cubby filled with wires and chargers. Everything so organized, all the tools to record, log, and edit. So why did I feel wildly out of order?

IT STARTED WITH A SMALL PROMPT ON THE MORNING OF DAY TWO. Ashley was sitting on a rocky outcropping with the sea behind her. In person her eyes were a little too far apart, her cheekbones too pronounced. But the camera loved the way those sharp angles defined light and shadow.

"What do you think of Kent?" Erika's voice from off-screen. I could imagine her perched on a rock, the puckered mouth, the thirsty gaze.

Irritation flashed across Ashley's face. "I'm really out here to prove myself. I've been working out." She flexed her arm, and her biceps popped. "I've been sleeping outdoors. I've been practicing with—bugs."

"Didn't you already hook up with Kent? At some charity thing?"

"Those charity events are basically drunken orgies." Ashley forced a laugh. She was trying to keep it fun, but I could see she was struggling for her life.

"Wasn't it hot when he made fire?"

"I mean—yeah, it was quite literally hot." Another forced laugh.

"Isn't making fire sexy? You're a wilderness girl. Surely you appreciate that?"

"Yeah," Ashley said quietly. "I definitely— Look, it was great that Kent made fire."

"Without even a fire starter."

"Yeah."

"Give me something, Ashley. You don't have to *mean* it." Erika's voice turned sharp. "This is what you promised us. I don't want you to be an invisible nobody. Again."

"Okay," Ashley said in a small voice. "Kent is—I think he's—really hot."

It was too painful to watch. I fast-forwarded away.

A few days later, Ashley was at beta camp, hunched over her knees. This must have been right after the first challenge, because bruises pocked her legs. Somehow she was more beautiful after starving for a week, like scrubbing away the tonics and treatments that enable the rest of us to look presentable to the world let her inner radiance shine through. I hated her even more.

"Kent really aced it today, didn't he?" Erika asked. "You almost had it, though."

"I was close," Ashley said. "But close only counts in horseshoes and hand grenades."

"Too bad you ditched him. The two of you would be quite a duo. And maybe then he'd have taken you on reward. Wouldn't you say you wish you'd never left Kent behind?"

"I would say I wish—" She was wary, choosing her words carefully. "I wish I'd never left all of that back there."

She gave a quick, hopeful look up at the camera, like she might have gotten away with it. I could imagine the tight shake of Erika's head. I thought of Miriam, and trying to get her to say one negative thing about Barb. That was different. That was for *Miriam's* sake, not to force her into some twisted storyline against her will.

"And Kent," Ashley offered up, defeated. "I wish I'd never left Kent."

A week later: "Wow, so Kent poisoned your water source. Wouldn't you say he's really playing the game hard?"

"Kent's playing the game *so* hard." Ashley giggled. I hate to use that word, but that was the sound she made. I could imagine Erika nodding, encouraging her to lay it on thick. "Poisoning, wow, what a great move." She looked up eagerly, searching for Erika's approval.

"When you do rejoin that camp—do you think you and he could get together?"

Ashley dug her toes into the sand.

"It doesn't have to erase who you are," Erika said gently. "You're incredible, Ashley. You amaze me. But getting with Kent—that could be something that lets you be who you're meant to be. The two of you together. A super-duo."

"I just—I really don't want my story to be about being some old guy's girlfriend." One last gasp of resistance.

"Better that than a story about being nothing," Erika snapped.

Ashley nodded. "I . . . do think we'll get together. Maybe we'll spoon really tight in the shelter." She giggled again, a sound that was half a laugh and half a sigh.

The resistance was gone.

Last night, Ashley shivered with no arm to comfort her while the monsoon raged. She was crying, and was I crazy to think they were real tears? To think that, raw and exhausted, after weeks of manipulation, she really was scared for her lost lover, who'd disappeared into the storm?

The last footage wasn't logged yet, but I knew how the story ended. Their passionate kiss, captured from multiple angles by two cameramen and a half dozen GoPros.

I sat back in my chair. The gray screens of the monitors stared silently down at me. How had I been so blind? Of course Kent would choose Ashley. He was exactly the man I thought he was at the beginning, a sad, faded bro, hanging on to the hot chick. Still—how could he lie so close to Miriam in that storm and moments later betray her? I felt heartbroken for her, and also for myself.

What about *my* storyline?

I WAS WALKING OUT OF THE PRODUCTION OFFICE IN A DAZE WHEN I heard the blaring horns of Stevie Wonder's "Sir Duke" echoing down the City's hallways. I followed the sounds of the trumpets into the dining room and came on the entire crew drinking and chatting. I'd forgotten tonight was Friedman's birthday. The tables were pulled back along the walls, coolers filled with beer had been dragged from the kitchen, and Benjamin the pilot had gone into Mud Town to purchase bottles of hard alcohol, which now saluted on a sideboard like an ordered regiment of glass soldiers. Everybody was dressed in the one fancy outfit they'd crammed into their duffels. The men had slicked back their hair, and Erika had somehow found a blow-dryer. The music blared out of a Bluetooth speaker connected to someone's phone. I saw the birthday boy, in a white dress shirt that was stained at the pits, and I forced a quick smile and a wave before beelining to Jacob.

He was talking to a group of junior production personnel but turned toward me smiling as I approached. He was wearing a black dress shirt and black jeans and smelled of soap and citrus cologne, and I became intensely aware of how foul I was from my night on the mountain.

"We missed you at dinner," he said.

"Did you know about this—romance between Kent and Ashley?"

"Of course." I could smell the alcohol on his breath. "What an epic moment for the show."

"It's barely in Erika's hot sheets."

"Haven't we been talking about this since the start?" He seemed genuinely confused. "You look like you could use a drink." He put his hand on the small of my back and guided me to the liquor bottles. They were all cheap well brands that I hadn't seen since college, and he apologized—cable TV budgets—as he poured vodka and soda water into a red Solo cup. I had no choice but to accept it, but I wasn't ready to let the issue go.

"All that footage I have of Kent and Miriam is going to be useless." I took a sip. The antiseptic taste of cheap vodka flooded my mouth. He'd made it strong.

"We're only on day nineteen. Not even halfway. It's okay to follow a few side stories while we see what develops. There's plenty of time to get on board with Erika's story."

"So it *is* Erika's story."

"It's too early to say. You know that. You can only tell the story backward, after it's over. Beck, you're new to this crew. I want you to be able to follow your instincts, and you're doing a great job, but you can't expect to jump in and have the final cut."

I could feel my outrage slipping away, but I wanted—I needed—to hold on to it. "I just thought—" I said again, impotently, not sure what I thought. "I thought Kent and Miriam— There was something—" I took another drink, the alcohol already blurring the edges of my sleep-deprived brain.

"Beck." Something in the way he said my name made me shiver. His typical expression of enthusiasm and encouragement, like he would always be your number one cheerleader in your quest to become your best self, was gone, replaced with a ferocity. "I need this show to be epic. This is my comeback. This is *our* comeback. There are plenty of wilderness shows where you can watch people starve in the outdoors and fight off bugs. This has to be a *Jacob Malibu* show. That means star-crossed romance. That means betrayals and heartbreak. That means blood and guts."

"Blood and guts?"

"Well, metaphorical blood and guts. And honestly? I don't know what you're doing out there. Ashley and Kent—they were *cast* to be lovers. That's what the network wants. Ruddy is sabotaging everybody. We've got a teary exit and a nighttime medical emergency. And you're going—*hiking*?"

I blanched. "I thought there was a story there. This unlikely friendship. I thought you . . . liked the idea. The mountain. The literal peak and the— For some reason I thought you had actually—" I was exhausted and tipsy. I knew there was something wrong, but I couldn't articulate quite what. "Didn't you tell me to—"

"I definitely didn't tell you to do anything. That's not how I work with my team. Maybe I asked you a question about what you were thinking of doing. And you're right, maybe there is *a* story there. But is it a Jacob Malibu story? I know you're a great producer. Push harder. Where's the Beck Bermann who let a dog die for the perfect shot?"

I didn't know what to say. Jacob was right. There *was* such a thing as a Jacob Malibu reality show. *Extreme Pregnancy* and *America's Favorite Murderer* showed people in moments of desperation and danger. What was I doing, going hiking? Yesterday, the mountain seemed meaningful. And really, I thought he was the one who suggested it—but in my bleary state, it was hard to piece it together.

"We found something up there," I ventured. "An old temple."

"Oh, right! I hope you got that on tape. The Art Department really outdid themselves. If you got a good shot of Kent discovering that temple, that alone may make your trip worthwhile."

"I think I got a good shot. There are monkeys living there. They chased us off."

"Us?"

"The contestants. Them. Me too. It was terrifying."

"A monkey chase. I love it. See? That's gold. Maybe your footage *will* make it. I have so much faith in you, Beck."

He turned as one of the junior crew tapped him on the shoulder, and I walked away. Had I even filmed the monkeys? I was fairly certain I'd been too busy running in fear. I wandered at the fringes of the party, struggling to make conversation with whichever crew member happened to be nearby. The music stopped, and somebody restarted the playlist. At the other side of the bar, Friedman was slow dancing with the ponytailed PA, and I watched his hand wander from her mid-back downward until by the time the playlist restarted again he was firmly grabbing her butt. Afa approached Erika and extended his hand like he was asking a lady to dance at a ball. I felt that acute loneliness that you can only ever truly feel in large gatherings. The laughter of the crew, the smiles and jokes surrounding me. I patted my pocket for my phone, but it was lying lifeless in my bungalow. I had another drink. Then another. Maybe I had been getting complacent, trying to paper over my own failures with this naive little story about two friends.

I was sitting on a couch when Jacob sat beside me and handed me a red Solo cup.

"I thought you could use one of these."

My mind was swimming. I tried to think of something to say, failed, and took a sip. My lips puckered at the sour wine.

"This is terrible."

"Hey—that came from one of Mud Town's finest boxes."

Somehow the wry remark touched me, and my emotions gushed out. "I'm sorry. You're right. I can do better." I hoped I wasn't slurring my words.

"*I'm* sorry if I was harsh. I want you to know that I believe in you."

I shook my head and my eyes started to tear, and I realized I was very drunk.

"I should go," I said, supporting myself against the couch as I stood.

I stumbled out of the dining room and to the door of the hotel. It was pouring outside, again, the rain coming down in vertical sheets. I was preparing myself for the mad dash across the muddy ground when I became aware of Jacob standing behind me.

"Don't go out in this," he said. "You'll get soaked."

"I have to get back to my room somehow."

"Come to mine. Until the storm passes." I could smell the cheap gin on his breath. He was smiling that generous smile, like he really was merely offering me a roof over my head. *Until the storm passes.* Of course I knew what it meant to follow him upstairs. But to my drunken brain, the reasoning made sense. I kept repeating the phrase—*until the storm passes*—in my head as he took my hand, as he pulled me up the staircase, *until the storm passes* as he guided me down the concrete hallway and turned his key in the door, only stopping when he pushed me against the wall inside and started kissing me, and I couldn't stop kissing him back.

"This is a bad idea," I murmured, half hoping he'd stop and half hoping he wouldn't hear me. "I smell terrible."

I reeked of dirt and sweat, but Jacob sat me down on the bed, gently, and started kissing my neck. He unbuttoned my shirt and kissed his way along my rib cage, and I shivered at his lips against my skin. He unbuttoned my pants. Even as all the consequences of sleeping with him played out on the screen of my inner eyelids like a disaster reel—he was my boss, what would we say in the morning? would I just go back to writing hot sheets?—I also—I deserved this. This tiny moment of human connection. I had Jacob's full attention and all his approval. Especially after my fuckup. *Take that, Erika*, a small, bitter part of me thought. He was moving his head downward, his lips brushing my hip bone as he went between my legs.

I pushed him away. "No."

"No?"

"I haven't showered in two days."

"I don't mind," he said.

"Just—put a condom on."

"You want to have sex?" he asked.

"That's traditionally what a condom is for."

"I want to be sure you're okay with this. Can I have sex with you?"

"Oh my god. Shut up and do it."

To be honest, I wasn't even sure if it was good sex or merely sweaty. It was so hot, he lost hold of my ankle a few times. It was so hot, I almost surfed off his chest and straight into a wall. For a second, when he was behind me, I heard the sounds of the jungle screaming outside and I started crying out too.

Afterward, we lay side by side. I felt like I might drip off the bed into a puddle, but I nestled into him. For the first time since my helicopter landed on the island, I was safe: inside a concrete hotel, wrapped in Jacob's arm. I could feel myself sinking asleep.

"The network is concerned too," he said. "They need a hit."

"What?" I mumbled, barely awake.

He was sitting upright. "I don't want you to think this is only about my ego. The show's not intense enough. They want us to push the contestants harder."

"I still think there's something with Miriam," I said. "Give me another shot."

"Of course. It's not another shot. It's the same shot. I believe in you. Really. But remember. Blood and guts."

We stayed like that for a few minutes, Jacob running the tips of his fingers up and down my rib cage. My body ached from my night on the rocks, and it felt like if I lay there long enough he might stroke all that pain away. Again I started to drowse off to sleep.

"It's stopped raining."

"Mmm?"

"You can go back to your room, if you want."

I felt the taste of my breath in my mouth, the sickly sweetness of too much liquor. "Oh–right. Good."

"You don't have to. You can stay here. I was only thinking–in the morning that–the crew–"

"No. You're right. I should go."

My pants were crumpled in a ball. My shirt was draped over his chair. I staggered around the room, dressing, as he watched. I couldn't find my underwear. I decided to leave it.

"Thank you," he said. He kissed me on the forehead.

I wobbled down the stairs. Thank god the lobby was deserted. A few red plastic cups were scattered around the floor, and empty bottles were tipped over on the wood-veneer table. The night's trash. I stepped out of the hotel and stood under the reeling sky, struggling to breathe. My brain sprinted back and forth through the hotel's corridors. I'd made a terrible choice. It was so transparently dumb. Sleeping with your boss. And there was no way to undo it.

I heard a small sound at the end of the porch. An ember lit the tip of a cigarette. In the faint glow I saw pursed lips and sharp eyebrows.

"I guess I know how *you* got the job."

Erika's cigarette seethed like a tiny star.

"Have you been . . . *sitting* out here, *waiting* for me?"

She said nothing.

"It's not what you think," I said.

"It's not?" The sly mockery in her voice had a bitter edge. "If I had any doubts about you before—" She gestured with her cigarette toward the hotel door. "It's *exactly* what I think."

She was right. Every nasty judgment was totally correct. I ran off the hotel porch and across the sand. The dark jungle fizzed with chattering insects. I slammed into my bungalow. There was a rustling in the rafters.

I was bleary-eyed from exhaustion; from drunkenness; from tears. But I blinked away the blurriness, and for the first time, I saw her. She was crouched, almost vertical, on one of the cabin's main posts—massive, a foot and a half long, the pads under her claws clinging to the wood. Her skin was brilliant aquamarine mottled with tangerine speckles. Her mouth was purple. The animal screamed poison. She was beautiful, and she was terrifying, and in my sleep-sodden, half-drunk misery, I felt a strange kinship. We were both toxic, hiding. I'd spent so many nights imagining and dreading the gecko that seeing her made me instantly sober, and I realized with a brilliant clarity how exhausted I was from feeling out of control. I'd been allowing myself to slip passively from bad decision to bad decision. For the past two and a half weeks, I'd been struggling with a sweet little fantasy and ignoring the dark and wild world around me.

"No more," I said out loud to the gecko, and I had a sudden vision of how I could salvage Miriam's storyline. No more stupid friendship stuff. No more cute hiking trips or splashing in the stream. I could see the sketchy outline. Miriam would surpass Kent and take his role. *She* would be the hunter. Kent would go mad with jealousy. She would take center stage. *I* would take center stage. The gecko darted up the post and disappeared back into the rafters.

Blood and guts Jacob asked for. Blood and guts he would receive.

ACT THREE
BLOOD AND GUTS

CHAPTER 35

BECK

DAY 20

The pig looked more like a house pet than a wild animal. It was the length of a medium-sized dog and was covered in brown hair with mottled black patches. The tip of its nose was bright pink and tender, and it had a marking beneath its eye that looked like George Washington's profile from the quarter.

Its dark, black eyes were alive with intelligence and terror.

"Couldn't you get something—I don't know—less adorable?" I said.

"Less adorable?" Million asked. His high forehead dripped with sweat.

"This thing looks like it belongs in children's movies. Nobody wants to watch the hunt for Pig Bambi."

My crew and I were in a small clearing by the mangrove swamp. I thought the clustered trees and mucky ground would be the perfect backdrop. Moody, bleak. In the shifting gloom, the twisted roots looked like fossilized ancient eels that had thrashed ashore from a primal sea. The pig shivered in its wire cage. As I approached, it started to scream.

"Okay, okay." I backed away. My head was throbbing. I'd skipped breakfast and stayed inside my bungalow with a bleary hangover that felt like tiny monkeys were throwing their shit grenades against the inside of my eyeballs. I knew that my eyes were puffy, that my face was flushed, and that my skin stank of booze as I sweated out last night's mistakes in the day's sticky heat.

"Next time I get the monster pig," Million said. "Today we have the pretty pig."

"I'm hoping there won't be a next time. How you feeling over there, Tarzan?"

Miriam stood at the edge of the clearing, leaning heavily against Kent's spear, her face a mixture of exhaustion and misery. Her lab coat was covered with dirt. All the contestants were looking grimier, skinnier, more ravaged by the insects. Every day erased their pancake-fed, body-lotion-scrubbed first world existence. But looking at Miriam, I was struck by how her collarbones jutted from her chest and how many red bites swelled up and down her toothpick legs. She gave me a weak thumbs-up.

I was going to shoehorn her back into this story before she was shipped home in a body bag.

I'D NEVER FILMED A WILDERNESS SHOW, BUT I KNEW THE TRICKS OF the trade. The survivalist Cody Lundin had sued the Discovery Channel and revealed that *Dual Survival* faked its animal encounters, like carting in a rattlesnake in a box for the contestants to stumble upon on a trek. A producer friend from a different show told me he'd wanted to film his survivalists hunting a beaver for the vanilla flavoring from its castor sac (right by its anal gland). A neat little survival trick. The problem was that the only beavers they could find on location were frozen. The crew had to film the shot from far away while the survivalists "hunted" a frozen beaver corpse in a stream.

So that morning, I told Miriam to get the spear. She'd be hunting a pig.

"I'll grab Kent," she said, too eagerly.

"No," I said. "Only you."

"But Kent's the hunter."

I gestured to the shelter, where Kent was feeding Ashley morsels of coconut while Erika's cameraman Aleister hovered over them.

"Think about *your* journey," I said gently. "Don't you want to do something for yourself?"

She looked at them again, as though if she stared hard enough, the image might blur and dissolve. "I've never actually hunted anything before," she said quietly.

"That's why we're here." I gave a stupid half bow and led her into the dragon fruit grove, where Million awaited.

The first step in spear throwing is to find the spear's balance point, Million explained. He placed the long wooden shaft on his wrist. If you tried to balance it too close to the blade, the spear tipped backward. If you placed the spear too far back on your arm, it tipped down to the front. At the balance point, the spear wobbled but didn't fall. That was where you gripped it. Point your left foot at the target. Hinge your right arm back. And then—with a twist of his shoulders and a pivot in his hips, Million bull's-eyed an X that he'd carved on a nearby palm.

"Got it," Miriam said. "Grab it perfectly, toss it expertly, and hit the bull's-eye."

Still, she gamely took the spear, and while her first few attempts went wild, within a couple of hours she was throwing straight enough to hit close objects. It was midday already, and soon the light would dim, so I decided it would have to be good enough. We filmed a few shots of her stalking through the swamp, the spear gripped in her hand, mud seeping up the sides of her shoes. Then we brought her to the clearing.

"LET'S WALK THROUGH HOW THIS IS GOING TO WORK," I TOLD THE crew. "Friedman—you position your camera here at the edge of the jungle. Million, you tie the pig to that bush, so the camera can't see the rope. When I give the signal, you let go of the pig, who will thrash around until Miriam nails him with the spear. Right?"

"If God is willing," Million said.

"This is reality television. We're the gods here."

"Wait—what?" Miriam said. "You said I'd be hunting. But this pig is—in a cage? Tied to a bush?"

"You're still hunting the pig." I tried to filter the frustration out of my voice, to sound patient and calm. "You're throwing the spear. Think of how this will look on television. You're going to be a hunter. A provider. People are going to go crazy on social media. We're going to hashtag the hell out of this. Hashtag island hero."

"I don't care about social media. I don't want to kill *anything.* I've never killed—"

"You killed a snake. You can kill a pig." I cut her off. If she couldn't articulate her objections, then she couldn't object. "Animals die all the time. Every cheeseburger you ever ate was once a living thing. You're *starving.* Is it better if your food's straight from the slaughterhouse? At least this animal is in the wild."

"That pig is in a cage!"

"Well, it was free at one point." I was feeling nauseated too as I looked at the squealing pig. It was hard not to think of snuffly Buster the bulldog, hard not to remember that pigs were said to be even smarter than dogs. Could Pig Bambi understand that I was condemning him to death? But there was an enormous difference between a dog I was filming—my subject, my responsibility—and the wild animals hunted by a contestant on a survival show. Blood and guts, Jacob said.

"Do this for yourself. Kent's been leading you on. This is *your* chance to be a hero." Hurt flashed across her face. "Here's how it will go. We'll set the shot. Million releases the pig. Then you—" I made a jerking motion with my hand. "And you can't tell anybody about this, because people will think you're cheating—and we'll have to take all your prize money away."

She looked around frantically, like some kind of escape might reveal itself in the mangrove trees or the coiled roots. For a brief instant, I thought she would run away. But she didn't go anywhere. It was as though the force of our cameras and the fact that she was holding the spear meant she couldn't leave. In six months when this aired, America would be collectively high-fiving her. Million opened the cage and coaxed out the cowering animal. The pig writhed and squealed while Million tied him to a branch.

"Are you ready?" I asked my crew.

"Ready," Friedman said.

The pig was screaming. It was so hot. I just needed to get through this moment so the rest of my plan could move forward.

"Miriam, are you ready?"

"No!" she said. Her whole body was slick with anxious sweat. But her left foot was pointing forward, and her grip was tight. That was all the confirmation I needed. "I really don't want to—"

"Now!"

Million let the pig go and ran out of frame. The pig darted forward, straight toward Miriam, a squealing blur of pink snout and dappled hair. It caught against the end of its rope and was yanked backward, its hooves sprawling. *Now*, I willed her. And like a puppet, she moved. Her arm hinged at the elbow. The pig thrashed in the bush. With a look of misery, she threw.

The spear grazed the pig's flank. "Get him!" I shouted. The pig screamed louder, desperate and wild. A stitch of blood trailed down his thigh. Miriam, trapped in the moment, ran to grab the spear, but she slipped in the mud and crashed into the thorny bush. The pig yanked desperately against his tether. Again the rope caught him short. He pulled harder, squealing. The branch broke. I cursed. Pig Bambi raced away, the branch bouncing behind, the blood slicking down his thigh.

"Oh god, oh god." Miriam stood with her hands on her knees, panting, staring around with a wild, confused look like she was surfacing from a nightmare. A sob coughed out of her and then another, and she ran back to camp.

My crew stood awkwardly in the clearing. Friedman and Afa fiddled with their gear. I tuned my radio to Erika's channel, to hear if Miriam said anything when she got back, but I didn't think she would. Who would she confide in? Mario leaned against a tree, digging a hole in the wood with his pocketknife. I had to say something, but I had no idea where to start. I thought of Erika tonight at dinner, overwhelmed with gossip. Did she tell everyone that I slept with Jacob? Or talk first about my disastrous pig hunt? Screwing and screwing up. Maybe the real reason Jacob hired me *was* that I was an easy lay. Maybe it had been obvious to him with his expert producer eye. *Good enough and available*, I'd told him on the phone when he first called. My hangover pulsed in my eyes. The light failed, and the trees lost their outlines, becoming spectral in the gathering gloom.

Friedman broke the silence. "What are you going to tell Jacob?"

"We can't tell him anything." It was an instinctive reaction, but the moment I said the words, I knew they were true. If Jacob heard about this botched pig hunt before I could fix it, I'd be on the first plane back to New York.

"Can't tell Jacob? He's the executive producer," Afa said, like he was the only person who knew the org chart.

"We can't tell anybody. This has to be—this has to be a secret operation." I realized that I needed to produce my team as much as I produced the contestants. I had to make them believe in *their* storyline too. And what group of adult men didn't love a secret op?

"I talked to Jacob last night," I continued. Afa and Friedman exchanged a look. "You know what he told me? Blood and guts. Jacob wants more from this show than a bunch of people starving on an island. He needs drama. Danger. Betrayal. We're here to make the best possible show. A *Jacob Malibu* show. But in order to do that, I need to trust you, and I need you to trust me. Sometimes, to push the boundaries, things have to get messy. I'd love for our crew—you, Friedman. You, Afa. You, Mario. And of course, you too, Million, you're with us on this one—to be able to go back to Jacob and show him an epic moment of primal drama. Miriam the nerd killing a pig. Imagine how thrilled he'll be. But to do that, I need you to give me three days. Three days with no gossip back to base camp. Three days of believing in my plan. Because if we go back to Jacob now, we *all* look like fuckups. But if we go back to Jacob in three days, we're going to be a part of solid-gold television that he'll love."

I put my hand out like it was the end of a team huddle.

"I'm willing to see where this goes," Friedman said. "But I'm not putting my hand in the middle."

"Has to be with hands."

I wasn't sure if Mario understood a single word I said, but now, maybe triggered by an instinctive teenage devotion to sports clichés, he put his hand on top of mine.

"Well, if the kid's in." Friedman put his paw into the huddle. Million followed.

"Afa?"

The mixer rolled his eyes and placed in his heavy hand. "Only because I don't want to be part of this mess. I'll give you a chance to fix it."

WHEN WE GOT BACK TO CAMP, KENT AND ASHLEY WERE SPLASHING together in the shallows, and Miriam was stripping off her muddy clothes. She dove into the water and began scrubbing herself. Her face was streaked, and her skin was scratched. I could almost feel the salt water burning her cuts and scrapes.

"Where've you been?" Kent asked. "Planning your escape?"

"You say that like it couldn't possibly be true."

"Hey. No offense. Just curious."

"I was—practicing my spear throwing."

I exhaled in relief. I had her.

"Spear throwing?" Kent repeated, with a hint of alarm. "Did you hit anything? I could join if you're thinking of hunting."

"You were—here." She gestured to Ashley.

Kent took a step away. Both of them looked confused. I could see the pig lie building inside Miriam, like the pressure might be too much to bear.

I walked into the surf with my camera. "Miriam, could you get out of the shot?" I called. "I'm trying to film Kent and Ashley."

She swam away. "Wash my back," Ashley said to Kent, and for a moment Kent hesitated, before he let Ashley draw his attention back to her.

"I forgot my soap."

"With mud, you doofus."

"You want me to wash you with dirt?"

"Have you *not* been washing with mud? That explains the stink."

"See, I always thought mud was the thing we wanted to wash off."

"It *exfoliates.*"

"Are you sure that's safe? I don't want to be responsible for exfoliating anybody before their time."

Ashley turned her back. "Scrub some mud on me, you idiot."

The evening was becoming cold. They'd have to leave the water soon if they wanted to get dry before nightfall. But for a few minutes longer, Miriam treaded water and watched Ashley and Kent play, letting the salt sting her fresh wounds.

CHAPTER 36

MIRIAM

DAY 21

For their fourth challenge they have to race through a jungle obstacle course holding a torch. "This is about keeping your light alive through adversity!" Jacob exclaims, as the contestants wobble across the rickety rope bridge, trudge through the swampy muck, and shimmy through the tunnel of thorns. Of course Ashley wins—a key, two additional oars, and food. Of course she chooses Kent to share her reward, and the two of them are set up ten feet away from the shelter on a blanket, with a carafe of milk and a picnic basket of peanut-butter sandwiches. Miriam can't bear to look. The reward seems like it's designed not only to feed them but to humiliate her, and when Friedman turns his camera's cruel lens toward her she walks into the surf and dunks her head under the waves.

When she gets out of the water, Barb's pants, which she's been wearing, are missing, and Ruddy is gesturing to her from the border of the trees.

"I'll bet you're wondering where your pants have gone," he says.

No, she is not wondering.

"I took them," he says slyly. "But I'm willing to give them back. *Both* pairs. If you go along with my plan."

More than anything, Miriam feels annoyed. "Is stealing pants your only move?"

He bristles. "*Listen.* Here's my idea. I take Barty out for a swim. You run up and grab his clothes. Wham, he's left shivering in his red skivvies. He'll quit in a day."

"You're the expert clothes thief. Why do you need me?"

"I don't *need* you. But–look at all the camera time those two are getting." He nods down the beach, to exactly where she's trying not to look. Kent and Ashley are splayed out on their picnic blanket, laughing. "So what if we set ourselves up a showmance of our own? You're not my first pick, but right now there's nobody else–"

"Keep the stupid pants." She walks away in disgust. A week ago, Ruddy loomed large in her imagination as the show's villain. Now Kent's spooning with Ashley at night. Now Beck is telling her to kill a pig. Her heart aches and her head is spinning, and Ruddy's sad attempts at drama feel tiny, like a play within the play, the most ridiculous characters acting out their inane theater.

Back at the shelter, the fire has dimmed to its embers. Miriam bends over the firepit and blows. At first a tiny whirlwind of ash gusts across the coals, but she modulates her breath, and soon an orange spark flickers. The kindling crackles, and a flame snaps to life. She carefully adds more twigs. The flame builds.

So: She can make fire, at least from the ruins of someone else's fire. She lets herself luxuriate for a moment in her newfound woodcraft, making a few unnecessary adjustments with the poking stick. Kent is licking peanut butter off Ashley's fingers. Miriam bites the inside of her cheek. It's what she always does to return herself to the concrete world when she's about to let her emotions spiral out.

The toothpick stab of pain grounds her in the real. She never actually had anything with him, she reminds herself again as she walks down the shore to forage. They slept close when it was cold. They destroyed Barb's raft. They climbed a mountain. But anything deeper—where was the evidence? It wasn't the first time Miriam declared herself to someone and was left humiliated. She still twists with embarrassment when she remembers the time at the gym, on the elliptical, listening to hype songs on her headphones while she worked up the courage to approach the hot guy she was sure had been checking her out. Not "gym hot" but skinny, with glasses and a *Battlestar Galactica* T-shirt. Approachably hot. "I don't know if you'd be interested in going on a date," she said, "but if you are, we should get a drink. And if you're not, we should get coffee." The guy looked totally flummoxed. The people around them doing arm curls were slyly looking at them in the mirror. She hadn't realized how flushed and sweaty she was. "I guess coffee?" he said. Why had she even included the second half of that offer? The worst part was he followed through, out of, like, pity, and they'd had to sit in a Starbucks talking awkwardly for an hour. Someday this would be the same, not so painful, merely another humiliating memory to turn over endlessly before sleep.

Down the beach she finds two full coconuts and carries them back under her arms. She splits one with the knife by levering the blade into the shell and using a large, flat rock to push it through. Kent can halve the coconuts with a quick machete chop, but this is the way Miriam must do it. Patiently, slowly. When the coconut splits, she sips the milk and retches. The coconut is sour. She tosses it into a nearby grove that they have turned into a trash pile of husks and fruit rinds. The pile gives off a rotten stink, and at night she tries to ignore the sound of skittering claws.

The second coconut is sweet. She drinks deep, careful to avoid spilling the juice over the rim. When she's finished, she hands it to

Bartolo in the shelter, who passes it to Ruddy, who passes it back to her, looking her in the eyes with a challenge, like he's somehow humiliated her, rather than the opposite. With the machete's tip, she slices the coconut flesh into squares and levers out small shards. She tries her best to peel off the bark, but the brown husk clings to the flesh. She carries the pot to the shore, crouches in the wet sand, and fills it with an inch of seawater. Of course Kent wanted the giggly pretty girl. Miriam was a placeholder, someone he would chat with while he waited for Ashley, just like Ruddy was now begrudgingly looking to her as the only other female left.

Ashley and Kent rejoin the group while they cook the coconut shards, gallantly insisting they won't eat any, they're simply too full. The salt water will give the boiled coconuts a different flavor and texture than the raw flesh. Three weeks in, any slight variation in routine feels like awakening to life anew.

"Coconuts are a natural laxative," Bartolo says for the millionth time.

"My guts are already as lax as they can possibly be," says Ruddy.

"The coconuts are the most miserable part of this experience," Bartolo expands.

"The *food* is the worst part?" Ruddy asks. "See, for me, the lack of food is the worst part."

"The worst part for me is the mint gum," Ashley says.

"You have gum?" Ruddy asks. "I would murder you for gum."

"Not me. Erika chews gum in the morning, and I can smell it on her breath. It smells–fresh. Like hair conditioner."

The group takes a moment to luxuriate in the glorious ideas of mint gum and hair conditioner. When they decide that the coconut is cooked, Kent wraps his hands in his shirt and pours the water from the pot. Ruddy, Bartolo, and Miriam fish out their pieces, careful to avoid the burning sides. Ashley leans back against Kent and takes his hand, and a cameraman runs over to capture this priceless moment, and Miriam heads back up the beach to forage again because every time Ashley and Kent make physical contact, her tongue finds the gap between her teeth, and she feels even more acutely her horrific awkward height and the flab around her midsection, which somehow is still here after three weeks of starvation, like it's the most essential part of her, like her bones themselves will dissolve before she tones her belly.

As she walks down the shore, her mind returns to the pig hunt. Why did she throw the spear? Her body seemed to act on its own. Miriam always defined herself by her brain and her logic, but what if she was now discovering a deeper self that knew things that were opaque to her conscious intelligence? That all her overthinking and inner monologuing had been a distraction, and now—out here, with her brain listless with starvation—her essential self was at last surfacing? Wouldn't that be wonderful? And isn't that why she's here?

She feels a tickle and looks down to see a tiny crab making its way across her feet. It's white, almost translucent against her tanned flesh, like it's been bleached by the sun. Watching it pass, her mind wanders back to a Chinese restaurant in Bemidji that her parents took her to as a child. At the entryway sat a tank full of crabs, their pincers rubber-banded shut. She would press her small nose against the glass and stare through the moss-green water. Every so often, a black-suited waiter would plunge his hands into the brackish water and pull one out, its carapace dripping, its neutered claws waving into the sky, and Miriam would run back to her parents in tears.

If that tank were here on this beach, she would grab every one of those crabs and throw them together into a pot to boil. Beck was right about the pig. Who was she to offload the moral weight of killing her meat onto a faceless corporation? At least she could look the pig—Pig

Bambi, Beck called him—in the eyes. Her stomach growls, and she wishes desperately she'd taken the hunt more seriously. Her body knew what to do, so why hadn't she listened? That poor pig was probably lost and starving in the jungle. It wasn't like it could run back to its pig family for pig brunch. The thought hits her: Where one crab goes, others are sure to follow. Miriam follows the crab's pinprick tracks through the soft sand down to the shore and the volcanic boulders that cluster up the beach at the water's edge. Three more sun-bleached crabs shuffle along the edge of a large, flat, half-submerged stone. She bends down, grips the stone with both hands, and lifts.

Underneath is a dragon's hoard of jeweled crustaceans. There are sea snails clinging to the dripping black surface, a massive oyster with whorls and ridges like a half-folded fan, an opalescent conch shell. She runs to camp, closing her eyes to whatever romance novel cover art Ashley and Kent are reenacting, and returns with the pot. She fills it with ridged and spiny oysters, with crabs that try to clamber over the sides, with handfuls of snails. She practically struts back down the beach. The pot is filled with food. Maybe she didn't hunt, but she has gathered this—

"We have to go." Beck intercepts her, looking manic. "Come with me. We have another pig."

Her brief sense of self-sufficiency dissolves. "But—" She holds up the pot of shellfish.

Beck wrinkles her nose at the dirty pot filled with squirming mollusks. "You can come back to whatever this is later. The crew's waiting."

Beck turns around and takes off without looking back. And so Miriam follows. Didn't she just come to terms with the idea that she wanted to hunt a pig? So why does she feel so confused? More than anything, she has the feeling she always gets with Beck, as she trips after her through the twisting trees, less like they're walking together, and more like she's being pulled along, sucked forward by the force of Beck's movement, like debris in the wake of a passing jet.

When she gets to the clearing and sees the hulking form trapped inside its cage, reeking of smoke and dirt, she goes rigid.

Million has found the monster pig. Thick black bristles mohawk down its back, and two yellow tusks curve from its lower jaw, the right one chipped at its point. Its hair is hoary with age. Its cheeks are covered in fungal scales. It slumps against the wire bars, and its eyes roll in its head.

"Good god." She feels nauseated. "He looks–sick."

"Not sick." Beck laughs, high and wild. "Drugged. So he'll–it–will be easier to hunt. No more . . ." She gestures to the thicket where Pig Bambi escaped.

The boar wheezes in its cage. Miriam feels the bile rise in the back of her throat.

"Absolutely not."

Beck puts a hand on her shoulder. "Everybody's starving. You'll be feeding the entire group. Think how good this meat will taste."

The boar rolls one eye up to stare at Miriam. Its iris is the copper color of a penny.

"I'd rather starve than– Can we even eat this? It's half-dead."

"So it shouldn't be hard to make it fully dead." Beck laughs, again too loudly.

"No." The clarity feels affirming. Every part of her, mind and body, refuses. "Find someone else."

"It's got to be you," Beck insists. "This is why you're here. Listen. Right now there's footage of you trying and failing to hunt a pig. If we don't get footage of you *killing* a pig, then what's going to go on TV is the part where you screw up. I know you don't want to be a screwup."

Miriam feels a tremor at the idea that her boss at the startup and her college roommate Penelope will watch her failing on national TV. But ultimately, she is not going to execute this animal. "What if you don't include any of the footage?"

"If it were only me, that's how I would do it." Beck looks pained. "But the footage exists, and–I know how these people operate."

"You're blackmailing me," Miriam says.

"I'm helping you. We can fix everything in the edit to make it all look like one successful hunt. You'll be a hero."

"These two animals look nothing alike."

"You're lucky that our editing software is so good. *Please,* Miriam. If you won't do it for yourself, do it for me. I'm going to level with you: I've put everything on the line because I believe in your story. My boss–my crew–" Beck gestures at the cameraman and sound guy, who stand there impassively. "They think I'm crazy. Because I believe in *you.* Please–don't . . . let me down. My career . . ."

Miriam's heart wavers. Over the past three weeks, Beck's been her only true ally. Beck put everything on the line for her after the raft debacle. It would be ungrateful to ruin her career for some stupid moral compulsion. What is she really asking? To close her eyes and stab? Animals die all the time, she repeats to herself. Every cheeseburger she ever ate . . . Her stomach rumbles.

"Please," Beck says again.

She walks leadenly into position at the edge of the clearing, the spear in her hand. Again Million opens the cage and guides out the animal. "Careful, careful," Beck says. *No,* Miriam's mind shouts. The boar struggles to breathe. Million ties its rope to the thicket of brambles where Pig Bambi disappeared. The boar lurches a few steps forward and collapses on its side.

"Stab it!" Beck shouts.

Her heart is racing, and her mouth is dry. She tries to lift the spear but she can't, like her arm is paralyzed.

"How will this look good? Me murdering this half-dead animal?"

"Trust me," Beck says. "We'll edit it together. We'll have the other pig running. You throw the spear, lean down to pick it up. Then cut to you stabbing down, and a dead pig on the ground. Nobody will tell one pig from the other."

Beck clasps her hands like she's pleading, and again Miriam tries to lift the spear, but her body refuses. If her body is the ultimate judge of her true self, its message is clear.

"Please. For me," Beck begs. "This is how things work. How do you think Kent solved that puzzle in the first challenge? I told him."

"What?"

"You think he solved it himself? I gave him a clue."

Where moments before she felt clarity, now her mind is a confused jumble. "He's been lying the whole time?"

"Yes! You think he can do *anything* himself? How do you think he found the fruit grove on day two? I led him there."

Miriam's overwhelmed with disgust. The spear is still heavy, but her arms can move. The beast is wheezing, suffocating under its own weight. Miriam closes her eyes. It looks like Kent, she thinks, bloated and useless.

"Don't you need food?" Beck urges.

We need food, she tells herself.

"Why should you let *him* be the hero, when *you* could be?"

Yes, she thinks. *This.* She wants to be the hunter. And a small, bitter part of her also wants to take this from him, to wound Kent, who lied to her, who let her believe in him and then went running to Ashley the moment she declared herself, that disgusting fraud.

"Do it!" Beck shouts.

She closes her eyes and stabs downward. The animal's flabby flesh is nothing like the snake's thick band of muscle. Its scream is mournful and dull with sedative. Miriam pulls out the spear and opens her eyes. The boar whimpers out its final breaths as blood pours from its side. She feels lightheaded and weak.

"What are you feeling?" Beck shouts. Her voice is spiky and wild.

"Did you get what you need?" Miriam is yelling too, but she feels far away from herself.

"Tell the camera what you're feeling!" Beck shouts again.

"I'm feeling–feeling–" Miriam can't finish the sentence. The boar's tusks are coated with blood. Flies are already settling on the wound. "How the hell am I supposed to get this thing back to camp?" she sobs.

MILLION CARRIES THE CARCASS ON HIS SHOULDERS DOWN THE PATH to camp. Beck flutters around her, reminding her again and again not to tell anybody, on pain of edit, what really happened. She went hunting. She surprised a boar in a clearing. "Repeat it into the camera," Beck says, putting the handheld right up to her face. She does, weakly, like she's making a vow to the TV gods. All the rage at Kent, the desperate wanting, and the need to placate Beck have faded to a nauseous sense of disgust. Watching TV at home, Miriam always assumed that reality producers manipulated from the sidelines, but this is beyond what she ever imagined. She thought that she would still be Miriam, but pushed to become her best self. Now when Beck looks at her, it seems like she's barely seeing *Miriam* at all. She's projecting someone else entirely.

At the edge of the trees, Million drops the carcass. She struggles to lift it, but the deadweight is too much. The fat black flies scatter and settle again onto the boar's side while she tries to figure out how to carry it. Finally, she grabs it by its legs and pulls it furiously down the path. The boar's face drags through the dirt, its cheek pulling back into a half smile.

When she steps past the trees and out onto the beach, there's a confused moment before the other contestants understand what's happening. Then Bartolo cries out.

"A pig!" he shouts in triumph. "We've hunted a pig, my friends! We've done it!"

He runs from the shelter, followed by the others, who crowd around her asking how it happened, giddy at the prospect of food.

Their enthusiasm makes her feel even more disgusted with herself.

Kent is the last to approach. "*You* . . . killed this pig?"

Miriam starts to say something, pauses, reconsiders, and nods.

"So there are pigs out here." He stares off into the jungle. "I looked everywhere."

"Looks like you missed one," she says, trying to control the anger and shame.

Ashley gives her a giant hug, and the blood from Miriam's coat smears across Ashley's dress, a darker stain against the strawberry-red fabric. "Who would have thought? Our little scientist."

She wants to hurl Ashley into the sea.

"Is that my spear?" Kent asks.

"The tools aren't *yours*."

"But I made the spear. Excalibur."

Kent looks like a lost child, and she feels a swell of sympathy. "Maybe you can help me–roast it?"

"Like I'm your servant?" He clenches his jaw. "You're the big hunter. You do it. Anyway, if there's pigs out there–" He grabs the spear and stalks toward the jungle.

"Babe!" Ashley calls after him. "We don't need you to hunt. We've got all the food we can eat with Miriam's pig."

"*Miriam's* pig," Kent says in disgust, and disappears into the trees.

CHAPTER 37

BECK

NIGHT 21

"You've heard me say this before, and you'll hear me say it again. We're blowing through our Purell line item. I'll direct you to row thirteen, column C."

Logistics Brian paused for dramatic effect. The production meeting quieted as we skimmed our spreadsheets, searching for the big reveal.

"Two tubs a week! I don't think I need to remind you that hand sanitizer doesn't grow on trees. Well, aloe does, of course, but not the alcohol. Although technically, I suppose, alcohol does *grow.* But not on trees. Anyway I don't think I need to remind you that you only need a light press to kill ninety-nine percent of germs. Tell your crews—no more giant squirts!" He mimed the appropriate motion. "Isn't that right, Dr. Callahan?"

"A little squirt should be fine," Callahan agreed. "But on the margin, I'd rather people sanitize more than less. Infections can get nasty quick. I once was working on an island not unlike this, and a man had a staph infection so big that—"

"Well, of course we want them to sanitize," Logistics Brian cut in.

"I don't think I need to remind you how expensive medical care is. Why, Kelly-Anne's visit to the hospital alone—all I'm saying is, two squirts and done." I glanced over at Jacob, our eyes met, and my heart flipped. But he looked at me with no more interest than if I were another cell on Brian's budgeting spreadsheets. Row Bergmann, column Beck. It was such a parody of a stereotypical guy. Warm words, then drunken sex, then complete emotional shutdown. I wasn't expecting our hookup to explode into romance. All I wanted was acknowledgment, a recognition of a special connection. Still, I wasn't angry at him. I was furious with myself—and I was still on edge from the pig hunt. The moans of the old boar had joined in my head with all the other jungle sounds—the chukking of the gecko, the tree frogs' screeches, and the cicadas' chirps—to form a jungle cacophony that looped at the base of my skull over the mental loudspeakers typically reserved for irritating advertising jingles.

"Thanks so much, Brian," Jacob said. "This is important stuff for everybody to remember. Let's definitely try to institute a 'two squirts' rule. Callahan, how's Kelly-Anne doing?"

"Hand's healing beautifully," Callahan said. "She's resting up at the Holding Pen with Carl and Barb. No lost limbs yet!"

"Great. Let's keep it that way. Beck, what's going on in your world?"

I took a deep breath, tried to shut out my feelings, and relayed the story of the pig hunt as I'd craft it in the edit. Miriam stalking through the jungle. The pig's dart through the undergrowth. Miriam's cry and the stab into his side. Nothing about a botched first try, or Pig Bambi, who was right now roaming free across the mangrove swamp. I told the story like it was the most epic hunt you'd ever imagined. I knew Jacob would love it. It was exactly what he'd asked for. As I talked, I kept glancing over at Million, the one person here who could reveal the ellipses in my story. But he was sitting silently, playing with his crowded key chain like a rosary, his fingers running along the metal grooves of one key before flipping it and toying with the next.

"When I told you I wanted blood and guts, I didn't mean that literally," Jacob said when I finished.

My stomach dropped. "This is the first part of a bigger narrative I'm planning. Besides, I like the literary resonance. You know, *Lord of the Flies*."

"I think we all get the 'literary resonance,'" Erika said. I could feel the laughter choked up around the table.

"I thought—hunting was the lifeblood of a wilderness show," I said.

"Hunting's great," Jacob said. "But for your major storylines, I want your focus to be on the *people*. Big, human emotions."

"Trust me, this is setting up some very big emotions."

"*Trust* you." Erika scoffed. "Rumor has it that this—pig hunt—had an abortive first attempt? How many pigs had to die for your literary resonance?"

"Fucking Afa," I said.

"I'm not going to reveal my sources," Erika said. "But I'm not surprised that the dog killer, now a pig killer, couldn't even—"

"They're *nothing* alike," I said. "This is a survivalist story arc. Geek to—"

"Okay, that's enough," Jacob said. "Beck, keep going with whatever bigger narrative you're planning, but remember—*people*. Big feelings. Erika, what have you got?"

"I'm glad you mentioned big feelings, because that's exactly what I've been following with Kent and Ashley," Erika said. She described the latest developments in the island romance: the moonlit strolls, the whispered nothings. Jacob nodded along, peppering her with follow-ups. I couldn't believe that he was more interested in this insipid camp fling than in an epic pig hunt.

"I'm also following Ruddy," Erika said, "who's still plotting to–"

"Actually, about Ruddy?" I'd been waiting for this.

"Excuse me, but I was–"

"I wasn't sure how to bring this up," I continued. "I was doing some clicking around online, and I happened to notice that Ruddy has liked some pretty nasty and offensive posts on social media."

The table went silent.

"He hasn't said anything bad *himself*," I added. "But he definitely supports horrific viewpoints. I'm worried what it will mean for our show if he's one of our breakout stars and the press gets ahold of this. It could be terrible publicity."

Jacob lowered his yellow legal pad. He looked deeply thoughtful in a way I hadn't seen before, not like he was analyzing a spreadsheet but like he was assessing a philosophy.

"What the fuck does that have to do with our show?" Erika asked. "Ruddy is a *villain*. Of course he's not going to be a choirboy on 'social media.'"

Jacob rubbed his eyes. "Beck's right." He looked very tired. "It's one thing to be a villain on-air. But we can't celebrate bigots."

"Are you kidding?" Erika said. "We have the freaking dog killer on staff."

"We all know it's different when it's a contestant," Jacob said. "Ruddy's plots are fun, but they're not worth jeopardizing the show. It could be a disaster if the media picked it up."

The last few years had seen a lot of this. The press would discover bigoted old posts from reality stars. Offensive comments from a *Challenge* contestant. Slurs from a suitor on *The Bachelorette*. A scandal materialized–in part driven by genuine outrage, and in part by the press's need to generate clicks. The contestants apologized. They were educating themselves. Every step of the ritual gave another article, more clicks. Invariably the story of the tweets eclipsed the story of the show itself. The season would have to be reedited to remove the contestant and minimize their storylines. Better to get ahead of it now.

It was poetic, I thought, to harness the medium that had brought me so low. Late last night I'd gone into the computer room and done a search through Ruddy's history, figuring with a guy like him, there had to be *something*. I was tired of seeing Erika weaponize her minion against my contestants.

"We're not going to yank Ruddy from the show," Jacob said. "But he can't be our biggest character. Maybe . . . de-emphasize him. Don't blow any more air on that fire."

"But he's been amazing television! All the plotting and backstabbing," Erika said. "I've been producing him for weeks!"

"I trust you can find other great storylines." Jacob could barely hide his irritation. I thrilled at my triumph. "Million, what's the news from our local liaison?"

After an awkward pause, Million gave his update. The tourism board was planning a US ad campaign to coincide with the show's debut. Then Jacob adjourned the meeting. I pushed my chair back and lingered outside the dining room door, waiting for him. I wasn't sure what I planned to say, or how it would come out of me—in a rational exposition or a series of frantic bursts.

I never had the opportunity to find out. Erika intercepted me.

"What the hell are you doing?" she demanded.

"Doing?"

"This Ruddy bullshit? You and I both know that you weren't 'clicking around.'"

"I'm looking out for the show," I said.

"And this fake pig hunt. Are you out of your mind?"

"I told you. It's a work in progress."

"Isn't everything with you."

We were standing at the top of the staircase, and in the lobby below, junior staff were drinking and laughing by the bar. A few looked up when they heard us and elbowed one another knowingly. I didn't want to make a scene. There was already enough gossip about me ping-ponging around the City. I leaned in close and lowered my voice.

"What is it with you?" I asked. "Ever since I got here, you've been undermining me at every opportunity."

"Undermining *you*?" She laughed in disbelief. "You literally just wrote out a storyline I've been tracking since day one. I feel like I'm in crazy town. You killed a dog on your last show, and now I have to rely on you? I knew you were going to be chaotic, but I'm still shocked by your total lack of professionalism."

"I've known producers like you," I said. "You think being cynical and mean is the same thing as being a professional."

"And I've known producers like *you*. Believe me, lots. You think your weird fixations mean you've got a big heart. Do you think you're the first producer Jacob ever fucked?"

I finally saw it. Of course. It had been jealousy all along. "So you and he—"

"Yes, he and I. And he and I again. And again and again. We're not exclusive. I just thought he'd show a little more—taste. You are spiraling out of control, and if we're not careful you're going to destroy this entire show." She turned on her heel and disappeared into the hotel. I had to suppress a smile. I'd turned Miriam into the hunter. Kent was going mad with envy. I'd kneecapped Ruddy.

I was completely in control, more in control than I'd ever been.

CHAPTER 38

KENT

DAY 24

Again he drags himself into the jungle, the sweat drenching his shirt, the mosquitoes shrieking and the tree frogs screeching, the sickly sweetness of decaying leaves saturating his senses, his mind jittery with Mydayis—did he take one already today? He should take another to be sure. *CRUSH HIM*, he thinks, *DESTROY HIM.* "Crush who?" he says aloud. There's a banyan at the start of his route that is mocking him, its branches hiked akimbo in a confused shrug. "I wasn't asking *you*," he tells the tree. Every day he follows the same route, up through the palms, left at the mocking tree, straight until he reaches a dense copse of ironwoods, turn right, the grass and moss and leaf litter so trampled by his passage that it's become a recognizable path, even as he is aware of how insane that is, to walk the same paces and expect a different result. It's not like he actually thinks he'll find a pig. He doesn't believe there *are* pigs in this jungle. Most of all he's certain there's no way Miriam found a pig. She took a spear for two days and expertly stabbed a boar? Impossible. But the corollary is more awful, that *she* has been anointed by the producers as the hunter, the provider. He isn't hoping so much to find a pig as to prove that he is worthy of being gifted one, like a prayer or a penance, a pilgrim walking the stations of the cross in search of salvation. The sweat drips down his face. The sun is too bright. How can so much sunlight penetrate the canopy? His eyes ache. His vision blurs, and—

He is in an interview with Beck, sitting on a cracked volcanic boulder at the edge of the sea, wavelets crashing against the rocks behind him.

"How did you feel when Miriam came back to camp with her pig?"

The light off the bounce spears into his eyes. His head throbs. "I was happy!" He shouts to be heard over the waves, even though he knows that the hovering boom mike will capture his every whisper and sigh. "Happy we got food," he yells. "Happy for Miriam! *SO* happy!"

The spray from the waves leaps and dances with the joy of all his happiness.

"You aren't bothered that Miriam killed a pig and you haven't?" Beck shouts back.

"No!"

"Kent, you know I need you to say complete sentences!"

"I'm not bothered that Miriam killed a pig and I haven't!" Why did Beck force him to do this interview here, where he has to yell the most painful, obvious lies? "I do wonder where *I* can find a pig, though!"

"And Miriam took your spear to do it?!"

"It's not my spear! We share the tools!"

"But you made it!"

"It's not my spear!"

"Do other people treat Miriam differently now?!"

"I really think that if pigs are out there, I could–"

"Does *Ashley* treat her differently?!"

Ashley is spooned against him, her leg hiked over his hip, while he lies on the edge of the shelter staring at the strips of pig carcass that dangle from the crossbeam. They roasted the boar and ate so much that their shrunken stomachs bloated with the excess, and smoked the rest of the meat. He used to love the smell of pork, eating bacon and eggs on a Sunday morning with Margaret was their weekend ritual, but now in the intolerable heat the world feels oversaturated with the stench, and the ache pulses outward from his right eye.

"Babe, let's go rinse." Ashley leans in to kiss him at the base of his neck, and then hammily recoils. "You stink."

Yes, he thinks. Go to the water with the girl. This is why he sacrificed Miriam. This is why he sacrificed his marriage.

He doesn't move.

"You can scrub mud on me." Her tone sounds worried in a way he doesn't like. Kent Duvall doesn't need your concern.

"Maybe I should ask Miriam." She flops away onto her other side.

Ashley's right to be frustrated. The whole premise of their "relationship"–big air quotes, even in his internal monologue–was that they were acting out the prescribed beats of island lovers. When Ashley kissed him, it seemed like the simplest, most straightforward solution to all his problems. With one move, he could be the man he wanted to be, and he could irreparably end things with Miriam, saving them both. Plus–there was something so–intense about Ashley's attraction to him that, on a purely physical level, was impossible to resist–a desire so straightforward and unhesitating that he couldn't believe it came from the same girl who a few weeks before dismissed him as a "gentleman in his later days." Of course he kissed her. It was amazing. Her lips were soft. Her tongue flicked into his mouth teasingly. He barely noticed her terrible breath. And the following days he kept on kissing her, kissed her harder every time the voice at the back of his head wondered what it would be like to be kissing Miriam—until Miriam strode back into camp with the boar, and his whole identity collapsed.

Ashley pulls herself on top of him so that their noses are touching, and her eyes are so close to his that they blur together into one giant eye. "I was kidding about Miriam."

He can't stand her judgy cyclopean glare. Like she's wondering how she ended up narratively lashed to a lump. Miriam believed in him. Miriam encouraged him to be his best self. If it was Miriam, he could get up and go to the water, because it would mean something. It wouldn't only be for the cameras. The world feels hazy at the margins, and he closes his eyes for an instant—

And he is hanging from a log over the ocean. His arms and legs are looped around the beam, which is suspended above the water by two poles. His forearms chafe against the rough wood, and gravity is pulling his shoulders from their sockets.

The strategy of these endurance challenges is simply not to allow the possibility that you'll fall. Your arms will go numb, you'll suffer permanent nerve damage, you will actually die before you let yourself drop. Normally Kent focuses on a repeated phrase to distract him—"You can do it!" or "You're the man!"—but now fragments of ". . . Baby One More Time" keep looping through his brain, and it's making everything worse.

My loneliness is killing me . . .

Damn you, Britney Spears.

"Ruddy slips and falls and is *out*!" Jacob shouts from shore. "Only Kent and Ashley left!"

Here's his path back to himself. Winning a challenge—wasn't that always who he was? The challenge beast? He'll win the planks of solid wood, the private spa day, and a *second* key. Let Miriam be the hunter. Although dangling beside him, Ashley looks almost peaceful, barely straining as her lips flutter to her own mantra. Meanwhile his forearms are numb, and lightning bolts of nerve agony jolt up his calves.

"You've been going twenty minutes!" Jacob shouts from shore.

Twenty minutes? Surely twenty hours? Has time itself slowed to a crawl? Or has his consciousness expanded to take in more time, too much time, so that every second is an infinity?

When I'm not with you, I lose my mind.

"Ashley starting to slip on that beam!"

"You got this, Ash!" Miriam calls from shore.

His heart breaks.

His arms slide.

"Stay strong, Kent!" Miriam shouts now, as though she's cheering them both on, but it's secondhand, she didn't mean it. *Oh, baby, baby, I shouldn't have let you go,* he hears as he slips from the beam and drops—

Again Kent stalks past the mocking tree. The sun hangs immobile at the center of the sky.

He feels an animal prickle along his skin.

Something is out here.

Close. Breathing, panting.

The boar. At last.

He pushes into a thornbush to watch, when from the corner of his eye a flash comes flying toward him. He tries to run but the thorns grip at his skin and tear his flesh, and as the spear plunges into him he realizes, clawing upward from the dream, that *he* is the boar and Beck–

He jerks awake. It's night. He's lying in the shelter. Beside him on the beams the other contestants sleep peacefully, but something is wrong with the sky. It's–green. The entire landscape is blanketed in green, green reflects off the mist, and at the shoreline the water throbs with a vivid neon green so intense that he has a moment of panic that the bombs have dropped. He pushes himself off the shelter beams and walks toward the water, into the heart of the light, the throb of the green becoming so painful that he has to shield his eyes. He feels like he's pushing into an awful mystery, and every part of his skin prickles with the sleep-sodden yearning that maybe the veil of the world has been pulled back and he will step into something pure and good, but when he reaches the water, the green is only the lights from a fishing scow, bobbing peacefully offshore. He stands for a few minutes on the sand, watching the men on deck in their bucket hats and wet T-shirts, marveling at their expertise as they gather in the net that bulges with writhing squid, every motion as practiced and purposeful as a dance, calling out to one another in a language he can't understand but whose companionate banter is unmistakable, and it fills him with an envy so profound, compared to his own solitary aimless life, that he wishes the sea would swallow him right there.

He is walking with Beck down the beach, farther than they've ever gone for an interview, past the tide pools where Miriam is gathering mollusks, Ashley beside her stooping to hold a rock while Miriam twists snails off its surface. The women wave as they go by.

"That's interesting," Beck says as they pass.

"What is?" Kent asks.

"Oh–nothing."

"You can't say 'that's interesting,' and then tell me it's nothing."

"Truly, it was nothing. I was talking to myself."

She leads him to where her crew has set up, positions him against a tree, and takes her seat on the sandbag.

"What was interesting?" he demands again.

She raises a finger to wait for Afa's moment of silence and stares studiously into her notebook. The lingering anxiety from the pig dream makes her terrifying, her eyes sharp and deadly.

"So, Kent–" she begins.

"It was something with Ashley and Miriam."

"I'm really not allowed to say."

His skin prickles. "You can tell me. You have to tell me."

Beck stares at her notebook for a long while. "Okay. You don't think Miriam–and Ashley–might be–"

"Might be *what*?"

"Well–together?"

He bursts out laughing. "Together–like girlfriends?"

"Or allies. Planning a move. We did see them together by the rocks."

"And at mealtimes, they're together around the fire. There aren't too many places to *be* out here. Somehow I've gotten the impression that Ashley likes me. And Miriam . . . used to."

"But you know better than anyone how Ashley seeks attention. First she followed Ruddy. Then you. And wouldn't you say that Miriam is kind of–no offense–the star right now?" She sighs. "I wish I could show you my footage."

His heart accelerates. "You have–footage?"

She shrugs, like the banyan, mocking him.

"You have to show me."

"It would totally violate my responsibility as a producer."

Friedman shifts uncomfortably by the camera.

"Damn your responsibility as a producer," Kent says. "What about on the mountaintop? Wasn't that a violation?"

"*Please.* Kent. You promised you wouldn't use that against me."

She looks afraid. The hunter has become the hunted. Whatever this footage is, he needs to see it. "Don't make me use it against you."

She sighs heavily, with a sad, resigned look. "This is totally against the rules. But—I do think you deserve to know."

"Beck, what are you doing?" Friedman demands from behind his camera.

She waves him away. "Don't worry about it."

"Beck, this is really illegal," Friedman says.

She unholsters her handheld camera and turns the viewfinder toward Kent. There in the small rectangular screen is Ashley. She looks different on the LCD, even more beautiful, he thinks, a two-dimensional miniature perfectly framed against the sea and the sky. What has he been doing, spending his days in the jungle looking for an imaginary pig, when he has—

"I'm really connecting with Miriam." Her voice comes out small and tinny from the handheld's tiny speakers. *"Honestly, we have something so real."* The clip seems to jerk and jag, or is that his eyes? Now she's speaking over B-roll of herself walking down the beach. *"Kent is jealous of Miriam. We're going to leave him behind when we escape."* Back to the interview. Her hand is to her mouth, laughing at her boldness.

"Play it again," he whispers.

"Beck—you really can't do this!" Friedman says.

"I need to see it again."

"I'm sorry," Beck says, to him or to Friedman he doesn't know.

The jealousy moves through him swiftly and violently, like a swallowed shard of glass. This is the woman he's been cuddling with at night, feeding coconuts to. But Beck's right. Of course she betrayed him. Ashley's the girl who flashed her boobs for Reddit. Who went along with Ruddy's torture. Who forgave him for trying to poison her. She would do whatever it took to get the best story arc.

The real heartbreak is Miriam. *How could she*, he thinks, even as he's aware that he did the literal exact same thing to her. He remembers her hopeful, expectant eyes as she confessed herself to him on the mountaintop. It makes his whole body ache with longing. Why couldn't he simply lean down and kiss her? He wills his past self to move an inch lower—his lips were so close, two centimeters away from everything being different. But what if—*she* was playing him the whole time too? He remembers how right before she spoke, she looked over her shoulder, directly into the camera. At the time he thought she was nervous, that she hated for her vulnerable confession to be recorded and exposed to the world. But maybe she wasn't worried that the camera might be recording. Maybe she wanted to be certain that it was, that she was manufacturing *her* big TV moment. *"You watch your ass with that one,"* Barb said. He doesn't know anything about any of these people. They're all strangers, speaking to each other through masks, hoping that the edited and chopped-up selves would—

Edited and chopped up. It hits him. The clip could be a Frankenbite. After you've been on the show, you know what to look for. The little dips and rises in a person's inflection that show that two audio clips have been stitched together to create a meaning their speaker never intended. Ashley might not have said any of it. It might all be a lie.

"Let me see it one more time." He'll know what to look for.

Beck shakes her head sadly.

It doesn't really matter if it's real or fake, he thinks, if that's the story the producers are telling. The fake will become real. Ashley and Miriam will escape without him. He thinks of Margaret, sitting in their apartment, where he no longer lives, watching this all play back on the sixty-five-inch LG OLED television that he picked out from BestBuy.com after exhaustive research about screen burn-in and pixel density, but that he no longer owns because it was on her credit card. He has nothing. He *is* nothing. He sees that now. He only exists in the minds of others. He feels wobbly and unfocused, like slime dripping into the earth's hollow cracks. He needs—a shape. He needs a big moment, something that can be his alone, that he doesn't owe to Beck, that can't be pitched as somebody else's subplot. They're never going to give him a pig.

What else on this island is there to kill?

Kent Duvall dips his head beneath the surface of the water, Excalibur in his hand, forcing his eyes to stay open despite the salt sting. He wants the water to be refreshing and cool, but the sea is as hot as a bath. He swims out past the tide pools. Normally the shark is here, circling for prey.

It was obvious once it hit him. The shark's been waiting for him. He feels like Dorothy discovering her ruby slippers. They were there the whole time. He laughs to himself, remembering Megadeth, so many months ago, insisting he already killed a shark. Maybe the man caught a glimmer of the future through his TV screen. Why not? Crazy people had visions. Or maybe he's in a time loop, he thinks, and on his next go-around he'll be able to narrate to Megadeth this moment exactly, how the sandy murk under the surface was dead and barren, how his lungs burned, but how certain he felt, this time at last, that he was pulling toward his destiny. *That's not how I remember it*, Megadeth will still probably say.

There. A flash of gray. The reef shark's two feet long, and its fins are fringed with black. Kent surfaces, gasps air, and descends toward the bottom. The shark has buried its head under a rock, wriggling after hidden prey. Or maybe it senses a greater predator. He pulls downward, struggling to angle the spear against the water. The shark pushes its head deep under the rock, twisting from side to side. He punches Excalibur into its back.

Joy floods through him as blood pours from the wound. It's the release he's been craving for weeks. The shark corkscrews its body under the rock, but before it can disappear, he releases Excalibur and grabs its tail with both hands. For an instant its skin is slippery and smooth, but as the animal thrashes, its sandpaper scales scrape against his palms. He grips harder. He plants his feet on the rock. Blood spills through the water, enveloping him. He pulls upward, wrenching the shark from its hideout into the air, where Kent gasps oxygen and the predator writhes for its life.

When he makes his way to the beach, grinning wildly, the shark held aloft like a trophy, still desperately twisting, Friedman is onshore, working to fit his flippers over his wide, flat feet. His underwater camera sits idly at his side. "Oh shit. You got it already?"

Kent holds the shark higher. Its thrashes are beginning to slow.

"Well—can you—do it again?" Friedman stands up and takes a few awkward flippered steps toward the ocean.

"Do what again?" Kent asks.

"Get the shark."

"But I've got the shark."

"But I didn't film it." There's a slight whine to the man's voice.

"Can't you film it now?" Kent holds out the shark, and Friedman instinctively flinches.

"You do what you like," Friedman says, getting huffy, "but if you want anybody to see you actually catch that thing, we need to redo it. Otherwise it looks like it just appeared. And you know what people will say about that."

The two of them stare at each other mutely. He remembers meeting the cameraman years ago, at a finale party for *Endure*. *"Friedman,"* he introduced himself–as though it were his only name, like Madonna or Cher. He had a grizzled, hard-bitten thing that Kent found appealing, his craggy nose and the lines around his eyes like geologic features sculpted by the winds. He got into reality from nature documentaries, he told Kent at that party. *"Aren't you bored watching us sit around?"* Kent asked. *"Brother, my normal days are eight hours in a blind hoping a snow leopard idles by. You assholes bickering is high drama."* Now with his flippers and goggles, he looks like a skittish tourist at a resort. Kent's hands are red and throbbing from the sharkskin lacerations. His arms are raw and inflamed. But the shark is faded, almost dead. He can catch it again.

"Tell me when you're actually ready," Kent says, not bothering to conceal his irritation.

"You don't have to be a dick about it."

"Just give me the thumbs-up, okay?"

"I'll give you a signal."

Friedman paddles into the ocean and ducks his head under the waterline so Kent can only make out the tip of his snorkel. A few moments later, his hand pops out of the water, waving his middle finger. *Asshole.* The shark is barely moving. Hopefully it doesn't float to the surface the second he lets it go. He walks back into the ocean, where Excalibur still bobs, takes a breath, and dips below the waves.

As soon as it's underwater, the shark jolts to life. The needles of its skin slice his inflamed hands. Kent loses his grip–only for an instant. The shark rockets free. He grasps after it, but the water is like molasses. His fingertips brush the fringe of its tail. The shark spirals forward, hurls itself out of the water with the glee of a dolphin, spins three times in the air, and splashes into the waves. *No,* Kent thinks with horror. If it escapes, he has nothing, no footage, no shark, no food, the whole encounter erased from reality except for his injuries. He takes the spear and strokes strongly after it, but of course he can't outrace a fish. Then, incomprehensibly, the animal flips its trajectory and swims down, back to the same rocks it was hiding in before, back to where he can grab it. He surfaces, gasps air, and pulls downward, making sure Friedman is watching, the cameraman's middle finger still extended while he grips the bright yellow underwater cam. He holds Excalibur tighter and stabs at the shark's back. He grazes its skin. The shark, wild with confused frenzy, pivots and charges. *Come at me, bro.* Kent braces to catch it head on. This is the man versus nature showdown he's been waiting for. But the shark dodges past his guard. It bites into his side. He screams under the waves. Pain lances up his torso. He grabs the shark and tries to yank it off, but its serrated teeth are latched onto his flesh, so that pulling is even worse, he is tearing his own stomach. His blood spirals into the sea. Kent pushes upward, struggling into the air, his lungs burning. He breaks the waterline, sucking oxygen, still bracing the shark in his hands, its skin slicing his palms. He stumbles onto the sand with the shark attached to his gut and collapses to his knees, blood pouring from them both, and the last thing he sees before he loses consciousness is Friedman in his face filming, still flicking him off, capturing all his agony and failure as he loses consciousness, and his final thought before he passes out is *Thank god, I can sleep.*

CHAPTER 39

DAY 28

In Kent's earliest memory, he is two and a half years old, sitting in the sunken den with its white-shuttered windows and low blue couches, the cathode-ray television in its recessed wood-panel housing, surrounded by his family. His mom and dad are there, holding hands, a rare display of real affection, and his paternal grandparents, Grandmère—"mare," she said, which made Kent think of her as a noble white-maned horse—and his grandfather, Grand Richard, which Kent sensed was a joke but never quite understood at whose expense, leaning over the narrow dry bar with his elbows propped on the marble counter. He can't remember what anybody was talking about. He can't even picture himself, in the way that in most of his memories he sees himself in third person in the scene. But the memory always evokes a feeling of extreme contentment, of being safe and secure, surrounded by the people he loves most, until Grandmare announced she had to go upstairs to shower. He remembers that anxious feeling, like a fragile glass snow globe was being pushed to the very edge of a shelf. He asked her in his tiny two-year-old voice to please come back when she finished, and Grandmare assured him she would. But he heard the shower stop and the blow-dryer, and still she didn't return, and the phone rang and his father took the call, and his mom went upstairs because she needed to get ready too, and he asked her to come back, and she also said she would, but she didn't, until it was himself and Grand Richard, and the old man picked Kent up, dangling him by his hands in the way he hated, and deposited him in the corner with his trucks.

That feeling never left him, of struggling to hold on to something that was slipping away.

Now as the pontoon motors Kent into the dock by the Holding Pen, and the eliminated contestants stand onshore whooping and cheering for him, he feels like his deepest wound may be starting to heal. This is his new family, his reality TV family, who will be there even at his lowest moments. It's a cloudy night, and the reflection in the water of the dock's wavering orange lights looks like torches flickering beneath the sea. The wound in his stomach throbs. Eighty-seven black stitches circle the angry red gash. Callahan, the doctor, sits next to him on the boat, explaining how this is nothing, one time he had a patient who'd been mauled by a tiger. His neck feels naked without his lavalier necklace. Onshore, Barb is belting out a welcome song, and Carl hoists a margarita into the sky. He steps off the boat. Kelly-Anne runs up the dock and gives him an air hug, so as not to hurt him. He's back, he thinks. He's safe. The game is behind them. "Oh, Kent, we're so sad for you and happy for us that you're here!" Kelly-Anne leans in close, and he's ready—so desperately ready—to be consoled. She whispers into his ear, "Was everybody talking about me after I left?"

"I got you a whiskey." Barb hands him a plastic cup. "I figured you'd need the hard stuff. But first you gotta tell me. The real reason, none of the in-game bullshit. Why'd you break up my raft?"

"Jesus, Barbara, give him a chance to breathe before you interrogate him," Kelly-Anne says. "But the snake. It was a big moment, right? They must have asked you about it in an interview."

"I was so close to that money," Barb says. "I could damn near—"

"I guess my question," Kelly-Anne asks, "is how *many* interviews?"

Carl shoulders the women aside and grabs him by the hand. "Let me show the man to our cabin." He yanks him bodily up the sloping beach to a row of small wood huts that overlook the shore. "We're bunking together," Carl says, and Kent's bleary gratitude leaps to the behemoth. "Those birds have been squawking nonstop. Barb won't shut up about money. How much she should have won. Or if production will give us a stipend. I need money too, but I don't keep yapping about it. Kelly-Anne, it's about her edit. 'Am I a big character? I bet they're still talking about me.'" Carl wags his head slowly with wide eyes. "I begged them to send me home. I may have to cut my ears off."

Kent laughs. It's a side of Carl he's never seen, edgy, funny. He's been too hard on the guy.

"I do have one question," Carl says. "Ruddy. He's going to quit any day now, right? That puny weakling can't last another minute."

"Is this our cabin?"

"He's not a warrior," Carl says. "Not like us."

No, Kent thinks, he hasn't misjudged Carl. The man's eyes burn with the same lunacy that Barb feels, that Kelly-Anne feels, that he himself is starting to feel more intensely with every second he's out of the game.

WHEN KENT WAKES THE NEXT MORNING, HE'S GROGGY AND CONFUSED, like he's just awakened in a foreign time zone. It's been two days since he had Mydayis, and his brain feels both sluggish and spiky. The cabin is empty. Carl's gone. The wound in his stomach burns, but he barely notices it. The plasticky pillow and thin mattress feel like the greatest luxuries of his life, and he snuggles in the sheets for a few minutes longer before getting up to situate himself. Inside his suitcase are the extra clothes he packed in case he was eliminated early, two pairs of jeans and three T-shirts and four sets of socks and underwear, a haphazard mix of random things he grabbed from his closet because he never believed he would actually lose. But here he is. He's out of the game. The game is over for him. He lost. No matter how many ways he tells himself, it still feels like it can't possibly be true. He stares at himself in the bathroom mirror. His cheeks are sunken, and his eyes look hollow and worn. He looks like someone who has survived a great trauma, not competed in a game show. Rain thrums on the hut's corrugated tin roof, pocks the sand outside, and exhausts itself into the sea. The sad gray drizzle is even worse than the wild torrential downpours, like all the jungle's grand energies are spent.

He finds the three other eliminated contestants lined up under the awning on the Holding Pen's main porch. It's eight a.m., but they are already well into their drinks. Behind them, Callie from Casting sprawls on a cushioned deck chair. She glances over her Kindle with the half-hearted concern of an annoyed chaperone. The air is sweet with griddling banana pancakes and excess gas from the open-air skillet.

"I bet they're *freezing*," Carl says. The blended ice from his margarita sticks to his beard hairs in a fringe around his mouth. "No way can they keep a fire going. Not in this. I could. Maybe you." Carl gestures toward Kent, welcoming him to their huddle. "But not—Ruddy." He spits the name like it's poison in his mouth.

"Ten grand each." Barb drinks deep. "That's not much. They have to give us something."

"Stop obsessing over the money," Kelly-Anne says. "I love you, Barb, but that's shortsighted. The only thing that matters is the edit. Right, Kent?"

Kent touches his wound, which throbs. This isn't him, sitting here with them, this can't possibly be real—and for a brief instant his brain flashes, and he is still at camp, he can see it perfectly around him—there is the firepit and there is the shelter and Miriam is reaching out to offer him her hand, smiling—but he shakes his head, and the vision dissipates, and he takes his place beside Kelly-Anne and waggles a finger at the bartender to bring him a margarita. He's positive it's the elder from the stilt house, only now dressed in jeans and a T-shirt.

"I was the one who came up with the desertion." Kelly-Anne slices the edge of her fork into a banana pancake. "They *have* to give me credit."

"They'll give it to Ruddy," Carl says. "*He's* the villain."

"It was my idea."

"And was it your idea to torture me?" Carl asks. "To use *my girls* against me?"

"Jesus, Carl. It's not always about you."

"They can't last much longer." Carl stares at the ocean. "Not in this."

The bartender hands Kent his margarita, and he sucks it down. His brain aches from the ice.

"They have to give us *something*," Barb says.

THEY ARE THE CONTESTANTS LEFT IN THE GAME. *THEY* IS THE NETwork, who owes them nothing, but has to—simply has to—pay them a stipend. *They* are the producers, who will edit the show and dictate their storylines. *They* is the one-word sum-up for all life's divinities that have rendered them here, trapped at the Holding Pen, living in tiny huts whose shower, toilet, and sink are one combined spigot and drain. For weeks the four of them were the heroes of their own stories. Now they've learned the story isn't about them at all. They are B characters, brief complications for the real protagonists, condemned to agitate on the sidelines while they wait for Bartolo to sail to victory, his mythic Coke bottle hoisted high.

"KENT, ARE YOU SLEEPING? KENT? KENT?"

He jolts awake.

"Are you sleeping?"

"I'm not sleeping *now.*" His sleep has been disordered and confused. He's not sure if he's withdrawing from the Mydayis or the game. He fingers his neck, still hoping to find the lavalier necklace.

Carl is staring at him from his bed in the dark.

"Kent—we're warriors, right? Us. Me. I'm a warrior?"

You quit, he wants to say. *I'm the warrior. I was medically evacuated after facing down a shark. You got beaten in the sitting-still challenge by the nerd. You're a quitter and for the rest of your life that's what you'll be.*

"My girls. They'll think I'm a warrior, right?"

"You're a warrior, Carl," Kent says.

THE WOUND IS SPREADING OUTWARD. IN THE FOGGED-UP BATHROOM mirror, he watches the angry red border expanding across his stomach. It's hot and painful to the touch. Of course he can't heal while he's here, he thinks, surrounded by loser energy.

THE WORST PART OF THE HOLDING PEN IS THE FOOD. KENT FANTASIZED for weeks about the bacon cheeseburgers and pizzas and chocolate chip cookie dough he would gorge on after the game, but the menu here is reheated meat patties sandwiched in stale bread, banana pancakes, and a red curry that at first tasted delightfully exotic, hints of basil and lemongrass, but now he sees as gristly meat chunks drowned in limey soup.

The worst part of the Holding Pen is the smack of Barb's gums as she sucks the salt from the glass rim of her margarita.

The worst part of the Holding Pen is Carl waking him up every night to double-check that they're still warriors.

The worst part of the Holding Pen is the nightmares and headaches, his body craving the Mydayis's sharp-edged blade.

The worst part of the Holding Pen is the afternoon they take the pontoon out for a sunset toast of wine and cheese, and Carl somehow gets it into his head that there will be brownies. But when all Callie offers them is a box of cheap wine and three squares each of bland cheddar, Carl stands in the boat shouting, "I demand brownies!" and when Kent tries to calm him down he starts stamping his foot, rocking the boat from side to side so that Kelly-Anne clings to an awning pole screaming. "If they respected us, they'd give us brownies!" Carl shouts. "Can't any of you see?!" Afterward, when Carl finally calms down, the four eliminated contestants pose for a picture and swear that they'll always remember this foursome, the true legends of the game.

The worst part of the Holding Pen is how the pink cliff looms over the whole island, beckoning him to a world that doesn't exist for him anymore.

The worst part of the Holding Pen is that three legends of *Endure* have been outperformed by Ashley, a first boot, who in their minds deserves to be eternally a first boot.

The worst part of the Holding Pen is the endless circling, the endless second-guessing, the endless assessing of every single instant in the game and where it could have and should have gone differently.

The worst part of the Holding Pen is that nobody is here to record him. On the show, every morsel of food he ate, how long he slept, every passing whim or frustration mattered urgently to the producers. It was how life should be, all the purposefulness of a religion, that the trivial opinions and feuds of your tiny existence mattered in the eyes of God.

THE WORST PART OF THE HOLDING PEN IS THAT WHEN HE TURNS IN his bed at night, Miriam's body isn't there, her legs aren't wrapped around his, her breath isn't hot against his forearm.

CHAPTER 40

BECK

NIGHT 33

We'd wrapped our production meeting, and Jacob was escorting me to my bungalow. Our meetings were getting shorter with so much less story to track. He was quiet beside me, and I wasn't sure what to say. We still hadn't talked about Erika and his relationship, or what our hookup meant, or even about the alleged "plan." There were so many weighty things I wanted to ask him that it felt impossible to ask anything at all.

On the beach, the junior staff were smoking cigars, playing poker, and swapping war stories.

"The hardest-core producer I ever saw was a guy who literally shit himself so he didn't interrupt a scene."

"He couldn't hold it?"

"This was Nicaragua. He had dysentery. We all did. A contestant the whole cast loved was eliminated in a duel. All the contestants started crying. Full-on waterworks. Meanwhile—my man *really* had to go. I watched the stain spread down his shorts. But he did *not* ruin the shot."

"Is that hardcore? Or disgusting?"

"What about the *Naked and Afraid* EP who got bit by the fer-de-lance?"

"I saw those pics. His foot literally rotted."

"The hardest-core producer I ever saw"—a PA raised his voice as we approached—"was the stone-cold icon who spent the night in a monsoon on a mountaintop."

"Is that the *same* legend who filmed a dog dying?"

"I hear that woman swam into a scene because she wanted a workout."

I couldn't help but smile as we passed.

"You're getting a reputation." Jacob tapped me on the hip. My whole body tensed.

"Me and the pants shitter. Two legends."

"Beck, you're giving me gold. I was skeptical about Miriam and the pig. But I never guessed how beautifully it would play out. Kent goes crazy with jealousy and tries to kill a shark? Amazing."

"Thank god this time we got it in HD."

"Friedman. King of the shark shots." He laughed. "This is exactly the big human emotion we need. Jealousy. Revenge. Desperation. You're doing better than I could have hoped. Keep pushing."

I disgusted myself by how much I valued his approval. I was like a dog that couldn't control its hind leg when it was scratched. "I'm getting worried there's not too much to push anymore. I was hoping the Kent–Miriam rivalry would last a few episodes. Give us a big blowup confrontation. Now he's at the Holding Pen, and things have stalled. They're mostly lying around. Miriam's gathering food. Bartolo is ridiculous. Ashley's showmance is over. Ruddy is—kind of a blob now."

"He's really wilted without Erika to egg him on."

Again we walked in silence. I wanted to ask if he was mad at me about Ruddy, but I didn't want to seem needy or whiny. The sound of the conversation dimmed behind us, until there was only the stillness of the night, the chittering insects, and my looping internal monologue.

"I was—annoyed about the Ruddy thing," he said, like he was reading my mind. "Not at you, though. Casting should have caught it, and it's better to get ahead of these things. Story with the contestants is slow, but you got it to spark before."

As we walked along the shore, I couldn't imagine what that spark would be.

We reached my bungalow, and he stood outside the door while I fumbled with the lock. "So?" he asked. "Are you going to invite me inside?"

I looked back toward the dark shapes of the crew clustered on the beach. We were far enough away that we wouldn't be more than blurs to anybody watching. Jacob edged closer to me and hooked his index fingers into the waistband of my pants. My heart accelerated.

"Someone could see us," I said.

He laughed. "Everybody knows."

Everybody knows. Somehow that statement made it okay. This wasn't a random hookup. It was an established thing.

"What about Erika? She implied you guys have a—relationship."

He smiled sadly. "I've known Erika a long time. Yes, she and I fool around. That's life on location. I worry she maybe . . . takes it too seriously. None of that changes how I feel about you."

"You've been kind of a jerk over the past couple days."

"A jerk?" he asked in mock indignation. "Am I being jerky now?" He slipped his hand lower beneath my waistline, to the top of my pubic bone.

I pushed his chest, but not hard enough to push him away.

"When we're at work, I can't treat you differently than everybody else. Maybe I overcorrect because I really want to be fair. If so, I'm sorry. You know how much you impress me."

God, his arrogance was irritating. And yet some idiotic part of me believed that if we had sex a second time, it became more than a one-night stand. By making the same mistake twice, I could transform it from being a mistake. I would wrap myself in Jacob's acceptance. I could start to believe this whole experience wasn't a slowly unfolding disaster and that I really was killing it.

"Apologies in advance for the gecko shit," I said, and opened the door.

CHAPTER 41

KENT

DAY 34

A boat pulls up to the Holding Pen's dock, and the staff psychologist steps off. He's trim, with neat blond hair and the hopeful wisps of a beard. He wears a paisley short-sleeve button-down that pulls too tight across his chest, in a way that suggests a boy who hasn't yet bought the right size clothes, though probably he's showing off his pecs.

Kent's been worried about the staff psychologist ever since the Kimpton Hotel. This is the man who diagnosed him pregame as meek and fearful. But it's been six days at the Holding Pen, nearly a week of feeling lethargic and depressed, while his shadow world becomes ever more vivid, so that he will go for minutes at a time watching himself pilot a raft over the choppy seas toward Treasure Island, and he will *feel* the waves wobbling him, while the red-and-black wound, a little green now around the stitches, burns with pain. So when it's his turn, and the staff psychologist sits across from him in a plastic chair outside his hut, ticking his way along a notepad down the bubbles of Kent's psyche—"How are you sleeping? Any suicidal ideation?"—

Kent's taken with the sudden idea that he should confess himself utterly.

"I am—having trouble sleeping," Kent admits. "I keep waking up in the night. I can't—actually be here. I keep seeing—another me. Still out there. Still on the beach."

"Sleep is unsatisfactory." He checks a box on his pad.

"The problem is, I can't possibly be *here*." He fingers the wound and winces. Should he tell the man about his desperate craving for a drug he's been stealing? Or the spreading infection? Best not to mention either. They'll take him to the hospital, and it will close his access to the true world. "You have to send me back into the game."

"Mm-hmm," the staff psychologist says.

He's waiting for more, Kent thinks. *Give me the deep stuff*, his silence seems to say. Maybe if he spills it all out, empties himself, the staff psychologist will say something that will end his relentless longing and give him the consolation he craves.

"There was a girl. Kind of—a nerd. Miriam. But we sort of— There was something—but it was getting too serious, and so I went for the hot girl instead. Like, really hot. And I thought we'd ham it up for the cameras, and I could go home, and be . . . I don't know. It's embarrassing. But now I'm stuck here, and I miss her so much. Miriam. The nerd. I think I—love her? You have to send me back. I can get the girl. I can win the game."

"Can win the game," the staff psychologist repeats. Kent absentmindedly pushes down on the wound, and the pain is overwhelming, and the staff psychologist fades into blackness and he's *back*. Miriam is smiling at him. He's on the raft. Both of them are. They're stepping onto Treasure Island and opening the chest, and his stomach throbs—

No. He's in a wobbly chair at the Holding Pen, speaking to the staff psychologist, who is apparently doodling in his notebook. "I need this to end," Kent pleads. "I'm—losing my mind. Please. How can this end?"

"Sorry, buddy. We're all stuck here until the game's over and the contestants get that chest. You think *I* want to be here?" The man pats him on the shoulder and heads to the main lodge to play beach volleyball with Callie.

KENT WAKES IN THE NIGHT TO THE SOUND OF MUSIC AND SHOUTING. How can that be, when he's still in the shelter, spooned between Miriam and Ashley? *You're not in the game*, he tells himself. Does he know that—for sure? He can *feel* Miriam's fingers as he squeezes them tight.

He lies there quietly, his eyes wide open, sensing her beside him, even as his inner monologue won't stop—*You lost, you're a loser, you're at the Holding Pen, which sounds like it was made for animals.* But that's not possible. Kent Duvall isn't a loser. The "Woo-woos!" and screams from the lodge get louder. He slips on his pants and a T-shirt and goes outside.

Walking down the scrubby path, he's met by a cool sea breeze, and he has the wild thought that he could race down the beach and leap into the ocean and swim to Treasure Island. He imagines himself floating, the tide pulling him out, the infection sucking out of him, the sense of blissful infinity as this self—the loser self—dissolves into the horizon.

He walks down the slope away from the lodge to the edge of the shore and strips to his underwear. The water is warm. The sky is brilliant with stars. He swims until he can't touch the bottom and he's bobbing on the tide. His eyes are bleary. The black night stretches to infinity. The salt water burns the wound. The infection is creeping outward, he knows, but he can't show them. His thoughts feel fractured, like looking through a kaleidoscope. Simple images and scenes are fragmented into a thousand colorful pieces. Miriam—the treasure chest—the wisps of the staff psychologist's beard. Suddenly he is a child, with his mother, together around a clear plastic cup filled with tiny squiggles no bigger than an eyelash. Caterpillars. A butterfly-growing kit. He must have been four years old. Every day as they peered into the cup, his mom would ask him, *"What do you notice?,"* and they discussed like it was serious business—the color and shape of the oblong forms, how those squiggles became bigger and bigger until at last they inched their way up the sides of the cup and hung from its roof spinning brown cocoons.

He feels silly getting teary-eyed about the memory, yet one of the things he misses most about being a kid is the sense that these experiences mattered. That it mattered how much attention he paid to the caterpillars, that it mattered how much he loved his mother—that every experience was leading somewhere, that even as he aged into his teens and twenties, every activity was building a personality, a life. Now he's diminishing—he has diminished—and even this magnificent starlit sky is purposeless. It goes nowhere. There is nothing left for him, here, at home, anywhere. The horizon beckons. He feels the undertow pull against him, dragging him down. Somehow, he has to escape.

As he swims back to shore and pulls his clothes over his wet body, but before he discovers the rolled-up parchment that's been left in his crumpled-up shirt, a hand-drawn map back to the game, and in the pocket of his pants a bottle of Mydayis, he is still with his mother, the day they release the butterflies in the backyard. One of the butterflies lands on her arm and pauses there fluttering its orange speckled wings, and Kent thinks—then and now—that it is the most beautiful thing in the whole world. *"Again, again,"* he says, but the butterfly ascends and whirls into the sunlight.

CHAPTER 42

BECK

DAY 35

The next challenge was gross insects. Our crew filled a clear plastic trough with beetles and roaches and spiders and pale, wriggling grubs. Were spiders even insects? I was pretty sure not. The contestants had to dunk their heads into the trough, pick up the insects with their mouths, and run to their individual platforms, where they'd spit them into their buckets. Whoever filled their bucket fastest would win a pizza feast, a key, and canvas for a sail. Ashley let out a small scream when she saw what we had in store, took a deep breath, and reminded herself, "I've been practicing."

"Once they're in our mouths, can we eat them?" Ruddy asked, and made wiggly fingers at Ashley, who smacked his hand away.

I felt anxious that morning, for no reason I could quite place. Maybe it was the mist pouring out of the trees in the cold morning air, the impression I always had on these days that the island itself was burning. I couldn't keep still, and I shoved my hands into my pockets to contain my restless fingers while I watched the feeds from Video Village, really nothing more than a tent with seven iPads relayed from a Teradek.

"Go!" Jacob shouted. The four contestants dipped their heads at the same time. Bartolo promptly surfaced. "Not for a man of my stature," he said, and immediately quit, brushing a beetle onto the ground. The other three ran with mouthfuls of bugs and spat them into their buckets.

"I've been practicing," Ashley kept saying, on each return trip to the trough.

"Mmm, crunchy!" Ruddy shouted.

The whole crew was tetchy that morning. Maybe the coffee had been off. Maybe it was the disgusting challenge. Maybe the atmosphere itself held an electric charge. Erika was smiling sweetly and greeting all the staff with big hellos, which at first I took to be a sign of the apocalypse, but when Jacob pushed into the tent and didn't look at me, I started to draw even worse conclusions. He'd said he was busy the night before. Now he kept fiddling on his radio, feeding directions on our shared production line and muttering into a channel I wasn't part of.

The challenge lasted half an hour. Ashley dominated, forcing her head deep into the trough to take enormous mouthfuls of bugs, which she gagged back up into her bucket. "I did it!" she cried, looking around in wild-eyed wonder as Jacob presented her with the pizza and her second key. "Pizza" was a gross exaggeration. It was damp cheese over hard dough, yet when Jacob offered Ashley a celebratory first bite, she looked euphoric. Then he tapped me on the shoulder and gestured me away, leaving Erika behind to deal with the logistics.

"We've found him," he said, as soon as we were in the van.

"Found who?" I often felt with Jacob that I'd missed vital information and was struggling to catch up.

"Kent. Didn't you hear? Last night. He left the Holding Pen. Million saw smoke coming from the mountaintop."

"He—escaped from the Holding Pen?"

"Not escaped. It's not a prison. Who do you want to take to confront him? Maybe Miriam? You've been building that confrontation."

I was certain that I was misunderstanding something. "Isn't he out of the game? You, me, and Million should fly up there and—"

"He didn't quit. The contract doesn't even mention the Holding Pen."

"So he can just come right back and start playing again?"

"If it's not illegal, then it's legal."

"But what if—he's not exactly stable right now?" Outside the window, the mist was so thick that the trees seemed to dissolve at their edges, like projections fading from a screen. "I could go up there myself and see—"

"This is a huge moment," Jacob said. "It has to be from a contestant's perspective. We think he may be building a raft."

"On a mountaintop? It sounds like he's having a psychotic break."

"That's why you'll be there. Beck, you know we can't swoop in and solve every problem. This is narrative gold. Big, boundary-pushing moments like this will define our show."

"I'm worried this has gone past the show."

"There's no such thing as 'past the show.'" Jacob clicked his jaw back and forth in irritation at the mere idea. "Why don't you take Miriam?" he said again. It wasn't a suggestion.

"But things could escalate even further with her."

"Things escalating is literally the point. And—make sure that she does something about that raft. If there is one. I love Kent coming back to the game, but he can't *win*. That wouldn't be satisfying for the audience."

"Right, we can't have him sailing off a mountaintop to victory."

What I didn't want to tell Jacob was that not only was I worried about Kent's psyche, but my relationship with Miriam had also become fraught. Since the boar, our interviews had lost the bantery back-and-forth that I'd worked so hard to establish. She seemed wary of me. Whenever I sat across from her, in a jungle glade or on the beach, I could tell she was choosing her words carefully. Still, I thrilled as she gathered mollusks or tended the fire. She and Ashley had bonded over both feeling confused and jilted by Kent. They were working together to run the camp, two strong women collaborating. She was thriving, exactly as I'd hoped, becoming the person we both wanted her to be.

After I went back to the City for supplies, I found her spearfishing by the tide pools, poised on the edge of the low cratered rocks with Excalibur held high. She'd lashed the small knife to the spear tip to make it sharper. I felt like a proud parent watching my child across the quad on a college campus. A flicker of orange and red shivered through the water. She threw. The fish scattered. She jumped into the water to retrieve the spear, set her position again, waited—and threw. Again, the fish dissolved. She seemed so focused out there, and happy, even without actually catching anything, that I felt filled with my own vicarious joy. I waved to her and called out. She looked over, and her smile soured.

"We need to go." I knew I sounded brusque and annoyed, but I felt hurt.

"Go where?" she asked coldly.

"Up the mountain. Kent. He's building a raft. You have to stop him."

"Kent was medevacked."

"Well, now he's building a raft."

She looked at me clinically, like she was diagnosing a disease. "Someone else can deal with it."

"Miriam, please—it has to be you. You're the one who—"

"Stop. I don't want to hear it. Whatever's going on with Kent is not my problem anymore."

"I'm not supposed to tell you this. But Kent loves you."

She laughed bitterly. "If this is about love, maybe Ashley should go. I'm staying here." She turned her back, jabbed the spear angrily into the water, and pivoted around again to face me. "I'm not a—prop in whatever's going on with Kent."

It hurt to hear her sum up the situation so precisely, but that was exactly the reason it *had* to be her. Jacob was right. Purely from a storytelling perspective, Miriam needed this confrontation with Kent. It was the capstone of her journey. I had to say something that would get her into the scene. I had to appeal to her humanity, her decency, the values that were at the core of her being. Of both our beings.

"Miriam, Kent's up on that mountain, and he needs help. To be honest, I think that our production team should rescue him. But my boss is insisting I take you. So please, come with me. Not for my sake. Not even for your own sake. But for Kent's sake." I had the instinct that if I argued with her, gave her a chance to say why she shouldn't come, she would argue back. But if I simply went, she might follow. "I'm going to help him," I told her, and I started walking confidently up the beach.

I was at the curtain of palms heading into the jungle before I heard her behind me.

CHAPTER 43

We moved up the mountain quickly. It was easy now that we knew the terrain. Miriam was still carrying Excalibur, and she used it to propel herself up the incline, stabbing the sharp end angrily into the dirt. Jacob tuned in through her lavalier mike to listen, and throughout the climb he kept chattering on the radio in my ear. *"What do you see? What do you see?"*

"Mostly rock in my face." I was trying to be glib, although the feeling of apprehension I'd had all day only intensified as we neared the top. The thick mist was closing around us, and in the distance I heard a strange hollow echoing sound. *Chok-chok-chok. Chok-chok-chok.* Three beats and a breath. Three beats and a breath. As I pulled myself over the lip of the summit, I could barely see anything. It was like walking through gauze. I edged forward carefully, trying to get my bearings. *"What do you see?"* Jacob asked. For the moment I saw nothing, only a few feet of cracked sandstone.

I almost tripped over the body.

"Oh hell. There's a—dead monkey," I radioed.

"Film it. What's the number one rule? Keep rolling."

I put the camera to my eye and filmed. It was a large male. Looking at the scene through the viewfinder leveled out my heartbeat. His eyes were half-open, and his hands turned upward as though begging for his life. It was footage. *Chok-chok-chok* echoed across the plateau, coming from the copse. What if Kent was *eating* monkeys? A lifetime of anxieties had taught me too much about the hemorrhagic fevers that made their zoonotic jumps from animals to humans through bushmeat. It was footage. There was a time code on the bottom and margins on the side. I could zoom out or change focus.

I called Kent's name.

"Have Miriam make contact," Jacob said in my ear.

I swiveled the camera. She was a few feet behind me, on the plateau's edge. Through the viewfinder I could still see her as a character. Her scrawny frame. The oversize glasses. The wild hair and filthy lab coat. My geek to hero, approaching her climax. She was leaning on Excalibur, breathing heavily after the climb. She hadn't seen the monkey yet. I moved away from it and started walking backward toward the trees, filming her.

"I need you to call Kent's name," I said.

"I'm not here to—make television. I'm here to help Kent." She sounded more irritated than scared. It was amazing to me—and frightening—how the contestants trusted we could protect them, even as we'd failed again and again.

"How can we help Kent if we don't reach out to him?" I asked.

"You call his name. If you really care."

"Kent!" I shouted.

"Beck, you can't be the one to talk to him."

"Miriam won't do it."

"Jesus, Beck. Make her talk. Produce her."

"Forget it. We can edit it in post." It would be simple. A shot of the mountaintop. The sound of Miriam's voice calling his name, taken from any of a thousand earlier times at camp. Cut back to her tenta-

tive face as she inched forward along the plateau. Viewers would connect the narrative dots. I'd be invisible. Blissfully erased.

Chok-chok-chok.

Inside the copse it was even harder to see. The mist steamed from the close-clustered trees. The monkeys were gone. At the doorway to the hidden temple lay ten logs lashed together with vines. *Chok-chok-chok.* It was the relentless beat of a machete chopping wood.

"You were right. There's a raft," I radioed to Jacob. *"A good one. Not sure how it would get down the mountain, but it's solid. And also a—map of some sort."* It was hand-drawn on parchment, like a pirate's guide to hidden treasure. Dotted lines marked the path from the Holding Pen to here.

"Make sure she destroys the raft," Jacob radioed. *"It's one thing for Kent to escape from the Holding Pen, but if he actually wins, our viewers—"*

"I get it." I swiveled around to film her again. "Miriam, I need you to destroy this raft. We can't let Kent win—"

"What don't you understand about what I'm saying?" Suddenly, she was furious. "Now it's about rafts and the game. Let him win."

"Miriam, no—look—we can help Kent. We are going to help Kent. But if he sails away, then you leave here with nothing."

"That's not even true."

"The four of you are going to split, what?" I quickly calculated. If Kent left on day thirty-five, that would take seven hundred thousand dollars, leaving . . . "Three hundred thousand dollars? After all this time? And Kent could wait until day fifty, sail out in the morning, and take everything."

"I'm not talking about the money. I've learned things that will stay with me forever."

"Nobody cares what you've learned. Let's talk about your story. Viewers are going to—"

"You're unbelievable. Edit me however you like."

"It's not only the story on television. I'm talking about the story of your *life*. This is about you taking control of your destiny. Not letting someone else dictate what happens. You redeeming your past mistakes." *Us* redeeming our past mistakes.

I reached into my pocket and pulled out a skinny four-inch-long black cylinder, cold in my hand.

She froze like I'd hit pause. "Is that–"

I nodded. The ferro rod. The fire starter that was taken from her moments after the game began.

"Where–?" she whispered.

"It washed ashore." The rod had been sitting on my bedside table, reminding me daily about Miriam's unfair start. Today as I prepared for this journey, I realized that if Miriam was going to destroy a raft on a mountaintop, she needed a way to do it, and the ferro rod would be perfect.

"You get it?" I said. "You find the ferro rod. You use it to destroy the raft, stopping Kent from winning the game. Boom. Your screwup on day one is transformed into your big move on day thirty-five."

I offered it to her, and she snatched it before it could disappear again.

"That doesn't make sense." She hefted it in her palm. "How exactly did I suddenly find it?"

She was considering it. I had her. "It washed up. We'll film you later, picking it up from the ocean."

"This wood is too damp. It'll never light."

"Lucky for you, I've thought of everything." I pulled a tin flask from my backpack and unscrewed the lid. The gasoline seared my nostrils as I poured it onto the logs.

"How–do I strike it?"

I'd brought a knife from the dining hall, but now I had a better idea. "Use the knife from the spear. You run it along the edge to make a spark."

She unlashed the knife, laid Excalibur on the ground, and crouched in the dirt, turning away from the raft to protect the wood from sparks. Holding the knife in one hand and the rod in the other, she chopped downward at the black cylinder. The knife screeched against the metal. She tried again. Again the knife glanced away. I zoomed in so close that I could see the red-and-white mottled skin along her knuckles as she chopped and struck until she found the touch and caressed the blade along the rod in a fast flick. Sparks gushed off the metal. *Chok-chok-chok* came the sound through the trees. *Please, Kent, a few more minutes.* She only had to turn around and, with one swift stroke, the raft would burn. She ran the blade down the rod again. A cascade of orange sparks sizzled into the dirt.

She took a breath, stood up, and turned toward me. "No. This is wrong." She gave me back the ferro rod.

I wanted to scream. She was so close. "It's not wrong," I said, trying to mask my desperation. "It's your story."

"I'm not a character."

"You *are*," I insisted. "It's a *show*."

She dropped the knife onto the dirt. "Let's find Kent."

I could see the decision had hardened in her eyes.

"Fine. *I'll* do it for you." I pulled a fluorescent green lighter from my pocket. Her mouth slacked open. Jacob had told me to make sure the raft was destroyed, and I wasn't going to disappoint him now. I could see Erika's smug smile at this morning's challenge. I flicked the lighter's wheel and touched the flame to the edge of the raft. The gasoline ignited. A pale orange tongue licked across the wet wood. For a moment, the raft sizzled as the moisture burned upward in gray-black smoke. Then it caught. Flames leaped over the ground. The raft burned.

I picked up my handheld. "Why did you set fire to the raft, Miriam?"

Heat warped the air so that her image in the viewfinder was blurred and hazy.

"You were standing over the raft. Now it's on fire. Tell me, why did you set fire to the raft?"

Miriam backed away, slowly.

"You were saving your game, right? By setting fire to the raft, you were—"

A scream erupted. I turned. Kent was sprinting through the trees, gripping a machete. "What are you doing?"

"We're here to help," I offered limply as his raft burned behind me.

"What have you done to my raft?" He stared at Miriam with fury and hurt. "I need to go! *We* need to go. Together!"

Miriam fought to croak out a response but merely shook her head.

"This was for us!" he shouted, pointing at the burning raft. The heat pulsed around us. He was in his underpants, and he had the emaciated yet bloated look of contestants who've binged food after starving for weeks. The massive wound along his stomach was hideous, green and purple and black. "This isn't supposed to happen!" He slashed the air with his machete.

As he advanced on Miriam and the hot air shivered around us, it seemed to me that the costumes had fallen off and I was seeing things truly. Kent wasn't a hero or a villain. He was a deeply unwell middle-aged man. Miriam was a terrified kid, skinny and wasted in her oversize lab coat. I saw myself, clutching the camera like it might protect me against the wild and frenzied world.

"Kent, no," I said hoarsely. "I set the fire."

Miriam was still shaking her head, stumbling backward toward the temple doorway.

"*I* did it!" I shouted. I stepped between them, positioning my body at the tip of his machete. "It was my fault. We're here to help you."

"Have Miriam say it," Jacob shouted in my earpiece. I'd forgotten he was listening. *"We can't use it if you're saying it."*

"Use it? Jacob, you have no idea—"

"Have Miriam say it!"

I put my hand to my ear to cover the buzz. Kent kept pushing forward, and while Miriam ran to the side, I retreated through the temple door. Inside, I saw how the "ancient temple" was a production trick, supported by cheap wooden scaffolding.

"Kent, we're going to get you medical attention. Please, let me help you. We'll fly you back to the States, and you'll be getting the care you need within twenty-four hours. You are in danger of—"

He shook his head. "They won't let me go until it ends. I have to be the one to end it."

"We'll take you home. I promise. Only—put down the knife."

"Beck, shut the fuck up," Jacob hissed in my earpiece. *"Let Miriam talk."*

Kent knocked away my camera with the butt of his machete.

"Miriam, run," I said. "Go. Down the mountain. Kent, please, drop the knife."

"Damn it, Beck, you're ruining it," Jacob shouted.

I turned off the radio and stepped forward. The point of the machete pressed against my sternum.

"Stay away," Kent said.

"Drop the knife. Please."

I could feel him trembling through the machete tip. He was like a cornered animal. His claws were out, but he wanted to de-escalate. I stood motionless. "It's time to go home."

"Home. Where is that?" He looked at me with such desperate longing as the tension leaked from his body. His hand spasmed, jerking the machete down. It cut through my shirt. Pain arced across my stomach.

"Oh shit," I said, and in one swift, reflexive motion I smashed the camera into Kent's head. The shock of the impact ricocheted up my arm. He reeled but stayed on his feet and shoved me deeper into the temple. I saw a red light in the darkness. He swung the machete hilt at my head. It cracked against my skull. My vision blurred. I fell to the ground.

Standing over me, holding the machete, he looked scared and furious and deranged. I screamed. An object flitted across my blurred vision. He reared up, waving his arms wildly, then dropped to his knees and slumped forward.

"Oh god," Miriam said from the doorway.

Kent opened his mouth. He started to speak but made a gargling sound. I tried to stand. I was too woozy and sat back down.

"Wait," I said, as Miriam ran from the temple.

I crawled to Kent. Blood was running down his neck. My skull was screaming. I was slipping downward. Invisible hands were pulling me into the rock. I groped along Kent's face, down his neck to the wound. The sharpened tip of the spear had pierced his throat. Miriam had hit her mark at last.

I fumbled to turn the radio back on. *"Jacob. Wounded contestant. Helicopter immediately."*

"Beck, what happened? We can't get a helicopter up there. It's pouring."

It was pouring? Outside the temple the mist had turned into heavy rain. *"Get medical up here."*

"Nobody can get up that mountain. Beck, are you rolling?"

I slipped into unconsciousness.

I wasn't rolling.

CHAPTER 44

KENT

Kent Duvall is bleeding out.

This was not the plan. He came on *Escape!* to win challenges. To spear a boar. To become his old self. He definitively did not come on *Escape!* to bleed to death on a cheap production set. His neck is in pain so severe that he cannot reckon with the feeling, but with each passing heartbeat it dulls, blissful numbness spreading outward, like his lips after dental work. A gentle suction pulls at him from above, as though he's being hoovered upward by a divine Dustbuster, until he seems to hover a yard above himself in the air. He looks down at his poor body, skinny and filthy and mangled. All the rage and confusion has disappeared. He feels total calm. A few feet away lies Beck's camera, and strangely it's the sight of that machine abandoned in the dirt that makes him realize, Kent Duvall is dying. *Good*, he thinks. *Let Kent Duvall die.* But then there is the closely related fact that *he* is dying. How extremely stupid. But isn't that life? His own beautiful mother died of lung cancer from his father's secondhand smoke. Everybody gets a stupid fate they don't deserve.

The camera. Everyone has to die, but not everyone can die on TV. He can transform his saddest, messiest moment into something historic. Give a few parting words. Sum it all up. One last epic whinny as the show pony trots into the sunset. He strains to twist to the side. The numbness fades, and everything is blinding pain. He stretches his arm. He rotates his hips, the light spikes into his eyes—

He is back in the glade on *Endure*. The boar blinks its patient, generous eyes. Its ears twitch in the warm breeze. Is this heaven? Blissfully stabbing this pig for all eternity? He raises his spear. "No," he says. "I can't." He—lowers the spear? Wait, this is not how he remembers this. But this is how it really went. He's watched this scene so many times over the past fifteen years, his epic pig hunt scored to soaring violins, that the edit overwrote his memory. But he said no. He tried to walk away, until the producer who was filming him insisted *you can, you must*, and he closed his eyes and stabbed—

He's yanked higher, up over the plateau, above Beck's prone unconscious body—*I'm sorry*. Hovering over the mountaintop, he notes that the temple looks even cheaper, balsa wood and duct tape. Far below, deep in the jungle, he sees Miriam. She's slumped against a tree. Look at her, lean and strong and powerful. God, he wants to tell her all of it, how deeply he cares about her, how marvelous she is. He tries desperately to float down, but he keeps going up. "Miriam!" he cries, but his voice only comes out in a whisper.

And lying in the dirt on the mountaintop, he struggles desperately to twist, to reach, to fight through the pain and turn on the camera. It's right there—

And on *Endure* he drags the pig back into camp, and the dairy farmer runs up saying, "Holy moly!" This is before that's become the man's catchphrase, before he's been featured in online ads for Sabra guacamole. And the skateboarder who in two weeks will be Kent's runner-up fist-bumps him, and together the three men skewer the pig on a spit while the bartender, who is five foot ten and looks like Naomi Campbell, builds the fire. And as the dark descends, they eat the cooked pork, and the Yale poet clears his throat and recites Robert Frost's "Stopping by Woods on a Snowy Evening."

My little horse must think it queer
To stop without a farmhouse near
Between the woods and frozen lake
The darkest evening of the year.

He gives his harness bells a shake
To ask if there is some mistake.
The only other sound's the sweep
Of easy wind and downy flake.

At home he'd be rolling his eyes, but here and now he can hear the bells tinkling along the horse's bridle, and he feels . . . perfect, like the misshapen puzzle piece of his self has finally found its fitted slot. *This* was the moment, he thinks, floating through it. The eight of them around the flame. He'd forgotten it because it didn't make the edit, but when he first watched his season, he cried because it wasn't there. He'd become lost inside the idea that he needed to kill a boar, but killing the boar was really about opening the door back to here—

Miriam—he wants to shout to her. *We had that.* That feeling of perfect belonging. He had it with her.

And lying in the temple dirt, he realizes he can tell her on camera. If he can only press the red record button, he can let the whole world know that this is what it's really about. Togetherness. Contentment. He strains with all his might to turn, the pain sizzling up and down his body, his finger hovering so close he can almost feel the button depress—

And back at the campfire the hot Boston lawyer is telling a ghost story, and it's terrible, the stupidest ghost story he's ever heard. In six months when he wins, she'll take him to her hotel room after the finale party, strip down, and meow. Not make the *meow* sound, but actually say the word "meow," and what, is he supposed to say "woof"? But now around the campfire they all groan at her awful story and she says, "Fuck you, I'll see you in court."

"Roses and thorns," says the neurosurgeon.

"Kent's meat is my rose," says the hot Boston lawyer.

"Heh heh heh, Kent's meat," says the skateboarder.

"What about your lifetime roses?" the neurosurgeon says. "The rosiest rose you ever rosed."

And at the time Kent said, "Killing that boar," and they all snapped their fingers, but now lying in the dirt in excruciating pain, and now hovering over the jungle watching Miriam recede into a tiny speck, and now sitting around that campfire, Kent wants to tell them this was it, being there with them, that was the best moment of his life

and also

the orange speckled butterfly flapping its wings on his mother's freckled arm

Margaret's frozen tears of laughter after wiping out on the sled

in the sunken living room with Mom and Dad and Grandmare and Grand Richard

squeezing Miriam's fingers

her sweaty palm squeezing him back

If he can only twist a little farther, he can hit the red record button and tell them all. His hand slips into the dirt. And as he's pulled higher and higher, the world recedes into a speck, and all he can do is whoop and whoop and whoop until his vision collapses inward, and all he sees is darkness surrounding a flicker of light.

Kent Duvall is approaching the campfire. His friends' and loved ones' shadowed forms are waiting. *I have so much to tell you*, Kent thinks, and he steps into the circle surrounding the flame.

CHAPTER 45

MIRIAM

At first her way is choked with brambles and creepers, but farther in the underbrush thins, and the trees gather close. It's pouring out, but the canopy is so dense that only scattered droplets sprinkle from above. The sound of the cicadas grows louder. What started as a distant buzz becomes a metallic whine that crowds out her thoughts. It reminds her of the pig, though it sounds nothing like the pig's noises, which were animal and familiar. This is high-pitched and jagged, like a rusty nail being scraped across thin metal.

She killed Kent. She killed a human being, and not just any human being, but a man she loved. She is a killer. As she stumbles past trees, her feet catching on the roots and the stalks of bushes, she feels like she is tripping from one nightmare to another, worse nightmare. The light dims, and the trees jut from the dark landscape like the limbs of an ancient creature. The smell is sweet and foul, the dank stench of moldy earth and rotting vegetation. At first her only instinct is to run, to outpace thought, but the sound of the jungle is a physical force, like an insect clawing to enter her, until it's too much, she can't go farther but she can't go back, and breathless and soaked with sweat, she slumps against a tree.

Next to her hand, a millipede makes its way through a pile of brown leaves. It's three inches long, its segmented body striped orange and black. If you look at insects close enough, with their thousand limbs and tiny beaks, the garish colors, body parts with names that sound like an alien species, like the thorax, you start to see that monsters are real. They're just very small. She watches it weave up the tree while dark descends, and—as she prays that no snakes or predators find her—her eyes drift downward, and she falls asleep.

CHAPTER 46

BECK

I woke with my stomach on fire.

Callahan was crouched over me. He'd lifted my shirt and was cleaning my wound with a cotton swab.

"Kent," I said. My head was cloudy, yet all my animal senses had jolted into overdrive. I could smell the antiseptic bite of the alcohol. I heard my pulse throbbing along my stomach wound. I closed my eyes, but my eyelids continued to ache from the pressure of the sun.

"He's gone," Callahan said. "Eyes open. There you go. Look at me. How's your head?"

"Gone?"

"Dead."

Dead. One simple syllable couldn't contain the end of a life, the erasure of Kent's existence, the nullification of the man who had stood on this mountain, gazing across the island and wishing he could stay here forever. I felt hands reaching into my skull to drag me back to the earth.

Callahan slapped my face. "Don't go to sleep, love!"

"Miriam . . . where's Miriam?"

"We were hoping you'd know. Eyes open!"

I kept my eyes focused on him until I heard the helicopter's rotors outside. Jacob stepped into the temple. He crouched down and kissed my forehead.

"Jacob–Miriam–" I started.

"Hold on." He took his camera from its holster and began panning.

Kent's body was splayed on the ground, twisted like he was reaching for something, though the closest object was my camera ten feet away. The blood from his throat seeped down his chest. As I watched, a blue butterfly fluttered into the temple, alighted on his skin, and swirled away into the sunlight. I blinked, afraid I was hallucinating. Had I witnessed an actual miracle? Kent's soul ascending? More butterflies flew into the temple and crawled lightly on Kent. No, I thought. It wasn't his soul. The spirit of the jungle was reaching out to say farewell.

"It's beautiful," I whispered.

"They're puddling," Jacob said.

"Puddling?"

"They're feeding. On his salt."

I staggered over to Kent and waved my arms, scattering the butterflies and almost collapsing on top of him. Jacob and Callahan supported me by my armpits out of the temple, past the charred wreckage of Kent's raft, and toward the helicopter.

"Miriam," I said. "She ran–away. I don't know where."

"Shit." Jacob spoke into his radio. *"Jacob for Million."*

"Go for Million," I heard faintly through his earpiece.

"Miriam's missing. In the jungle. We need your team scouring everywhere. May be injured."

"Roger that." The radio clicked off.

"I don't think she was injured," I said.

"She could be now." He turned again to the radio. *"Jacob for Erika."*

"Go for Erika."

"Miriam's disappeared. I need you to—"

"Disappeared? Another Beck masterpiece? I know you thought she'd create good chaos, but I told you she would—"

"Not now," Jacob snapped. *"Check all the cameras for any footage."*

"I told you," she hissed, and clicked off.

On the helicopter ride to the City, I kept looking out the window, hoping I'd find Miriam among the trees, but we were too high. The jungle below us was a solid sea of green. My mind flickered through the last few days, like home movies on a worn-out projector. I thought that I should cry, but I felt too desolate even for that. Why did terrible things happen to everyone around me? It was like my entire life was rubbing against the grain of the universe.

The helicopter set down on the edge of the City. I asked to join the search party, but Callahan insisted I was injured and needed to rest. Jacob escorted me back to my cabin.

"What about Kent's body?" I asked as we walked.

"Benjamin will go back for it."

"And then what? We ship him back to the States?"

"We'll cremate him here."

"Won't his family want to say goodbye?"

"Kent doesn't have any family," Jacob said. "No kids. His parents are dead. There's a wife, but they're separated. None of our contestants have anybody close."

"*None* of them?"

"Carl has kids. But otherwise, they're all orphans. If you can call eight grown adults 'orphans.'"

"Surely someone will want his body. A separated wife is still a wife."

"We're in the jungle. It's not like we have a morgue. He's already decomposing."

I prayed his coldness was due to his professional instincts clicking in. When we arrived at my door, Jacob looked out across the beach. "I hate to even ask but—did you get it?"

"What?"

"The footage of the fight. Did you get it?"

"The *footage*?"

"We owe it to Kent's legacy that we show how he died."

I shook my head. "I got—something? I honestly don't know what." I paused before asking, "What do we tell the contestants?"

"We don't tell them anything. If we provide any information, it violates the ethos of our show. We don't reveal what they haven't observed with their own eyes. Besides, we can't have them panicking."

"Our *show*? You can't seriously want to keep filming."

"We have to. This is *reality*, Beck. Kent's death really happened. Reality TV doesn't have to be boiled down to some—kitschy competition with gross-out challenges. Don't you see? We're disrupting the entire genre. This is a reality show that is *real*."

"Kent died," I said. "Miriam *killed* him. Now she's god knows where in the jungle. We need to shut this production down."

"Beck, this is the very stuff we've been working toward. Capturing the raw vitality of the human experience."

"Kent *died*."

"People die on TV all the time."

"*Fictional* people."

"Exactly! People love scripted TV because of the drama. The only danger on reality TV is who's getting voted out of the singing competition. People die doing extreme things every day. They drop dead running a marathon. From playing video games too long. People *die*. It's the fundamental human condition, and *we* have an opportunity to document it in a new way. This is why reality shows are considered trash while scripted content is high art. We can't turn our cameras away right at the moment we're capturing the vital thing. Beck—you got this. This is genre defining, and it's your story."

Had I missed something in my hazy concussed state? Jacob could be intense, but this was insane. "Is that even legal?"

"What *we're* doing is absolutely legal. We're documenting. What Miriam did is another matter, but with the clear case of Kent's erratic behavior, supported by our connections with local government—"

"We can't pull strings and make this go away!"

"I'm not making anything go away. The exact opposite. But if the local officials, after being fully informed of all the facts, don't think Miriam did anything wrong—if it's not illegal, then it's legal. I hate to be the one to say it, but I'm doing this for you too. You were the one who pushed Kent to the edge. If we shut down production, the narrative ends with your fingerprints everywhere. And with Buster, you now have a pattern. You *have to* see this through to its conclusion." He stamped his foot impatiently in the dirt. "Don't you see, Beck? We're making history. You did this. It's extraordinary."

He was so excited he was almost trembling. He grabbed my waist and pulled me close. He was hard. My whole body recoiled. I pushed him back, stepped inside the bungalow, and slid shut the rusted latch.

Who even was that man quivering outside my door? And what had he seen inside me, that he thought I'd be turned on too? This "vital thing" that we were going to show society. That a sick middle-aged man had a psychotic breakdown? It was brutal and exploitative. It only showed how horrifically you could abase someone. All I'd wanted was to create simple sweet stories where people got what they deserved from this terrible world.

But if that was true, why had I twisted Kent into circles? Why had I told Ruddy to weaponize Barb's dead son? Why had I set fire to Kent's raft?

Jacob was right. I'd pushed Kent. I had killed Buster. I'd ruined

Miriam's life too by making her a killer. I'd been telling myself I was a good person for so long, and I let myself do the most awful things to prove it.

No. "Let myself" was a lie. I'd loved it.

Like a subconscious tic, I opened the video on my laptop to calm myself down.

My mother was crouched beside me, dropping marshmallows into my pink ceramic cup.

"Okay." My dad's voice. *"Rebecca's first-ever hot chocolate."*

"Am I going to like it?" I asked.

"You're going to love it." Mom moved the cup to my lips.

"Mmm!" I held up my elephant stuffie. *"Can Ellie taste too?"*

For the first time I could remember, I let the video play straight through.

I was belting out "The Itsy-Bitsy Spider" while Mom made the hand gestures. *"Down came the rain—to wash the spider out!"* She tickled my tummy with her spidery hands.

Who was I to choose where the video stopped, what parts to see and what to ignore?

I was jumping from our living room couch onto a beanbag chair.

"Here comes the big jump!" Mom said. I leaped as high as I could.

"Can I have more hot chocolate?" I asked from the beanbag.

"Sweetheart, you already had a cup and so many delicious marshmallows. We'll have more tomorrow."

"But I want more now." My toddler whine.

She put a gentle hand on my ribs. *"We've already had our treats for today."*

"Now! I want more now!" I was bawling.

"Sweetie, calm down."

I pushed her away. *"I'm going to hit you!"* I flung my hand out.

"We're not going to have treats if you're going to throw a tantrum every time."

"I. Want. More. Hot. Chocolate!"

"Michael, can you help?"

"I *don't know what to do,"* Dad said. He never did.

"Maybe start by putting down the camera?"

"You don't have to snap at me, Evelyn."

"You're a bad guy!" I shouted at my mom. *"I'm sending you to jail!"*

"I'm not snapping, Michael. I'm asking."

"Tone, Evelyn. We talked about this."

"Put down the freaking camera!"

"You're a bad guy!" I shouted again.

The screen went black.

It was the only footage I had of my mother, my final memory of her alive. My last words, repeated forever, lashing out, and making my parents fight too. I had always been a monster.

In real life there is no story arc. Only disaster.

Oh god, where was Miriam?

CHAPTER 47
MIRIAM

DAY 36

In the morning, still half asleep, Miriam realizes that her body has become rooted to the earth and that her consciousness has diffused through the bushes and trees. When she opens her eyes, she will see the universe kaleidoscoping through a billion fluttering leaves. She will see the tree frogs camouflaged against the bark with their throbbing throats, she will understand the mosquitoes' endless complaint, and everywhere she will be aware of the tiny cicadas and their unceasing song. She has transcended. She will take in at one knowing the multiplicity of life.

But when she at last lifts her painful eyelids, she is still herself. She is still a panicked killer, alone in the jungle.

She fled wildly and aimlessly, and now she has no idea where she is. She must gather her wits and return to camp. She'll be sent to jail, but what else can she do? Live on the lam in the wild? "Hello," she says into her lavalier necklace. "This is Miriam. I'm in the jungle . . . somewhere." It's painfully vague, and who knows if the mike can even transmit from where she is all the way to production. Her best bet is to walk straight and hope that somehow, she reaches something. The sea, a river, a road. And fast, because she's becoming severely dehydrated.

The body is like any system in a laboratory. It seeks its equilibrium. The high heat means she is sweating more to cool herself, but in the humidity, the sweat can't properly evaporate, so the body keeps sweating. She's covered with a sheen of moisture on the outside and parched internally. She can already feel the ache at her temples and the blurring behind her eyes. She needs water.

She walks for what feels like hours without coming on even a muddy hole. She passes a tree heavy with the poisonous green fruit. She plucks one and digs a finger into its skin. The flesh is yellow and pulpy and plump with juice. The fruit is poison. Still she can't convince herself to leave it behind. She drops it into the pocket of her lab coat and presses on.

By midafternoon, her vision has blurred to the point that she is witnessing the world through a translucent film. Her tongue is jagged. She needs water. The fruit is in her pocket. Does she know for certain that it's poison? It made her mouth numb, but the risks of dehydration may be greater than the danger of the numbing agent. Kent used it to "poison" the Deserters' water supply, but nobody drank from it, and for all she knows that may have been a production ruse to get them to live together, one more lie in an endless cascade of lies.

Using a stick, she cuts a gash in the skin, puts the fruit to her mouth, and sucks. Again her lips numb. But the juice is sweet, like lime. The trickle passes along her parched throat. The squirt of liquid eases her headache, and the sugar jump-starts her brain. Yes, she killed Kent, but clearly in self-defense. Well, defense of Beck. She has no idea what counts as justifiable homicide in this country, or really, any country. What will the other contestants say? She imagines Ashley, wailing in misery. Miriam wants to break down, but she can't, and so as she pushes onward through the jungle she keeps thinking of

Ashley, like an imaginary outlet for her grief. At least her parents aren't alive to see this. She always thought there was something sad about her mom and dad, their narrow life trimming their rosebushes. But they were happy. Why couldn't Miriam accept her life, just let herself be?

It's dusk when her stomach surges through her throat. She heaves up the fruit on her hands and knees, retching bile onto the dirt. Kent is beside her, laughing hysterically, wiping his finger on a leaf. No. Kent is dead. She killed him. She catches her breath and tries to stand but falls again. The screaming of the cicadas is too much, too loud. She slumps onto the ground, where she sees scattered images of Kent in the shelter, Kent in the stilt house with his mouth stuffed with meat thing, Kent standing beside her on the mountaintop leaning down, almost kissing her, Kent dead on the temple floor.

CHAPTER 48

BECK

Jacob and I were standing at the helipad, wearing our sunglasses, watching the chopper descend. "I had to give the network a heads-up," he explained. "They believe in what we're doing, but they wanted to send their own guy. You know how they like to meddle."

What we're doing. What was I a part of? Was this a horrible accident that Jacob was capitalizing on, or was documenting a death the plan that Jacob had been pushing toward all along? At least I could help fix the catastrophe I'd caused. Looking up, I thought back to my own first views of that jungle. A few weeks earlier, the island had been a crucible of possibility and promise. Jacob had bounded across the turf, taken me into his arms, and held his hug at peak clench. Now the rotors were gusting sand across my face, and Jacob felt like an icy blank as he waved his exuberant greeting into the sky.

The helicopter door opened, and a pale man stepped out in a tailored suit. He squinted into the brilliant light, slipped on sunglasses from his breast pocket, and squat-shuffled toward us across the field. *Oh no.* I recognized this shuffling, elegant form. It was Jeremy Englander, the network employee from *Surf Dogs.*

"Jeremy, meet Beck," Jacob said as the whirring blades faded into the distance. "She's been the main producer on the ground for this. Jeremy will be guiding us through this crisis."

"Beck, can't believe we're meeting again so soon!" Englander said, grasping my hand and slapping me on the back as though we were the oldest of friends. "Christ, it's hot. So much respect for you guys on location. Did you find her yet?"

"We're looking," Jacob said. "All hands on deck."

"Find her fast," Englander said. "You know that Oscar Wilde quote—to lose one parent is a misfortune. But to lose two looks like carelessness?"

Jacob did a good job of pretending to laugh. I grimaced. I couldn't believe that Jeremy Englander of all people had descended once more into my personal hell. Was it a cosmic coincidence? The small world of cable TV? Or maybe he was now considered an expert on dead reality contestants, specifically those murdered by Beck Bermann. It was becoming a genre. As we bounced along the road, he smiled broadly at every shock and bump, like it was a reflex.

Production companies and networks enjoy a symbiotic, combative, loving, tense relationship. Like any marriage. The prodcos see network suits as penny-pinchers and meddlers with no clue how to tell a story. Network execs see producers as arrogant auteurs who can't understand the demands of building an audience, scheduling a season of programming, and monetizing the industry. But in times of celebration, like smash ratings and Emmy wins, or in moments of crisis, like this one, the codependent pair closes ranks like any self-respecting dysfunctional family.

When we got to the City, Jacob led us upstairs to the room Jeremy would be staying in.

"There's an extra room?" I hissed as we walked down the hallway.

"It's reserved for the network," Jacob whispered.

"And has been sitting empty for a month."

He unlocked the door, and Englander peeked inside. "Love it. The authentic experience." He set his suitcase on the edge of the bed. "Beck–you and I should chat, so we can sort out what's going on and plan our best response."

Englander's last attempt to sort things out had resulted in my being fired from my job and pilloried by the media. I looked at Jacob, waiting for him to save me.

"I'll leave you guys to it," he said. "Beck can show you around the City when you're done. I've got a contestant to find."

I followed him into the corridor.

"I need to be out there looking for Miriam," I said.

"I know you want that. But I can't send you into the jungle with your injuries. It would be irresponsible. I need you here, keeping Englander out of the way. Everyone else is looking. Even the kitchen staff. Erika's crew has locked down camp, and–"

"What do the contestants think is happening?"

"They're worried," Jacob said. "As far as they know, Kent is still at the Holding Pen. But Miriam's disappeared. Bartolo's talking about organizing a rescue mission. We're coming up with a challenge to keep them occupied. See how long they can stand on a log or something. But the last thing I need is to babysit a network suit. You may not believe it, but you're playing a crucial role."

"Fine." But as I pushed back into Englander's room, I thought of Miriam, starving or attacked by an animal or bitten by a snake, and felt desperately helpless.

Englander motioned me toward the flimsy wooden chair beside the room's bare table. "Beck. I'm truly sorry about how it all ended with *Surf Dogs*. I knew in my heart you weren't to blame. This time's going to be different. Jacob won't stop gushing about how you're such a vital part of our show's success. That's why I've flown ten thousand miles to this—hotel. To support you. So why don't you start by telling me about the incident?"

Everything I do is terrible, I wanted to say. *The world is broken and terrible.* I started tearing up.

He moved to put his hand on my shoulder, but before he touched me he caught himself, like he remembered the network's sexual harassment guidelines, and so his hand hovered there. In spite of myself, I sobbed out a laugh.

"Sorry," I said. "I mean, thanks."

"Just do your best. I know this is heavy stuff."

I felt a sudden strange affection for this awkward bureaucrat. Maybe what I needed most *was* a messaging expert, someone to weave the wild catastrophe of the last few days into words that made sense. But where should I begin? How could he make sense of anything if I started with the climb up to the mountain plateau? Maybe I should start with my arrival on the island, or, better yet, begin with the last time I spoke to Englander himself, from the Surf On Inn. Maybe I should start with finding my mother dead in my living room.

"Kent—" I said. My voice choked. "He . . . had an infection in his stomach. From a shark bite. And he was having a psychotic break. He escaped the Holding Pen and got it in his head that he could still win the game, so he was building a raft. Jacob wanted Miriam and me to go up the mountain—" I broke down again.

"There, there," Englander said perfunctorily. "Did Jacob explicitly tell you to take Miriam?"

"Yes. We were driving back from a challenge. He said, 'Why don't you take Miriam?'"

"So it was more of a question."

My skin prickled. "At the time, I heard it very much as a command."

"Let's not sweat the details. What happened when you got there?"

"Like I said, we found this raft of Kent's. And Miriam—" I paused, wary. I had footage of Miriam striking the ferro rod and standing beside the flames. "She set fire to the raft. And then . . . Kent attacked us. I tried to get him to calm down, but—" My voice choked up.

"It sounds to me like you were a real hero," Englander said softly. He hovered his hand above my shoulder again.

I shook my head.

"You said Kent was having a psychotic break. I remember him from *Endure.* Solid guy. I have to ask. Did you maybe push him a *teensy* bit too hard?"

At every moment I'd been pushing Kent and prodding him. But my warning signals were pinging like crazy, and my instinct for self-preservation took over. "I never told Kent to do anything. My job is to ask questions. That's what producers do."

"But there must be at least *one* instance that comes to mind." His eyebrows crept up his forehead. A smile played across his face, as if we were best friends sharing a secret. "I need to know, so I can protect you."

Englander's fingers tapped along his pant leg. His mouth was open just a little, like he couldn't wait for my response.

I was being produced.

He hadn't traveled thousands of miles to make sense of a catastrophe. He was here to find the fall guy. *Erratic producer with a record of pushing too hard.*

"Good luck in your investigation." I stood up.

"Beck, hold on. I must remind you that you have a pattern—"

Jacob's words. I let the door slam behind me. I needed a drink, even if it was unsafe after a head injury. The bar was crowded with PAs. I couldn't bear to be near them, so I walked into the kitchen and opened the fridge. I pushed my hand past the bags of meats and veggies, hoping my suspicions were wrong.

There it was. Another tiny bottle of champagne. I could feel the hard cold glass of at least three others. Who knew how often Jacob had led people to his room and painted the illusion of a private confidence? How many times he'd clinked his red plastic cup with theirs and told them they were saving his butt. I popped the cork and drank straight from the bottle, focusing on the sweet-sour fizz curling down my throat until my head started spinning and I couldn't focus on anything anymore.

CHAPTER 49

MIRIAM

DAY 37

She wakes in the morning to a rustling. She instinctively flinches, but when she opens her eyes she sees small hooves shuffling through the leaf litter. Not twenty feet away, his snout digging through the rain forest decay, is Pig Bambi. Miriam blinks her swollen eyelids, half-sure that the animal is a fever dream. Even in a few weeks, the pig has changed. It's bigger, and coarse hairs have sprouted along its back. Small tusks edge outward from its mouth. Miriam would think it was a different animal entirely, if not for the little rope still tied around its leg, and the outline of George Washington etched below its eye.

She is silent, motionless, watching. When the pig moves, Miriam forces her gummy limbs upward and follows. For a few moments, she is freed from the crippling question of *why*. The pig moves. She follows. That is all. The cicadas sing their iron song, and the rain-choked trees gaze at this unfamiliar trespass as she follows the pig, which winds its way deeper into the heart of the jungle.

At first she hopes that Pig Bambi is leading her to water, but at a certain point she realizes she's hunting the pig. If she can kill the pig, she can drink its blood and hydrate herself. *Drink its blood*, she thinks with disgust—but what other choice does she have? How even to kill an animal? She scans the ground as she walks, looking for a sharp object. She picks up a fallen branch, but it's damp and rotten, and termites race out of tiny cavities in the bark. She drops it and continues to follow. Later she finds a branch that is less rotten than some, whose point is sharper than others. She picks it up and follows the pig, which snuffles carelessly forward.

When the pig pauses to graze in the dirt, Miriam inches as close as she dares, hinges back her arm, and throws. The sharp branch flies true and hits the animal at the back of its shank, but the wood is too rotten and breaks before it drives deep into the flesh. Pig Bambi squeals and bolts. Miriam follows, and for a moment she is the act of running, without consciousness, nothing more than the feel of legs pedaling through the air. What if she could exist like this, no past or future, no *story*—mere being? They race through the trees, the pig slowed by the pain from its wound, Miriam's head pounding. The problem with her spearfishing, she realizes suddenly, was that she was trying to spear the fish where she saw them. But light warps as it travels through water. The fish she was seeing wasn't really where the fish was at all. It's all an illusion—everything, not only the show, not only the hunt, but her entire being is a jangled array of senses, *sensation*, *sensation*, *sensation*, and most of them wrong and meaningless. She feels—effortless. She is not a killer, she is not a chemist, she is not a daughter or a hunter or a marketing specialist. She is the throb of her temples and the ache of her feet, she is the pig veering before her, she is the whispering of the tiny birds through the air, the reptiles and the rodents scuttling along the ground, and beneath everything the scream of the cicadas.

The heat spikes. The pace slows. At times Miriam loses the pig and follows it by its sound among the dead leaves, or by the trail of blood that is now wide and clear. At times she walks within sight of the animal, which staggers before her. By early afternoon, she is spent. The adrenaline and the desperation have abandoned her. She sits on the ground and watches the pig shuffle away and knows that this is her end.

Get up. She hears Kent's voice beside her.

"Kent?" she says aloud.

It's only the wind.

But she hears it again, in Kent's clear baritone. *Get up. Get up.*

It is the wind, and it is Kent, and it is her, speaking to herself through the wind and through Kent. *Get up.*

She thought the lesson of the island was that there was nothing beyond the raw facts of her body. Now she sees there is another layer, even lower, when the body collapses. Below everything, there is the will.

"Okay," she says. She pulls herself up like a marionette. She demands that her limbs move forward. She is the animal and she is the storyteller; she is the experience and the summary. She follows the animal's trail.

By late afternoon, Pig Bambi has lost too much blood. He moans and wobbles, he collapses and staggers to his feet, and at his end, he turns toward Miriam and stomps the ground and hunches his shoulders. Face-to-face with the boar at last, Miriam has no idea what to do. She has no weapon. Around them the ground is a layer of rotten leaves, not even a stick.

That's when she hears the sound, louder than the cicadas, booming down through the trees, racing along the wind like the voice of the jungle itself. It is the sound of Kent's whoops as he jumped off the boat; his shouts of celebration at building fire; the bellow he made before leaping into the waves at the second challenge. It is a human sound beyond words that sings in Miriam's ears and echoes along her heart. The sound passes through her and over her. It is her sound; she joins her own voice to the chorus and, whooping, she rushes at the pig and grapples with the animal as it writhes and kicks for its life.

CHAPTER 50

BECK

I woke up tangled in my mosquito netting and drenched in sweat. I'd been having an anxiety dream, one in which the oozing infection in my stomach repulsed a room full of doctors, and as soon as I jolted awake, I massaged the line of my cut. It was swollen and hot, and my entire torso was covered in bug bites, but as far as I could tell, no wasting illness. The wind had blown open my rotten windows, and the mattress was wet. It was dark out, but I had to pee, and I lay in bed debating whether to hold it or go relieve myself in the porta-bins down the beach. They were filthy wooden boxes surrounded by big lazy flies, and I wanted to gag every time I stepped inside one, but the pressure in my bladder was too intense.

Outside, the night was brilliant and clear, and I considered squatting in the pine scrum behind the cabin, but down the beach I could still see the three guards clustered around their radio. The endless sports match continued. I waved to them as I passed, and one of the men said something in his language, at which the other men laughed.

Neither of the porta-bins had a seat, and as I squatted over the hole I held my nose to stop myself from retching. Afterward I walked down to the beach and sat on the sand, gulping in the clean night air and looking up at the endless canopy of space, another grim reminder of how tiny we are in a vast and impersonal universe. It had been two days since Miriam disappeared. I couldn't bear to think about it. Instead my mind kept looping back to those moments on the mountain. How did Kent get a machete? And where did that map come from? Most of all, I remembered the feel in my hand of the camera hitting Kent's skull, the reverberations echoing up through my wrist and into my arm. And I could see in my mind's eye a glowing red light in the temple darkness.

The hotel was silent, but when I walked into the production room, Ralph the PA was logging footage.

"You're still up?" I asked. "You're practically nocturnal."

"Jesus. Don't sneak up on me," he said, taking off his headphones. "Here, I could use an outside opinion. Listen to this. Is Bartolo saying coconut *chop* or coconut *shop*?"

I liked Ralph. He reminded me of a small forest creature, like something out of Narnia. He handed me the headphones. On the monitor, Bartolo was talking to Ruddy in the shelter about opening a coconut in his typical roundabout way, where he somehow managed both to imply his own expertise and to demean the person he was speaking to, all while asking for help. I watched the scene and smiled. There was something so perfectly innocent about Bartolo trying to preserve his dignity while Ruddy made him twist. These tiny personal peccadilloes, set against the backdrop of the jungle, were the types of stories I'd expected to tell out here.

"I hear coconut *shop*," I said. "Now I have a question to ask you. Have you seen the latest memory cards from the mountaintop?"

"What cards from which mountaintop?"

"Isn't there a camera in the mountain temple?" I asked. "When I was up there the other day, I was pretty sure I saw a camera."

"Not that I know of," Ralph said. "I haven't seen any footage. The producer who you replaced, Stellan, was all over the island placing remotes. I guess it's possible that he left one up there? It'd definitely be out of batteries by now, though. Jacob would know."

"Thanks. I'll ask him," I said, and left the room. Asking Jacob *would* be the normal way to approach this problem. But the more I turned those final moments with Kent over in my mind, the more certain I was that the red light was a camera, and that it was recording. Ralph was right. If it was an abandoned motion-sensing rig, the batteries, triggered by the monkeys, would have long since been depleted. That meant someone had to be replacing the batteries. So why didn't Ralph or I know about it?

I lingered in the lobby until Ralph went into the dining room for breakfast. Then I slipped back into the production office, sat down at a computer, and sent Stellan a message on Facebook: *You there? This is Beck Bermann. Quick question for you.* It was twelve hours earlier in New York, which meant that it would be early evening for Stellan. He should be up, though I wasn't sure if he'd even receive my message, let alone respond to it. I leaned back in the chair and waited.

Across the hallway, I could hear the crew gathering for breakfast. I couldn't bear sharing a meal with them. I thought the entire camp would be up in arms over Kent's death, frantic for Miriam, or at the very least blanketed in a mournful hush. But there they were, rattling plates and backslapping in the buffet line. They were *excited* to be part of this so-called grand television experiment. To the crew, Kent's death was a tragedy in the way a news event was a tragedy, in the way that hearing an acquaintance had lost a grandparent was a tragedy, and not the deep and personal indictment of each and every one of us. No, worse, it was an opportunity, a boost for their careers. At first, there'd been a slight modulation. People would be subdued when they sat down. But the conversations quickly escalated to the usual jokes and war stories. Plus Englander would be in the dining hall. I couldn't possibly eat watching him spin out my PR fate while he swirled the milk in his cereal bowl.

After about a half hour, my computer pinged. *Let's chat*, Stellan wrote.

He came through pixelated over the poor Wi-Fi—a pattern of flesh-colored boxes that roughly approximated the outline of a man's face. His staticky voice spiked and distended as the signal wavered, so that some of his words sounded high and screechy while others dragged in a deep bass.

"Beck Bermann," he said. "I'm mad at you."

"Me?" I asked. "How's your injury?"

"Injury?"

"Your infection?"

"What are you talking about?"

"They told me you were injured and had to be evacuated."

The line went silent. I worried for a moment that I'd lost the connection, but the flesh-colored boxes shifted and re-formed. "I was fired."

"But Callahan said—"

"They canned me and hired you. They said it wasn't a 'personality fit.' With your track record—no offense, but I was pissed. It was three or four days after your . . . viral moment."

That didn't make sense. Why get rid of Stellan and bring me in? And why lie about it? The timing didn't add up either. Jacob had called me the day after Buster died, right after his funeral, not a few days later.

"I'm so sorry," I said. "I had no idea."

"It's fine. I got another job at the same network, actually. On a show about a family of interior decorators. People always assume Scandinavians know everything about design. I'm just saying 'hygge' a lot. What's your question?"

I had a thousand of them now. I was trying to replay all my conversations about Stellan. I remembered Callahan, shifting uncomfortably on our walk down the beach when I asked about the producer who left. But I had to stay focused before the Wi-Fi evaporated or someone came in. "Do you know anything about a camera in that temple on the mountain? The one the Art Department made?"

"I never went up there," he said. "You should ask Jacob. He was weirdly excited about that spot."

I apologized for the misunderstanding and wished him luck on the new show. Then I walked down the stairs, past the noise from the dining room, and out onto the beach.

Maybe I was being paranoid. It could all be an innocent misunderstanding. Maybe the story about Stellan's medical evacuation was a polite lie. People could be awkward about firings. Maybe I'd imagined the red light in the darkness. Surely after a lifetime of reality TV, I knew better than anybody how unreliable memory was. Two different people could recount the same experience as if living on two different planets, and neither of them would remotely match what we'd recorded. And I'd suffered a blow to the head.

Or maybe Jacob Malibu had fired stoic, reliable Stellan to hire the crazy dog killer. He saw the news about Buster, he streamed the online footage of me acting erratic as I confronted Dave at the funeral, and he thought that here was a producer who would drive things to extremes. Here was someone who could take the fall if a tragedy "happened" to occur, because I'd already shown the world I was unsafe. He'd said in the story bible he wanted to push the show to new places. Jacob had done what every great producer does, what he told me and Erika to do on the first day—take the opportunities you see to drive the story. He first made sure I could sign on, and then he fired Stellan, not the reverse. He couldn't know for certain it would end in a death, but it was a possible outcome he anticipated. One he hoped for. And he placed secret cameras to record the crucial moments. I was positive that before the fight with Kent, I'd seen a camera's red glow. If there was a secret camera, that meant there were memory cards. Where would Jacob hide them? For all I knew, there could be a hidden room piled high with mountains of cards, looping spools of film dangling from the rafters, a jungle of secret tape. But for something so confidential that Ralph and Stellan and I didn't know about it? He had to be hiding them in his room.

I heard the cough of the vans revving on the other side of the City and ran out front. Jacob was walking out the hotel door. He looked like he always did, springing down the steps with the wild enthusiasm of a golden retriever. Maybe there was a straightforward explanation. He'd simply forgotten to mention the mountaintop camera. A lot had happened in the last few days.

"Jacob!" I called out.

He skidded to a stop and jogged over to me. "Hey. Englander told me you gave him the slip. It was probably insensitive of me to saddle you with him. I'm sorry about that."

Even with a fleet of vans waiting for him, even with a contestant lost in the jungle, all his attention was on me. "I just– I wish we could know what happened on that mountain with Kent," I said. "Why did he go up there? What he was doing before we came? If only we could replay it." I yearned for him to take my hand and explain how it was all a tragic mix-up.

"You're like me," he said. "We get so used to hitting rewind and fast-forward that we forget that real life doesn't work that way. Some things we have to let go." He squeezed my hand and then spoke more forcefully. "Really, Beck. Let it go. I need you to take care of yourself. With one contestant dead and another missing–it's a reminder how dangerous it is out here in the jungle. Especially in your condition."

Despite the heat, my body went cold. His whole face was concerned and kind, and yet I'd never felt more threatened. He trotted back to the van, but before he got into the passenger seat, he called out. "By the way. I asked Million to take care of that gecko in your room. You've got enough to worry about."

"Take care? You mean—"

"It's a reminder that I'm here for you, and we're keeping you safe."

He closed the door, and his van sped away.

I sprinted through the hotel and down the beach, the cut along my stomach burning. *Take care of*—it sounded like a mafia hit. A warning. As I approached my bungalow, I heard shouting from inside. Then one of the three camo-clad guards burst out of the door, screaming and waving his arm, a blur of bluish-green stapled to his hand. Behind him came the two other guards and Million. The injured man went sprinting into the ocean and plunged his hand into the water, but when he pulled it out, the gecko still hung off him where she had fastened her teeth. Million was yelling, gesturing for the guard to stop, but he kept flailing his arms, trying to fling the gecko away. One of the other guards grabbed him from behind in a bear hug. The gecko hung there, her feet paddling helplessly, fury in her orange eye. Million carefully pried open her jaws. With one hand, he held her behind the front legs, as she twisted and snapped. With his other hand, he took her head between two fingers. I felt all the motive power leave my limbs. I tripped in the sand and fell to my knees.

"Wait!" I shouted. "No!" The gecko wasn't monstrous. She was a desperate animal.

Million stopped. "Jacob said to—"

I got to my feet and stumbled forward.

"Please. Let her go."

Million gestured at the injured guard, who had stripped off his shirt to bandage his bleeding hand. "He's going to be very angry."

"Please."

Million held the gecko away from his body. Her rear legs paddled uselessly in the air. He tapped her belly and nodded. "It's very bad luck to kill a tokay gecko."

I followed him into my bungalow. One of the bedposts had been smashed, and the mattress sagged onto the floor. The old cooler that was nailed above the sink was rolling on the ground, beside my clothes and toiletries and the wreckage of the nightstand. But it was all irrelevant. Million reached up into the rafters and opened his hands, and the gecko disappeared.

"I'll get somebody to—" He gestured at the mess.

"Thank you. I appreciate that. Let me ask you one quick question." I wasn't about to be threatened into silence. I would find the incriminating footage. This was how I would avenge the loss of Kent. Of Miriam, if the worst had happened. Even of Buster, in a cosmic sense of righting the scales of justice. This was how I could redeem myself. "You have keys for all the rooms, right?"

Million nodded.

"I—left something in Jacob's room. When I was there—the other night."

"You wait here. I'll get it."

"It was actually . . . my underwear." I blushed and dragged my foot, trying to imitate an embarrassed girl. "I don't want to put you in an awkward position. But maybe I could— It's *sexy* underwear," I whispered.

Million smiled a big knowing grin. He reached into his pocket, pulled out his cluttered key chain, and flipped through the ring before detaching a small room key.

"Please don't tell anybody," I said. "I'm so embarrassed."

"I'm going to look for the lost girl," he said, still chuckling and nodding to himself. "Give it back when I return."

CHAPTER 51

I knocked loudly on Jacob's door and called out his name. The hallway was silent. I slipped Million's key into the lock, turned the handle, and closed the door quietly behind me.

The room looked the same as when I first saw it. The bedsheets were tucked. The books were neatly stacked on the bedside table. The butterflies kept their silent vigil from their frame on the wall. Out the window, on the beach below, I could see two of the security guards, including the one with the bandaged hand. At a signal from Jacob, they could charge in here, and I'd be trapped. I had to move quickly.

I started with the wooden drawers beneath the television. I went through the bundled socks and the underwear laid out in neat rows. One drawer was filled with button-down moisture-wicking shirts in a variety of neutral colors. Another had six sets of folded gray technical pants. I've always found something a little moving about laundry. No matter who we pretend to be with our clothes on, every morning we're naked bodies. I tried to imagine Jacob selecting his shirt and combing his hair, but I struggled to picture him alone. What image met him in the mirror before he put on his smiling mask? Was the face he saw reflected back vicious and cruel, lined with hard-hearted decisions from his twenty-year career? I reached into the back of the underwear drawer, expecting to find a secret cache of hidden memory cards. My hand rapped against bare wood.

I opened his bedside table. There was an open packet of condoms—five missing, more times than we'd had sex—a bottle of melatonin, and my underwear, folded neatly like a trophy. I pocketed them. I got down on my hands and knees and looked under the bed. Dust bunnies and a discarded sock. *The sock!* Hiding the evidence in plain sight, the ultimate trick. I flipped it inside out.

It was a dirty sock.

A scream came from outside. I banged my head against the bed before sliding out and creeping to peer through the window. A pair of seabirds were swooping in from shore. I couldn't see the guards. They could be on their way in to stop me.

On the edge of Jacob's sink were vitamins, hair-loss pills, a comb, and pomade. The mirrored medicine cabinet was crowded with Neosporin, Band-Aids, antibiotics, antidiarrheals. The usual.

I searched through the pockets of Jacob's folded pants. Nothing. What about the books? Could there be a hollowed-out compartment? I leafed inside them, almost embarrassed at myself. I'd read too many spy novels. I was too desperate for something to explain away my failures. Jacob was expressing genuine concern for me, and my addled brain had turned it into a threat. Maybe the red light in the temple was a reflection of the fire. Or there might not have been a red light at all, and my subconscious created a false mystery to distract me from the very real tragedy. Maybe Kent drew the map himself and found the machete somewhere at the Holding Pen, and I had misjudged Jacob, just like I had misunderstood the butterflies puddling on the mountain—

I almost laughed out loud when it hit me. The butterflies! Of course. It was one of those insights that producers sometimes have, years of instinct and training aligning into an absolute certainty. He had hung the butterfly box on the wall himself, his one piece of personal decoration. That first night in his room, as I walked over to examine it, he came up to me from behind. I thought he was being flirty, but was he protecting a secret?

I lifted the cabinet off the wall, careful not to disturb the insects. Behind the frame was a rusty nail.

I sighed and plopped onto the bed. There was nowhere else to look. My only remaining move was to tidy the room and leave without being spotted. If there were hidden cards, I might never find them. As I lifted the butterfly cabinet onto the wall, I angled the box to align the nail with the hole. Taped to the wood on the back were three microSD memory cards.

CHAPTER 52

The production office was silent.

The entire crew was either looking for Miriam in the jungle or filming at camp. Even the hotel staff had been press-ganged into the search. As far as I knew, I was the only person left behind in the City, other than the guards and Jeremy Englander, who had commandeered a box of white wine and established himself in front of his room fan. Still, every sound—from the chugging of the generator to the wind rattling the cheap wooden hotel doors—was the sound of Jacob's footsteps, and reflected in the blank screens, I saw the flickering movements of people sneaking up from behind.

On the whiteboard in the corner, the season's major story beats were written out in red marker. *Arrival + ferro rod + fire. Camp desertion. Poisoning. Barb quit. Escape attempt 1. Snake + Kelly-Anne evac. Kent + Ashley first kiss. Kent vs. Miriam fight.* There was a smudge of red marker where Ruddy's storyline of backstabs and betrayals had been erased.

My pulse was pounding. Without turning on the lights, I pulled one of the cards from my pocket and stuck it into a computer. When the image opened on my screen, I gasped, even though it was exactly what I was expecting. A grainy grayscale from inside the dark temple. For a moment, Kent Duvall was alive again. Pacing and muttering. He wasn't miked, but the camera did a good enough job of picking up his audio. His raft was at the edge of the frame. I had an impulse to rewind, to let him live at least here on the screen. Instead I fast-forwarded, scrolling through an hour of him standing, sitting, and lying on the ground, until Jacob walked into the shot.

My hand jumped on the keyboard, making the video scroll backward a few seconds, so that he walked into the shot again.

Kent stared at him, wary. Jacob crouched down and took out his handheld.

"Kent, I think it's really smart of you to stay here until you're ready to escape. Going back to camp could be risky. Wouldn't you say they're all against you?"

"I . . . would say they're all against me."

"Every one of them?" Jacob asked. *"Even Miriam?"*

He hesitated.

"Wouldn't you say Miriam turned on you when she started hunting that pig?"

Kent stared out the door toward the raft.

"Do you really think you can trust any of them?" Jacob walked toward the camera until he filled the screen. The tape went black. He must have changed the batteries and swapped cards. I was about to switch to my next card when I heard a sound in the doorway.

"I thought I heard someone in here," Afa said. "What are you watching?"

"You're back?" I asked idiotically.

"For lunch."

We stared at each other across the room.

"Did you know about this?" I rewound the tape.

He walked over and peered at the screen. "What is it?"

"There was a hidden camera in the temple on the mountain."

"So? There's cameras everywhere."

"Why was this card hidden?" I asked. "I found it in Jacob's room. He's in it. He was interviewing Kent. Working him up."

"Why were you in Jacob's room? Does he know you took it?"

On the surface his questions were reasonable, but they felt charged with menace. He stepped close. The hump of his shoulders, his jawline like the blade of a bulldozer, the garish Hawaiian shirt, the crust of dirt under his ragged nails, the fuzz of black hair down the back of his neck, all these small physical details crowded in on the overtaxed circuitry of my limbic system, and I felt a surge of animal panic. I pulled the card out of the machine and jammed it into my pocket.

"Wait, give that back," Afa said.

"Stay away from me."

"Beck. Calm down."

"Stay away."

He took another step toward me. I was like the trapped gecko, twisting and snapping. I grabbed a monitor and sent it crashing toward him. But the monitor snagged on its power cord and shattered onto the table. Afa stepped back and threw up his hands to protect his ears. I darted around him, down the stairs, and out of the hotel. I ran down the beach, past my bungalow and toward the guards.

"Help me," I shouted, but they merely looked at me and laughed. One pointed behind me, and I knew that Afa was coming. I could hear him now, shouting at them to stop me, but they didn't understand him either. The announcer of the eternal game was shouting *"GOAL! GOAL! GOAL!"*

The cut across my stomach ached. It started bleeding through my white shirt. Past the guards' station the shore ended in a jag of black volcanic rock. I plunged into the ocean and started to make my way around the point, clutching the memory cards in my hand.

"Beck! Where are you going?" Afa shouted. "Come back!"

I edged my way between the sea-carved rocks. The ocean floor was slippery, and the current slapped against me. A wave forced me up against the headland, and I reached out to brace myself with my free hand, slicing my palm on a barnacle. I barely noticed. I was focused on my footing. If I slipped, I could hit my head, fall into the water, and drown. One tiny misstep and–

Afa was in the water behind me. He was more solid against the waves, but he was running, and he slipped on the rocks. "Beck!" He spat out seawater. "Stop! This is dangerous!"

When I reached land, I took off down a muddy path between two boulders and crashed into the jungle. The spines of the creepers slashed my exposed skin, but I was running headlong, not even thinking where I might be going or why. The ground sloped down, and the humidity spiked. I ran full out, not daring to look back. I could feel the trees gathering close. And then I was in front of it: the thick wall of brambles that closed off the heart of the jungle. I pushed aside the creepers and plunged inside.

The mosquitoes were everywhere. They landed on the back of my neck and my arms, on my legs where my pants bagged around my ankles, and across my forehead. The chirruping of the cicadas was deafening here, and below all that, there was another noise, a whirring sound.

The terrain sloped down, and I followed, ducking under branches, tripping over massive roots. I heard a noise. People talking. Who could possibly be having a conversation so deep in the trees? I briefly imagined a long-lost civilization. But then I thought about the mountain temple. The only mysteries on this island were produced by my colleagues. I followed the sound forward, trying to move quietly, as though that mattered at all against the jungle's cacophony.

I followed the voices to the edge of a steep slope. At its bottom, at the very base of the island, I could see a clearing. Miriam was sitting at its center. She was alive. Thank god. Across from her sat Jacob. Friedman was crouched behind his camera. Million stood to the side.

They were filming an interview.

The air around the group looked blurry, as pixelated as a bad connection. I rubbed my eyes, but it wasn't my vision failing. The glade was clouded with thousands of butterflies, so many that they clotted the sky. The beating of their wings was making that mysterious sound, like the rustling of a million sheets of paper.

I ran down the sharp slope, skidding into the glade's wet grass. "What's going on here?"

"Beck?!" It only took half a heartbeat for Jacob to move from surprise to concern. "You're supposed to be resting."

The worry on his face—I could see beneath the mask. He was a demon, the best producer in history, able to shape-shift his every expression and word to trigger the exact responses he wanted. He hadn't been worn down by life from the young hotshot with the ripped-up jeans. He had intensified—he had crystalized, and I had the terrifying thought that he only looked like a kind middle-aged man to me because that was what I craved. Perhaps to Erika he was a strapping hunk. It was a glamour he could weave at will. I looked away. I had to find out what was happening, before he could soothe things with his blanket of words.

I turned to Friedman. "*You* work for Jacob?"

"What are you talking about?" Friedman said. "We all work for Jacob."

Jacob walked across the clearing and laid his hand on my shoulder. "Beck, you've experienced a traumatic event. You need rest. You—you're bleeding. You shouldn't be running through the jungle. Especially not here." He waved his hand and brushed aside a butterfly.

"I found your videos of Kent on the mountain. I knew there was a secret camera. I saw the red light–"

For the briefest of instants, I swear I saw through the illusion, and Jacob was furious. Then he was back to being the kindest, most concerned paternal figure in the world. "Beck, I didn't want you to see that footage. It's too upsetting." His voice sounded like my father's again. Had he snuck into my cabin and watched the video on my laptop, learned to mimic Dad's precise intonations? "For you especially. You're overdue for a good rest–"

"And the map Kent had? You wanted him to escape the Holding Pen. He had a machete!"

"Yes, I gave Kent a map to the mountain. I had Peter the staff psychologist leave it for him. We left the machete in the temple, so that he could actually survive up there. Isn't that what you wanted? You said how disappointed you were that you never got your big blowup between Kent and Miriam. We couldn't have dreamed that events would take such a tragic turn–"

"You're *in* the video. You told him not to trust Miriam! And then you told me to go up the mountain *with* Miriam."

"I only wanted to reinforce your story."

"Then why keep it a secret?"

"I didn't want you to think that I was stepping on your toes. Because I believe in you."

His gentle grasp on my shoulder was too comforting. I stepped back. There was a missing connection here, I was sure, something I could say to make the puzzle align. Behind him, Miriam was sitting still where they had posed her, staring blankly into space. She had to be in shock.

Afa scooted down the slope into the glade, looking sheepish.

"Thank god you're here," Jacob said. "We're going to need your magic to level out this lunacy."

"You made Kent and Miriam fight," I said.

"Beck, *you* made Kent and Miriam fight," Jacob said. "It's your story, and it's a great one."

"A contestant is dead. You've been angling for it the entire time." I could feel the pressure building behind my eyes. "You told me to push myself past my limits when my group didn't have any food. We—Kent—I *poisoned* the Deserters. You told me to take Kent and Miriam hiking up the mountain. Then you told me it wasn't dramatic enough. Every meeting you criticized my stories, then told me how great I was. You . . . fucked me, then kicked me out. You've been keeping me off-balance—"

"I definitely agree you're off-balance. We're going to get you home, but I need those memory cards." He extended his palm.

"I was behind you in the woods, with Erika. At the spiders. I heard you—you said I was the perfect person. I wondered why you hired the dog killer. Now I know."

"You're mad at me for calling you perfect?"

"The perfect fall guy. You knew you could manipulate me into doing something wild. I don't think you plotted this out exactly, but you knew with enough pressure that something bad would happen." My voice was rising. "You kept pushing me, so I kept pushing them, but your hands are clean. Other than these cards."

"All I'm doing on those cards is asking questions. Now, please, give them to me."

"Why did you fire Stellan?"

"He was—the wrong fit. Too passive. I shouldn't have lied about it, but it really wasn't his fault, and I didn't want him to have any stigma. When I heard about you, I felt like—we could go bigger than a normal show. You're right. I want a spectacle, a show that pushes people to their limits. I've told you that all along. I knew you had that in you, Beck. I didn't know exactly how you'd get there, or how far you would go—"

"I'm getting off this island, and I'm taking the cards with me." I looked around at the rest of the crew, but no one would make eye contact. The butterflies were everywhere, batting against my cheek, making it hard to focus. "If you're innocent, why are you so desperate to keep them?"

"They're footage for the show we're making."

"No. No, no, no, no. You always have such reasonable explanations." I was crying now. "And why did you warn me to stay away from the heart of the jungle?"

"Very bad bugs," Million said.

"Bad bugs?"

"Mosquitoes. Cicadas." Jacob waved his hand in front of his face. "Butterflies."

"You warned me away because of all the butterflies? I find that–"

"And snakes," Million said. "There are venomous snakes out here."

"We were only looking out for your safety," Jacob said.

"If this place is so dangerous, why are *you* here?"

"Million found Miriam and radioed us."

"Oh, and you decided to bring a camera crew," I said.

"Of course," Jacob said. I looked at Miriam. The butterfly swarm was centered behind her over an animal carcass. Puddling, like Jacob had explained. Feeding. She looked–different. Her clothes were covered in dirt and ash, her shirt matted with blood, and even from feet away the smell of her was overpowering. But it was more than that. She was sitting up straighter than normal, and her hands–usually so active–were cradled in her lap. She was smiling too, and for the first time, not bothering to cover the gap in her front teeth with her tongue.

"I'm taking Miriam, and we're getting off this island," I said. "You can't make me disappear. *I'm* not an orphan."

"We are most assuredly getting you off the island," Jacob said. "You are in need of serious professional care and a long rest. But Miriam stays. She signed a contract."

"She killed a man!"

"Consider your own culpability." His tone shifted from patient to threatening. "Based on your history with the two contestants, it's irrelevant whose hand threw the spear, since the real question is who controlled the hand. If you try to take Miriam—"

"I knew I was set up to take the fall. Send me to jail. I am responsible."

"If you won't think about yourself," Jacob said, "think about Miriam. She'll be accused of *murder.* As I mentioned, we have a good relationship with the local government. We can keep her out of legal jeopardy, but she needs to remain part of our organization."

I shook my head. All that mattered was getting Miriam away from Jacob. We would sort the rest out later. I would take the blame. I would say I killed Kent. In a way, I had.

"Miriam," I said. She was sitting on the ground with her legs crossed, watching me. "Please. Come with me. Let's get out of here." I took her hands and pulled her to her feet. That was as far as she would budge.

"Keep rolling," Jacob said.

"I'm not going," Miriam said. Her voice came out flat and far away. "Jacob promised to keep me safe."

"You can't trust him." I knew how that must have sounded. There was not a plea I could make to convince her that *this* was her pivotal moment—not all the other times I'd asked for her faith. I had exhausted every rhetorical strategy. I had no tricks left in my bag.

Instead, I told Miriam the truth.

I started with our early days on the island, about how I immediately felt a connection with her after Erika shoved her into the water.

How Erika stole the ferro rod. How hard I busted my ass to bring Kent and her together, and how I worked just as hard to drive them apart. I mapped out the ways our production manipulated them at every turn—encouraging the fights, sabotaging Carl and Barb. How Erika orchestrated Kent and Ashley's first kiss. I expected Jacob to interject, even tackle me to shut me up. I hoped he would. It might have shocked Miriam into action. But Jacob merely regarded me with the same intense interest as always, while Friedman filmed.

When I finished, Miriam smiled so serenely that I worried she had gone insane.

"None of that changes my decision," she said. "I've climbed a mountain and gathered food. I was buried alive. I've endured more physical misery than I could have imagined, and I found the inner strength to move forward. I—I found love. And I heard a voice—"

"You see that it's all a lie, right?" I was desperate, almost feral. How could she not see the truth?

"My *experience* isn't a lie. You can't control how I feel. What it was like to make it through that rainstorm. What that means to me now after all that's happened. You claim you were in charge of everything. Were you in charge of the monsoon?"

"In a way! Yes! We brought you here during monsoon season."

"I still experienced it. Were you in charge of the snake I killed?"

"Actually—that one," Friedman said sheepishly. "I was filming B-roll with that snake, and it . . . escaped. I never thought it would—"

"Don't you see?" I said. "This whole production—"

"Beck," Miriam said. "No talk about production."

"Miriam killed a pig with her *hands*," Jacob said. "She saved herself—she saved the whole group—she saved you—from a crazy person. Miriam's a hero. The whole world will see her as a hero. Beck, isn't that the story you wanted all along?"

CHAPTER 53
MIRIAM

DAY 44

She stands in the center of the raft, the sail fills with wind, and they scud across the sea's small ripples toward Treasure Island. The salt air smells fresh and new, like clean laundry. Water seeps between the beams and sloshes over the sides, but the lashes hold. For once, nobody has slashed them. A drone swoops overhead. Beside them, in the growling yellow Zodiac, Friedman stands as firm as a saluting soldier, with his rig to his eye. The beach behind her is crowded with producers and cameras, but she won't look back. A bird screams from the canopy, one final farewell from the restless jungle's boiling cauldron, but still she doesn't turn. The island is behind her now, where it will remain forever.

Where *he* will remain forever.

Oh, Kent. She still wakes in the night to the weight of his arm around her waist or the pulse of his dick against her back. She still hears his whoops and cries on the wind. She can even see him now, as if he's at her side, a hazy outline in sea spray. It's as though there's a thin curtain separating this world from a different one, where he's still alive, and where they spent the last days complaining about how hungry they were, splashing in the stream, going on endless hunts for nonexistent game, and fantasizing about the first meal they would share after the show, when she took the train to Providence.

At first Miriam thought using Ashley's sail was a terrible idea. She had no sailing experience and wanted to use their replacement set of oars that Ashley had won. But Bartolo insisted he had unique expertise. "Wind power is mightier than arm power," he said. *We're going to drown*, she thought. Amazingly, Bartolo was telling the truth. He directed her to the perfect palm to fashion into a mast and found a fallen log that he hacked and scraped into a serviceable boom. What if his boasts were *all* true, she wondered, all his tall tales, all his expertise? She laughed at the absurdity. Together they secured the canvas to the mast with vines and the remnants of cordage, then threaded a makeshift rigging. Now Bartolo looks almost glamorous with his hand on the ropes, squinting into the rising sun. He's lean, with a gray-and-white beard, and his gray roots have pushed out his dyed black mop to give him a vaguely piratical air. For a moment she loves him. The raft skips across the water to the wind, as Bartolo tacks and adjusts. Above them, the Coke bottle is lashed to the mast and refracts the sunlight into rainbows.

It's day forty-four, nine days since she killed Kent. "Why today?" Bartolo asked her that morning. Because Kent was forty-four years old. Because she wanted to pay him that small tribute. And because the two of them wouldn't last another week. For days it's been only her and Bartolo in the shelter, their two emaciated bodies shivering against each other in the wet cold.

Ashley quit the second she learned Kent had died, when Miriam followed Jacob back to camp after her final conversation with Beck in the glade. She wailed inconsolably on the beach while waiting for her boat. Maybe she really did love him, Miriam thought. The two women shared a hug before she left. "Bring it home," Ashley whispered in her ear.

Erika helped her orchestrate Ruddy's elimination, convincing her to hide his clothes until—exhausted, miserable, and mostly naked—he quit the game. "You're a stone-cold killer. First Kent, now me," he told Miriam as he waited for his evacuation. "And here I thought *I* would be the Big Bad." She felt guilty being so vicious, but—well, it was Ruddy. It was only fair.

Erika was different these days, happier. Afa was on her crew, and once, emerging from the jungle after an interview with Jacob, Miriam caught the pair of them sitting side by side on the edge of the shelter, so close that their knees were touching.

"We could go to Paris?" Afa suggested.

"The rude fucking waiters." Erika shook her head in revulsion.

"Santorini?"

"Drugged-up scenesters."

"Patagonia," Afa said.

"We'll do it all. Every disgusting last one." She wrinkled her nose as she picked up his hand and kissed his fingertips. Miriam snuck back into the woods.

With Beck gone, Jacob took over her interviews. She grew strangely attracted to him. He was masculine but nerdy, a hybrid of Kent and the New York men from the apps. They filmed one confessional where she compared her castmates to the characters in Shakespeare's *The Tempest*. Miriam didn't remember the play that well, but Jacob fed her the details. Ruddy was obviously the wicked Caliban. Bartolo was Trinculo, the fool, and Carl was like drunken Stephano. Kent was magical Ariel, the spirit of the wilderness. "Would you say that makes you the magician, Prospero?" Jacob asked.

"I guess I *would* say that I'm Prospero. If only because I'm going to escape."

Inevitably the topic returned to Kent, and Jacob acted more as a counselor and a friend than as a producer. "You weren't only saving Beck," he reminded her again and again. "You were saving yourself. He was coming for you next—and god knows who else." Occasionally, he insisted she hadn't killed Kent, not really. "He was dying—that wound on his stomach was infected, but he wasn't telling the doctors. I believe—in my heart—this was how he wanted to go." Legally speaking, Jacob had taken care of everything, and she was in the clear. She worried at first that he was the next Svengali in a line of manipulators from her boss at the startup to Callie to Beck. But when Jacob suggested she abandon Bartolo on the beach and win the game solo, she experienced such a clear and deep sense of indignation, she was certain she'd discovered her moral core. "No," she responded, recalling how Kent stood by her when the Deserters had abandoned camp. "You said you wanted me to be the hero of this show. To be a hero, you have to save someone." He nodded, letting her make the last crucial decision for herself.

The water shallows, its hue brightening from navy to turquoise to clear as a bath. Miriam jumps over the side of the raft before it can come to a stop. The three palms and sandy beach flecked with sea grass look like the desert island in a cartoon. Jacob and his crew are already here filming, and Miriam adjusts her expression to the proud and triumphant countenance of an explorer reaching a fabled land. The treasure chest sits where the three palms meet. It's a simple wooden box, almost too simple. The sides are worn and weathered, but only cosmetically, like the show's Art Department sanded it.

"As the captain of this craft, I insist you do the honors," Bartolo says with a bow. But she can see how desperately he wants to be the one to crack the lid, and she bows back at him, extending to him the golden key, and after a brief bow-off, Bartolo accepts. He kneels in the sand and inserts the key into the lock. It slides in with a satisfying click, and the mechanism turns smoothly.

"We've done it! We're rich!" He flings the top open. Inside lies a pile of fake cash, the bills so crisp they look newly minted. "We escaped!" he exclaims.

"Toss it in the air!" Jacob says, and the two, laughing, throw the stacks of fake money into the sky.

Eight hundred and eighty thousand dollars. Split two ways, that's four hundred and forty thousand each. She'll give Barb two hundred and forty thousand. For David. That leaves two hundred thousand to pay off her student loans and give her a nice cushion. Though after taxes–Bartolo races off with Jacob for a confessional. The other side of the tiny islet is steps away, and she can hear him explain how he navigated the treacherous currents, dodged sharks, surged over monster swells . . . Staring at the cash, she feels a moment of total deflation. Of course she's *excited.* She *won.* But–now she goes home. She can hear Kent on the mountaintop. "That's life. Normal life. Out here–it's *more.*" She hasn't even left the game, and she already wants it back. They'll eventually have an *All Star* season. They'd *have* to cast her, right . . . ?

No. She won't allow herself to think that way. She's taken what she needs from this experience. The next adventure is applying those lessons. She'll quit her job. What then? She knows she wants kids, and she wants to be a young mom to see them grow into adults. That means finding a relationship with someone she loves and trusts, who shares her passions for board games and books–and hopefully has that special impossible spark. These are life's real challenges, because they're not manufactured, the rules aren't clear, and there aren't producers coaxing you at every step. Maybe that's what she really takes from the island, she thinks. She's learned to tune out the Beck Bermanns of the world and to search instead inside herself.

And she still gets to have the show in her life. In five months, Miriam will throw a premiere party. She'll invite everyone, they'll toast with champagne in plastic flutes, and together they'll watch the edited, color-corrected version of their adventure. Barb will showily forgive her and tell her how she's set up a pediatric cancer fund in David's name with the money. She's using her momentary fame to become a motivational speaker. Bartolo will share how he's used his winnings to retire. He's now a doctor of dance emeritus. Kelly-Anne will give them an update on her hand—all healed!—and share how her mindfulness seminars are oversubscribed. Carl will show them pictures of his girls. The first time the show airs him roaring, he'll roar in person, and they'll all share a group roar together. Ruddy will have brought a new pair of pants to gift Miriam, as a gag, but he'll fall silent as they watch the show and he learns how invisible he is in the edit. Ashley will still be forlorn over the loss of Kent. But she'll also be giddy when she sees her first interview and can tell she's being set up as a major character.

And Miriam's college roommate Penelope will be there too. She'll smile indulgently when Miriam falls off the boat, but it will be okay, Miriam knows, because it's only the beginning of her story.

EPILOGUE

BECK

6 MONTHS LATER

The camera sweeps across the island. Down from the pink sandstone cliff, the smiling rain-carved faces on the lintel of the temple. Over the dark cathedral of the jungle, around the shimmering water of the shore, the shadows of fish slipping beneath the aquamarine. Then over the bare spit of a beach, where a lone crooked palm beckons in the sand.

A gravelly baritone voice-over cuts in.

"In the remotest region of the Pacific Ocean, near the heart of the storm-tossed Dragon's Triangle, await the dangers of the island. The ruins of ancient civilizations. A treacherous and forbidding jungle. Eight Americans are about to step onto this beach for the ultimate test of their bodies, their hearts, and their souls. Can they survive the ravages of the wild and the challenges of each other? Will they last long enough to make it off the island and claim the million-dollar prize? Find out this season on . . . ESCAPE!"

In the distance, across the sea, a speck of yellow. As the announcer speaks, it grows larger. A Zodiac cuts through the waves, jouncing over the swells. A red-and-green bird screams in the sky. The boat nears the shore, and one of the contestants leaps over the side and runs to the beach and whoops, his machete in the air and hunger in his eyes.

One point eight million people watched the premiere, which made the show a decent success for the network but not a ratings bonanza. It was another show on the network's lineup of shows, competing against the hundreds of other programs on networks and digital platforms that aired on Tuesday nights at nine. It was one more story among the thousands of stories with which we're bombarded every day.

I was not one of those 1.8 million viewers.

The end of my time on the island unwound like a tape playing in reverse. The chopper ride back to the mainland, Benjamin the pilot making the same oblivious jokes. An evening in Mud Town's International Hotel, where I locked the door and watched the video of my mom. I played it straight through, over and over, with the compulsion of a conspiracy theorist, like if I watched it enough, its hidden secret might be revealed. And then I returned home to New York, back to my Williamsburg apartment.

I gave Jacob the memory cards after I quit. Standing in that glade with Afa, Friedman, and him glowering down at me, I didn't think I had a choice.

I practiced meditation. I sat on a chair in my living room in the lotus pose and counted my breaths, begging my brain to stop endlessly cycling through every moment on the island. I downloaded apps that were supposed to clear your mind. I immersed myself in New York, trying to catch myself up again in the flood tide of humanity, the mad bustle of people elbowing their way through the city. The harried mom struggling to get her stroller down the subway stairs. The anxious businessman in the ill-fitting suit who pushed past her, late for his meeting, peering down the tunnel for his train. So many stories interweaving in the city's ceaseless drama. But it all felt blank to me.

I reached out to Kent's wife, Margaret, looking for—I wasn't sure what. Someone to blame me? Someone who could make me feel better by ripping me to shreds? Technically I was violating my contract, but the lawyers could already destroy me at their whim. Margaret only sighed sadly. Yes, a man from the network had informed her. She was trying to move forward and not think about Kent anymore. She had a new fiancé, a doctor from her hospital, whom she was very happy with. I wished her well.

The single episode of *Escape!* I watched was the one where Miriam killed the pig. I cooked a dinner of chickpea pasta and salad and sat down on my white couch, hunching over my coffee table. The editing was masterful. Shots of Miriam creeping through the jungle. The music soared. The first pig—Pig Bambi—leaped from the bushes. Miriam hurled the spear. Then there she was, bent over the body of the sick old boar. I could see the seams, but your average viewer wouldn't notice. The audience would only see the narrative connecting them from point A to point B and never question what happened in between, that zag from one reality to another in the blink of an eye. One point eight million people would say they saw Miriam kill that pig, they saw it on their TV, and nobody would be able to convince them otherwise.

Kent's death would air in two weeks. Already the show's promos were hyping "the most shocking moment in the history of television." I was the network's insurance policy. The executives were waiting to assess the backlash before they decided what to do with me. If the public thought the death was a powerful moment, raw humanity at its most essential, then Jacob and the network would take full credit. But if the outrage spiraled, I was an easy scapegoat. Kent was yet another victim on the dog killer's murderous rampage. They had footage of me egging him and Miriam on at every step of the way. They had my final moments on the show, when I broke the fourth wall, stepped into the scene, and confessed everything.

So I waited, living off my savings, partially hoping the American public really was bloodthirsty and numb, and part of me praying for all our sakes they weren't. I wasn't sure what came next for me professionally. I watched police procedurals on television. Their tidy structures used to calm me. In act four, the cops realize they've been chasing the wrong guy. In act five, the villain confesses. Now it all seemed too pat.

One day in the spring, my father called. We hadn't spoken since Buster died. My instinct was to let it go to voicemail, because what kind of consolation could he possibly give? But an inexplicable urge made me answer. He told me he was planning a trip to New York, and would I join him for dinner? I knew he wanted to snap my life back into place with the same mechanical simplicity with which he could reset a joint. In spite of myself, I said yes. I made reservations at a stuffy bastion of New York fine dining. Dad liked to be surrounded by white tablecloths, obsequious waitstaff, and heart-stopping breaded chicken dishes. I figured that the restaurant's well-heeled clientele of hedge funders and charity doyennes would never have heard of *Surf Dogs*.

"Is anybody staring?" I asked Dad once we were seated.

"At us?"

"At me."

"Nobody's looking at you. You're not the center of the universe."

"Can you at least check?"

Dad made a big show of peering around. "Nope. Still not the center."

Over dinner—his chicken cacciatore and my salade frisée—I told him everything. He looked pained as I spoke, and at the end he sighed and said, "I'm glad you quit. I always said it was beneath you. Dogs dying. And you're telling me a person was killed?"

"It was my fault, Dad."

He grimaced and looked away. "I know that's not true. That's not the woman you are. It sounds like this Jacob—"

"It *is*," I told him. I couldn't stop squirming in my seat. I didn't know what I'd been looking for. Forgiveness was too much, but maybe understanding? Acceptance? "It *is* the woman I am. Or part of who I am. And I have to live with that."

The waiter came over to hand us the check. We weren't even finished with our meals, but Dad always thought it was more efficient to pay while we ate. Dad squinted at it and fumbled for his reading glasses in his jacket pocket. In that instant, I saw him as other people must. He was wearing a light gray sweater and dark slacks, and his frame still hinted at a lifetime of exercise. But the liver spots on his forehead; his yellowing teeth. It was like all our history and resentment melted away, and I could see him as everybody else in this restaurant did, another old man.

"I love you, Dad," I said. "I know that when Mom died, you lost the love of your life—"

"Don't be ridiculous." He peered appraisingly at the check through his reading glasses. "Your mother wasn't the love of my life."

"Oh god." How idiotic of me to try to start a sincere conversation. I wanted to crawl under the table and shrivel into a ball. "Please. Don't. I don't want to hear about whatever college love affair—"

"*You* are." He looked down awkwardly, the way he always did at moments of genuine emotion. "Since the moment you were born. You're the love of my life," he told his chicken cacciatore.

He wasn't the father I'd needed, and I wasn't the daughter he'd imagined, but as I opened the door to outside and the cool wind breezed in, and the bar crowd pulled their coats tighter and cast us nasty looks, I slipped my arm into his with such an upswell of gratitude that he was mine, and that he was incapable of saying the right thing, because when he did speak from his heart it felt like a piece of the broken world had been mended.

That night, feeling buoyed by my father's love and two glasses of wine, I finally sorted through my luggage from the island. The evening had turned rainy, and I was feeling grateful again for the roof over my head and the heat chugging through my radiator. As I sorted through my bug-gnawed tank tops and the filthy pants that still smelled like woodsmoke, I came upon the ferro rod, and suddenly, my mind shunted back to the island so violently that my whole body started shivering.

I saw it all unspool. That first moment I landed, when Jacob criticized me for a benign remark about Benjamin the pilot, then love-bombed me with praise and affirmation. Sitting there in the clattering dining room while he picked apart my storylines, and then walking down the beach afterward hearing him gush over my work. The day he prompted me to take the two contestants up the mountaintop, and the next day, at Friedman's party, how he berated me for such a terrible idea, and minutes later, took me to his room. Now he had a show that pushed the boundaries of the medium, and the network had a perfect patsy.

I looked out my window across the East River to the Manhattan skyline. In one of those skyscrapers lurked the production offices, Public Relations Department, and executive suites of the network. I imagined Jeremy Englander working late, and that pantsuited executive, and in a conference room—not now, it was too late, but maybe tomorrow—Jacob would be pitching his vision for his next groundbreaking show.

How many of my decisions were my own and how many was I manipulated into pursuing? Every reality TV contestant had to ask themselves that very question. In this world of producers and manipulators, we were all asking it of ourselves every day.

Still, even if I was manipulated, I had to take responsibility. I'd made the choices that led to Kent's death. At times I'd loved making them. I'd done it to help people I believed in. To please the people I respected. I'd acted naively and idealistically and terribly. I was so focused on others' storylines, I hadn't recognized my own capacity to harm.

My eyes teared up. The lights across the river blurred. Instead of New York's brilliant skyline, my own reflection came clearly into shape in the window. I existed somewhere between the woman Jacob saw me as, the woman my father saw me as, and the woman I imagined I was, somewhere between my most vicious impulses and my most noble. I wouldn't ever have the story I deserved. Nobody would, because nobody could be reduced to a story. But I thought as I stared at my hazy contours, the wild chaotic blur that surrounded the sharp hawk nose I'd inherited from my mother, maybe if I recognized my worst self, I could start to guide myself toward my best.

That night, I played back my home video again. *"Rebecca's first-ever hot chocolate,"* Dad said. I sipped the marshmallows from my ceramic cup. Then there I was belting out "The Itsy-Bitsy Spider" and jumping on the living room couch. The video wasn't about my mother. It was about me. My parents were beaming their love through the camera lens as they documented their brief journey together caring for their child. The video was about us, as a family. Now I was shouting at Mom, calling her a bad guy, telling her she would go to jail, and my parents were arguing over how to calm me down. It was all there, our best and worst moments, our hopes and our mess, the highlight-reel highs where we felt most connected, and the blowups where we hurt each other more than we could ever mean.

I would have to learn to embrace all of it.

What other choice does anyone have?

ACKNOWLEDGMENTS

First I need to thank Maya Ziv, my editor, who combined superhuman positivity with unerring cuts and revisions. Your edits made this book find its true and final form, and your kindness kept me sane through the work. To everyone at Dutton: Alice Dalrymple, Erica Rose, Melissa Solis, Emily Canders, Caroline Payne, John Parsley, Stephanie Cooper, Amanda Walker, Ella Kurki, Gaelyn Galbreath, Daniel Brount, and Justina Vasquez, you have my unending gratitude.

Thanks to Michael Heyward and the team at Text for embracing this book.

Thank you to my agent, Kent Wolf, for his guidance, insight, and patience, as well as Eloy Bleifuss Prados and the team at Neon Literary.

To my parents, Connie and Ron. Now that I'm a parent, too, I see how much effort and care go into every choice. Thank you for filling our home with books and a love of learning.

To my aunt Kathy, who has been unflinchingly supportive at every step of this tortuous path. I would never have finished this novel without your encouragement.

To my brother, Daniel. The first time I ever wanted to write was watching you and your friends make up silly stories on our Apple llc. Thank you for making writing seem cool.

To my in-laws, Marian and Stuart. Thank you for turning the DC swamp into a welcoming family oasis.

To Will Allison, Patrick Ryan, Hannah Tinti, Maribeth Batcha, and the entire community at *One Story*, thank you for gifting me my debut publication, which has opened every subsequent door. Thanks as well to Bill Henderson and the Pushcart Press for honoring "To Sharks." To Garth Greenwell, thank you for finding the emotional architecture of the story that became this novel.

To my many friends who read iterations of this book: Claire Hoffman, Graham Ballou, Elliott Bueler, Cal Shook, Kira Procter, Liz Riggs, Shanteka Sigers, Hayley Phelan, Sanjay Agnihotri, Thomas Mannella, Eric Simpson, Scott Stubbs, Jackie Gilbert, Brian Carso, Laura Schechter, and Johannes Lichtman.

To John Cochran, Benjamin Lorr, Margaret Miller, and Suzanne Wrubel. Thank you for all your creative counsel and calming text messages, for this novel and for countless projects across the decades.

To Jonathan Safran Foer, Nathan Englander, John Freeman, Katie Kitamura, Deborah Landau, Lisa Gerard, and the entirety of the NYU low-residency MFA program.

To Thomas Mallon and the community at Bread Loaf.

To my college professors Harold Bloom, Leslie Brisman, and Jane Levin, who taught me to fall in love with the mysteries of literature, and my classmates Daniel Pollack-Pelzner and Greta Gao, who nurtured that love in late-night sessions debating the meaning of a near-rhyme.

To my freelance editors: Alexandra Shelley, who made me believe I could publish a novel, and Robert Siegel, who gave me the courage to finally hit send.

To Stephanie Feldman, whose Catapult class on novel structure helped me discover this book's story arc.

To Stephen Friedman, who gave me my first job and has supported my creative endeavors across multiple stages of my life.

To Andrea Boehlke, Sophie Clarke, Erinn Moss, and Shirin Oskooi, thank you so much for your honest conversations about the woman's POV on shelter spooning.

To all the producers, contestants, camerapeople, and audio professionals who gave me expert insight that animated this book.

To Drew "Scooter" Ackerman and the *Sleep with Me* podcast, I literally could not have written this without your soothing help on the long anxious nights.

To Jeff Probst, Mark Burnett, Matt Van Wagenen, Joe Lia, Meredith Fisher, and Lynne Spillman, as well as the entire team at SEG and CBS, thank you for gifting me the opportunity to explore this reality TV landscape that has come to define my life. I only gained the courage to write this novel when I was violently ill in the middle of a tropical monsoon on *Survivor.* I had the epiphany that if I was willing to suffer so much for reality television, how could I not have the fortitude to write a book?

To Rob Cesternino and the *Know-It-Alls* podcast listeners, thank you for supporting me and this book with such enthusiasm. Being a part of the *Rob Has a Podcast* community has been one of the most joyful parts of my entire reality TV experience.

To my wife, Julia. I only know a fraction of the sacrifices you made to give me the time and space to write this novel, from long nights awake with the girls to taking entire vacations without me. You are the life partner I could never have dreamed of. I love that you are truthful and unflinchingly honest–and I appreciate even more that you betrayed those deep values to pump me up with false praise when I needed it most.

Last of all, thanks to my daughters, Margot and Prue, whom it's all for.

ABOUT THE AUTHOR

STEPHEN FISHBACH is a Pushcart Prize–winning writer and former television executive. A two-time *Survivor* contestant (voted onto the show the second time by millions of fans), he's worked on the network side as a vice president at MTV and freelanced for a reality producers' trade group. He cohosts the *Survivor Know-It-Alls* podcast as well as the literary podcast *Paraphrase.* Stephen graduated with honors from Yale and received a master of fine arts in fiction at New York University. His short story "To Sharks"—an excerpt from *Escape!*—was published by *One Story* and garnered Stephen the Pushcart Prize. He lives in Washington, DC, with his wife and two daughters.